THE DRAGON'S DEN
THE METAFRAME WAR:
BOOK 3

Graeme Rodaughan

Published by System Zero Productions Pty Ltd, 2018

Trade Paperback ISBN-13: 978-0-9945952-6-3

EPUB Edition ISBN-13: 978-0-9945952-7-0

Cover art by Huw Jones

For Linda, for her unfailing love and support that always leaves me in awe.

I would like to thank a number of people who have assisted with my progress as an author, including Alex, Tim, Lisa, Lena, Marie, Eldon, Michael, Christopher, Perry, Nick, Andrew, Laura, Daniel, Ginger, Jody, and the regular crew of Beta and ARC readers at the Castle Dracula group and my many friends and followers on Goodreads. You have all contributed more than you know to my craft and your support and encouragement are invaluable for this journey.

Books by Graeme Rodaughan

The Metaframe War Series

A Subtle Agency
A Traitor's War
The Dragon's Den
The Day Guard
The Crane War
The Key of Ahknaton

Omnibus Volumes

A Subtle Agency Omnibus (includes A Subtle Agency, A Traitor's War, and The Dragon's Den)

Forthcoming Books in the Metaframe War series

The Metaframe Adept

Dramatis Personae

The Ancients

Ahknaton, Ruler of the Southern Realm, High Priest of the Temple of Thoth. Master Architect. Ramp Master.
Hakron, Second prince of the Southern Realm. Master Scribe. Ramp Master. Ahknaton's brother
Mekra, Princess, Ahknaton's wife.

The Vampire Dominion

Cornelius Crane, King of the Vampire Dominion
Chloe Armitage, General, The Americas, ex Order of Thoth and Crane's chief enforcer
Haras Mosule, General, Middle East, ex Red Empire warrior of the 3rd rank
Dieter Franz, General, Western Europe
Clayton Maze, General, Africa
Shen Zhen, General, East Asia
Marcus Drake, Chloe's aide de camp

The Order of Thoth

Ramin Kain, Head of the Order of Thoth
Samuel Luther, Ramin's chief of staff and aide de camp

The Exiles

Arthur Slayne, (Exiled) Master Strategist, Force Leader, Weapons Grandmaster, Speed Talent.

The Mirovar Force Team

Francis Mirovar, Force Leader, Weapons Master
Juliette Mirovar, Loremaster, Netmaster, Combat Surgeon
Yvette Mirovar, Operative
Jay Creeley, Operative, Weapons Master
Peter Lamb, Operative, Armorer, Strength Talent
Chiara Romano, Operative, 2nd Combat Surgeon
Anton Slayne, Order novice
Li Wu, Order novice, Weapons Master

The Walker Force Team (UK)

Richard Walker, Force Leader
Joan Lewis, Loremaster, Netmaster
Mary Turner, Operative, Netmaster,
David Wilkinson, Operative, Weapons Master
Karen Chapman, Operative
David Khan, Operative, Weapons Master
James Cox, Order novice
Michael (Mikey) Wilson, Operative
Francine (Frannie) Parker, Operative

The Red Empire

Shabbah al Ahmar, aka 'The Red Ghost,' aka Dalien Morte. Head of the Red Empire
Al Ghurab, aka 'The Raven,' Operative inserted into the Order of Thoth
Thueban Kabir, aka 'The Great Serpent,' aka 'Taipan,' Weapons Grandmaster, warrior of the 3rd rank
Nasr al Dam, aka 'The Blood Eagle,' Fist team leader, warrior of the 2nd rank
Tamsah al Ramil, aka 'The Sand Crocodile,' Fist team leader, warrior of the 2nd rank

Shadowstone

James Haley, Head of Operations, United States
Louise Wesson, Operative
Gordon Heathmont, Director Shadowstone United Kingdom.
Frank Quiver, Major, Command Officer Squadron F
Victoria Hansen, Flight Officer, Blackwidow pilot, Squadron F

Other Players

Justin Blake, Force Leader (South West) Weapons Master, Strength talent. Former student of Gang Wu

Gracie Williams, Flight Lieutenant, RAF
Tom (Tommie) Wilkes, RAF Regiment, soldier

Prologue

The Armitage Manor, England, July 5th, 1856, 22:25

A single shaft of moonlight cut through the summer air. It glimmered through an open bedroom window, caressing the curves and angles of two lovers entwined on white sheets. One was an exquisitely beautiful young woman; the other was something that was ancient before she was born.

He stilled, his skin becoming hot to touch. He was ramping. Chloe followed his lead, dropping into silence and accelerating her mind. Time slowed. Exquisite bliss bloomed throughout her being. The silence deepened, her joy intensified, and surface reality evaporated away.

He was a fiery, golden light, shuddering in rhythmic waves and she became the same. All sense of corporeal reality disappearing completely, like the night giving way to the dawn.

There was only golden light, a steady drumbeat of time, glorious bliss and union.

Then hot kisses on her throat. A sudden gasp of air into oxygen-starved lungs. Her fingers plunged into his long dark hair, bringing his head up. Their mouths met for a long, lingering kiss.

She moved slightly, turning and resting her head on his shoulder, holding him gently.

"Oh my God!" she whispered. "What just happened?"

He stiffened for a moment, then relaxed, kissing her quickly on the lips. He slipped out of bed, and before she could react, he was on the balcony. A moment later he was gone.

"Cornelius?" she whispered.

There was only the promise of two nights hence. Longing filled her heart. What was he waiting for?

* * *

Armitage Manor, England, July 7th, 1856, 23:34

Crane's vampire attack had weakened Chloe past the point of being able to take action. She was powerless to resist.

Chloe had first met Crane three weeks before. It was a warm summer night, she was practicing with her weapons in the moonlight, pistol, longsword, and rapier. Crane emerged from the shadows and offered himself as a training partner. Intrigued, Chloe accepted, and they fenced throughout the night. He was clearly a champion of the blade, and a seasoned Ramp master. Time flew, and before long the first glimmerings of

1

dawn appeared in the east. Crane frowned and begged her leave to depart. She allowed it, on the promise that he return the following night.

Crane was true to his word, returning the next night and every night after that until two nights past.

At first, she believed he was a Ramp master, an unknown member of the Order of Thoth, but quickly, she understood precisely who and what he was – one of the most powerful vampires alive. By rights, she should have followed her allegiances to the Order and fought him to the death.

But her loyalty to the Order had died along with all hope for the Order's eventual victory. Confirmed as a full member of the Order of Thoth at sixteen, the youngest confirmation on record. She'd taken little more than a year to come to the conclusion the Order would lose the war. The Red Empire was larger and more ruthless, and the vampires had the unbeatable strategic advantage of rapid recruitment. It took years to grow and develop new Ramp masters. One vampire could create another in minutes. No matter how many vampires the individual heroics of the Order killed, vampire numbers could always swell faster than the Ramp masters could destroy them.

Chloe couldn't see her life spent to an empty purpose, to someone else's broken dream. She set her sights on becoming a vampire and using her gifts to master the vampire world. To rule vampires and men – for she would never submit to the rule of another. Only one question had remained, when would her transformation occur?

The appearance of Crane answered that question, but then he'd delayed, and delayed again. He was waiting for something, something he needed before he could proceed to the next step; the arrival of Jean Philippe Allemande.

Chloe lay dying of blood loss on a divan in her library.

Crane stood over her, his generals a respectful distance beyond him. He pulled a glass vial filled with a dark red fluid from his vest pocket. He uncorked it, upending it over the twin bite wounds on her throat. The 'blood,' crawled over her skin. Running in tiny rivers, the animated fluid seeking the holes in her neck. In moments, the blood had vanished, dark lines tracking beneath her skin in its wake as it flooded through her diminished bloodstream.

"What is this? What have you given her?" the blond general asked, his face rigid with suspicion.

Crane held up his hand in abrupt dismissal.

The chamber flickered around her. Shadows stretched across her vision before a searing white light washed them away. Shrill screams and gasping silence competed with each other while every bone in her body splintered and renewed itself. Fire surged along every nerve, muscle fibers tore and then knitted anew. Time fled and eternity reigned a world of suffering. A rapid trembling rippled over her limbs. Her eyelids fluttered. She sighed once. The transformation was complete.

All new things are born in agony.

Chloe opened her eyes to a wondrous world of superb clarity, every sense perfectly attuned to the world around her. Someone was speaking in a strange language, each word cutting her mind like a razor.

"Who's speaking," she whispered. "I didn't—"

Allemande's face leered above her, his voice a dreadful whisper as he pronounced the final words of the binding curse. Faint rainbows flickered, the light of the room faded, shadows blooming before her eyes. A veil wrapped itself around her mind, extinguishing any ability to directly harm the man who stood beside the Haitian sorcerer, staring at her with obsessive interest.

Crane had been hunting her for some time – her transformation was not a whim, but the result of a carefully laid plan. It galled her to realize he'd duped her. He'd promised her so much more, but had instead delivered her into slavery to his will.

Pure rage flooded her; she conceived her attack in a moment – Allemande's curse be damned. Her nostrils flared, a vast lust for violence throwing down her mind. She stared at Crane, her eyes flashing with hatred, but before she could move another need overwhelmed everything else.

Cowering in the corner of her library, his hands and feet bound, his mouth gagged, crouched a brigand. Recently captured and brought to her manor. A man no one would miss, and certainly not missed by anyone who could do anything about it.

Chloe rose from the divan, rushing over to where the brigand cringed, his face white with terror. She grabbed his lank hair with one hand, drew his head back, exposing his throat. She arched back, her nostrils flaring with the scent of prey. Her mouth gaped open, brand-new fangs flashing in the lantern light. Filled with an overwhelming, hideous need, she crunched forward, sinking her fangs into his neck. His hot blood flooded into her mouth. She swallowed desperately, instinctively smacking his chest to keep the heart flow coming until she drained the last available drop.

She found herself on the floor, the brigand's body limp and pale beneath her. She bounded to her feet, the others in the room staring at her with curious interest. A new power coursed through her being. She screamed in exultation. Opposite her stood Crane and his minions. Her gaze flicked over them. There was Allemande, the voodoo priest, a smug smile on his face. She silently promised herself, *you will pay for your curse, this I swear.* Beside the Haitian stood a powerfully built African, a slimly built east Asian, an athletic Persian, and a tall, strong northern European. All were Crane's generals, and he'd cursed them all as he'd cursed her.

Crane and his servants. She despised them all. Crane had tricked her. The binding lay like a hot net around her soul. She locked gazes with Crane, his eyes narrowing slightly – waiting for her response.

She drew upon her Order training, now enhanced with extraordinary vampire strength. Reaching up and sweeping an ancestral sword from the wall, she whirled toward Crane. His generals, immediately drew weapons, reflexively blurring forward to defend their master. She evaded them, faster than the eye could see. Her thrust carved through open space toward Crane's heart. Lightning crackled; rainbow flecked shadows danced through the room. The air shuddered, blowing her backward against the wall. The sword, livid with flame, fell from her nerveless fingers and crashed to the floor.

She staggered back to her feet, the stench of burning metal ripe in her nostrils.

Crane's voice cut through the silence in the room, "Such perfect ferocity."

"What have you done?" the blond general asked. "What was that blood? I've never smelled its like."

Crane blurred forward, grasping Chloe's shoulders possessively. He stared hard into her eyes and declared, "You will enforce my laws, even unto my generals. I have given you the strength to carry out my edicts."

They stared at each other for a long moment.

A hot vow sprang from the depths of her soul. *Never, never, never will I serve you. I will have my freedom, and you will regret this night before you die.*

She paused for a moment, her mind spinning – she would have to deceive Crane, now and until she'd broken the curse, and restored her liberty. She stood tall, stepped back from his grip and relaxed; a slight smile caressing her lips. Bowing respectfully, she said firmly, "My Lord, I will serve you."

Crane smiled triumphantly.

Rising from her bow, she glanced up at him, her face calm.

Beware my fury – for I will never rest until I am free to live my own purpose and not yours.

Chapter One

Customer Name: R.I.S.C Enterprises Pty Ltd
Job: Transport
Priority: Urgent
Security: Secured/Armed
Pick Up Address: Hangar [REDACTED], Logan International Airport, Boston
Destination Address: [REDACTED], Chicago, IL
Pick Up Time: 09:00, Wednesday 23rd August
Description of Goods: 16x palletized crates of machine parts.
Mass: Not more than 20,000 lbs. (est. 18,000 lbs.)
Insurance Value: $40M
Vehicle Type: Semi-Trailer
Container Type: Large
Quoted Price: $79,900.00
Customer Contact: James Halifax.
Customer Contact details: [REDACTED]

– Quote metadata for contracted secured transport of 'machine parts,' from Boston to Chicago

* * *

South of White Hill, Maine, August 21st, 21:20

The engines of the two SUVs idled quietly.

Anton Slayne lugged a strong box filled with FN P90 submachine guns and magazines with a mix of high-performance armor piercing and silver ammunition into the back of the rear SUV. Every fifth bullet was silver, a general-purpose magazine load for when you could not be sure what you might be facing.

Peter threw a dark brown, leather battle vest on top of the box. He'd loaded his vest with his favorite weapons, a pair of razor-sharp battle-axes and four tri-bladed throwing axes.

Anton closed the tailgate, and they walked around the big vehicle to join the other members of the Mirovar force team.

Francis Mirovar stood on the doorstep of the log cabin. Gripping Justin Blake's arm, he asked, "Can I convince you to come with us? You could make a real difference to our chances."

Justin frowned, shaking his head. "Not this time my friend. I have to see to my team and organize the next Order conclave."

"When will it be?"

"Two," Justin shrugged his heavy shoulders, "perhaps two and a half weeks. You'll all be back by then." He leaned in close to Francis and requested with a wry grin. "Make sure you bring Ramin Kain back in one piece, I would like to see him squirm during an impeachment."

Francis nodded; his eyes flat. Necessity drove the rescue of Kain, not concern for the man himself.

Anton halted a couple of feet back from the two force leaders. Li Wu appeared at his shoulder. She carried the Blue and Green Dragon swords and thumped him hard on the side with the Blue Dragon as she thrust it into his hands. She stared at him for a moment, before flicking her head back at the log cabin. The message was clear – were you going to leave this behind?

"No," Anton whispered. "Of course not."

Li lifted both eyebrows skeptically. Coldly pushing past him, she hugged Justin.

"Bye, Uncle. Keep safe and kick ass."

Anton shook his head in bewilderment. Why was Li upset with him? She wasn't even talking to him.

Justin hugged her back. They broke apart. Putting a big hand under Li's chin, his face became serious, and he said quietly, "Take care Li, it's one big trap over there, and we don't know what Armitage's real target is."

"What about the inquisition?" Li asked. "Is that still hanging over my head?"

Justin sighed. "Unfortunately, yes. However, we must put it aside until we either get Ramin Kain back in one piece or we hold the next conclave where the Head of the Order will resolve all these matters."

Li's face fell, she backed away from Justin, joining the rest of the team standing near the two SUVs.

Juliette stood next to Francis, one hand resting gently on his arm. A far-away look flitted across her eyes, and she reported, "Joan is aware of the situation. The Walker force team have pledged their assistance."

Francis smiled grimly. "A second force team will even the odds. Are all the other loremasters aware?"

"Yes. The news will filter through the rest of the Order over the next few days."

"See – you don't need me," Justin remarked, striding away from the porch and onto the track. He stood in the headlights of the front SUV, shouldered a backpack, put on a pair of Order nightglasses and called out, "Godspeed to you all." He jogged off down the track, quickly vanishing into the dark.

Anton stepped up next to Francis and inquired, "The Walker force team?"

"The English team. Just like us," Juliette answered. "Joan Lewis is their loremaster, and Richard Walker is their force leader."

Luther pushed himself off the wall of the log cabin and stated derisively, "A real force team, one the Order can count on."

Anton's lip curled. He was about to respond, but pulled himself up short, thinking, *I can't let this guy get under my skin.*

Francis stepped toward Luther. His hand flashed out, hitting Luther hard across the face. Luther's head rocked to the side, and he staggered back. Francis snarled. "I've had enough of your disrespect."

"What the hell," Luther snapped, blood dribbling past his lips. He blurred forward to tackle Francis. Francis met his attack, flowing around Luther and bringing him to the ground with a thud.

Kneeling on top of him, Francis pressed down hard on Luther's right arm, twisted up high behind his back. "Shut up, or I'm leaving you here."

Luther grunted, and gritted his teeth. "You can't do that."

"I damn well can."

There was a long moment of silence.

"Are we clear," Francis added.

Luther nodded and grunted again.

Francis released his hold, allowing Luther to regain his feet.

"Ramin Kain is not a traitor," Luther asserted hotly, glaring at the others. "I will keep this mission honest."

"Yes, you do that," Juliette remarked, sweeping past him and taking a position in the front passenger seat of the lead SUV. "Peter, come up here with me and drive."

"Sure," Peter agreed.

Francis stared at Luther for a second and shook his head. "We can't waste more time. We're leaving now, everyone on board."

Anton got into the back seat of the front SUV and sat next to Li. Chiara jumped in beside him in the last remaining seat. Peter put the SUV into gear rolling forward along the track to the main road. Li turned her head away, looking out the window. Anton decided not to press the issue, it was clear she was upset with him about something. He thought back over the night's events. *I protected her when she couldn't fight, what is she so upset about? ... Oh, I ran off after Drake.*

The pieces finally dropped into place.

"Damn," Anton whispered.

He'd abandoned her in the middle of a battle.

"Li," he whispered. "I'm so sorry."

Li stiffened for a moment and then sighed. She turned her head forward, not looking at him. Her eyelids half-closed, she declared in cutting tones,

"You will be if you do it again. What would have happened if they'd turned on Peter and me in numbers too high for him to handle? I couldn't fight, not properly. The Red Empire could've killed us and just because you'd run off to satisfy 'what?' … I don't know. How often do I have to ask myself, 'what were you thinking?' You're too smart to be losing it like this. Get a handle on your emotions before they cause damage to the team you can't repair."

Anton frowned for a moment, and promised, "I will. I understand what you're saying. It won't happen again."

Li tilted her head and looked at him askance. "Don't make promises you don't know how to keep."

"I'll keep it," Anton vowed, looking forward through the car's windscreen.

The SUV turned onto the main road and accelerated away, the second SUV following tightly behind it.

* * *

The Spike 512 supersonic business jet flashed through the night sky over the Atlantic.

Chloe Armitage glanced at the monitor seamlessly merged with the front wall of the cabin. It was 22:30 on Monday night in Boston and 03:30 on Tuesday morning in the United Kingdom. Stats streamed along the bottom of the screen. Altitude 51,034 feet, Speed 1253 miles per hour. In another two hours, she would be landing at her private airfield outside the town of Goathland, ten miles from her ancestral home near the town of Whitby – Armitage Manor.

It had been more than a century since the property had been known by that name. She'd begun obfuscating her personal history back in the 1890's but still owned the manor house. It was the home of her human retainers, including the pilots who flew her plane. She'd made it almost impossible to discover who really owned 'Armitage Manor.'

She didn't need Shadowstone to hide her own tracks, she'd been doing that for most of her life.

Her smartphone pinged, there was a message from James Haley that read, 'Tech crew dismantling the 3rd blackwidow. All deaths attributed to Order actions. Remaining Red Empire personnel en route to a Shadowstone safe house in Boston.'

She responded with, 'Noted.'

The four Red Empire assassins in Boston, a fist team led by Nasr al Dam, aka Blood Eagle, would no doubt prove useful. Having a secret force in reserve in North America was an edge over her opponents. Chloe hungered for every advantage she could establish. Regime change was no easy task, and while she believed in her eventual victory, she had no illusions about the difficulties, risks, and challenges that lay before her. If Crane ever discovered what she was doing, he would surely kill her. Events had gone too far. There was no going back now. There would be no opportunity for forgiveness and redemption. He would cut her in half with his blade and rip her living heart from her chest – and there was nothing she could do to stop him. Jean Philippe Allemande's curse ensured Crane was the one man she could never defeat in open combat, the one man she couldn't fight against and win.

Everything was at stake. The game was live, and there would be only one winner.

At the back of the cabin under the watchful gaze of Marcus Drake sat Ramin Kain, head of the Order of Thoth. Kain was awake, bound and gagged. She could've drugged him, but she wanted him conscious, aware and frightened. She needed to break him before the Mirovar force team arrived at her manor house.

There were many questions to answer. After the battle at the Boston docks where she'd killed the Order grandmaster, Gang Wu, it had become clear the Order had managed to partially corrupt the feeds to the Panopticon. They'd demonstrated their capacity to shield operations from Panopticon surveillance on the night of the second battle in Boston where she'd killed Crane's praetorians. Just how the Order had accomplished this feat was a question at the top of her list. A list which included, where were all the Order safe houses? What was the disposition of Order forces? Who were the Order loremasters? Where and when would the Order hold their next conclave? These and many other questions she expected to answer today.

Chloe would have to wait until she got Kain into the dungeon beneath her manor house before she could begin the interrogation. The supersonic Spike 512 had bought her another three hours of lead time. She was six hours ahead of her pursuers.

Chloe tapped her fingers on the arm of her seat. There would be some necessary preliminaries before she could properly put Kain to the question. Then there were the inevitable preparations and final checks on the trap for the Mirovar force team she'd ordered built by the Red Empire assassins currently occupying the manor house. James Haley and the Spike 512 had delivered a four-man Red Empire fist team and a host of specialized equipment to the manor before completing his flight to Boston with the rest of the Red Empire assassins. She needed to be sure the trap was ready and fully functional – she'd explicitly designed it to condition Anton Slayne into a living weapon against Crane.

Li Wu's death at the hands of vampires would be the final straw that would break Anton's restraints, making him completely vulnerable to Chloe's will.

She paused, frowning. With all the checks and preparations, her six-hour lead could easily become four, would it be enough time to learn everything she needed to know. Interrogating the Head of the Order of Thoth was a once in a lifetime opportunity, well … once in a human lifetime. Still, she should not waste the opportunity, and four hours would pass quickly and may prove to be insufficient.

She needed more time.

Her fingers froze, her eyes widened. She'd made a mistake. She was not six hours ahead of her pursuers, she was at best two hours ahead. Once the Order realized that the Embraer jet carrying the decoy GPS signal was not heading toward London as per its flight plan, they would look for another landing site. Once the pilots in the Embraer posted their changed flight plan to land in Goathland, the information would be accessible to anyone with Internet access.

The United Kingdom had its own members of the Order of Thoth. She was well aware of the existence of the Walker force team. Their center of operations remained hidden in the sprawling metropolis of London. The initial flight plan of the decoy Embraer should keep them there. They would only begin to move once they became aware of the new flight plan to Goathland in Yorkshire, and London was hours away from Yorkshire.

How much time she had to question Kain rested on the capacity of the Order to realize the decoy Embraer had changed flight plans and transport the UK force team to Yorkshire. It was a capability of the Order that was currently unknown.

Chloe didn't like unknowns in her plans, and she hated relying on the inefficiency of either the Mirovar or the Walker force teams.

It was safest to assume the worst and plan for it. The Mirovar force team would already be in communication with the Walker force team. They would pass on the decoy GPS signal, and the UK team would track it to Goathland and from there to the town of Whitby and her manor house. They could move into position to attack the manor house and rescue Kain. But would they attack immediately, or would they wait until the arrival of the Mirovar force team to ensure they had an overwhelming force?

Unless Walker was stupid, or desperate, he would wait. Whether the Order attacked or waited for reinforcements, she needed to consider and plan for either possibility.

The four Red Empire assassins she'd stationed at her manor house would help. They were a second, elite fist team. Like the team led by Nasr al Dam who had all bar one survived the battle at the Maine safe house, they were an elite squad, a notch above the regular fighters of the Red Empire.

As effective as they were, they were too few to prevail against a full-sized Order force team, especially one that was prepared for combat.

She needed to keep the UK team, and the Mirovar force team separated for as long as possible, and she would need to deter an early attack by the UK force team.

Chloe frowned. She would have to deliberately delay the pursuit by the Mirovar force team. What were her options? The Spike had long overtaken the decoy Embraer business jet transporting Kain's phone. The decoy plane would arrive at Goathland at 08:00 UK time. The GPS signal of the phone drawing the Order to the airfield. She could divert the decoy to another site, but then how to reacquire the Mirovar force team and draw them back to Armitage manor and the trap that waited there? She could get her staff to transport the phone, but what if the UK Order caught up with them before they arrived at the Manor. No, the decoy plane had to complete its mission, delivering the GPS/phone to her private airfield and from there to her manor house.

She had to throw something in Mirovar's way, something that would give her enough time to drain Kain's mind, but not so strong they would never arrive. Her fingers drummed the armrests of her seat. Focusing her gaze beyond the cabin, her mind raced through a dozen options before she settled on a new plan.

She commanded her phone, "Call James Haley."

The phone rang three times before James answered, "Yes, Ma'am?"

"Where are you?"

"Logan airport overseeing the teardown of the last blackwidow. What do you need?"

"Good. Delegate it. I need you to keep an eye open for the arrival of the Mirovar force team."

"Yes, Ma'am. If they have a helicopter—"

"They don't have one. They will come by car … expect them after midnight, one a.m. at the latest."

"And when they arrive?"

"I need a photograph of 'Anton Smith,' getting on whichever plane they're using to follow the decoy. Once you have that, bypass the Panopticon and alert Shadowstone UK to arrange a welcoming committee for Anton's arrival in UK airspace."

"Yes, Ma'am, will do. Anything else?"

"Yes. Don't send the photo too soon; make Shadowstone in the UK wait. I want them rushed and under pressure."

"Copy that. Anything else Ma'am?"

"I need you to intercept any communications traffic from UK Shadowstone to Crane's personal line for the next twenty-four hours. I need Crane isolated from the UK, and I need a very plausible excuse for it."

James' breathing whispered hesitantly over the line. "… When do you need the intercepts to start?"

"As soon as possible, but not later than your notification to the UK of the imminent arrival of an Order of Thoth operative."

"Yes Ma'am, there is a way this can be done."

"Thank you, James, that will be all," she said, disconnecting the call.

Now it's time to focus on extracting everything I can from Kain.

Chloe smiled, her eyes shining with anticipation.

Her phone vibrated in her hand; the screen indicated a call from Crane. She tapped the answer icon and put the phone on speaker – there was nothing here she wanted to hide from Marcus or Kain.

"Yes, Sir. What can I do for you?" she asked.

"Where are you?" Crane responded.

"Over the Atlantic."

"Are you in a drone?"

"Personal jet. I wasn't anywhere near Fort Dix when Kain decided to fly to the UK."

"What the hell is he doing?" Crane demanded.

"I don't know. I'm following him now. I'm sure to find out soon."

"What happened in Maine? It's a mess over there."

"Shadowstone hit a live Order safe house. The first in years. There have been Order casualties."

"Was it Mirovar?"

"Yes," Chloe replied, rising lithely out of her chair. Walking casually down the aisle toward Kain, she held her phone in front of her. "But at least some of the Mirovar force team survived, perhaps the majority of them. I will know more soon; it appears they're also following Kain."

"Remember what I told you – keep Kain safe. We need the stability of the secret detente for another year. It is essential you keep Kain alive until the Day Guard is ready. Of course, afterward, he will be of no further use."

Kain's eyes bulged above his gag, his face flushing red.

Chloe tilted her head slightly, staring at Kain and said affirmatively, "I can guarantee he's perfectly safe right now."

"Excellent. Keep it that way."

Chloe smiled slightly. "Yes, Sir. I will do my best."

"See that you do," Crane said and hung up.

Chloe arched an eyebrow at Kain. Turning on her heel, she strolled back to her seat. Crane's call had been unexpected but useful. Events were tracking well toward her goals. She would remain vigilant to ensure that remained the case.

* * *

Electric motors hummed; the hangar doors grinding along their tracks with a low rasp.

The Order owned Embraer Legacy 500 business jet, taxied through the opening and out onto the tarmac. Everyone in the Mirovar force team was on the plane. Peter and Anton were in the cockpit. Behind them in the main cabin sitting in pairs along the aisle were Francis and Juliette Mirovar, Jay Creeley and Yvette Mirovar, and Li Wu and Chiara Romano. Sitting by himself at the back, Samuel Luther stared out the window.

Juliette leaned back in her chair and engaged her mind palace. The external world vanished, an internal landscape blooming into view. Recent events since the arrival of the Order traveler Deon Lamar, at the destroyed safe house in Maine, flashed before her.

She 'reached,' for what she needed. The abduction of Ramin Kain by the Red Empire and their escape in a nightfalcon helicopter arrested before her. She leaped up into the nightfalcon's cabin, the helicopter behaving as a solid object in her vision. The surviving Red Empire assassins stood around Kain's body, slumped on the floor. One of the assassins quickly bound him. The tallest of the assassins let his cowl fall back to reveal a head of close-cropped blond hair. It was Marcus Drake; he went forward to the helicopter's cockpit. Chloe Armitage emerged from the cockpit and stood near Kain. Kain moaned, beginning to wake up.

Her mind flashed forward to Logan airport. She was standing alone on a runway. Racing toward her was an Embraer business jet, it lifted off, zooming overhead. Turning around she tracked its ascent into the night sky. A sheath of light glimmered around it, before streaking over the horizon. The plane was bound for England. She followed the light, her mind palace providing an intuitive leap. The light split in two, one strand heading to London, the second, brighter strand, heading toward the northeast coast.

Yorkshire? The manifest for this flight indicated London as the destination, but Yorkshire is more likely.

Juliette briefly dropped out of her mind palace. Francis reached across to touch her forearm and asked, "Are you okay?"

"Working," she replied.

She flipped open her laptop and logged in. The implant in her right forearm completed the routing, giving her access to everything on the Internet. Less than two minutes later she identified a private airfield near the village of Goathland in northern Yorkshire as the most likely destination of the Embraer jet.

Is Kain, Armitage, and Marcus on that plane?

Numbers flashed through her mind. The projected arrival time approximated 08:00 am in England, more than two hours after sunrise.

Is Armitage planning to transport herself off the plane in a box? She was in control of the schedule for the attack on the safe house. What was her exfiltration plan? Surely, she would have planned better than this.

A second plane?

Only a supersonic plane could deliver Armitage and Drake to England in time to beat the sun. That restricted the options. Juliette used her implant, laptop, and the Internet to directly feed her mind palace vision. She remained at the end of the runway, the airport around her now inactive and silent, shrouded in shadows, the dark of night closing in. A half dozen aircraft appeared arrayed around her in a broad semi-circle. The Spike 512 stood out. Designed in Boston and locally produced in England, possibly favored by someone with an English heritage. It could take Armitage to Yorkshire before sunrise. She checked departures from Logan airport. A Spike 512 had left at 21:35. A time that conveniently matched the flight time of a nightfalcon from the Maine safe house to Logan International Airport with a few minutes to spare.

Juliette took a step, the runway vanished, and she was back in a hangar similar to the one she'd just left. There were two planes, a Spike 512 and an Embraer business jet before her. Marcus Drake was carrying an unconscious Ramin Kain onto the Spike 512. A tall, dark-haired woman turned at the top of the stairs into the supersonic jet. It was Armitage, leading Drake and Kain onto the plane.

Armitage had the Spike 512 waiting at Logan International airport and had used it to beat the sunrise in England.

She's further ahead than we thought. More like six hours, we are far behind her.

Juliette paused for a moment, using the implant in her forearm to send a private message to Joan Lewis, the loremaster in the English force team. 'Armitage arrived in a supersonic jet before sunrise. The Embraer is a decoy carrying a GPS beacon only.'

She dropped out of her mind palace and declared, "Francis, we need to go to Goathland in England."

Francis nodded. "Peter, set course for Goathland, UK."

"Sure, Boss," Peter replied. "I'll file a new flight plan once we take off."

"Good work."

Juliette sat back, she had two main questions to answer. What was Armitage's plan, and who was the Red Empire spy? It was clear that Peter, Yvette or Chiara was an opposing agent, but she couldn't identify who. The team couldn't afford to drop all three due to the risk of one. It was clear that whoever was the spy had provided Armitage with the information to compromise the safe house sensor array – it could have got them all killed – and yet it hadn't.

Armitage had been in the perfect position to wipe the team out but had failed to do so. She'd achieved a stunning victory against the Mirovar force team and had kidnapped Ramin Kain from under their noses. The obvious part of her plan was that she could torture Kain to reveal a host of sensitive information about the Order.

The obscure part of her plan was using Kain as a lure and providing a trackable GPS signal to follow. If she wanted to kill the team, she could have done so already – it had to be something else – but what? What were the implications of Armitage keeping the Mirovar force team alive, and how much longer would she stay her hand?

Juliette re-entered her mind palace and began searching for answers. What were the patterns in everything she knew? What were the gaps in her knowledge? She found herself in the midst of a large, well-lit hall. The rest of the Mirovar force team appeared in a circle around her, their faces impassive. A door opened on the far wall of the room. The light in the room retreated, casting everything into gloom. Armitage walked into the room, striding purposefully toward the team. The shadows deepened until only Armitage, and the members of the team were visible before the surrounding darkness.

Armitage slowed as she approached the edge of the team. She slipped through the ring. Walking past Juliette, she approached someone behind her.

Juliette whirled around.

The world shifted violently.

The shadows vanished. Juliette stood before a massive warehouse. Bright lights seared between the weathered gantries overhead. Dead men in matt-black body armor littered the Boston docks. Armitage stepped forward, putting her hands on the shoulders of two young people standing casually together, dragon swords in their hands.

Anton and Li! Her plan is about Anton and Li. But what does she want with them?

Juliette dropped out of her mind palace, turned toward Francis and whispered urgently, "Her plan is focused on Anton and Li!"

"… We still have to rescue Kain."

"We have to block her plan."

Francis nodded, his lips pressed firmly together, he whispered, "Strategy my love, we need to vary our strategy." He stood up, turned around and addressed the rest of the team, "Everyone, you have three hours to get some sleep. That will leave us with two and a half hours to prepare before we land in England. So, get some rest while you can."

The team responded by reaching for pillows and blankets. The lights in the cabin dimmed, someone flicking a switch for the team.

Juliette reached across the aisle and found Francis' hand heading toward her own. They squeezed each other's hands, and she caught his gaze in the shadows. His eyes lay shrouded with serious thought. He wouldn't get much sleep tonight. She closed her eyes, knowing she wouldn't get much sleep either, her mind bedeviled by a single question. What does Armitage want with Anton and Li? She didn't know, and she felt in her heart that this was the most important question to answer.

She sighed and drifted off into a restless sleep. Sleep disturbed by a dream where Chloe Armitage wore a delicate golden crown, and to her left and right stood Anton and Li. Both wore black armor emblazoned with a red dragon on their chests, their dragon swords sheathed at their waists, and long vampire fangs resting over their bottom lips.

She woke with a start, whispering hoarsely, "No. Never."

No one else heard her.

* * *

The Embraer business jet sat on the tarmac waiting for permission to take off. Peter and Anton sat in the cockpit. Peter began preparing a new flight plan – they were going to a private airfield outside a village named Goathland in Yorkshire, England.

Anton slapped his knee, and declared, "We have to take the initiative, we're always on the back foot."

Peter flicked a button on the console, setting the communications with the air traffic control tower to receive only. They would tell him soon enough when it was time to leave.

"You're right. The last few months have been crap," Peter agreed, raising an eyebrow and looking at Anton wryly. "Ever since we met you on the Boston docks. It's probably all your fault."

"Peter – I'm serious."

"Yeah, I know," Peter sighed. "We just got our asses kicked. We should be dead. They cut through our sensor array like it wasn't there and took us by complete surprise."

"How did they do that?"

"I hate to think, but seriously, someone had to have told them how to do it."

They sat back in silence for a moment.

Anton's heart sank and he whispered, "Who would've done that? Everyone's loyal, aren't they? Look how we fought together against those gangster vamps a couple of weeks ago, and tonight – everyone fought against the Red Empire and Shadowstone. Who could do that? Who could put their lives on the line in battle and then turn around and betray us?" he shook his head. "It doesn't make any sense."

Peter paused for a long moment, staring out through the aircraft's windscreen before replying, "There's only one conclusion I can draw. I'm sure I'm not the only one in this team to put two and two together and come up with four. There must be a spy in the team. Someone is working for the Red Empire or the Vampire Dominion, or both – whoever they are – they're buried deep."

Anton looked hard at Peter. "How deep?"

Peter grinned. "Well, of course, it wasn't me."

"You wouldn't admit it anyway."

Peter's grin evaporated. "Well, that's true enough. You'll have to make a decision about who you really trust."

Anton paused for a long moment, frowning.

"I'm cut – we share a room. While I haven't exactly saved your life, I did clean up after you with a vamp who was escaping that apartment building a couple of weeks ago."

Anton remembered Peter's battle axe flying past his shoulder, tumbling end over end before it sheared through a vampire's skull in the midst of a battle in Boston. He hit Peter on the shoulder. "Yeah," he shrugged his shoulders, "it couldn't be you. I would be dead by now if it were you. You could've killed me a hundred times by now."

"What makes you think that I would reveal my hand by killing a novice. C'mon, if I was a spy, why would I reveal myself over a small fish like you?"

Anton smiled briefly, then frowned.

"Hey, you opened this can of worms," Peter noted.

"Yeah, it's a problem I can't solve at the moment, but getting back to what I really wanted to say. I'm never going to defeat Armitage unless I can seize the initiative."

"That would be 'we.'"

"Yes … unless we seize the initiative."

"What are you proposing?"

"We need better weapons. I mean, you're an armorer, can't we be doing something more? What about using a lot more silver?"

"Silver?"

"Yeah silver. Why aren't we using silver weapons across the board?"

"We used to decades ago."

"Huh! What's the problem?"

"Well think about it. Imagine a force team carrying a lot of silver and then match that up to a vampire's sensory ability. Their sense of smell is far more powerful than a human, and they have a massive aversion to silver. They would typically detect the Order team well before we found them. Add in modern air combat systems like helicopters and drones, and they simply stand off and vector in air attacks on us. That's when we really dropped the use of silver, the advent of aerial weapon systems killed its usefulness. The Order had to give up using a lot of silver as it kept giving our position away and getting us killed. It was more trouble than it was worth. We can get away with using a small amount of silver in bullets and in specialized traps where the silver is well hidden. Otherwise, it's more of a problem for us than it is for them. The Order has been well and truly down this path time and time again. We've already optimized our combat systems. There are no special weapons modifications that are going to give us a decisive edge."

"Oh," Anton noted. "At best, we can get away with a carefully concealed silver weapon."

Peter nodded.

Anton sat back in his co-pilot's chair. There were no easy fixes for seizing the initiative away from Armitage. He shook his head and asked incredulously, "Why didn't she take the opportunity to destroy us in Maine? She could have done both. She could have abducted Kain and killed the Mirovar force team. This is a critical point. The Mirovar force team being alive suits her goals."

"Clearly, but what's her plan?" Peter asked.

"Precisely, if we knew that, we would know what to do to counter it."

"And there you have it."

Anton stared at Peter for a long moment. "But how do we find that out?"

"It's an age-old question in any war. How do you find out your opponent's plans?"

Anton looked out the windscreen at the runway stretching in front of them. "There has to be a way. I don't accept that she's always going to be ahead of us."

"You and me both."

"Juliette said it's a trap. We can anticipate that and plan for it. How's she going to maximize her advantages?"

"She'll want to shut down our situational awareness and divide us up into smaller groups. Then pick us off one by one." Peter paused. "But, in her case, splitting us up into pairs would be enough."

"She's that good?" Anton asked, "Gang almost killed her."

Peter sighed. "Her skills are legendary. Gang was a rare talent with the sword."

The two young men fell silent for a long moment.

"We used fireworks in the warehouse at the Boston docks to haze the vampires," Anton reminded Peter, his gaze intense. "She'll use darkness."

Peter nodded. "Our nightglasses won't be enough. We'll need portable lights."

"Small ones we can keep hidden, so she doesn't realize we've got them until it's too late."

"We've got flashlights on board, but they will be a little too obvious."

"Do we have time to pick up some portable LEDs?"

"We'll see."

The voice of an air traffic controller came across the comms link. It was time to take off. Peter switched the comms link back to bi-directional, acknowledged the command and pushed the throttle forward.

The pursuit was underway.

"Once I take off and get this ship on auto-pilot, I'll get you to take the first watch, wake me up if anything seems off. I'll grab the spare seat in the cabin. I've got to get some sleep; I'll relieve you in a couple of hours."

"Sure," Anton agreed.

"Hey – don't crash the plane while I'm sleeping."

Anton rolled his eyes. Peter grinned at him and said, "Oh yeah, one last thing." He reached into a document holder and pulled out a booklet. "Read this, its got public data on the details of the latest tech deployed with the UK military. Shadowstone typically uses the same gear as part of blending in with the locals."

Anton took the book. On the cover was a menacing twin-barreled main battle tank called the 'commander.' He put it aside to read later. He focused his attention on assisting Peter with taking off. A minute later the aircraft was off the ground and winging its way toward England.

* * *

Chloe Armitage still trusts my loyalty.

The Raven fitted a U-shaped pillow around their neck and curled up underneath their blanket. Doing their best to get comfortable in the reclined chair. Their mind was on fire, their emotions roiling in fits and starts. Less than six hours before, they'd discovered the Red Empire had allied with Chloe Armitage and Marcus Drake. Shabbah al Ahmar's second agent in North America was Armitage, the right hand of Cornelius Crane, king of the Vampire Dominion. The Raven had flip-flopped between belief, denial, elation, and despair a dozen times since the battle in Maine had revealed the truth. They didn't want to believe it. Surely their father, the Red Ghost, could not have betrayed everything the Red Empire stood for. An alliance with a vampire was anathema and no true follower of the Way could allow such an arrangement to persist. It would have to end and soon, and even then, they could only expiate the stain on their father's honor in one way – through his death.

What had happened to the Red Empire in their absence? Could things have changed so much in a little less than ten years? What of the elite warriors of the 'fist' teams, why hadn't they done something to stay the Red Ghost's hand? Were they all so swayed by his aura of command, to lose sight of the essence of their faith?

The Raven had been little more than a child when they'd left the Red Empire. The question loomed before them. Had they misunderstood the true nature of the Red Empire? Only understanding what a child could understand. Albeit, a clever, talented child, but a child nonetheless. Had they only seen what their instructors allowed them to see?

The Raven shivered beneath their blanket. Finding precious little comfort as they pulled it tighter around themselves. Slowing their breathing, turbulent emotions steadied, ebbing away, evolving into profound loneliness. Wherever they stood, they now stood alone.

They glanced around the dimly lit cabin. The Mirovar force team was now the only real family they knew, but the relationship was one-sided. The Raven knew them, they didn't know the Raven, only the mask the Raven wore. The Raven shuddered beneath their blanket. Their heart sank — there was no hope of acceptance if they revealed who they really were. They'd done too much damage, revealing how to bypass the sensor array to Armitage, and inviting the devastating attack that had destroyed the safe house and taken so many lives.

The Raven resolved to earn their forgiveness, to redeem themselves. They could do it, especially if they managed to thwart Armitage's current plans.

Her trust is the one lever I have that could change everything. I must be watchful; a critical moment will come where she will rely on what I know. It will be at that moment I will be able to betray her to her doom.

The Raven sighed, everything would rest on a single decision, they would have to make it count. With that in mind, they closed their eyes and drifted off to sleep.

Chapter Two

"The mind palace relies on two interlocking factors. The fundamental mind palace discipline, and the use of the implant-laptop-Internet cloud to access massive data. The first is personal training and discipline, and the second is technology. The human-machine interface has a quirk. There is no way you can physically access the raw data and comprehend it as a totality. The technology creates a gestalt experience, essentially a vivid, lucid dream, where the information is presented in metaphorical imagery. A skilled loremaster can guide and interpret the dream to establish an augmented view of reality that approaches precognition." – Juliette Mirovar, loremaster of the Order of Thoth.

"One caveat – without due care, lucid dreams can easily become nightmares beyond your control." – Juliette Mirovar.

* * *

Private airfield, Goathland, Yorkshire, August 22nd, 05:31

Overhead lights gleamed off the sleek body of the Spike 512 supersonic business jet as it rolled to a stop in the middle of the hangar. Within moments, an upright rectangular seam appeared in the white skin behind the cockpit. A door emerged from the body of the aircraft and swung down to the ground with a faint hum. Stairs pushed up from the inner surface of the door.

Chloe Armitage walked through the Spike's open doorway and descended the stairs. She wore her dark-gray combat fatigues from the night before. Before her stood five men. A loose knot of Red Empire assassins, wearing their traditional garb and weapons. A four man 'fist' team led by Tamsah al Ramil, aka the Sand Crocodile. The fifth man, was tall, lean, much older than the others, with sandy-gray hair and dressed in a well-made black suit. He stood at attention next to a dark-blue Rolls Royce.

Behind Chloe, Marcus Drake hustled the struggling form of Ramin Kain from the plane. Kain's head twisted this way and that, hidden beneath a tight-fitting black hood with a single opening over his nose.

Chloe came to a halt before one of the Red Empire assassins. He was the shortest of the four, barely five feet six inches tall, but thick-set, a veritable barrel of muscle and grit.

He looked up at Chloe with a pair of dark brown eyes like flat river stones, and introduced himself, "Ms. Armitage. I am Tamsah al Ramil, you may call me by that name or by Sand Crocodile. My men and I are at your service."

"Please, Mr. Tamsah. Call me, Ma'am."

"Yes, Ma'am."

"Your master's instructions are clear? You are fully aware of our rules of engagement?"

"Yes, Ma'am. We are to serve you unto death, or if you order us to attack each other or the Red Empire – whichever comes first."

"… Indeed," Chloe observed, a slight smile caressing her lips. She looked intently into his eyes. "Are all the preparations made?"

"Yes. We have built the trap you requested."

"And tested?"

"Yes, of course. The Red Empire does not lack advanced engineering skills."

Chloe's left eyebrow arched quizzically. "Of that, I'm sure." She glanced briefly at Kain. "But you will show me while Marcus ensures our guest is properly attended to."

Tamsah al Ramil nodded. "Yes, Ma'am."

"Then let's proceed. Time is short."

Chloe strode to the Rolls. Her driver bowed low and declared, "Ma'am. It is good to see you home again."

"Yes, David, it is good to be home. Now please make haste for there is much to do, and little time to do it."

"As you wish, Ma'am."

Chloe slipped into the rear of the Rolls Royce saloon. Marcus, Kain and the Red Empire assassins went to a pair of Land Rovers. In less than thirty seconds, all three vehicles left the hangar in convoy heading east to Armitage Manor.

* * *

Ramin Kain's heels dragged down a set of stone steps, clunking one after the other all the way to the bottom. He counted twenty steps curving to the right as they descended, clearly a spiral staircase. He sucked in air, there was a faint aroma of sea salt, the ocean must be nearby.

In a moment of clarity, he was thankful Marcus Drake wasn't dragging him feet first into whatever hellhole the vampire was taking him to. The stairs ended, Drake pulled him to his feet, a grip like iron on the back of his neck.

"I'm sick of hauling your carcass around. You can walk from here," Drake declared, his voice heavy with irritation.

Ramin obeyed. Drake could rip his head off faster than he could think about it. The only thing stopping him from doing so was the will of Chloe

Armitage. Ramin had no illusions about bargaining his way out of this mess. His only hope was to stay alive long enough for the Order of Thoth to rescue him. The Walker and Mirovar force teams would try to find him. Within a day or two, the other force teams would mobilize resources. He hadn't lost yet, he still had options. Armitage would question him, that was obvious – he would have to spin it out as much as possible. Keep her thinking there was more to learn, keep giving her a reason to keep him alive.

He stumbled on a bit of rough, ancient flooring. "What the hell!"

"Shut up, and keep moving."

"Do you think someone could build a level floor?"

A fist slammed into his gut, he jack-knifed forward, gasping for breath. Drake dragged him back upright, his heels coming off the floor. "Shut up, I said. Was that not clear enough for you?"

"Uh huh," Ramin grunted.

He staggered forward. Drake helping him along with a ruthless slap here and there to guide him around corners and along corridors. A barely detectable breeze whispered past him – somewhere there was an opening to the outside – and a possible escape path. As bleak as things looked, Ramin had not given up on the idea of escape.

Drake twisted him around and pushed him hard up against a cold stone wall. Something swished through the air and the bonds on his wrists fell away. Drake instantly pushed his right hand up high. A new manacle snapped around his wrist, a chain clinking against the stone. Drake lifted his left hand up and manacled it too. Then Drake locked a third brace tight around his throat with a loud click. The big vampire kicked his right foot back, a fourth manacle snapping tight around his right ankle. A second later, his left ankle was bound with a fifth manacle.

Ramin leaned forward. The chains attached to his throat rattling with him over the rock, jerking his hands back hard. The chains were all attached to each other behind him. If he pushed his face forward, his hands would pull backward, and vice versa.

He ramped hard, testing the strength of the chains, but without success. No matter how hard he struggled, there were no obvious means of escape. The black hood became wet with perspiration, clinging to his face like a mask alive with his growing fear. He took a deep breath, exhaled, sinking back against the cold stone of the wall.

A hand gripped the top of the hood, ripping it off Ramin's head. He blinked owlishly, his eyes adjusting to the bright lights strung along the ceiling. He stood chained to a solid stone wall. The chamber was four yards across and six long. There were two open entrances, one to his left and the other to his right. Drake and Armitage stood behind a waist-high wooden table in the middle of the room. A brown leather satchel and a large white bucket sat on the table.

Armitage reached into the satchel and withdrew a large carving knife. She regarded it skeptically for a moment and remarked to Drake, "This looks a little blunt." She sniffed with disdain. "But I suppose it will have to do."

Ramin's eyes widened; he pushed back hard against the cold stone of the wall. All thoughts of 'toughing it out,' evaporating like snowflakes in the summer sun.

Armitage fished around inside the satchel for a moment, then withdrew a large hypodermic needle and lifted it up to the light, studying it closely. She asked Drake, "Has this been cleaned since we last used it?"

Frowning and shaking his head, Drake sucked air through his teeth. "No, Chloe. I'm pretty sure it hasn't."

Ramin shivered.

Armitage sighed, raising an eyebrow. "Do we have any tourniquets?"

"Sorry – it's another mess."

"Really Marcus?"

"I've been rushed," Drake offered, shaking his head. "It's been the very devil lately to keep up with events."

Armitage stroked his cheek lovingly. Leaning up, she kissed him. "It's alright my dear. We'll make do with what we have."

Armitage and Drake dropped their embrace, turning to stare at Ramin, their eyes flashing, their grins sporting long fangs.

Ramin wondered what had gone wrong. The last twenty years had proceeded smoothly, beginning with the assassination of George Madison, the previous Head of the Order of Thoth, and his lover Mary Creeley. The framing and exiling of his chief rival, Arthur Slayne, had ensured his rise to the Head of the Order. For nearly twenty years, he'd subverted the leadership of the traditionalists and promoted men loyal to his cause. Establishing a secret detente with Cornelius Crane had been the last step in his master plan.

The goal was the transformation of the Order of Thoth into an efficient fighting force under his unquestioned rule. With most of the old traditions thrown into the bin of history where they belonged, he could wield the force teams as their sole commander-in-chief. The force leaders would be his trusted lieutenants. Then he could use the detente with the vampires to draw their forces into a deadly trap and victory would be his.

His plan was the fruit of genius and deserved to succeed. It would have succeeded if it hadn't been for the insane arrival of Anton Slayne. A plague on his damned family. He had to see the Slayne family line stopped, and extinguished to the last leaf on the last branch. If he ever managed to get out of this mess, he would see to it personally.

Anton Slayne gripped his imagination. An insolent, head-strong boy; no match for a man of his genius, and yet, Slayne was walking free somewhere while Ramin languished in a vampire's dungeon.

A deep sense of injustice boiled within his soul. Incredulous rage ripped through him, making him bold. Ramin stood tall and called out, "Do your worst Armitage. Once Crane finds out that you haven't kept me safe, you're done for."

Armitage laughed briefly. Blurring forward, she halted six inches in front of his face.

There was a slight pressure in his groin. He glanced down, the carving knife was in the crease of his thigh, pressing his trousers against his skin.

Armitage arched a quizzical eyebrow and asked, "Shall I cut left, or right? Shall it be a quick death, or shall I make you into a ... what was the word you used?" her eyes sparkled with delight. "A girly."

Oh my God! She remembered that.

Ramin's testicles attempted to retreat into his body cavity. His anger vanishing, replaced with frigid tentacles of terror writhing in his gut. He pushed back hard against the stone wall and gasped out, "You will pay for this."

Armitage stepped back for a moment, twirling the knife in a circle with her right hand. "I don't know what it is, everyone keeps saying 'you will pay,' and yet, it never happens."

The knifed flashed in the overhead lights; the blade slicing through the skin and muscle an inch below the inner crease of his right thigh. Ramin gasped in shock, it all seemed so unreal. A part of his mind had never admitted this could actually be happening; not to him, not to Ramin Kain, not to the smartest man in the room. Not to the one who always managed to get away with everything. The sight of his own blood spraying onto the flagstones of the floor and the ravenous fingers of pain radiating up from his groin destroyed any remaining doubts.

Armitage flashed away. Drake rushed forward with the white bucket. He placed it underneath the wound, catching Ramin's blood as it rushed through his severed femoral artery.

Perspiration slicked Ramin's forehead, a bead of sweat rolling into his left eye. His heart raced. He gasped for air, his life draining away with every beat of his heart.

Armitage scrunched back the left sleeve of her dark-gray combat fatigues, exposing the fair skin of her arm. She picked up the syringe, pressing the needle against the vein in the crook of her elbow. She applied more pressure and broke the skin. Drawing back on the plunger, the syringe filled with her blood.

She stared at Ramin; her eyes filled with intent. She was not playing with him anymore – the real game was about to begin.

Ramin's skin paled with blood loss. His heart began to struggle to find blood to move through his veins. His breathing was almost useless. Armitage appeared in front of him, the needle of the syringe plunging between his ribs into the left ventricle of his heart.

It was like pouring nitrous oxide into a hard-revving V-8 engine. His heart surged. Armitage's blood began spreading throughout his body. A ravishing fire sweeping through him, burning away all vestiges of his humanity. Transforming him into an apex predator, a creature of the night, a vampire.

Reality strobed, flashing in and out, bounded with utter darkness and searing light. The agony of the transformation went beyond sensation – becoming unutterable – beyond words and forms, shattering all distinctions, and rendering Ramin mute. Time disappeared, his mind fled, but there was nowhere to run to. There was only the experience of boundless suffering. A thing unto itself, overwhelming his reality and throwing down the walls of his sanity.

Ramin drooled, his lips trembling, mouthing words he couldn't utter. His body vibrated. The chains binding him rattled and scraped across the cold stone.

The agony peaked, then evaporated away. Ramin sucked in a great breath and released it all at once. The transformation was complete.

Hard light lit the room, the angles sharp and clear. Down a corridor to the right, a noisy mouse scurried along the base of a wall. Its musky scent indicating it was moving into a fertile cycle. Waves were slowing breaking against the stony beach far to his left. The salty aroma of the sea was everywhere. Above him human voices talked in the Manor house – every word was crystal clear. Armitage stood in front of him, poised, immaculate, filled with dreadful purpose. Drake loomed beside her, relaxed, alert, and deadly.

The smell assaulted him like a hard slap in the face. His own blood, in a bucket near his feet. He lunged for it, blurring forward, the chains snapping taut dragging his hands back. Drool splashed from his mouth; he grinned a harsh joyless grin of ultimate effort. His tongue flicked desperately over his lips, his gaze focusing hard on the bucket. His nostrils flared, the need flooding through him was equally exquisite and horrible. A cavernous desire, an overwhelming force demanding immediate action.

"I must feed!" he shouted, staring ravenously at the bucket of blood. "Feed me. Give it to me. I must have it."

Armitage dipped a handkerchief into the blood, wetting one corner. She placed it an inch in front of Ramin's face. He strained to reach it. She moved it closer, a drop trembling on the corner of the cloth.

Ramin strained, the drop of blood fell onto his outstretched tongue.

Ambrosia! Nectar of the gods! His eyes fell shut for a brief moment as he savored his first taste of blood as a vampire.

Ramin swallowed, but there was almost nothing there. The thirst for blood, the ravenous hunger returned, now doubled in strength for he'd tasted its release. He wanted to tear at his face with frustration, but his manacled hands couldn't reach. He stared at the still damp cloth in Armitage's right hand, and at the bucket of blood behind her.

He panted, reflexively straining against the manacles and chains, but to no avail – they were beyond his new vampire strength to break.

Armitage leaned forward slightly and declared with avid interest, "Now we're ready to begin the interrogation. Tell me, how does the Order haze the Panopticon feeds when conducting operations?"

Ramin stared at her in helpless desperation.

She waved the bloody cloth before his nose.

He started talking.

* * *

Richard Walker, the force leader for the United Kingdom arm of the Order of Thoth, scanned the private-airfield hangars with high-powered binoculars. He descended into silence, activating a partial ramp to become perfectly still.

Joan Lewis, the Walker force team loremaster sat on a fold-away stool next to her commander. Her laptop was open, and her implant lay warm in her forearm. She studied the private airfield and waited for Walker's directions.

There were two hangars. A larger one, its doors shut, and a smaller one that had recently accepted an Embraer Legacy 500 business jet. A jet chartered out of Logan International airport by one Ramin Kain, a New York City businessman, or so stated its public flight plan.

A single, dark-blue Rolls Royce left the open hangar. Driving sedately through the private airfield's main gate, it turned onto the main road heading toward the town of Whitby. The driver, dressed in a dapper black suit with sandy-gray hair was the only occupant.

"No sign of Ramin. Where's the GPS signal?" Walker asked in a gravelly voice.

"Within the Rolls," Joan replied. "Just as Juliette said, the Embraer is a decoy. Armitage's jet will be in the other hangar."

Walker lowered the binoculars, put his hands on the well-maintained wire fence surrounding the airfield and asserted confidently, "We can't trust everything the Mirovar force team says. They've been compromised."

"My own analysis concurs with Juliette's."

Walker scowled. "You're both coming from the same information. You have the same blind spots."

"I know the mind palace is not perfect. I take that into account."

"Still," he remarked, "we'll send in Wilkinson and check the hangars before we follow the car."

Joan glanced down at her laptop. The Rolls Royce was continuing to Whitby. The small town on the coast of Yorkshire was its most likely destination.

"Don't worry," Walker directed. "You can haze the cameras along our route. Wilkinson will be in and out in five minutes, and then we'll follow the car." He turned away from the fence and strode purposefully toward a pair of dark-gray, late model Range Rovers occupied by the rest of his team.

Joan snapped her laptop shut, flicked a stray strand of dark-red hair out of her eyes and followed after him. Her lips thinned, frowning, she tried to reconcile her force leader's words with the honesty and trust she'd felt in Juliette's mind over the implant link.

There was no betrayal or falsehood in Juliette Mirovar. Whatever Walker believed about the Mirovar force team, it didn't extend to their loremaster.

Reaching the front Range Rover, she paused at the door, glancing down the road to Whitby. The second most famous vampire alive was somewhere down there waiting for the Order to arrive. They would be following a GPS signal provided by Armitage in an attempt to rescue Ramin Kain. At twenty-three years old, Joan was the youngest of the loremasters and had only recently joined the Walker force team after their previous loremaster committed suicide.

She hesitated at the car door, her every sense taut. The gray sky lowered oppressively, shadowing the road with threat. Her mind palace hung like a web behind her eyes, ready to activate at a moment's notice. But no awareness, examination, or predictive foreknowledge could shift the dread pooling within her. At the end of the road waited the most dangerous foe she'd ever encountered.

She shivered, blinked and got into the car.

Walker rubbed a hand over his close-cropped gray hair and asked, "Are you okay?"

"Yes," Joan lied; she knew her force leader was in no mood to hear anything else. *I'm not okay. Not okay at all. We don't know enough to be sure of what is going on here. There are too many unknowns. Too many open questions and the answers could kill us all.*

"Good," Walker noted. "The last thing I need is another loremaster cracking up on me."

Joan looked out the car window, cold fingers of fear working their way around her soul. She clenched her fists and hoped she would be strong enough to deal with whatever may come.

* * *

Tamsah al Ramil and his fist team had been at Armitage manor for just on six days.

It was a very short timeframe for implementing the trap in the dungeon underneath the manor and running an isolated network of cameras along the road from the airfield. They'd worked feverishly, like men possessed, in accordance with the plans and requirements provided by James Haley. The camera network was brand new and disconnected from the Panopticon. Whatever technique the Order was using to haze the feeds to the Panopticon would be unable to impact his dedicated camera network.

He sat alone in a pleasantly appointed drawing room near the main entrance of the manor, a small water-cooled server rack whirring softly away in the corner. His laptop fed a pair of twenty-four-inch screens sitting on a table in front of him. A window on the right screen switched from camera to camera, tracking two dark-gray Range Rovers heading from the airfield to the Manor house. If they kept coming, they would arrive in about fifteen minutes. Order operatives packed the vehicles. He counted nine of them and suspected the eldest was Richard Walker, the elusive head of the UK force team.

He stroked the closely-cropped dark beard on his chin, his gaze flicking over the other windows on his screens. There was a multitude of camera feeds including an aerial view from a small drone shaped like a peregrine falcon flying a thousand yards above the manor. A map of the immediate vicinity of the manor showed where his men were. Three small red circles indicating the locations of his own team members. They were all men who had grown up in the Red Empire, their loyalty beyond question.

All the members of his team had passed the first level of the test of the Olgoi Khorkhoi. An initiation that demonstrated survival capabilities and raised them above the common ranks of the Red Empire. A second fist team, accompanied by a group of young recruits and led by Nasr al Dam had deployed on a mission to the United States. He shook his head slowly, the recruits had barely completed their ramp mastery training, to send an inexperienced force suggested they were expendable and expected not to survive.

His team was the more capable of the two fist teams sent by the Red Ghost, more experienced, more highly trained, more exposed to combat. He trusted that whatever happened to Nasr al Dam's mission, his own team would fare far better.

Tamsah al Ramil had earned his name, 'the Sand Crocodile,' from the Red Ghost himself after passing the second level test of the Olgoi Khorkhoi. His reward had been leadership of an elite fist team. If he survived, and the Red Ghost released him from this mission he would commit to the training necessary to submit for the third and final level test of the Olgoi Khorkhoi. Surviving the final test would raise him to the level of a prince of the Red Empire, second only to the Red Ghost, and equal to the likes of Taipan.

Shabbah al Ahmar had personally selected him for this mission. It was a great honor, and of course, he'd accepted. The orders of the Red Ghost were as law. There was no option to decline, and success would bring great honor to his name. Shabbah al Ahmar had instructed the Blood Eagle and himself on what to expect. The arrangement with the vampire general Chloe Armitage was an elaborate ruse. A game of advantage that would see the Order of Thoth and the Vampire Dominion both diminished and the vampire king, Cornelius Crane destroyed.

The Red Ghost valued the mission highly enough to release for use the most advanced and secret technology the Red Empire possessed. Tamsah frowned, he was uncomfortable with exposing the capabilities of *Gossamer*, especially to the vampires.

Such thoughts bordered on insubordination and were inappropriate for a Red Empire assassin, especially one who had passed into the second rank.

Questioning your superiors was not a normal practice for a loyal warrior of the Red Empire. The Sand Crocodile considered himself to be exemplary in his loyalty, and yet, he found himself harboring doubts. He'd assessed Chloe Armitage on meeting her. She was clearly the most capable and deadly vampire he'd ever encountered, and he wondered if the Red Ghost may have underestimated her.

Underestimating your opponent was not something the Sand Crocodile was vulnerable to. Growing up shorter than most had led others to underestimate him, he understood it as a weakness that others could easily fall into. He vowed to himself to be wary of Ms. Chloe Armitage, general of the Vampire Dominion. She was a dangerous force beyond all reckoning, and he would maintain an escape path for his team in case she betrayed the terms of their engagement.

The two Range Rovers took a critical turn-off, there could be no mistake as to their objective. Tamsah al Ramil tapped his in-ear communicator and reported, "Ma'am. The UK Order team is heading toward the manor."

There was a lengthy pause, then Chloe Armitage commanded, "Hold your positions and observe. Expect them to stage their main force nearby and send in a two-man team to scout the manor house and the dungeons underneath. Guide the local staff to the upper floor and allow the Order scouts to come into the lower levels. I will deal with them there. If they do anything else, then call me immediately."

"Yes, Ma'am, it will be done."

"Excellent," she finished with, the line muting automatically.

Tamsah al Ramil sighed and went to work, issuing orders to his men. He put doubts about the mission aside, there was work to do and honor to win.

What more could a man ask for than that?

* * *

Frowning, Chloe Armitage muted her ear-piece and stepped back from Ramin Kain.

The UK force team were proving to be overly efficient. She glanced at a clock she'd positioned on the table, it was 08:35. She stared into empty space for a long moment. How best to deal with a second Order force team? If she played today to the best of her ability, she could deliver a victory over the Order to Crane, hide what she was doing with Kain and drive Anton Slayne into a fury of vengeance aimed at her king.

Outcomes, she considered well worth taking calculated risks for.

Kain struggled fruitlessly against his chains. They rattled and scraped, he leered at the bucket of congealing blood on the floor a yard in front of him. His left eye twitched, his tongue darting between his lips, his new fangs gleaming in the lamplight.

Chloe stood still, silently contemplating her options. She relaxed, a smile growing on her face. Picking up a blood-stained mug from the table, she dipped it into the bucket and lifted it to Kain's open mouth. The half-congealed blood slid thickly out of the mug. Slurping loudly, Kain tried to drink it all at once.

"Marcus, could you please call the staff upstairs and get them to deliver a couple of good-sized towels and a large bucket of fresh water to the first level."

Marcus nodded and vanished.

Chloe dipped the mug back into the bucket. Filling it to the brim, she fed it all to Kain.

"More," Kain whispered.

"No."

"More," Kain pleaded.

"No."

"More!" Kain shouted.

Chloe's open hand flashed out, a resounding crack echoing off the walls. Kain's left cheekbone shattered, his head almost spinning off his shoulders. "Enough!" she commanded, leaning in close to Kain's face.

Kain panted, blood dribbling from his open mouth. His cheek swelled into a deep purple bruise, which immediately began to fade as it healed.

"I have a deal for you," Chloe offered, arching an eyebrow.

Kain stared at her for a moment, his mouth still healing and said thickly past swollen lips, "You won't keep me alive. Crane would punish you for turning me."

"There are lots of things Crane doesn't know. You can be one of them."

"How could you hide me?"

"Oh – I can hide you. Have no doubts about that."

"I can't trust you."

Chloe sniffed disdainfully. "Are you still deluding yourself that the Order will save you."

Kain stared at her.

Chloe moved in close and whispered harshly into his face, "What hope do you have? The Order will kill you without hesitation. Your only hope of survival lies with me."

Kain hesitated. His eyes flicking down to the blood-filled bucket and back up to Chloe's face. Pride warred with fear on his face. Then something snapped within, his face fell, resignation filling his voice as he asked, "What do you want?"

"It's very simple. When the UK Order team come into the manor, start calling for help."

Kain's gaze lifted from the bucket. "Is that all?"

"Yes," Chloe smiled, her eyes dancing.

Kain murmured defeatedly, "Right. Got it."

Marcus blurred into the room, coming to a halt next to Chloe. He had a pair of soft, white bath towels and a bucket of fresh water.

"Clean him up," Chloe directed, picking up the bucket of Kain's blood and moving to stand next to the exit back to the manor house.

Marcus set to work, Kain looked longingly at the bucket as Chloe carried it away. In moments, he was clean of blood. Marcus turned and sloshed the remaining water across the floor, disappearing any blood splashes.

"Now remember," Chloe said, "the Order are trained killers who will cut your heart out as soon as they understand what you are. Marcus and I will be nearby, we will make sure they don't hurt you, but you must first call out for help and draw them to you."

"I'm bait?" Kain asked.

Chloe's face crinkled into a smirk, her answer hanging in the silence between them.

Kain nodded once, water dripping from his soaking clothes to the floor. "Yes, yes, I'll do it."

Chloe and Marcus turned away, walking into the corridor. Chloe put a finger to her lips and mouthed, *quiet*. She grabbed Marcus' arm, taking him down a side corridor away from the spiral staircase to the upper level of the dungeon.

We have to hide, she mouthed silently, pointing to the solid wall at the end of the corridor. She took a remote control from a thigh pocket on her dark-gray combat fatigues and pressed a stud. The lights in the side corridors dimmed to almost nothing, except for Kain's prison chamber and the main corridors.

They vanished into the shadows.

* * *

Someone was shaking Anton's shoulder.

He woke up, opening his eyes wide. Chiara was leaning over him, her brown eyes luminous in the half-light of the Embraer's cabin.

"Time to get up big guy. We have to do strategy," she said. "C'mon you need to be involved."

"Sure," Anton replied, throwing back his blanket. "How long before we land?"

"Ninety minutes. 11:30 local time."

Anton sat up, facing forward from the back of the cabin. Francis Mirovar stood in the middle of the aisle facing most of the team. Peter sat alone in the cockpit, leaning to the side, listening in – the plane flying itself on auto-pilot.

Juliette sat next to Francis, having swiveled her chair one hundred and eighty degrees. She faced the team with her hands in her lap and a serene expression on her face.

Francis declared, "We have made contact with the Walker force team. They have stationed off a manor house just outside the town of Whitby in Yorkshire. We will be landing at," he lifted his eyebrows to emphasize the next words, "a private airfield about ten miles west of Whitby." He paused, looking at the team. "Walker confirmed there was a supersonic Spike 512 business jet at the airfield. It looks like Armitage owns or at least operates this specific 'private airfield.'"

A low murmur swept through the cabin.

"The Order will provide local transport. We will join the Walker force team and prepare for a joint assault on the manor house."

"What's the disposition of opposing forces?" Jay inquired.

"How can we be sure Kain is even in there?" Anton asked, frowning.

Luther snapped, "The GPS signal."

"C'mon," Anton asserted, "The GPS signal could be faked."

Francis declared, "The GPS signal is real, and Richard Walker is verifying the status of Ramin Kain, we'll soon know if he is alive or dead … or worse." He glanced at Jay. "They haven't encountered any hostile forces yet. They're sending in drones to scout the site."

"Drones. That's good," Jay observed.

"We will soon have confirmation that the GPS signal is associated or not with Ramin Kain, and who or what guards the manor house."

"We'll know if Ramin is alive and what we're facing," Juliette stated. "We're not going into this blind." She stared down the aisle at Luther. "We know this is a trap. The trick will be to steal the cheese without springing it."

Luther grimaced sourly.

Anton spread his hands wide and asked, "What if Chloe Armitage is just waiting for two Order force teams to show up, and simply blows up the place with a fuel-air explosive?"

Juliette locked eyes with him. "That's not her plan. She's playing a subtler game."

The knowledge implicit in Juliette's gaze sent a cold shiver up Anton's spine. He gasped out, "How do you know?"

Juliette stared at him for a moment, a glimmer of fear passing behind her eyes. She shook her head once and remained silent.

Juliette's concern washed off Anton. The lash of fear fled before a thrill of anticipation. He wondered if today would be the day he would confront Chloe Armitage with her villainy and extract vengeance for her crimes against his family.

It was about time; he was sick of waiting.

* * *

The shotgun blast rang out, the aerial drone fragmenting into a haze of metal and plastic.

"Damn! They took out our last drone," Mary Turner swore, adjusting her Order nightglasses. She sat with her back against a tree, across from the manor house resting atop a cliff on the Yorkshire coast. The nightglasses networked with mini-cameras on the drones, providing her with first-hand visuals of whatever they encountered – while they'd lasted.

"Maps? How far in did you get?" Richard Walker demanded. He glared in annoyance as his second netmaster worked feverishly over her laptop.

"Not far enough. Our second flier got about forty yards into a large open space leading from the cliff face over the ocean. Add that to the ground drones we got to the front door, and we still have a lot of unexplored territory under the building. There's a couple of levels of cellars, dungeons or something else down there."

"How many humans did you count in the floors above ground before we lost our first flier?"

"Ten. Four on the ground floor, and six on the upper floor."

"Anyone running cold? Any sub-37? Any vampires?"

"None. But they could be far enough below ground to be out of reach of our drone's sensors."

There had been rumors the Red Empire had allied with the Vampire Dominion to wipe out the safe house in Maine. Calvin Woodstock had phoned him in the middle of the night to tell him the dreadful news of Ramin Kain's abduction and the Mirovar force team's inability to prevent it.

"Joan," Richard called out to his loremaster. "Analysis?"

Joan Lewis blinked, her eyelids fluttering for a handful of seconds. Dropping out of her mind palace, she said, "Any skilled shooters could be destroying our drones. There is no direct evidence of Red Empire presence here, but—"

"Good," Richard interrupted her, putting his hand up.

With all the drones destroyed, the only option remaining was to send in a squad, he called out to his best pair of warriors, "Frannie, Mikey, load up on silver, it's time to go in and verify the target."

"Yes, Sir," they chorused together. They donned Order nightglasses, picked up their weapons and blurred away. They would be going in hot and fast, relying on the Ramp's heightened senses and reflexes to keep themselves safe. Their nightglasses were equally effective in daylight or darkness and would transmit what they saw or heard back to the Order force team.

Richard stepped away from his loremaster and stared at the imposing manor house. He was confident he would soon know precisely where Ramin Kain was, and whether he was alive or dead. His lead combat team may even be able to extract Kain without risking the rest of the team.

He smiled broadly; it was a good day to fight vampires.

* * *

Joan Lewis moved over and sat down next to Mary Turner.

She fitted her nightglasses. The feeds from Francine and Michael would form images in front of her eyes. She stilled her mind and prepared to enter her mind palace with her eyes open. It was a difficult state to be in, drawing information from the external world and feeding it directly into her mind palace to generate inferences about what was happening. It was the best way she could help her teammates survive whatever was beneath the manor.

She wanted to do her best; especially if there was a weird alliance of the Red Empire with the vampires.

* * *

Francine Parker, Frannie to her friends, paused for a moment at the bottom of the spiral staircase. Her Order nightglasses, adjusting automatically to the improved light in the corridor of the second level of the dungeon beneath the manor.

She half crouched, sighting along the barrel of her FN P90. Fluorescent lamps bolted onto the stone ceiling a dozen feet overhead lit the corridor in front of her. Twenty feet in front of her the corridor branched to the left and right. Another thirty feet past the intersection, the corridor opened up into a well-lit room.

"Help! Help!" Ramin called from within the room.

He was somewhere in there, out of sight from where Frannie stood. She recognized his voice, it sounded real, like he was alive, but it could be a clever, high-quality recording. She needed to be sure before Michael Wilson, and she could take further action.

Frannie took a step forward, Mikey moving silently into the space behind her. His head swiveled, taking in everything else around them. Frannie would cover their front, and he would cover her back. They'd worked together as a team within a team for years; their combat awareness with each other honed to a fine edge.

She held up her right fist, Mikey halted. With two fingers, she indicated left and right. They would clear the corridors before they advanced into the room. Ramin called out again, his voice filled with desperation. Frannie ignored him for now. There was no way she was going to lead them blindly into a room, not for anyone, she was too experienced an operator for that.

Frannie sank into silence, accelerating her perception of time, and heightening every sense. Dust motes floated lazily in the pale light. The edges of the flagstones stood out in razor sharp relief. Waves crashed against distant rocks, and nearby chains rattled and scraped across stone. She scanned the floor, looking for tripwires, or a sensor lattice. The floor was clean, her nightglasses and enhanced vision picking up nothing but worked stone and ancient ant trails.

She blurred forward to the edge of the intersection, Mikey a step behind. The two side corridors were unlit. The whole site stank of 'trap,' the hairs on the back of her neck quivering in response. They'd almost reached Ramin, whatever was going to happen would happen soon.

There had been no sign of the shooters who had taken out the drones. All the people in the house had fled upstairs as they came in through a side door into a ground floor kitchen. The way into the basement level had been open, and Ramin's calls for help had been easy to follow. They'd cut through the first underground level in a couple of minutes, mapping the pathway through a maze of intersecting corridors and rooms for anyone else to follow. Their nightglasses recorded their steps, transmitting the information back to the team's netmasters.

Joan's voice whispered in their ears, sounding ghost-like through their ear-bud communication links, as she muttered from within her mind palace, "They're hiding, they're hiding in the walls."

Despite years of combat experience, the words sent shivers rippling over Frannie's skin. Her fingers found a stud on her FN P90. A flashlight slung underneath the barrel switched on, sending a beam of focused light down the left corridor. Mikey, facing in the opposite direction, immediately followed suit, illuminating the opposite corridor.

They moved their beams of light carefully over the nooks and crannies of the corridors – nobody was there. The corridor on her side ended in a stone wall forty feet away. There was nothing but featureless walls carved into the rock and a flagstone floor.

She glanced at her partner.

He shook his head.

Well, Frannie thought, *loremasters aren't perfect, sometimes they get it wrong.*

She signaled 'forward' with her right hand, moving across the intersection into the corridor heading toward Ramin's prison. Mikey followed, his eyes tracking left, right and behind them. Frannie reached the threshold, crouching down next to the right side of the entrance. Ramin Kain, his eye's wild, stood chained to the far-left wall. He was dripping wet, water pooling in the gaps between the flagstones at his feet. Opposite him stood a table on which sat a brown leather satchel bag, a clock, and a blood-slicked knife.

Ramin's face twisted with rage and desire, he screamed, "You took too long!"

At the corner of her left eye, a shadow moved across the floor. Twisting around, she darted to the left toward her target. Mikey was already blurring in the opposite direction, his own FN P90 coming up. Frannie hit her trigger, her FN P90 exploded into life, a stream of silver rounds raking the ceiling.

The lights went out, pitching the dungeon into utter darkness.

Afterimages faded in her nightglasses. The crimson outlines of two vampires scrambling like flying shadows along the ceiling. Diverging violently to the left and right as the silver rounds ricocheted off the stone between them. Her left hand ripped the submachine gun toward the nearest target, her right flashing to her shoulder where the handle of her katana jutted up.

She drew her sword free, her gun barking, the shots cracking along the corridor. She fell deeply into silence, the Ramp flowering within her.

It was time to fight.

* * *

Nothing beats vampire vision in the depths of the dark.

The Ramp masters blurred to the left and right, streams of submachine gun fire lancing up at Chloe and Marcus.

Chloe twisted hard right, letting go of the ceiling, dropping to the floor in front of the male.

He drew his katana from over his left shoulder in a sweeping vertical arc. His FN P90 flamed as he sprayed a second burst of 9mm silver bullets at Chloe's chest. The flash of each round leaving the barrel strobing along the corridor, the stone walls stuttering in the fragmented light.

Chloe leaned backward, almost becoming an upside down 'U' as her head dipped back toward the floor. Her left hand brushed the flagstones, her right hand bringing her sword over her in an arc. The bullets streamed above her, a stray one ricocheting off the immaculate blade of the Red Dragon, instantly fragmenting into a cloud of burning silvery dust.

There was no time to evade. Chloe shut her eyes and held her breath. Rebounding off the floor, she passed through the thin edges of the silver mist. The Red Dragon's arc completed, lancing forward toward her opponent.

Numbness bloomed across her skin.

Her blade beat past the Ramp master's katana, slashing through the center of his face, its blood-soaked tip emerging from the back of his head. His eyes bulged, his mouth gaped, he quivered for a moment. She drew her sword back with a wet swish, and he dropped to the floor like a stringless puppet.

Chloe staggered back to the nearest wall.

The woman blurred backward into the room letting rip again with her FN P90, the silver bullets spraying down the corridor in a disciplined 'S' pattern, while her katana lifted into guard position.

Chloe dropped to the floor, the bullets skittering off the stone wall above her head.

Marcus launched himself from the top of the wall, flying through the shadows above the stream of bullets. Landing beside the woman, his big hands grasped her head.

She started to scream, her katana blurring around in her hand.

His hands flicked left and right.

There was a sickening crack, she went limp, her submachine gun clattering to the floor. Marcus dropped her, and she fell in a heap over her smoking gun.

Marcus grunted, staggering backward. The woman's katana jutted from his right side where it pierced his body beneath his ribs. He dragged the blade clear, dropping it onto the floor. Blurring back to Chloe's side, he ignored his wound and bent to lift her from the floor. She leaned on his arm as he helped her back to her feet.

"Nu-u-mb," she muttered, shaking her head slowly.

"You, OK?" Marcus asked, his voice filled with concern.

"Ge-ar, kill … the … gear."

Marcus left her propped against the wall, where she wobbled on unsteady legs. The touch of silver had been fleeting, a minimal dose, but made worse by the bullet transforming into a hot aerosol after colliding with the much harder meteoric iron of the Red Dragon.

Marcus reached down, picked up the man's nightglasses and ear-buds, crushing them into powder with his hands. He did the same with the equipment worn by the woman.

Chloe touched a remote at her waist, and the fluorescent lamps flickered back on.

She took a step, standing straighter, the effect of the silver ebbing away. "Now … they've … proof of life."

Kain wrinkled his nose and stated with utter disgust, "God that stinks."

Marcus glanced at him, snarled and said, "Silver! Welcome to our world."

Chloe shook herself, took a couple of deep breaths and flicked the Red Dragon clean with a flourish. She strode forward, stood in front of Kain and declared, "Now that little interruption is over, let's continue. Please tell me more about the network of Order safe houses."

Kain grinned lopsidedly and said, "Sure, sure, I'll tell you everything."

"Marcus," Chloe directed, "fetch the blood bucket." She indicated the two dead Order operatives with a casual wave. "Refresh it with one of these two bodies; we have work to do."

Marcus blurred away.

Kain continued explaining everything he knew about the Order safe houses.

* * *

Everyone in the cabin of the Embraer jet watched Juliette Mirovar as she communed with the other loremasters. The implant on the inside of her right forearm linked wirelessly through the laptop on her thighs. A network of satellites transmitted the signal via an encrypted quantum cloud, enabling direct mind to mind communication with her peers.

Juliette started suddenly, then blurted out, "Two of our people just died."

Francis frowned, shocked. "Who?"

"Wait. Joan is sharing now," Juliette advised, her eyelids closing, her eyes vibrating beneath them as if she was dreaming. She sat still for a few seconds, then abruptly stood up. "Michael Wilson and Francine Parker are

39

dead. Vampires, most likely Chloe Armitage and Marcus Drake killed them."

Anton's eyes tightened with sharp intent, he asked, "The manor house is hers?"

"Is Ramin Kain alive? Is he safe?" Samuel Luther asked urgently.

Juliette glanced at Luther first and answered, "He's alive, chained in a dungeon." She turned to Anton. "Yes, most likely the manor house is something to do with Armitage. Perhaps her original home. It's a place she knows well."

"Home territory," Li said grimly. "A powerful advantage for her."

Juliette shook her head. "Richard Walker is enraged; he wasn't expecting this."

"He should have been," Anton chimed in. "He's a force leader, he should know better."

"Who are you to judge?" Luther snapped. "You're a novice, you know nothing of the world."

Anton took a breath, reminding himself not to rise to the bait. Li's response after the battle at the safe house had cut him deeply. He vowed to himself to remain mindful and focused on the mission. Ignoring Luther, Anton asserted, "Li is right. Armitage has the home ground advantage. She probably expected the Walker team to send in two people and just waited for them to show up. Now we know precisely what she wants us to know and nothing more than that."

Luther snapped incredulously, "You can't know—"

"Enough Luther," Francis declared. "Anton has made a good point."

Juliette nodded. "We know it's a trap and so far, nothing has happened to change our evaluation of the situation."

"It's hers. I'm right on this." Anton asserted, a grim smile crossing his face.

"All I've got on the manor house is that it's important to her," Juliette answered. "There is nothing tying it to her."

"All her tracks have been wiped clean," Anton declared. "She's been playing this game for decades."

"How do you know?" Jay asked.

Anton looked directly at Jay and replied, "We've been underestimating her every step of the way."

"You're just speculating Slayne, you know nothing," Luther declared, frowning, his voice rough with emotion.

Francis stood up from his seat, taking a position at the end of the aisle facing everyone in the cabin. "A high price has been paid," he declared to the team. "But the Walker force team has mapped the target environment, and we have absolute confidence Chloe Armitage, and Marcus Drake are in the manor. We may be able to rescue Ramin Kain and deliver a defeat to the Vampire Dominion at the same time."

"About time," Luther snapped bitterly.

Francis stared at Luther until Luther looked away. He looked approvingly at Anton and said, "Well done Anton, you've made an astute observation. While we don't know how long Armitage has been working on her current plans, it is clear she is prepared for our arrival." He glanced knowingly back at Luther. "Only a fool would think otherwise."

Luther sucked air through his teeth.

"Despite these losses, our plans stand. We will land at Goathland, join forces with the Walker force team and make a combined assault. Any questions?"

There was a long moment of silence.

"Very good. Do what you can to prepare, today we go to battle against a general of the Vampire Dominion."

Anton glanced at Li. She lifted an eyebrow, a slight smile curving the edges of her mouth, her eyes alight with anticipation. With the combined might of two Order of Thoth force teams behind them, trap or not, now was the opportunity to deliver justice for their lost loved ones.

Anton looked away from Li, his gaze going up to the ceiling. His fists clenched, a wild emotion surging through him. His soul flowed with it, a boat on a heaving sea of wrath.

He took a deep breath, letting it out with a sigh. The rage ebbed but did not go away.

He wondered if he would ever be truly free of it.

* * *

Gordon Heathmont's laptop gave a specific ping. He'd received an email from James Haley, the head of the US arm of Shadowstone.

While nominally at the same level within the worldwide Shadowstone organization, as the head of the founding United Kingdom arm of the service, Gordon saw himself as the more senior of the two men. Crane had created the UK arm of Shadowstone in the late 1880s, almost a full forty years before the establishment of the more junior service in the United States. If Gordon were able to have his way, the UK arm would subordinate the US arm. Certainly, he would not have led sixty plus men to their deaths in an Order of Thoth slaughterhouse.

The UK organization was too experienced and too careful to fall into such a trap. The gung-ho mentality the yanks had been born with had never infected the UK organization. The UK arm was old school, there was no way such a disaster would occur on his watch.

He clicked the email, a counter in the upper right-hand corner of the email started counting down from sixty to fifty-nine to fifty-eight. The email was self-obliterating with a sixty-second time limit once opened. In sixty seconds, the email and every track it had made from its origin point to Gordon's laptop would vanish. It would be as if the email had never existed. Haley was ensuring no one else, not even the Panopticon, would be aware he'd sent the email and that Gordon had opened it.

Gordon read the email, his eyes widening. He studied the attached photograph, committing it to memory. A young man, hooded, medium-tall, athletic, getting onto an Embraer Legacy 500 business jet. Anton Smith, a member of the Order of Thoth directly implicated in the battle on the Boston docks. He jotted down the aircraft's identification numbers, noting the flight plan had changed from London to a private airfield in Goathland.

The counter hit zero, and the email disappeared from his screen.

There was no way the Embraer was landing anywhere near Goathland. He lifted the phone and dialed RAF Command. Interceptors would be taking off in another five minutes.

There was no time to waste, he must organize a suitable welcome for Anton Smith. He would be waiting to see a member of the Order of Thoth taken into custody. He flipped his laptop closed, packing it into a protective travel case. He stood up from his desk, stepping around it to a nearby coat rack. Picking a long dark-gray coat, he put it over the beautifully crafted bespoke dark-blue suit gracing his slim frame.

Grabbing his laptop case, he strode from his office, calling to his men in the main room. In minutes, they would be on the road north to the RAF airbase at Coningsby.

The Order and Red Empire operatives possessed special skills and abilities. His men and the troops under his immediate command had graduated from the ultra-secret, Phase IV, Day Guard program. It was time to test them on Anton Smith.

Leading half a dozen suits from his office, he whispered to himself, "We'll soon see who's stronger."

Gordon was confident in his men, they could perform amazing acts of speed, strength, endurance, and healing. They would be a match for a single Order of Thoth operative, of that, he was certain.

* * *

Peter stared through the windscreen at the bright blue sky, rubbed his hands together and flexed his fingers. He enjoyed flying, but piloting a plane in a straight line, mostly on auto-pilot, was a recipe for boredom.

The comms-link to air traffic control squawked, "Flight N971AZ, acknowledge communications."

"Control, flight N971AZ acknowledges communications," Peter replied,

"You have a new flight plan. The destination is now RAF airbase Coningsby. Begin descent in ten minutes. Acknowledge."

Peter paused for a moment, somewhere, shit was hitting the fan. "Flight N971AZ acknowledges new flight plan."

"Control out."

Peter twisted around in his seat until he could see into the cabin. He saw Francis look up and caught his gaze.

"Hey boss, we've got a problem."

"What's that?" Francis asked.

"We've been redirected to the RAF airbase at Coningsby."

Juliette said, "They know who we are or at the very least suspect it."

The other members of the team leaped up from their seats, crowding the aisle just behind the cockpit.

"UK Shadowstone in action?" Jay asked.

"For sure," Yvette asserted, leaning past Jay's shoulder.

"Okay Peter," Francis directed, "do as they ask. We'll have to adapt our plans."

"Sure Boss," Peter agreed and began setting the plane up for the new flight plan. In another forty-five minutes, they would be landing at a major RAF airbase, surrounded by Shadowstone and regular UK military forces.

Peter sighed; this could get messy in a hurry.

* * *

Bright sunlight gleamed off an ocean of fluffy white clouds beneath an azure sky.

Flight Lieutenant, Gracie Williams' F-35 Lightning II interceptor did a slow looping roll over the Embraer Legacy 500 business jet. The maneuver allowed her to closely examine the plane. She was close enough to see the pilot, a big red-headed fellow. He nodded politely at her as she passed overhead.

She took a position to the left of the Embraer, her wingman mirroring her position on the right. She flicked a switch, opening the doors to her missile bays and tilted her F-35 slightly to show what she was carrying. Having bared her teeth, she righted her aircraft and looked at the red-headed pilot.

He was smiling at her with a dopey 'love at first sight' grin and gave her a thumbs up.

"What the hell," she whispered. It wasn't the sort of reaction she expected to see when showing off four MBDA Meteor ramjet air-to-air missiles. Just one of which could turn the Embraer into a smoking ruin on the ground.

The pilot grinned again, nodded and waved. He pointed down to the ground and then gave her a double thumbs up.

Gracie waggled her wings left and right. Message understood, there would be no trouble. The red-haired pilot of flight N971AZ would comply. She waited another handful of minutes, and the Embraer started its descent toward RAF Coningsby airbase.

She wondered who these fools were. The intercept orders had come from the highest operational ranks of the Royal Air Force. She and her wingman had been on duty and had scrambled their aircraft. She'd expected to see a Russian Tupolev bomber or a pair of Sukhoi fighters testing UK air defenses. She'd been surprised to discover they would be escorting a business jet down to her home base.

Whoever was on board the jet had clearly pissed off someone important. Gracie didn't know who that could be, it was a question well above her pay grade. She shrugged, getting down to business, the fine art of shepherding the Embraer all the way down to the ground. They wouldn't be able to do anything without her wingman or herself knowing about it.

* * *

The two RAF F-35s descended in close formation with the Embraer business jet just under two thousand yards above the ground. There would be no arguing with the escorts, they were all heading to RAF Coningsby and would be landing in less than ten minutes.

Organized chaos filled the cabin of the business jet. The Mirovar force team had opened a locker built into the floor and extracted eight stealthy wingsuit gliders. A set of parachutes remained in the locker, unusable in a situation requiring daylight capable stealth. The team members were variously checking weapons, clambering into their wingsuits, and checking each other's webbing and attached gear.

"Okay everyone," Francis called out. "Peter will set the autopilot to land the plane, and we will escape with our stealth wingsuits. They have the radar cross-section of a marble and are the next thing to invisible to the human eye." He looked at Anton and Li. "Don't worry about your lack of wingsuit training, just follow your guide closely all the way down. Anton pair up with Chiara, Li, your guide is Juliette, is that clear?"

Anton and Li both nodded, moving with their wingsuits to pair up with their guides.

"Furthermore, we will be landing in farmland to the southwest of the airbase. Once you hit the ground, evaporate the wingsuits, grab your gear and form up on Jay. Is that clear?"

"Yes, Sir," resounded through the cabin.

Chiara helped Anton with the final touches of his wingsuit. Checking the fit, adjusting the armored hood over his head and zipping him up at the front.

Anton said, "I've seen this on video, shouldn't we have parachutes? How do we actually land these things?"

Chiara smiled. "Don't worry, we just ramp all the way down. These wingsuits are super cool. They allow for a rapid brake just above the ground. Don't worry, you'll love it. Follow directly after me, mirror what I do, and be ready to brake when I do. Whatever you do, don't drop out of the Ramp, if your reflexes aren't in a heightened state – you won't brake in time, and you'll hit the ground."

"Hit the ground? How hard?"

"Hard."

Chiara and Anton looked at each other, Chiara raised a quizzical eyebrow, a slight smile curving her generous lips.

"Everyone ready?" Francis called out.

"We have a problem," Jay said with a frown.

"What?" Francis asked.

"We're one glider short."

"C'est un foutu bordel!" Francis swore. "What a mess." His eyes flicked over Luther, and he said, "Of course – we have an extra man."

Francis rubbed his chin. "We need a volunteer. Someone must stay on board, land the aircraft, breakout of the airbase and meet us at rendezvous site number two by 12:00 at the latest." He looked around the cabin. "You will have to make it on time. Our mission is time-critical. We cannot afford to leave Ramin Kain in the hands of our enemies – he knows too much about the operations of the Order."

Peter called out from the cockpit, "Hey Boss, I'll take the job."

Francis nodded. "Good man."

"Trust me," Peter asserted, loud enough for everyone to hear. "I'll see you all at twelve, don't be late – I don't like waiting."

"Francis," Anton said, "I could stay with Peter, with the two of us it would double the chances of escaping the airbase."

Francis shook his head. "No, it would double the chance of losing both of you." He reached out, grasping Anton's shoulder firmly. "You come with us. We put one man at risk and make sure the rest of the team escapes."

Peter called out from the cockpit, "Anton, take my battle vest with you, I doubt I'll be fighting vampires this morning, and I'll get it back off you later."

Anton snatched up the battle vest, tucking it inside his wingsuit. Chiara rechecked his fittings and nodded once; he was good to go.

"Ten minutes to landing," Peter advised. "I'll yaw the plane and make it look like I'm about to crash. It'll focus all eyes on me and make your escape easier."

"Good work, Peter. Okay team, get ready. Form up in a line behind Jay. We need to land outside the airbase. We have to go now. Peter – open the escape hatch!"

The team moved, in moments, they formed a line behind Jay. Yvette put her hand on Jay's shoulder. Behind her Luther put a hand on her shoulder, followed by Juliette, Li, Chiara, Anton and Francis at the end. An electrical whirr emanated from the floor just behind the cockpit. A six-foot seam opened up, exposing the cabin to the exterior, the air rushing past howled like a banshee. The seam widened to a three foot by six-foot hole in the floor. Jay leaped through it, immediately followed by Yvette. The plane began to yaw left and right. The line began disappearing through the hole. Chiara leaped through it, Anton didn't hesitate, he followed her, ramping hard as he did so. Time slowed, the world snapping into sharp clarity, the plane drifting away above him. A dozen feet below him, Chiara was already in position, her arms out in a 'T' and her legs spread in a 'V.'

Anton copied her, she was just visible, an outline against the verdant landscape beneath them. The stealth effects of the wingsuits were excellent, almost too good, Anton sharpened his focus, vowing to copy her movements all the way down.

They'd come out of the plane about fifteen hundred yards above the ground. The coating on the gliders would make them essentially invisible to radar. The color schemes would defeat human observers. Still, there was a window of risk where the RAF or Shadowstone could spot them. There was nothing else they could do, every other option led to the immediate capture of the entire team.

Anton had no time for thought as he dropped toward the ground. He watched Chiara closely, waiting for her signal to brake. The ground rose toward them, the Ramp reducing the sense of onrushing speed.

Anton eased off the Ramp slightly, it was fun, exhilarating. Then a thought struck him, *how the hell did they find us?*

He almost missed Chiara's brake. He sharpened his ramp, twisting in the air, his arms flinging out hard.

The wingsuit filled with air as Anton braked hard, a grassy paddock rushed toward him in slow motion.

"Damn—"

* * *

The F-35s roared overhead.

The Embraer business jet had already landed and was taxiing over toward a large hangar. Gordon Heathmont had ordered his men to direct the plane nose first into the broad cream-colored building. It was never going to fly again. They would impound it and strip it to reveal every last shred of information about the Order of Thoth. Men with flags indicated where the jet was to go, and it obediently moved into position within the hangar. The engines slowed to a stop. A big red-headed pilot clambered out of the cockpit, disappearing into the cabin of the aircraft.

Gordon studied the aircraft; it was the expected flight. In addition to the pilot, the Order of Thoth agent, Anton Smith, should be on board. He ordered his men forward. Six suited operatives armed with H&K MP5 submachine guns stepped forward and flanked him. Four squads of four Shadowstone operatives, wearing full tactical combat armor, and armed with H&K assault rifles, took up positions on the corners of a rectangle surrounding the aircraft. Beyond them, were another four squads of Shadowstone operatives armed with rifles with net throwers instead of grenade launchers. Outside the two rings of Shadowstone operatives were another thirty members of RAF regiment regular soldiers. At the hangar's main entrance, a pair of light armored RAF Regiment vehicles, armed with 7.62mm machine guns on their roofs, rolled in from Gordon's right. They faced the rear of the aircraft, blocking any escape in that direction.

All of his Shadowstone men, the suits, and the armored warriors were all participants in the Phase IV Day Guard program. His commander, Cornelius Crane, the head of Shadowstone, had provided the serums for the program a year earlier. Crane had hinted of a new program in the works. The Phase V program which would provide another leap forward in the capability of his operatives.

Gordon lifted a loud-hailer to his mouth and called out, "All personnel on board the aircraft. We have surrounded you. There is no chance of escape. Come out with your hands up, and you will receive fair treatment."

The plane's cabin door swung open with a soft hum, revealing a set of steps and part of the interior of the cabin.

The Shadowstone operatives tightened their stances. Their guns lined up on the open doorway. Silence fell over the hangar.

Gordon wondered if Anton Smith and the red-headed pilot were foolish enough to resist capture.

He smiled grimly and hoped they were.

* * *

Peter lined the Milkor MGL up on the tail of the Embraer and pulled the trigger.

A 40mm grenade 'chuffed' from the barrel of the launcher. It sailed along the aisle toward the back of the aircraft, trailing a plume of gray smoke. Keeping his finger on the trigger, Peter pulled the weapon slightly to the right. The first grenade passed through the left side of the luggage compartment at the rear of the plane, detonating immediately. The backwash of the first blast lit Peter's face with a fiery light. The next grenade launched as the explosion of the first was dying away. The shaped charge of each grenade directed the vast majority of its energy in a narrow cone, slicing through the aircraft's bulkhead. The second grenade flashed and boomed in the narrow space of the cabin.

Peter lifted his launcher, the third grenade chambered into the barrel and shot toward where the ceiling met the rear bulkhead. It struck the target like a God-driven hammer, slicing through the plane's spine with ease.

Peter ramped hard, blurring down the aisle toward the back of the plane. Smoke filled the cabin. Electrical cables hung sputtering from the ceiling. Light from the hangar cut through ragged tears in the walls and ceiling, gleaming off the smoke. The floor shook as he ran along it, the wounded plane trembling with each step. He hit the back wall with his hip and shoulder at full speed – and the fractured rear of the Embraer came apart like torn paper.

Around him, the tail of the Embraer fell away in pieces from the body of the main plane. Peter rolled out onto the concrete of the hangar floor, his eyes taking in everything around him. The Shadowstone operatives in close-fitting matte black body armor were already on the move, as were the suits armed with H&K MP5s. Beyond them, regular RAF soldiers were just beginning to react, their faces marked with shock, amazement and grim fear. The Shadowstone operatives were rushing toward him at faster than normal pace. The bastards had found a way to enhance their men. It was the sort of situation he would normally call 'target rich,' but today he'd no time for quips.

The main gates of the hangar were in front of him. A pair of uprated RAF Regiment Land Rovers stood in his way. He dodged to the right, sending his fourth and fifth grenades through the front radiator grills of each vehicle. The two grenades ripped through metal and piping, shattering the engine blocks. Smoke and flame exploded from the front of each vehicle. RAF soldiers shouted with alarm, spilling out of the cabins.

A slim gray-haired suit with a loud hailer shouted, "Take him alive."

Some of the RAF soldiers weren't listening, letting rip with automatic weapon fire, bullets whizzing through the air behind him. They lacked experience with shooting at a fast-moving target, their bullets slashing through a helicopter parked on the far side of the hangar.

Peter bounded to the top of the nearest vehicle, twisting, his right arm outstretched, firing the last of his grenades into the left wing of the

Embraer. Ninety pounds of reserve jet fuel exploded, most of the wing and half the body of the plane disappearing in a fiery cloud of fragments. A moment later, the reserve fuel in the right wing evaporated in a secondary explosion. The detonations blew through the hangar, men falling away with the wash of the explosions.

Peter launched himself forward, leaping off the top of the vehicle and out of the hangar. Bullets zipped past him, RAF Regiment soldiers firing wildly in the chaos within the hangar.

To his left and right, four Shadowstone operatives armed with net throwers ran to where he was landing. Peter landed on his feet, dug in and began blurring forward. The men fired their net throwers. Black, weighted nets flew through the air, spreading out as they approached him. Peter turned hard right, the first net missing. He twisted to the left; the second net flew past him. He leaped, the third one caught his ankles, flipping him mid-air. He started falling, the fourth net reached out, wrapping around him like a giant's hand.

Peter hit the ground hard. The four men rushed forward, firing tasers. He shivered and trembled as the electric shocks froze his nervous system. They rolled him in the nets like spiders trapping a fly.

In moments, he could barely move, Shadowstone had caught him.

* * *

Gordon Heathmont strode over to the red-headed man wrapped up in weighted nano-fiber cables. He reached down, plucking a pair of earbud communications devices from the man's ears. He wrapped them in a gel-impregnated cloth and put them in his pocket.

Gordon stared down at the man and demanded sharply, "Who the bloody hell are you?"

The man attempted to shrug, failed, and then replied, "Why would I tell you?"

"Where's Anton Smith."

The man's eyes widened, nonplussed. "Who?"

Gordon frowned. "Are you going to keep answering everything with a question?"

"Are you going to keep asking them?" he answered, one eyebrow raised.

Gordon glared at the bound man coldly, he indicated with his forefinger left and right to two of his suits. "Pick him up." He turned to a third man and commanded, "Call your van around, we'll take him to the Facility. We can question him properly there."

The first two suits dragged the Order operative to his feet. He was about the same height as his men, around six feet two or three, but appeared to be twice as wide. *Gods*, thought Gordon, *he's a big fellow, he must weigh two sixty, two seventy pounds, and there's no fat on him.*

He was obviously enhanced, faster and stronger than anyone Gordon had seen before. He'd almost got away. Only the closest of the Phase IV day guards had been in a position to stop him, and they'd almost failed.

Gordon stepped forward, stood as tall as his slim five feet, seven-inch frame allowed and stared into the man's eyes. They were blue, serious and filled with secret depths. A slight dusting of freckles ran across the skin of the man's cheeks, and a shock of thick, red hair framed his face. There was a reservoir of bold confidence in his manner at odds with his current helplessness. The young man stared back at him with a look that Gordon would have called insolence in anyone else, but there was something else about this fellow, an unwavering sense of purpose that was larger than both of them.

An uncharacteristic shiver ran up Gordon's spine. He held the man's gaze, but took a step back and said, "You won't be such an arse later today, not once we're done with you."

He looked away, a nondescript dark-gray Shadowstone van rolled to a stop next to them. In moments, his men hooded the Order operative and threw him into the back of the van, four of the enhanced Shadowstone agents leaping in after him. A second car, a late model dark-blue Jaguar sedan pulled to a stop behind the van. Gordon walked over and got into the luxurious rear of the car. The last two of his suits joined him, and the Jaguar rolled forward after the van.

He leaned forward, tapping the driver on the shoulder. "Make all speed to the Facility. There is no time to waste."

The operative, tapped his earbud, giving quick commands to the driver of the van. Both vehicles accelerated away toward the main entrance of the airbase.

As they approached the gates, Gordon stared out the window, silently vowing to break this Order of Thoth operative if it was the last thing he ever did. There could be no mercy shown to those who would oppose the agents of stability and control. They had to maintain a stable world order for the good of all. The only alternative was chaos and destruction, and Gordon Heathmont was willing to do anything that was necessary to defeat Shadowstone's enemies.

Chapter Three

"I can categorically affirm there are no military or paramilitary forces operating in this country without the express permission and knowledge of his Majesty's government." – The Prime Minister of the United Kingdom on the floor of Parliament.

* * *

Near Coningsby, Lincolnshire, August 22nd, 11:16

Anton awoke upside down, his cheek brushing against the warm fatigues of one of his teammates. He blinked, there was a break in the cloud cover, and the sun was shining.

Jay was carrying him over his shoulder on the edge of a slim bitumen road. On one side was a caravan park, on the other side, a river shone with a silvery light.

His head bounced painfully as Jay jumped over a pothole in the path.

"What the hell!" Anton said, squirming in Jay's grip.

Jay grunted, leaned over and stood Anton up. "About time, you've been gaining weight."

Anton glanced around, rubbing his head. The team was moving along a paved bike path toward a newly constructed industrial estate on the left past the caravan park. F-35s thundered to the far right, about a mile away from the Mirovar force team. Suburban housing and rows of low trees partially obscured the airbase.

Chiara handed him his slim backpack, Peter's battle vest, and the Blue Dragon, and stated matter-of-factly, "Here's your gear."

"Thanks," Anton replied, putting on Peter's vest and cinching it tight as it was easier to wear than carry. He shrugged on his backpack, carrying the Blue Dragon in its scabbard with his left hand. He glanced at Chiara and asked, "What happened to our wingsuits?"

"They self-immolate: smokeless, very little heat, a little bit of ash. How's your—"

"Keep moving," Francis ordered from the rear of the line, "and pick up the pace, we have to reach our first rendezvous point with the Order helper."

"Order helper?" Anton asked rhetorically, looking back over his shoulder. "That was quick. The RAF intercepted us less than an hour ago."

Francis shook his head slightly, and said, "Juliette and I switched everyone in the UK to active hours ago. There's a helper nearby."

Anton's eyes widened. The Order was more pervasive than he'd thought.

Three explosions cracked in a tight sequence from the RAF airbase on their right-forward flank.

"That'll be Peter," Anton said. "Damn, we shouldn't have let him go in there by himself."

Juliette brushed past him; studying the distant airbase. "He's still online. Check your earbud communications."

Two whip-like cracks ripped through the air. Another pair of grenades going off. A second later a powerful explosion echoed in the distance, and gray smoke billowed out of a hangar on the northern side of the airbase.

"Give 'em hell Peter," Anton whispered. He tapped his right ear. The earbud was still in place and activated with his touch. He picked up what was happening with his friend.

There was a sharp crackle of gunfire through the link, Peter had to fight his way clear. The noise abruptly stopped; they'd lost the communications link with Peter.

"What the hell," Anton snapped angrily. He shook his head, his face flushed. "This is a disaster."

Francis jogged past everyone to reach the front of the line, he put his hand out to signal 'stop.' He signaled 'silence,' by placing his hand over his mouth for a moment and then pulled his earbuds out, and indicated everyone do the same. In moments, all the team members removed their earbuds. Once out of contact with a warm human they shut down. He addressed the team, "They are attempting to compromise our comms. Everyone, put your earbuds back in and shift to our backup channel now."

Anton popped his earbuds back in and tapped his right earbud three times. The earbud gave a chirp as it switched to the backup channel. "But, what about Peter, he won't be able to hear us."

Francis looked at Anton and said, "His earbuds will have been taken."

Juliette brushed past Anton to speak with Francis, she said softly, "There is an opportunity here to deceive Shadowstone."

"Precisely."

Juliette nodded and put a hand on Anton's arm. "Don't assume the worst, it's not over yet, Peter is very resourceful. We'll go to the second rendezvous point and wait for him there."

Anton looked at her, his eyes questioning. "I really hope he makes it."

He wasn't comfortable with hope. Hope was one of the most useless and unreliable things in the world. He gripped the scabbard of the Blue Dragon, his eyes narrowing. There was no way he was leaving his friend to languish in captivity, facing torture or worse – not if he could do anything about it.

God only knows what's happening to Peter.

Anton vowed to find a way to rescue his friend. After all, his friends were far more important to him than Ramin Kain.

* * *

The Jaguar sedan passed through the northern gates of the RAF airbase and raced along the street behind the dark-gray Shadowstone van. They needed to get through the suburbs of Coningsby before they could hit the main roads heading south toward the Facility.

Gordon Heathmont dialed Cornelius Crane on his secured, private line. It was time to report the capture of a member of the Order of Thoth. His call rang out unanswered, it didn't even go to voicemail. Nor was the call picked up by Crane's executive secretary Ursula Zielinkski, or another functionary. In his thirty-two years with Shadowstone, the last nineteen heading the UK arm, Gordon had always been able to contact his commanding officer or a designated functionary.

He frowned and tried again. The call rang three times, and then blipped as it transferred to another Shadowstone phone. The familiar voice of James Haley, the head of US Shadowstone answered the call, "Hello Gordon, what can we do for you?"

An undercurrent of false conviviality flowed beneath the American's words. Gordon glowered with distaste, Haley had pitched the words perfectly to skate a thin line between insult and parody, leaving Gordon with no room to call the uncouth man out for his lack of manners. As to why the man had not resigned after his utter failure with the Boston incident on June the 11th was beyond his comprehension. The man had no breeding and was clearly little more than a trumped-up barbarian who had risen far above his natural station.

Unfortunately, and to his great dismay, Gordon still had to deal with him as an equal. It was an appalling situation and a sad indictment of the world that it tolerated the likes of Haley in positions of real authority. Gordon vowed to himself to do his utmost to see Haley removed and replaced with someone better suited to administrate a transnational security service. A man with the right background. A man with an Eton education and a doctorate in law from Cambridge University. A man who had come from a long line of serious men who had done great deeds of service.

A man like himself.

This will jam it right up him, the upstart bastard. Gordon's thin lips curled into a smug grin, and he declared, "I've caught an Order of Thoth operative, and it is imperative Cornelius Crane is notified."

There was a momentary pause before Haley replied, "Have you identified the operative?"

"Not yet, but we will. Where is Crane?"

"Cornelius Crane is unavailable at this time. Can you describe the operative?"

"Why is Crane unavailable?"

"There is a glitch in the communications system. No one can reach Crane."

Gordon paused, why should communications be down on the very day Order of Thoth operatives were landing in England? Had the Order managed to compromise the system? It beggared belief. He frowned; it was infuriating to have to deal with Haley instead of Crane. He sighed, submitting to answer the American. "Male, about six feet two inches tall, heavy, muscular build. Thick red hair, blue eyes, and an insolent, over-confident manner."

"His name is Peter Lamb," Haley advised. "He is a known member of the Mirovar force team."

Gordon's mouth turned down in a disappointed sneer. How did Haley know so much about the operative? He'd already checked the Panopticon, it was the first thing he'd done as his car crossed the RAF airbase from the hangar to the front gates – there was nothing on 'Peter Lamb,' in the system. Why hadn't Haley shared this information earlier? Was Haley deliberately withholding information from his peers in Europe? Gordon shook his head, he wouldn't be surprised to discover Haley had done precisely that, most likely motivated by personal ambitions to bring the US arm of Shadowstone to a position of global primacy with himself at its head.

Just another example of the hubristic over-reach of a small-minded man given too much power.

Gordon demanded, "Why isn't this information in the Panopticon?"

Haley ignored the question and asked, "Where are the rest of the Mirovar force team?"

Gordon glared at his phone. "What do you mean? The plane landed. Only one man came off it, and he is in custody. Anyone else on the aircraft would be dead. It's a smoking ruin in a hangar at RAF Coningsby."

Haley snorted.

Gordon seethed; *how dare he laugh at me.* "Answer me, man! What do you mean?"

"The Mirovar team are in England. They're on an operation right now. You have one of their number. There are at least another six to nine members in your vicinity. I don't know how they did it, but they evacuated the plane before it landed."

"Not possible. We intercepted the plane before it flew over England and then escorted it all the way down. No one left the plane."

"Well, it happened."

Gordon sniffed disdainfully. "If they're here we will soon find them."

"Or they will find you."

"I hope they do. They will discover we're able to defend ourselves."

The line was quiet for a long moment. "Don't underestimate them."

Gordon shook his head. "Not a chance. Now please ensure Crane receives this good news at the earliest opportunity."

"I guarantee it, I will pass it on as soon as communications have been restored."

Gordon stared at his phone as if the sheer intensity of his will could reach through the network and pin Haley down. "I'll hold you to your word."

"Of course."

The line disconnected as Haley hung up.

Gordon took a deep breath and let it out slowly. Calming himself; he considered a list of options in his mind. It was better to be safe than sorry. He would mobilize Shadowstone, and UK government agencies and military forces. He would set a net so tight that not even a mouse could fart without him knowing about it. If the Mirovar force team were operating in the UK, he would discover them, and then he would direct the full force of his Phase IV day guards upon their heads.

Gordon smiled avidly; he'd more than one ace up his sleeve. He pulled the captured earbuds from his pocket and fitted them into his ears. Before he marshaled his forces, he would see what he could hear from the mouths of his opponents. Of course, his enemies could have realized that their operative's earbuds had fallen into the hands of Shadowstone. Whatever he heard could be false information.

He was confident he would be able to tell the difference. His smile broadened as the communications link became live in his ear.

Today would be a special day.

* * *

The industrial park loomed before them.

Francis held up his hand, signaling the team to stop, he turned and directed, "It's time to start a ruse. Juliette and I will be the only ones involved. We'll be on our normal communications channel until further notice. It's important that everyone stays quiet."

Anton nodded with the rest of the team.

He half listened as Juliette and Francis discussed their plans to abort the mission and head to the west coast of England for a boat pickup with the remainder of the team. Their conversation touched on the loss of a single man, Peter, and their belief that he would have to be 'left behind,' for the good of the Order. They finished by declaring future communications silence to minimize risk.

Anton imagined catching up to Peter's captors and freeing his friend. He couldn't imagine doing anything else.

* * *

Jay took point as they trooped in a loose line along a street filled with various small factories and workshops.

Anton turned left with the rest of the team, following Jay into a laneway. A neatly painted white roller door began to rise up on the third building on the right. The building sported a bright red sign on a white background that read, 'Dogdyke Motor Repairs.'

The roller door pulled to a halt at the top with a clatter of chains. A young woman stood in the shadows inside the door. She'd pulled her dark hair back beneath a red scarf and wore dark, oil-stained coveralls, and black work boots. She nodded, gesturing for them to come into the automotive workshop. They all filed in, spreading around the workshop, wary eyes watching everything. The young woman punched a black button on the wall, and the roller door descended smoothly. In moments, they were alone with her and a pair of late model Range Rover SUVs resting on the cold concrete of the workshop's floor.

Francis approached the young woman and asked, "You already have our message?"

"Yes. Everything is prepared."

"Good work, show us."

The woman moved behind the charcoal-colored Range Rovers, lifted their rear doors and said confidently, "The fit out is the same for both cars. Full tank of fuel. Supercharged engines. Reinforced stealth body armor good against 5.56mm or 9mm ball, not so good for anything more potent than that. Top speed of a hundred and thirty miles per hour and zero to sixty in six and a half seconds. On board each vehicle, you'll find four H&K MP5s, each with two mags strapped together, and four extra mags of high-velocity rounds each. A .50 cal sniper rifle with thirty rounds. A Milkor MGL with six HEAP rounds, and one spare load of another six HEAP rounds. There's a satchel with a dozen AP hand grenades."

Francis frowned. "Define, 'not so good.'"

"Right," The young woman nodded. "Sustained 7.62mm fire will break through the windscreens and the armored panels. Don't go anywhere near depleted uranium rounds – they'll tear these babies apart."

"Any silver?"

"Only what you brought with you."

Francis nodded. "Thanks, you've done well."

The young woman nodded once without smiling, her brown eyes serious. She turned, striding back to the roller doors, she said over her shoulder, "Follow the street north along the river for about a mile. You'll hit a 'T' intersection, that's the A153, Sleaford road. Turn to the north and cross the Witham River, from there on, head for Whitby."

The team split into two groups, loading their packs, edged weapons, FN P90s and magazines into the two cars. Francis climbed into one of the Range Rovers, Juliette took the other side and opened her laptop on her knees. Anton clambered into the back seat behind Juliette, and Li took the other side, the Green Dragon joining the Blue Dragon resting between them. Anton looked to his left across the workshop, Jay had taken the driver's position in the second Range Rover with Yvette at his side, and Luther and Chiara were behind them. In moments, the engines were idling smoothly. The young woman, her dark eyes flashing beneath the fluorescents hit a black button next to the roller doors. They ascended in a handful of seconds. Francis gunned the SUV's engine. The Range Rover accelerated forward and into the street, the second car joining it a moment later.

It was sinking in. They were leaving Peter to his fate. His absence cut through Anton like a cold blade. "We need to find Peter. We can't leave him behind."

Francis replied firmly, "Peter accepted the mission. He knew the risks, and we haven't lost him yet. He may still escape his captors. We'll go to the second rendezvous point and wait for him there." He paused for a moment, his face still, but his eyes were alive with emotion. "We must forge ahead, speed is of the essence, Ramin may still be human, we must recover him as soon as possible."

Juliette twisted around in her seat to look Anton in the face. "We have a dilemma, no one wants to leave Peter. But, where is he? He could be anywhere. We have no way of knowing where they will take him or how soon he might escape."

"What of your mind palace? Surely you can do something."

"It's not magic Anton. I need something more to work with. There are too many options, but I'll see what I can see." Juliette turned back to her laptop and closed her eyes. Her eyelids fluttered like she was dreaming for about ten seconds. She opened her eyes, and her eyebrows lifted slightly. "Peter could still be on the airbase, but it is more likely he will be in transit right now. The only thing I can rule out is that he's not in the air. Clearly, no planes have taken off. There's not enough information to be more conclusive than that." She reached around and patted Anton's knee. "For now, we can do nothing to help Peter. He will have to help himself." She paused for a moment. "Do not doubt him. I would not want to try to hold Peter captive."

Francis declared, "We will go to the rendezvous point and see if he turns up. He's got another thirty-five minutes to get there."

Anton sank back in his seat. But what if they'd tied Peter up, or drugged him, or worse, and he was unable to do anything to get free? What then? He glanced knowingly at Li, she raised a quizzical eyebrow and then frowned, appearing torn between the mission and the option of rescuing Peter.

Whatever he was going to do, it was clear that he would be doing it on his own.

He could live with that. After all, he wouldn't be abandoning Li in the middle of a battle – he would be saving Peter.

* * *

The lead Range Rover pulled to a stop at a 'T' intersection. A weathered sign on the far side of the road pointed to 'Horncastle' on the right and 'Sleaford' on the left. Francis waited for the traffic to clear from the road on the right so that he could turn to the north.

Anton rubbed his forehead; he still had a headache from knocking himself out with a clumsy landing in the wingsuit. Gray clouds arched overhead from horizon to horizon. The sun rested; a dim orb vaguely present somewhere above them. The daylight dimmed like a sudden onrush of twilight. Anton wiped his brow; his hand came away slick with perspiration. A queasy feeling overtook him, and he rocked forward in his seat.

Li's left hand grasped his shoulder, and she inquired, "Anton, are you—"

Her voice trailed off as Anton's perception suddenly accelerated, time slowing down in a deep spontaneous Ramp. Anton shivered, his breath misting before his face. A nondescript dark-gray van was passing in front of the Range Rover.

The world faded, the van coming into sharp relief. It dragged his eyes with it as it rolled through the intersection in slow motion. Faint scratches were crystal clear on the almost immaculate paintwork. The rubber tires thrummed hard on the bitumen. Air rushed over the blocky vehicle. Near invisible smoke puffed from its exhaust. The two men in the front seats were both young, wearing suits and high-end sunglasses, the nearest was touching an in-ear communications bud with a well-manicured finger.

Conviction flooded through him; they were Shadowstone operatives.

Anton tried to drop out of the Ramp, he needed to tell everyone the van passing them right now was Shadowstone, most likely it had Peter in it. He couldn't do it, the Ramp had him in its grip and wasn't letting go.

Time almost stopped. Anton could no longer feel his heart beating – he could barely move; it seemed the slightest movement would require maximum effort. He stared, the men inside the van withered inside their suits, their skin shrinking back over their bones, their eyes darkening to gleaming black orbs. Black streaks stretched across the gray sky like the ill-formed fingers of a malevolent god's dark desire.

Thunder rumbled, lightning flashed, the side of the van corroded away. Inside was Peter, hooded in black, bound in cables and chains. The sky became flame, great gouts of fire storming over the world.

A dreadful terror filled Anton to the brim. Peter writhed on the floor of the van, screaming once in utter agony before collapsing into dust. Above, flames roared and lightning sheeted over the sky. A gust of wind picked up Peter's ashes, flinging them at Anton in a dark storm.

He tried to lean back out of the way but remained frozen in place. The ashes washed around him, ripe with the charnel house stench of death.

Peter was dead.

The Ramp collapsed. The vision vanished. Li's hand clenched tight on his shoulder. "—Okay?"

For an instant, the world felt less real than the vision it replaced.

Anton's head snapped around to face Li. "Peter's dead!" he shook his head. "No, he's not, he's," his left hand shot forward between Juliette and Francis' heads to point toward the van, but the van was no longer there. He twisted left. The van was disappearing southward down the road, closely followed by a dark-blue Jaguar sedan. "There, in that van!"

The Range Rover slammed to a halt. Francis and Juliette both twisted around to stare at Anton.

"What the hell are you talking about?" Francis demanded.

Juliette reached around, putting her hand on Anton's knee and asked, "Anton what happened?"

Anton shook his head, his voice rising, he declared urgently, "There's no time to explain." He glanced out the window. The van and the Jaguar sedan had disappeared around a bend. "They're getting away. We have to follow them."

Francis stared at Juliette intently. "Is there anything to this? Did you see enough of the van?"

Juliette's eyelids closed; her eyes vibrated behind them briefly as she accessed a tightly focused mind palace. She gasped and said, "Yes, mon amour." Turning to stare at Anton, she said insistently, "After this is done, you must tell me exactly what you saw."

Francis declared, "We need to be quick." He floored the accelerator. The supercharged engine roared, the SUV's big wheels smoking as the car shot forward through the intersection and raced away to the south. The second Range Rover with the rest of the team racing after them.

Luther's voice screamed over the communication links, "What are you doing? We have to go north."

Anton said, "We're getting Peter."

"Where is he?" Luther asked.

"In a van," Anton asserted with absolute confidence. "It just passed us heading south."

"A van? What? Are you claiming x-ray vision now? Hell, this is madness. Francis, what of the mission?"

Francis glanced at the clock. "We still have thirty minutes before we need to be at Peter's designated rendezvous point. Even if Peter is not in the van, we can still get back there in time without affecting our overall schedule because we would have waited there until noon anyway." He glanced knowingly at Juliette. "We have the information he is in the van on good authority."

"Mind palaces," Luther uttered in disgust. "They're unreliable. This is a wild goose chase when Ramin Kain needs our help."

Li chimed in. "Peter would never leave any of us behind."

"He's expend—" Luther hesitated for a split second. "Going to have to make a noble sacrifice for the good of the Order."

A chill silence fell over the comm links.

Juliette said clearly, "It's an unnecessary sacrifice when he is within reach."

"The mission has to take priority," Luther said, but the force had drained from his voice.

"Who are we?" Juliette asked as if instructing a wayward child. "What do we stand for if we can't even look after each other?"

Luther fell into silence.

A wave of relief rolled over Anton. They were going to save Peter. He sucked in a deep breath and sighed, left with the mystery of what had just happened. This had been the third vision he'd experienced in his life. The first one was an uncanny sexual encounter with Chloe Armitage at the homeless shelter. It had left him feeling violated, even though he'd given in to it in the end. The second vision occurred during the battle on the Boston docks, where Armitage had beckoned to him. What was going on? Where were the visions coming from? What did the first vision mean? Was Armitage inside his head? Was she figuratively screwing with him? Why did he give in to her at the end, did some part of him want her to win? What the hell was going on? One time he could dismiss as something freakish, twice as coincidence, but three times?

And what was the extreme Ramp experience where time external to the vision seemed to freeze? His mind must be racing through each event, and if the Ramp was involved, how on Earth had he had the first vision *before* Gang had initiated him?

He had no answers. The only thing he was sure of was he had to rescue Peter or something terrible was going to happen. Something terrible like the end of the world terrible. The shadows and flames in the sky had felt malignant as if driven by a horrific and malevolent intelligence.

Li was looking at him with a 'what the hell is going on?' expression on her face. His face froze, he would like to be able to tell her, and he would if only he knew what the answer was. He decided to talk with her later, and explain all three visions. No doubt, Juliette would want to know too.

He hoped they wouldn't think he was going mad.

He prayed he wasn't going mad.

He craned his neck, looking through the windscreen. There was no sign of either the dark-gray van or the dark-blue Jaguar sedan.

He whispered harshly, "Damn it."

* * *

"Where the fuck are we?" Luther asked, his voice dripping with contempt.

The pair of Range Rovers were flying along the road at well above the legal speed limit. There was no sign of the Shadowstone van or its trailing Jaguar sedan. Unless the Shadowstone operatives were hammering their vehicles or had pulled down another road, they should have caught up with them by now.

Juliette glanced up from her laptop and said, "No police radars on this road, … which in itself is an oddity. The UK is one of the most surveilled societies in the world. Why are there no cameras here, especially this close to a major RAF airbase?"

"Juliette," Francis stated, without taking his eyes off the road, trees, and farms whipping past like ghosts of the daylight beneath a gray sky. "We have a fork in the road coming up. Which one did they go down?"

Juliette touched a key on her laptop's keyboard, a GPS map swapped to front and center on her screen. Two miles ahead, the road forked. What would she give for a drone right now? She stared into the distance, dropping into silence and bringing her mind palace into being. Her mind integrating everything she had to hand.

Her mind palace bloomed into being, the external world dropping away. She found herself standing at an empty crossroad, the world was silent, a zephyr of a breeze tickled her nose. The sky hung low overhead, an oppressive grayness smothering the light.

She spun around, four roads, all seemingly identical. But it was a fork they were heading to in the real world, how could there be four choices? Was there another dimension to this problem? Something else, in the air, or underground? Alternate pathways in a mind palace vision could also mean something from the past or future intervening deeply in the present.

Shadows pressed in from each direction.

Despite her stillness, silence, and depth of concentration, Juliette shivered. There was something else here, something very dangerous was moving through her vision. Her skin crawled, loneliness bordering on terror sweeping through her. The real world receded further away.

Her mind palace deepened, the roads and shadows falling into sharp relief. She breathed deeply, sighed softly, and reached along the roads.

The implant in her arm burned like a hot coal, hooking through to her laptop, accessing all the available information. The nearest police camera was on one of the roads, the rest fell into deep shadows. It was the clue she needed, the road with the police camera was the wrong road.

The lurking presence receded into the darkness; the gray clouds lifted. She ascended out of her mind palace, the world snapping back around her. The fork in the road was upon them. "Left," she advised urgently. "Left, now!"

Francis turned the steering wheel slightly, the car careered forward along the left road.

The sense of threat hung around Juliette for a long moment after the mind palace had closed down. A rare frown hung over her forehead. She'd never experienced a mind palace so filled with portentous evil. Something dark and deadly was waiting in the near future – she was sure of it.

She stared through the windscreen. The Range Rover was eating up the miles. There was still no sign of the van or the sedan, but they were out there, somewhere in front of them. Driving at their limits to whatever destination they sought.

Wherever they were going, both Shadowstone and the Mirovar force team would be there soon.

* * *

A thick cloth hood clung to Peter's face, blocking all sight and dulling sound.

The four Shadowstone agents who shared the back of the van with Peter had barely said a word, giving nothing away. One had kicked him hard in the guts. Still immobilized by the nano-fiber nets, Peter had been unable to respond in kind. He filed the position of that agent away. If he got the chance, he would extract a little payback. Kicking a bound captive was beyond the pale, an unforgivable cowardly act.

When the fourth net had begun to wrap around his body outside the hangar, he'd flexed every muscle he could to maximize his size and give himself room to maneuver within the net. But the smart materials comprising the net tightened as he inevitably relaxed, eliminating the use of an old Houdini trick to deal with being bound.

As soon as the van started moving, he'd begun a one count per second count. He was already at one thousand and seventy-two, nearly eighteen minutes had passed since his capture. Lying on the floor of the van allowed

Peter to feel the vibrations of the motor, driveline, and the tires rolling over the road. He could sense acceleration and changes in direction. The engine was working hard, and the driver had barely touched the brakes. He was pretty sure they were heading south, and fast, at an average speed well over the speed limit. He estimated they were already at least twenty miles south of Coningsby. He would need to steal a vehicle once he escaped, otherwise he would miss the rendezvous with the Mirovar force team at 12:00.

In any event, he only had a little less than half an hour to affect an escape from the van and break contact with Shadowstone.

His hand reflexively went to rub his chin thoughtfully as he planned an escape but got nowhere. The inability to perform simple gestures almost irked him more than lying hooded and bound in the back of a Shadowstone van. He grinned at himself beneath the hood and chuckled softly.

One of the agents kicked him in the stomach again. "What are you laughing at asshole."

Pain shot through him; this could get ugly. He needed it to get uglier, and said derisively, "I was just thinking of your mother pleasuring the village idiot on the night you were conceived."

"Are you asking for it?"

"Of course," Peter snarked, "it wasn't the first time for her."

"Fuck you!"

The four agents started in on Peter with hard, booted feet and fists like steel. The kicks were relentless, they must have been crouching over him, giving him everything they could in the cramped space. Fists pummeled him remorselessly, the punches snapping in whip-fast.

Peter grimaced, waiting for his chance.

He crunched, lifting his head half a dozen inches off the floor. One the agents smashed him hard on the right cheek. He went with the blow, hitting his head against the floor of the van. Stars shot before his eyes, and he went limp.

"Check him," one of the agents growled.

A pair of fingers pressed against his throat, finding his carotid artery. "He's still got a pulse, damn slow but strong."

"He's out cold, you might have thumped him a bit too hard."

"Heathmont won't be happy if you've damaged him too much."

"Fuck Heathmont."

"Stow that shite, Collins."

"Yes, Sir."

The agents fell silent.

Peter continued breathing slowly. Let them think he was unconscious. It was a lever he could use to escape. All he needed was the slimmest of openings, the slightest mistake and he would be gone. He'd already shifted the situation in his favor. They were unaware he was awake and waiting for the first opportunity to take action.

They would regret underestimating him.

He continued his silent counting.

* * *

A flash of dark-blue disappeared around a broad-left curve in front of them.

"It's the Jag!" Anton asserted, pointing forward with his right hand between Juliette and Francis.

"We've caught them," Francis declared.

The two Range Rovers barreled around the corner, ten or eleven seconds behind the Shadowstone vehicles. The road stretched straight for half a mile before curving to the right. Halfway along was a turn off to the left. The dark-gray van slowed down, the Jaguar sedan with it. Francis tapped on the brakes, bringing the Range Rover back under the speed limit. The Shadowstone vehicles took the left turn, keeping their speed low as they moved along the side road.

There were thick screens of trees along both sides of the main road. Anton's SUV approached the intersection, a gatehouse and boom gate nestled down the side road emerged from the tree line. Camouflaged painted metal dominated on the far side of the boom gate, a pair of long gun barrels jutted out to the left and right of a bulbous turret, pointing down the side road toward the main road.

"A tank," Anton said, a nebulous idea sparking into being on the edge of his mind. He stared intently at the massive vehicle as the SUV approached the intersection. Details of the military manual Peter had given him to read on the flight over flashing through his mind. It was one of the newly deployed 'commander,' tanks, named for their ability to dominate and take command of a battlefield. It was the first tank deployed with a viable rail gun able to deliver a kinetic spike made of tungsten at nine times the speed of sound. It had a more conventional 105mm gun with high-explosive rounds, a 7.62mm minigun, and a belt-fed grenade launcher. Its weapon systems were largely automated, simplifying operations down to two people, a driver/gunner, and a commander. If necessary, the driver/gunner could operate the tank on their own. He crinkled his nose with thought. The commanding officer was probably just there to make sure the driver/gunner didn't get up to no good. A grin flashed across Anton's face and then vanished.

Francis took the SUVs past the intersection, as if they were just simple, law-abiding traffic with no interest in what lay down the side road.

Anton stared out the window as they passed by. The boom gate was up, the van and the Jaguar were passing beneath an arching sign that proclaimed 'Squadron F,' in large black letters. The gate guards obviously expected the two vehicles, waving them through without checks.

The commander tank sat on the right side of the gate, opposite the main gatehouse. One of the crew was climbing down the side of the tank, heading toward the gatehouse, leaving the turret hatch open. Fifty yards behind it, a pair of wheeled armored personnel carriers bristled with firepower and menace. Beyond them, the side road ran another fifty yards before turning to the right and disappearing behind a stand of trees stretching parallel to the perimeter fence. Anton counted heads as the Range Rover sped past at sixty miles per hour. There were four men in standard dark-gray combat fatigues manning the gate. Another eight men, wearing the standard matte black Shadowstone body armor stood on the far side of the gate. All of the men carried automatic rifles.

"It's a secret Shadowstone base," Li suggested beside him. "Hiding in plain sight."

Juliette nodded. "Most people would just see another UK military special forces base."

"Squadron F?" Francis asked.

"The Stateless Warfare Wing," Juliette answered, glancing down at her laptop. "Apparently a recently formed branch of the SAS, less than six years old."

"A great place for Shadowstone to hide," Francis said confidently.

Anton slammed his right fist into his left palm and declared, "Well we need to find a way in, and soon – anything could be happening to Peter in there."

"Yes, of course. But easier said than done." Francis said, keeping the Range Rover moving at speed. Soon they were traveling around the right-hand curve in the road and out of sight of the gatehouse.

Francis slowed the SUV, pulling it over and stopping on the loose gravel beside the road. Jay brought the second Range Rover tight in behind the first.

Francis twisted in his seat, glancing left and right at Li and Anton. He tapped his in-ear communicator to broadcast to the others in the second car and directed, "Okay everyone, we need to establish a good and careful plan to get Peter out of this base."

* * *

"Don't take any chances with him. He's enhanced somehow," The lead agent declared in the back of the van.

Tasers crackled in the dark.

Three sets of prongs lanced into Peter's flesh, sending hot electric current raving through his nerves. His muscles spasmed and drool wet the mask over his face. The tasers stopped, the rear door to the van burst open with a click and a pair of clangs. Strong hands gripped the nets wrapped around him, and dragged him from the back of the van. More hands grabbed his feet, lifting his legs, and together, the agents carried him bodily over the concrete floor. The faint echoes of their boots resounding within a large enclosed space.

"Drop him and stand clear," the lead agent shouted.

Peter thudded to the concrete. Tasers lanced forward again, the charges almost knocking him out. Lights and shadows flashed before his eyes. When his vision began to clear, he was free of the nets and hood.

A large tan vehicle loomed before him. A purpose-built semi-trailer rig attached to a v-hulled container. A pair of thick doors were open at the back of the container, bright lights illuminating a white and chrome interior with a striking resemblance to a dental clinic.

The agents dragged him up a set of portable stairs and into the rear of the container. He tried to ramp, but the half-dozen taser shots left his nerves too jangled to cooperate. They lifted him bodily, carried him forward, and strapped him into an oversized dentist's chair at the front of the container. Quickly wrapping heavy metal cuffs around his ankles and wrists, and strapping thick belts over his shins, thighs, chest and forehead.

A port into a vein on his left hand seemed to magically appear as the agents stepped back. A slim, plastic tube ran from the port to a drip feed of clear fluid in a bag hung from the top of a thick, chrome pole jutting up behind his left shoulder.

The agents left the chamber. Peter's mind cleared, and his nerves settled back to their normal functioning. He assessed the space around him. There were two men, one tall and lean, one short and round, dressed in white fatigues. *Med techs!* He nicknamed them Bud and Lou. The ceiling was about eight feet above the floor. The room was a narrow rectangle, about ten feet wide and thirty feet long. The chair he sat in was hard up against the front bulkhead. A pair of double doors with a spinlock dominated the rear end of the chamber. Halfway along the ceiling, there was a hatch a man could fit through; shut tight with a heavy spinlock. Along the walls were racks of equipment, much of it medical in appearance, the rest were mostly computers, recording, and communications equipment.

A pair of chairs sat either side of the rear doors with air-transport style harness seat belts.

Someone had designed the vehicle to keep its operators safe under acceleration and flying conditions. His mind ticked over; it was the right size to fit inside a large military transport aircraft. He shook his head once, and pressed his lips into a thin line of grim recognition. It was a mobile rendition unit, an MRU. A system designed to transport a prisoner anywhere in the world, to facilitate torture away from jurisdictions that would frown upon such activities.

The plummy voice of the lead Shadowstone operative who had spoken outside the hangar came over an intercom in the ceiling, "Prepare the prisoner with the truth serum."

Bud, the tall, slim technician said, "We have already started Sir, he'll be ready to question in five minutes."

"And the enhancers?" asked the voice over the intercom.

"About to start, Sir."

"Good work."

"Enhancers?" Peter asked. Whatever they were pumping into him wasn't anything like Truther, that took about two hours to reach full effect. A clock on the wall read 11:46. He had fourteen minutes to reach the rendezvous point to catch up with the rest of the Mirovar team. That was starting to look impossible unless he was able to escape immediately and capture a helicopter.

Lou, the shorter, rounder technician approached, and said with avid interest, "Pain enhancers." His eyes crinkled and he grinned. "This should be fascinating. I've never tried this on an Order of Thoth operative before."

"Cool," Peter observed drily, "I always like being first to try something new."

Lou snorted. "Well, aren't you a confident one."

Peter could just move his head and tilted it a little to the side. There was a lock unit, a small chrome lever on the arm of the interrogation chair, just below the manacle. Hopelessly out of reach for anyone strapped in the chair.

He ramped hard, his muscles bunching and straining. A drop of perspiration appeared on his hairline above his left eye and started to roll down his face. Did the right manacle budge? Possibly, but maybe it hadn't moved at all.

Lou watched him curiously. "What are you doing? There's no hope of escape here." He approached with a large syringe filled with a pink fluid and pumped it into the port on Peter's left hand. A cold fire ripped along his arm and just as quickly faded away. He followed it with another syringe of saline fluid to flush the port. The tech stepped back and reported to the overhead cameras and intercom, "Sir, the enhancers have been applied."

Bud stepped forward to Peter's right, grasping a device that looked a lot like a cross between a cattle prod and a stun gun in his right hand. He frowned dispassionately at Peter and pressed a stud on the top of the baton like device. A pair of blue arcs crackled between the prongs on its forward end.

Lou moved up on Peter's left and said matter-of-factly, "Don't worry, this won't knock you out like a taser would … even though you might wish it would do so."

The lead Shadowstone operative's voice came over the intercom and commanded, "Begin the interrogation process."

Bud lifted the baton toward Peter, the sparking end of it looming before his face.

Peter involuntarily winced in anticipation.

Bud pressed the baton forward.

* * *

"Whatever we do – we have to do it quickly, and we have to do it quietly," Francis instructed. He stabbed down toward the floor of the car with his finger. "No one knows we're here. We need to preserve stealth while we can."

He glanced at his wife. "Juliette, is there any way through the perimeter fence."

Juliette consulted her laptop. "There are public warnings about approaching the site, the fence is heavily electrified. There will be a control center on the base where they'll monitor the perimeter alarms. A site like this will also have active perimeter defenses."

"Such as?" Francis asked.

"Flechette guns are a popular choice for perimeter defense in the UK," Jay said, his voice crystal clear over the tactical comms link. "Imagine thirty or forty razor-sharp slivers of metal hitting you. They'll cut you in half."

"What about drones?" Chiara asked from the other car. "Has anyone seen one yet?"

"No. But we should assume they're there even if we can't see them," Juliette advised.

Anton squeezed his eyes shut for a moment and then pleaded with the team, "We're wasting time."

"Anton," Francis cautioned, "We can't rush in all guns blazing, we'll have these Shadowstone operatives all over us. We're not invulnerable, and a big enough force can easily swamp us."

Anton's eyes widened with barely contained anger. A ball of frustration burning in his gut. He had to save Peter, and soon. Anton didn't need the threat of terrible things happening to the world if they lost Peter today to motivate him. It was enough that his friend was in danger and he was able to do something about it.

The other's continued discussing the tactical parameters of the site.

Anton fingered the lace ends on Peter's battle vest. Even with the muscle he'd grown over the last three and a half months, the vest sat large on him. Peter would need his weapons and Anton would get them to him.

He quietly unlatched the SUV's door.

Fortune favors the brave.

Grasping the Blue Dragon in his right hand and one of the H&K MP5 submachine guns in his left, Anton pushed open the car door with his shoulder. Blurring away to the tree line, he disappeared between the trees, with the voices of his teammates shouting over the comms link.

It was time to kick in the front door.

Chapter Four

"Damn it – I'm just going to have a go. No one ever won a game without attacking the goal." – Anton Slayne

"The new commander tank comes equipped with the latest nano-ceramic, reactive-ablative armor matrix. This armored shell integrates with the command-and-control system, ensuring heightened crew awareness of protection levels in the face of the most lethal threats on the modern battlefield." – Commander Tank Sales Brochure.

* * *

The Facility, South Lincolnshire, August 22nd, 11:46

Peter screamed in agony.

His nerves were on fire, whatever the 'pain enhancer,' drug was, it was certainly effective.

Bud, the taller of the techs stepped back, and the Etonian tones of the lead Shadowstone operative came through the intercom in the ceiling above the chair. "I see you have begun to understand the nature of your confinement … Mr. Lamb. Are you feeling more relaxed now, more willing to tell the truth, more compliant?"

Peter grimaced, somehow, they knew his name. He gritted his teeth, admitting to himself that beneath the pain, he was feeling like a neighborhood gossip with a juicy bit of news. A strange urgency to say something was building within him. He bit back the first words that came to mind and said, "You know what? I really want some ice-cream … preferably chocolate."

Peter stared at a camera mounted next to the intercom. Presumably, he was staring at the man who was asking the questions. He grinned broadly.

"Very well, Mr. Lamb. I see there is still work to do," the disembodied voice said coldly. "Increase the pain enhancer dose."

"Sir," the taller tech said, "we've already given him the maximum recommended amount."

"Double it."

The tall tech frowned and nodded at his shorter assistant. Lou picked up a fresh syringe, loaded it with the pink fluid and pumped it into Peter's veins.

The cold fire assaulted Peter again and then faded away.

"Repeat the process," the voice commanded over the intercom.

Bud, the taller tech stepped forward once again. He surveyed Peter's face, looking for fresh skin. He adjusted his aim, caressing Peter's right ear with the coruscating tip of the baton.

Peter's world disappeared as white lightning surged through him.

* * *

Anton kept the perimeter fence to his right, blurring from tree to tree.

Francis and Juliette's voices were in his ears, urgently ordering him to return to the car. He ignored them, he was already committed to a course of action, and there would be no turning back.

He was going to get his friend Peter out of this place alive or die trying. He wasn't going to lose anyone else – not if he could help it. He came to the last tree and pressed his back hard up against it. Its trunk was thick enough to shield him from the guards at the gatehouse another forty yards away.

He scanned the woods in front of him. No one had followed him, not even Li. She had too much good sense, but damn it all to hell, he had to do something. All the talk in the car had got to him. A part of him acknowledged that it probably made very good sense to sit back and plan, but Peter could die while they talked. He couldn't stand it anymore, the waiting, the inaction – he had to go in and save his friend.

Francis' voice cut through his earbuds, and he ordered, "Anton, hold there. We'll come to you."

Anton checked his H&K MP5, it was ready to go, thirty high-velocity, armor-piercing rounds in the magazine. A second magazine was strapped upside down to the first with black duct tape to allow a quick reload. He held it in his right hand. The scabbard of the Blue Dragon lay strapped over his shoulder, the handle jutting up for a quick draw. He tapped his earbud and declared, "No, Francis. I'm gonna blow the power. The fence and the perimeter defenses will be down, and you can cut through it."

"Non, Anton—"

He centered himself, fell into silence, the Ramp flowering within. A brief break in the cloud cover let sunlight cut through the trees, spearing in bright shafts to the grass covered ground. He turned, rushing around the tree and forward to the commander tank.

He was beside it before anyone could react. He leaped over the 105mm gun mount to the top of the turret. The Shadowstone guards in their body armor started to move, lifting their assault rifles. His H&K was the first to fire, rounds cutting a line through the black-armored troopers. Two fell back, the rest ducked for cover, firing back at him with short, controlled bursts.

Bullets whistled past him, ricocheting off the armor of the commander tank. In one quick motion, he was inside. His feet dropping to the floor. The commander's position was empty.

The driver twisted around beneath him, shouting, "What the—"

Anton's left fist lashed forward, striking the man on the top of his head. He jerked down, unconscious. Anton grabbed hold of the man's uniform, dragging him out of the lower position and pushing him up and out of the tank. More rifle file struck the man's body with wet thuds before Anton pushed him out of the tank, and he disappeared limply over the side.

Something struck the tank, pinging off the armor. The slow stutter of a heavy machine gun firing resounded nearby. Someone was firing a .50 cal at the tank. The standard ball rounds making a lot of noise but not doing any significant damage.

Anton pulled off the Blue Dragon, and dropped into the driver's position, placing his sword next to him in the cramped cabin. The tank sat in hot standby mode. He picked up the controls which the tank's manual had declared, 'were specifically matched with those of a popular games console to minimize the cost of training operators.' A heads-up display appeared, painting a three-dimensional picture of the surrounding battlespace in a holographic bubble around his head. He turned his head, he could see whatever the tank's sensors could access, including feeds from the tactical links to the Shadowstone base.

He floored the accelerator, the tank responded, it's engine roaring as it surged forward. He swung the tank around in a tight circle to the right, taking out the gatehouse, Shadowstone troopers running to escape the collapsing building. The two armored personnel carriers began firing their main weapons, 25mm Bushmaster cannons, rapid fire rounds smashing off the commander's nano-ceramic armor. They were unlikely to destroy the tank, but they could blow off a track, bringing the tank to a halt, or damage the external weapons, or sensor arrays if they got lucky.

They were less than forty yards away, point blank range.

Anton used the console to select his first target and pulled the trigger.

Nothing happened. A flashing red line appeared and outlined the APC in the heads-up display. The word 'FRIENDLY,' flashed above it in bright yellow letters. A set of icons along the bottom border of the HUD caught his eye. One was marked IFF, 'Identify Friend or Foe,' he selected it. A disable option appeared. He punched it – the red line around the APC and the bright yellow warning message disappeared.

Anton pulled the trigger again.

There was a slight momentary hum to his right, then a whip-like crack as the rail gun fired.

Heat fins glowed hot behind his right shoulder, the rail gun system jettisoning waste heat. The eleven-pound tungsten kinetic spike traveling at two miles per second rammed into the middle of the turret of the APC on the right, which promptly evaporated in a fireball. The backwash of the explosion vibrated through the commander tank's hull. An ammo counter on Anton's heads-up display dropped from fifty to forty-nine. Another dial marking the heat dissipation spiked into the red for half a second before returning to green.

Anton didn't waste any time wondering how many rounds the rail gun could fire before heat became an issue. If he needed to break the tank using it, he would. He pivoted the tank's turret slightly to the left, bringing the rail gun to bear on the second APC. Its main gun continued to fire bravely, taking out the grenade launchers on the left-hand side of the commander's turret. The launchers exploded, a ball of flame enveloping the tank, obscuring Anton's vision for half a second.

The flames blew away, the APC resolved into view. The HUD indicated the target with red crosshairs painting the middle of the APC's turret.

Anton pulled the rail gun trigger, there was a slight recoil, the commander tank rocking back momentarily as the rail gun cracked again. The top of the APC disappeared, the wall of a building two hundred yards behind it imploding as the remnants of the kinetic spike tore it apart.

Anton floored the accelerator, the tank rolling forward between the burning wrecks of the APCs.

"I'm in," he broadcast over his in-ear tactical link to the rest of the Mirovar force team.

Anton fired up the full power of the tank's sensor arrays. The sensors connected to a high-flying drone and the base's tactical links. The main power substation for the site was clearly visible on an online map, less than four hundred yards from where he was now. There were at least two buildings in the way and no clear shot. Anton kept the accelerator hard to the floor, the tank surging forward along the road.

There was no time to waste.

* * *

Fire and lightning rushed along Peter's drugged nerves.

The physical transformation of the Ramp increased pain tolerance. A Ramp master still felt pain, but the Ramp transformation greatly enhanced the ability to act through the pain. Shadowstone had developed the drug administered to Peter using regular people as test subjects. As 'Lou,' the short and chubby technician had remarked, they'd never used the drug on an Order of Thoth operative. This was the first time they'd used it against a Ramp master. The results were unpredictable as Shadowstone science encountered ancient genetics honed in a far more hostile environment than the modern world.

The stench of his own burning flesh assaulted Peter. He'd been attempting to fall into silence, to find a secret center where he could master the pain, but the enhanced agony coruscating through his body destroyed every pathway to stillness.

The pain blew through all his barriers, wiping the emotional slate clean. A primal fighting rage exploded through Peter's consciousness, the pain evaporating like damp mist before hell's own furnaces. A dark lightning flashed unseen through nerves and muscles born to war. Something cracked like a whip, Peter's right arm blurring up and right.

Blood, bone, and brains splashed in a broad swathe across the clinical whiteness of the right wall. An instant later, Peter drove a stainless-steel spike through the head of the smiling, chubby faced, second tech on the left. He pulled back his right hand. It was still dripping blood and gobbets of flesh from the thick manacle and half its housing. Descending from the manacle was the lock unit and a half-foot-long steel spike covered in gore ending in a twisted, fractured finger of metal.

Peter glanced right and left. The taller tech's body, now headless, lay crumpled on the floor gushing blood in a spreading pool from the open remains of his neck. Of his head, there was no sign, except the lumpy dripping residue over one corner of the room. The shorter tech had slumped to the floor, blood spouting from two one-inch-wide wounds in his skull to mingle in a spreading pool emanating from the headless body of the other tech.

Peter reached around, pulling the small chrome lever underneath the manacle on his left hand. The manacle opened with a satisfying mechanical click. With his left hand, he freed his right, dropping the gore-slick manacle to the floor. Loosening the belts from his chest, thighs, and shins, he opened the manacles around his ankles and stepped out of the chair.

He rubbed his face with his left hand, and it came away bloody. His left eye was a little hazy, and the top of his right ear was missing. The rage had subsided from a tidal wave to a swollen river. His chest heaved, his eyes narrowing with deeply felt purpose. Explosions resounded dully, the sound struggling to penetrate the armored walls of the mobile rendition unit. Somewhere a siren began wailing in the distance.

"Hey, you pommy bastard, are you still listening?"

The intercom remained silent.

He smiled grimly, the Order had come to rescue him, and the local Shadowstone boss now had bigger problems to deal with.

Peter approached the back door. Its spinlock had four chrome handles jutting out of it. He grabbed them, his rage bubbling away in the background. He ramped hard, twisting the device counter-clockwise. Metal groaned, his face flushed with blood, but the wheel wouldn't budge. Above the spinlock was a retinal scanner. A small light above the scanner glowed a solid red.

"Damn." He had a sneaking suspicion luck wasn't on his side today. He dashed back to the chubby tech, picking his body up by the scruff of his neck, he carried him back to the rear door. In moments, he'd tested the dead tech's eyes with the scanner – the light remained red. He dropped the body, looking back at the wet, congealing splash across the front left corner of the chamber. Somewhere in that mess was a retina that could open this door.

"So much for plan A," Peter said, frowning.

He needed a plan B, and quick, before Shadowstone responded with knockout gas or something else to immobilize him.

Peter shook his head; he wanted his earbuds back. They were a loose end he needed to tie off, and catching up with the upper-crust Shadowstone vampire flunky who had stolen them was high on his to-do list.

But that would have to wait.

He needed to get out of this damned vehicle first.

* * *

All hell was breaking loose.

A wall full of screens told a tale of mayhem and chaos. Three screens, one fed by a high-flying drone, showed various angles on a commander tank accelerating away from the smashed remains of the gatehouse and the burning wrecks of a pair of armored personnel carriers. A dedicated screen revealed the butcher's abattoir the interior of the MRU had become. Somehow the red-headed Order of Thoth operative, 'Peter,' – if that was his real name – had broken free of the interrogation chair. A feat that was supposed to be impossible, but it had happened.

Gordon Heathmont's pale lips thinned into a grim slash, he thumped the desk in front of him and screamed, "Scramble the blackwidows. We have to kill that damned tank before it destroys the Facility."

One of his aides looked up from his command station and asked, "Sir, which wings should I scramble?"

"All of them!" Gordon shouted, staring at the man. He quailed before Gordon's gaze and issued the orders.

"Williams, get me a direct line to Major Quiver."

"Yes, sir," another young aide replied, establishing a secured communications link with the Head of Squadron F, the Phase IV Day Guard contingent in the UK.

The Major's voice came over the line, "Sir, what are your orders."

"We need to stop this bloody tank and secure the Order operative in the MRU."

"Yes, Sir. Consider it done."

"You have tactical command of our assets and full release of weapons. The defense of the Facility is in your hands."

"Understood sir, they won't get past us."

Gordon began to calm down. The defense of the base was in the care of the best men that Shadowstone could find.

He stared at the screens showing the tank. It was accelerating along a road toward a pair of logistics storehouses. That didn't make any sense, there was nothing of great importance in those buildings. The view in the screen shifted as the tank approached the storehouses, bringing into view what was beyond the buildings – the electrical power substation.

"Oh my God," Gordon whispered.

The blackwidows would be too late.

His guts tightened as he watched the screens, powerless to affect what was about to happen.

Gordon slammed both fists on the desk. "Damn! Damn! Damn!"

The Order of Thoth earbuds lay on the desk in front of him. He snarled and crushed them with his fists. They hadn't been aborting the mission and heading for the west of England for a boat pickup, and there was no doubt more than three members in the team. He'd sent half his forces in the wrong direction and would now have to recall them.

They've tricked me!

It was galling.

* * *

Anton didn't believe in doing things by halves.

The commander tank raced along the road belying its massive body. The HUD automatically and seamlessly updating what he could see. Shadowstone hadn't yet shutdown the data feeds, allowing the tank to automatically pull-down data about the base. The manual he'd read on the plane said he could give the tank verbal commands and limited instructions. Anton had no real idea how that would work, but he was determined to give it a try.

"Prisoners. Where are prisoners held?" Anton asked the tank.

In the electronic circuits of the tank a dedicated, natural-language-processing artificial intelligence responded, drawing a map overlay on the HUD. The prison section of the base was located on the southeast corner, almost directly opposite from the side of the base Anton was on. The AI drew two lines that zigzagged around the buildings to the prison section. It labeled one 4:46 and the other 4:58, clearly the amount of time in minutes and seconds it would take the tank to get there by following the roads.

"I've found Peter," Anton called out over the earbud link back to the rest of the Mirovar force team.

"We can't get past the automatic flechette guns, they're tracking too fast," Francis stated. "We're still outside the base."

Anton glanced at the location of the power substation and said, "I'll deal with that now."

He slammed the accelerator, the tank racing forward along the road. The speedometer running up to fifty miles per hour as the two logistics buildings passed to his right. The power substation came into view. He designated three of the biggest structures he could see as targets and set the rail gun to autofire. There was a hum, it fired the first kinetic spike which slammed through the center of a transformer the size of an SUV. The tank rocked slightly with the recoil of the rail gun. The transformer exploded in a shower of sparks. The second and third spikes followed the first at one-second intervals. The substation caught fire as more transformers blew up, streamers of sparks snaking along cables in all directions. The kinetic spikes cut through everything in their way, disappearing through the woods surrounding the base.

"Anton," Francis called angrily over the comms link, "those spikes just went over our heads."

Anton frowned. The heads-up display stuttered for half a second as the data feeds from the Facility failed for a second, then came back online. Batteries, backup diesel generators, whatever – taking out the power substation wasn't the knockout blow he'd expected.

"Get your heads down," Anton broadcast to the team. "I know exactly where you are now." He then asked the onboard AI, "Where are the backup power units? Show me a power grid."

Red lines snaked across the map on the HUD. There were three nodes spread across the base. The backup power in a redundant, distributed array. A slick solution, but not good enough today. Anton targeted all of the nodes, specifying the 105mm gun which began raising its barrel until it was pointing nearly vertical. It fired three times, the shells disappearing through the clouds, leaving smoke-ring indentions in the sky. They would be back in seconds. Anton floored the accelerator again to get the burning power substation out of his line of fire. He targeted the perimeter fence. The 105mm gun lowering, and firing another three rounds on a flat trajectory. The high-explosive rounds destroyed the fence and the flechette guns mounted along that section of the perimeter.

"Fixed?" he asked over the comms link.

Three explosions erupted in the base behind him as the initial three 105mm rounds returned from their highly parabolic flights and struck the backup power generators. Buildings crashed to the ground, debris blowing high into the air, thick plumes of dark gray smoke streaming into the sky. The data feeds from the Facility dropped out and didn't come back on.

There was a pause, then Francis said, "Jay is leading an exfil team to help you and Peter get out. Mon Dieu, Anton – try not to kill them."

Jay's voice came over the comms link, "We'll keep you appraised of where we are by voice. Where's Peter?"

"On the other side, I'm going to get him now."

The tank pivoted on its tracks. There was one functioning asset still feeding data, a Shadowstone drone flying high overhead. Four helicopter icons took off from a flat area on the southwest corner of the base map. The icons, now labeled Widow-1, through to Widow-4, began to accelerate toward him. The last thing Anton needed was four tank-killing gunships catching him out in the open.

"Give me a straight-line path to the prison."

The AI responded with a green line labeled 2:02, cutting from where Anton was through to the southeast corner of the base. A straight-line approach would cut two and a half minutes off the time to reach Peter.

The helicopter gunships were coming up on Anton's right forward flank. He punched the accelerator, the tank surging forward along the green line. A quarter mile away, the first building stood in his way, a long two-story office block.

"Identify structural targets."

A green rectangle marked the office block. Critical support structures popped out in red glows on the HUD. Anton pulled the triggers for the 105mm and the rail gun. The tank slowed momentarily as both guns fired. The kinetic spike hitting first, tearing through the main structural beam of the building before disappearing further into the base. The 105mm high-explosive shell hit next, the middle of the building evaporating in a fiery blast, collapsing to the ground, dust, fire, and smoke billowing into the air.

Anton drove the tank straight at the breach, hoping this new tactic would hold off the blackwidows. He whispered to himself, "Let's see if they'll fire on their own people."

The HUD flickered slightly; the drone data feed had dropped out. The gunship pilots had cut him off from his one remaining external source of data. He was down to what was directly visible from the tank. In seconds, the blackwidows would rise over the base, drawing line of sight on the commander tank. Anton expected they would begin by attacking him with their purpose-built anti-tank Hellfire III missiles. He selected another icon on the HUD, setting the 7.62mm minigun sitting on top of the turret to defensive fire vs missile threats. It might buy him some time against the blackwidows.

Time, he suspected he was rapidly running out of.

* * *

Li took a position on the fence line opposite the ruined gatehouse.

Shadowstone had abandoned the entrance to the Facility as they concentrated their forces on defeating the commander tank running amok through their base.

Li, Jay, and Yvette had left the breach in the perimeter fence alone, moving straight to the destroyed gatehouse. It was the best location to organize a quick exfil from. They only needed Anton and Peter to arrive, and they could all escape the base together.

She sighted along the top of the buildings with her .50 caliber sniper rifle. The handle of the Green Dragon jutted up over her right shoulder where it lay strapped to her combat webbing. Nearby, Jay and Yvette took up positions, armed with their katanas and a pair of H&K MP5 9mm submachine guns, and a Milkor MGL respectively.

Almost half a mile away, a ragged scar cut into the base. Judging from the smoke, explosions and the rapid-fire cracks of a 105mm cannon set to autofire, Anton, and the commander tank were almost a third of the way through the base heading directly for the southeast corner.

Four blackwidow helicopters were in the air, zeroing in on Anton's location, they fanned out in a loose semi-circle. Two new armored personnel carriers rushed along the road toward the smoking rip in the buildings.

Jay said, "Anton, we're at the gatehouse, and you've got another two APCs on your six."

Four Humvee-sized vehicles, with 7.62mm M240 machine guns on their roofs, and packed with fully-armored Shadowstone troopers followed after the APCs.

Li stared at the Shadowstone base and the forces beginning to swarm against Anton. *How are we going to get out of this? My God Anton, what have you done? At least they don't know the rest of us are here yet and their power is knocked out.* She called out over the tactical link, "Anton, Shadowstone are coming in numbers, move faster, there is no more time."

"Yeah, I got that," he replied, his voice calm.

He's becoming reckless and fatalistic.

She watched, powerless to help as gunships, APCs and Shadowstone troops converged on Anton's position.

What would happen now?

She had no idea.

* * *

Gordon ran through the open front doors of the command center, surrounded by his aides and Phase IV Day Guard security detail. The building next to the command center blew up in a tower of flame as successive high-explosive 105mm shells ripped it apart. Cutting through the noise of the explosions was the whip-crack of the commander tank's rail gun.

His jaw gaped open in horror as the rogue commander tank emerged into view. The heat dispersal fins at the back of the tank glowed a dull red, the air shimmering thickly above them. Beyond the tank, four blackwidows hovered in a fan formation about five hundred yards above the base. The formation allowed them to concentrate their attacks on a single target.

He could see them hesitating to fire. His previous order releasing all weapons for use against the commander tank had not been clear enough. They'd standing orders not to fire on the Facility itself lest they kill other Shadowstone personnel remained in place. They hadn't fired as they didn't have a clear shot that avoided friendly casualties. Gordon glowered; friendly casualties were a given at this point, there was no time to be overly cautious.

The commander tank disappeared into the wreckage, in less than a minute it would be breaching the prison section where the mobile rendition unit and the most high-value prisoner he'd ever captured waited.

Gordon fingered his smartphone as he ran away from the defunct command center, setting up broadcast links with Major Quiver and the pilots of the blackwidows. "Fire on that damned tank," he shouted. "Fire now men, be about it."

"Yes, Sir," Major Quiver replied. "Widows one through four, fire at will."

"Roger," chorused the pilots.

Gordon remembered James Haley's warnings. "Major Quiver, there's no doubt an Order of Thoth team is waiting nearby to exfiltrate their own operatives. Find them and deal with them."

"Yes, Sir."

Gordon glanced up; thin trails of white smoke were lancing across the sky. All four of the blackwidows had fired a volley of Hellfire missiles at the rogue commander tank.

The eight missiles darted forward. He stared at them, willing them to destroy the tank with every fiber of his being.

* * *

The 7.62mm minigun whirred above Anton's head, its six barrels rotating in a blur, spent shell casings spraying in a wide swathe to its left.

A long tongue of fire gushed from the minigun's throat as four-thousand rounds per minute of depleted uranium penetrators speared up at the incoming Hellfire missiles. The commander tank's onboard AI integrated the available missile tracks, calculating their future paths relative to everything else within reach of its onboard sensor arrays. It discarded two missiles as threats, their paths destined to intercept falling masonry, and other debris. The remaining six it methodically picked off from right to left. The last exploded half a dozen yards from the tank, the thermobaric blast momentarily engulfing the vehicle in bright fire.

Anton rocked in his seat as the ear-splitting explosion of the last Hellfire missile washed over the turret. An armor-integrity counter on the HUD dropped from ninety-eight to seventy-six and shifted from green to yellow.

The commander tank emerged from the flames, both main guns leveled at the last remaining barrier to the prison – a stone wall. Anton drove forward, the tank crunching over the smoking remains of a fallen building. The 105mm fired, the rail gun cracked, the last barrier fell before the barrage. The way was clear, Anton drove the tank through the last of the wreckage and into an open area before the warehouse that was doubling as a prison.

In moments, he would be through the prison wall.

Alarms beeped, the rail gun was down to five shots, the same with the 105mm. The minigun was at thirty percent and falling as it dealt with the last of a second volley of Hellfire missiles.

The final Hellfire missile in the second volley exploded a yard short of the hull. Anton lurched against his restraints, the tank rocking on its tracks as a wall of flame washed over it. Multiple alarms resounded through the cabin, half the indicators on the heads-up display were solidly in the red, the rest were a sea of yellow warnings with the occasional island of green.

In the ascending chaos, Anton gritted his teeth and pushed forward. The tank's tracks ripped through grass, soil, and concrete as he lined up on the wall of the prison.

He wasn't going to survive the next volley. The blackwidows were re-arranging their positions, taking up the points of a square and coming closer to minimize the vulnerable flight time of their missiles.

With the armor-integrity counter dropping to thirty-six percent and solidly red – time had run out.

* * *

Juliette's eyelids fluttered.

She sat next to Francis in the front Range Rover. Francis brought the vehicle into position to run hard past the Shadowstone base and pick up his team to head north. The second Range Rover with Luther and Chiara in it was a dozen yards behind them.

At least that was the plan they'd cobbled together after Anton had rushed into the Shadowstone base. In her mind palace, everyone was in terrible danger. Anton's precipitous actions had risked the whole team, and the probability of his own survival was close to zero. They'd lose Peter and Anton with him. She dropped out of her mind palace, cut deeply by what she'd seen.

"Mon, Dieu," she whispered, her eyes wide.

"Juliette?" Francis asked in worried tones.

"Soon my love, soon we must flee."

Francis' face was grim beside her, and he whispered harshly, "I had my doubts about Anton back at the safe house. We can't manage him – he's too much like his grandfather."

"Don't give up on Anton yet, there is something powerful working through him."

Francis stared at her. "What have you seen?"

"Not enough, but give him time. He could save us all."

"Or destroy us."

Juliette's eyelids dropped for a second. "That remains to be seen."

The future remained deeply hidden in shadows, unknowable, wreathed in darkness. Was there any room left for hope? Juliette knew where she would always stand – come what may. She grasped Francis' hands with her own, squeezed and declared passionately, "We will win through in the end."

"Will we be alive to see it?" Francis asked, his face betraying sudden doubt.

She looked in his eyes for a long moment, her heart filled with faith and promised, "Yes, we will."

* * *

Anton scanned the heads-up display, his eyes intense, his mouth grim.

He used the controller to direct the rail gun, and the 105mm gun at the two blackwidows moving into position in front of him and pulled the triggers.

His guts clenched tight as the third volley of missiles leaped from the hovering gunships at his tank. The minigun above his head whirred into life, its ammo counter descending through the low twenties toward zero percent. The 105mm gun fired first, a great tongue of flame leaping from its barrel as the round speared upward at the first helicopter gunship on the left. The rail gun was next, the kinetic spike flashing faster than an eye could follow at the second blackwidow on the right. Behind Anton, the tank's heat fins failed catastrophically, overloaded by the nearly continuous firing they blew apart in a brilliant shower of burning fragments.

The rail gun would never fire again.

Incoming Hellfire missiles, the 105mm high-explosive round, and the eleven-pound tungsten kinetic spike all passed each other in mid-air halfway between the commander tank and the blackwidow gunships.

Above the jagged remains of the heat fins, the minigun spewed fire, ejecting spent shell casings in a wide swathe as it rotated around to cover the incoming missiles. Its barrels were a blur of motion, the onboard AI dedicating every resource to defending the tank. Missile after missile blew apart mid-air as the minigun's depleted uranium rounds sliced through them.

The blackwidow on the right took the eleven-pound kinetic spike, through its nose. The tungsten slug shot through the cabin, instantly turning the crew into a pink mist. Without any visible loss of momentum, the slug sliced through the right-side engine, clipped the main rotor on the way through and disappeared somewhere into the next county.

The second last Hellfire missile speared through the minigun's defensive fire. The exploding warhead evaporated the minigun in a nightmarish thermobaric glare. The rail gun cracked along its spine, and all the tracks on the right side of the tank blew off. Ablative, ceramic armor around the main cabin disintegrated; partially dissipating the force of the Hellfire missile blast away from the crew.

Anton rocked in his seat, a wave of heat washing over him. Sparks flew from shorting equipment. The heads-up display failed. The stench of singed hair filled his nostrils.

The blackwidow on the left took the high-explosive 105mm round in the middle of the cabin, the resultant explosion scattered the gunship across the roof of the prison facility in a cloud of burning fragments.

The last of the Hellfire missiles struck the front of the commander tank. The thermobaric explosion dislodged the 105mm gun, cracked open the hull and ripped apart the front half of the tank. The turret canted backward at a twenty-degree angle, its ablative ceramic armor stripped away, exposing the bare metal of the cabin shell.

The stricken gunship on the right, its crew vaporized by the kinetic spike, its right engine shooting flames like a giant's toy firework, fell like a stone. Diving nose first onto the edge of the prison building, it promptly flipped over toward the ground. It never reached the concrete pathway beneath it, exploding in a huge fireball as the rest of its munitions and fuel detonated in a blinding glare.

The commander tank stood silently, canted to the right on its shredded tracks. Its 105mm gun barrel sloped crazily away to the left, the rail gun was a useless tangle of steaming metal on the right. Heat waves shimmered off the rear of the tank. Smoke and steam issued in plumes from ragged holes over the engine bay.

A gaping hole in the prison wall, next to the burning wreck of the second gunship, stood directly in front of the tank. Behind the tank lay a long, thick trail of smoking ruins.

The last two blackwidows peeled away, racing toward the front gate and their next engagement with the forces attacking the Shadowstone base.

* * *

Gordon Heathmont watched in horror as two of the blackwidows fell from the sky in flaming ruins.

There was a bright glare next to the prison section as one of the helicopters blew up, a plume of greasy smoke rising high in the air. Scattered fires and burning debris lit the prison section's roof. The surviving blackwidows veered away from the battle and raced toward the front gate.

They must have destroyed the rogue commander tank, or else the blackwidows would have stayed there to continue the fight.

Gordon fitted a pair of Shadowstone earbud communicators slaved to his smartphone, all his comm links became live.

Major Quiver's voice came over the tactical link, "Sir, our overhead drone has identified three intruders near the main gate, I am vectoring the remaining blackwidows onto their position."

"Get the MRU in motion. The base is without power. It's indefensible. Get the prisoner to Coningsby airbase. We have an A400 transport inbound, I will re-purpose it to this mission. We can airlift the prisoner out of the country and out of range of this Order of Thoth team. It's imperative the prisoner gets to the airbase alive. Ensure the blackwidows guard the MRU."

"What of the three Order operatives at the gate."

"Kill them if the opportunity presents itself, otherwise ignore them – three can't make a difference. The MRU and the prisoner are your sole concern now."

"Yes, Sir," Major Quiver growled. "… I've given the order. The MRU is in motion."

"Keep me in the loop. I'm evacuating this base with my security detail."

"Roger, that."

"Good man – now protect the prisoner."

"Yes, Sir."

The line muted. Gordon climbed into the back of his dark-blue Jaguar sedan. Three members of his security detail came with him. The rest boarded a pair of four-wheeled, armored Humvee-sized MRAP vehicles armed with 7.62mm M240 machine guns on their roofs. He would follow the MRU and ensure it made it onboard the A400 transport aircraft. He would fly out with the prisoner. Where would they go? Saudi Arabia was always helpful, but shockingly hot in the middle of August. He frowned, unfortunately, the kingdom would have to do; the Saudis had one key advantage, he could trust them to turn a blind eye and see the bigger picture.

Once on the plane and safely in the air, he would phone ahead, making sure the local Shadowstone cells were active and positioned to deal with the prisoner. He was sure Peter Lamb would eventually break and would be a treasure trove of information on Shadowstone's enemies.

The information inside the Order of Thoth agent's head was of primary value. He'd just about sacrifice anything to keep it within his reach.

Gordon stared through the car window and ignored what was outside the vehicle. The next hour would be the most important in his life. It would be pivotal in determining the future of the secret war between Shadowstone and the Order of Thoth.

Of that, he was sure.

* * *

Anton surfaced into agony, the darkness ebbing away.

A terrible ringing was clawing at his ears. Half-dazed, Anton shook his head and then swore mightily, his hands rising to cover his face. Moving his head had been a mistake.

He wriggled his fingers and toes – everything hurt like hell, but everything also moved.

The interior of the tank felt like a sauna on overdrive. A dull red light, running off emergency battery power filled the cabin. The air was thick with smoke, Anton wheezed and coughed, tasting blood in his mouth.

He reached up, punching a button next to the top hatch. Explosive bolts fired, the top door of the commander tank promptly blowing off. Grabbing the Blue Dragon and his H&K MP5, he jumped up onto the top edge of the tank. His boots sizzled on the hot metal, and he immediately leaped onto the ground.

He fell to his knees, coughing hard again, spots of blood appearing on the torn-up ground in front of him.

"That's not a good sign," he observed, pushing himself up onto one knee.

Juliette's voice sounded in his ears – a precognitive whisper, "Peter's being moved." Her voice firmed. "Everyone, head for the main gate; they're taking him from the site. We'll pick you up, exfil now!"

Anton had fought his way to a standstill to reach the prison, and now he had to go all the way back. He stood up, blinking his eyes, gritting his teeth and sucking air in through his nose. He started jogging back along the trail of devastation left by the tank. His ribs hurt abominably with every breath. He grimaced in pain, whatever was necessary – he'd get the job done.

Peter wasn't free yet.

The ringing in his ears was dropping away, and his lungs started to clear. He fell into silence and managed to Ramp. In moments, he was blurring over the rubble of the base back toward the entrance.

* * *

A turbine ignited and began spooling up with a steadily increasing whine.

"This thing's jet-powered?" Peter asked incredulously. He put his hands on his face, then jerked them away. His face was still painfully tender after the ministrations of Shadowstone's torture techs.

The truck started moving, rolling smoothly forward over the concrete floor of the prison section. The engine gave a low throaty rumble. His enemies had built the mobile rendition unit for speed and protection, it would be hard to stop.

He needed to get out of this mobile prison, the longer he stayed in, the worse his chances of survival were. He reached up to the wheel lock on the overhead hatch. With the ceiling only about eight feet off the floor, he could reach the arms of the spinlock. But with his arms extended over his head, he had virtually zero leverage.

The spinlock on the overhead latch was half the size of the one on the rear door. Peter grinned; it might be within his ability to literally tear it apart. He needed to solve his lack of leverage. He crunched hard, pivoting upward, planting his big boots to either side of the hatch in the ceiling. Crouched upside down from the ceiling, his big hands wrapped around the chrome handles of the spinlock, he plunged deep into silence. The Ramp flowered within, power flowed along muscles and nerves already configured for extraordinary strength. His muscles bulged; his veins popped – the wheel didn't budge.

He strained for another ten seconds, then dropped back down to the floor.

Wiping perspiration from his brow with his forearm, he declared with a measure of respect, "Damn, they built that tough."

The truck turned hard to the right, the wheels began running over a rougher surface and started to pick up speed. There were no windows but it was clear the MRU was outside the building, and on a road, before long it would be off the base.

"I need a lever."

Peter started looking for something within the chamber he could use to break the spinlock on the top hatch. Then an idea struck him, and he smiled broadly.

He dashed to the back of the chamber to check the larger spinlock. If the spinlocks had the same basic construction, he might have a way out.

* * *

The two MRAPs burned on the right side of the road, seventy yards inside the base. Half a dozen black-armored troopers lay scattered around them.

Yvette hunkered down under cover of the smoking hulk of one of the armored personnel carriers. She pushed the last of her reloads into the Milkor MGL and glanced over to Jay and Li sheltering next to the second APC on the other side of the road. They'd completed their ammunition reloads and were ready for the next attack. A pair of Shadowstone troopers – the faster than normal ones – were hiding behind their wrecked vehicles waiting for reinforcements.

Jay, Li and Yvette's position was indefensible. They had to break contact with the enemy and make an escape as soon as possible. The sound of approaching gunship helicopters screamed it might be too late. A single hellfire missile fired at their position would wipe them all out.

Juliette's voice came over the comms link, "I've hacked their drone. Two blackwidows are inbound. They're providing top cover for a convoy approaching your position. There is a lead vehicle, looks like an armored version of a semi-trailer rig with an armored trailer – it's a mobile rendition unit. There are two APCs and four MRAPs following it. Prepare for immediate exfil."

Yvette risked a quick glance around the edge of the APC. The convoy was passing the destroyed buildings on the edge of the main base, where Anton had driven the commander tank on his quest to rescue Peter. She pulled herself back, a three-round burst from an assault rifle pinging off the armor of the APC. The two surviving troopers near the burning MRAPs had her position under their crosshairs.

"I'm on, I'm on," Anton shouted across the comms link.

"Where are you?" Francis growled.

"I'm on top of the MRU. Peter's inside, this is what they're using to transport him."

"... Agreed," Juliette observed. "It's the most likely way they would move him."

"You're mad!" Luther declared. "... Not you Juliette, I mean Slayne."

Francis demanded, "Anton, what do you hope to achieve?"

"This truck has to stop sometime, and I'll be waiting to get Peter out."

"Don't try and do this by yourself," Li warned.

Yvette looked across the road at Li. The novice loremaster's face creased with growing desperation. Too many of her friends were at risk. Yvette glanced knowingly back at Jay, a decision passing between them in an instant. They would not leave Anton to fight this battle alone.

The specially designed armored truck slowed to turn the corner facing onto the road beside the destroyed gatehouse.

"The truck! Get on the truck!" Jay shouted urgently.

Li nodded; her face filled with intent.

Yvette readied herself, as soon as she moved from cover the troopers would start shooting at her, she would have to be faster than they were. Slinging her Milkor MGL over her shoulder, she adjusted her katana shoulder straps and silenced her mind. The Ramp overtook her, time slowed down, and she waited, still as stone for the right opportunity to move.

The MRU was the first vehicle in the convoy. It drove between the two APC wrecks, its powerful bulk moving between them like a great white shark indifferent to anything else in its domain. The rig's turbine engine rumbled, its metal flanks armored and curved, an indomitable steel beast seemingly from another world, it passed her, towing the armored trailer behind it.

Yvette wasn't sure if what Anton had just done was bold or crazy – perhaps it was a bit of both. She accelerated forward along the road, leaping onto the side of the armored MRU trailer. There were multiple service handholds for maintenance staff, she grabbed hold of them. Bullets whined past her, striking sparks off the trailer. She scrambled to the flat top of the trailer as it accelerated past the ruins of the gatehouse.

Anton was already there, hugging the top of the vehicle and looking like he'd passed through a furnace. The left side of his face lay raw and bloody. What remained of his hair clung half-burned to his scalp. Lines of dried blood ran from his nostrils and the corners of his mouth over his chin. His eyes burned wild and hot with a fearsome resolve.

Jay and Li both appeared on the other side of the roof at the same time, a fraction of a second behind her, bullets and tracers flying overhead. The height of the trailer created a sheltered area on the roof above the trooper's angle of fire.

The MRU approached the main road, its great horn blaring. It barely slowed to take the corner to the right. They straightened up; they were on the road heading north. A pair of blackwidows angled in to pace the convoy.

They were heading back to the RAF airbase at Coningsby.

Yvette looked around herself, her lips thinned. *Frying pan, meet fire.*

Chapter Five

BREAKING: Explosions reported at UK MOD site

There are reports of multiple explosions at a Ministry of Defense site in South Lincolnshire.

Published 08/22 11:52

Witnesses report a massive pall of smoke rising over the base of the recently formed Squadron F.

— Breaking News article on the Internet.

* * *

North of the Facility, South Lincolnshire, August 22nd, 11:52

The two charcoal-colored Range Rovers motored along at sixty miles an hour.

Francis had positioned the remainder of his team ahead of the approaching convoy. There was no point being behind the convoy with half of Shadowstone UK between the rest of the team and himself. All he needed to do was stay in front and identify an opportunity to help the team escape.

Scanning her laptop, Juliette stated, "Panopticon hazing has begun. That will hide our SUVs from their drones and any other cameras and sensors. We've got about fifteen minutes, twenty at best." She nodded; her lips pursed. "Shadowstone cyberwarfare units out of Beijing, Saint Petersburg and Seattle have already begun counter attacks."

"Fifteen minutes will have to do," Francis observed.

Chiara spoke up from the second SUV, where Luther was driving, and she was keeping watch, "I don't know if we'll have fifteen minutes. They're coming fast, eighty, ninety miles per hour, and the APCs and MRAPs are keeping pace."

Francis pushed down on the accelerator; the Range Rover's supercharged engine responded with effortless power. The SUV surged forward, the speedometer climbing to eighty-five miles per hour.

"The two blackwidows are flying top cover," Chiara added.

"How far back are they?" Francis asked.

"About half a mile … and closing slowly."

Francis accelerated to ninety miles per hour, the SUV racing along the road. There was no traffic heading in either direction, had Shadowstone blocked the roads? He asked Juliette, "Sitrep, any police roadblocks activated in front of us?"

"Got it," Juliette said, her fingers flashing over her laptop. "Yes. Connecting roads between the Shadowstone base and the RAF airbase at Coningsby have roadblocks. That's the confirmation we've been looking for, they're taking Peter back to the airbase."

"They'll fly him out of the country."

"And half our team is on that truck."

"C'est un foutu bordel!" Francis swore. He didn't need to wonder how the team had ended up in their current position – Anton Slayne. Despite Anton's disobedience, the objectives remained clear. Get Peter back, break contact with Shadowstone and disappear back beneath the Panopticon's radar – and do it all in the next fifteen to twenty minutes – while Juliette's cyberwarfare attacks hazed the Panopticon.

Then they could get back to the main mission, rescuing Ramin Kain, or more correctly, stopping him from leaking all the secret knowledge of the Order of Thoth to the Vampire Dominion.

He broadcast to the team, "Anton, Jay, Yvette, Li. Report in."

Howling wind came over the earbuds, then the voices of the team members clinging to the MRU cutting through, enhanced by technology to pick out their words against any background noise. Jay shouted, "We're on top of the truck."

Yvette and Li reported in, then Anton yelled urgently, "Guys, we've got to move!"

What else was about to go wrong? Francis glanced into the rear-view mirror. A futile gesture, everyone was too far away for him to see what was happening.

Chiara said calmly, "The blackwidows are descending to flank the MRU on both sides."

They're sitting ducks up there.

Francis' heart leaped. There was nothing he could do.

* * *

The mobile rendition unit raced along the road, a pair of armored personnel carriers and four MRAPs hot on its heels.

Victoria Hansen, a flight officer for the aerial wing of Squadron F, lowered her blackwidow helicopter gunship to three hundred yards above the ground and about two hundred yards to the left of the MRU. Her wingman mirrored her position in the second blackwidow on the opposite side of the road. Four Order operatives clung to the roof of the trailer section, barely holding on as ninety-mile-per-hour winds lashed them. Their weapons included a sniper rifle, some submachine guns, and a Milkor MGL. It was primarily the MGL she was concerned about. Without specialized ammunition, the other weapons wouldn't be able to penetrate her gunship's armor. She was at least three hundred and fifty yards away from the MGL; on the practical limits of its range.

"Select your targets," She ordered her gunner. The man was already staring at the four enemy operatives, the right-side minigun pointing directly at the roof of the MRU. With a squeeze of his trigger finger, he would scrape those vermin off the top of the trailer with an irresistible stream of 7.62mm depleted uranium penetrators.

All she needed now was permission to fire. The fight had passed beyond the Facility and was now in open civilian territory, the rules of engagement had changed. She opened her comms link to Major Quiver and Director Heathmont, and reported, "Sir, we have the targets lit up. Ready to take the shot."

Major Quiver ordered, "Weapons are cleared for—"

"Belay that order," Director Heathmont interrupted, cutting across his subordinate. "Widow dash Three, what munitions are loaded in your miniguns?"

"Standard 7.62mm penetrators, Sir," Victoria answered.

"Major Quiver, what is the hull rating on the MRU trailer?"

"Protection up to and including .50 caliber ball, Sir," Major Quiver said.

"The MRU is not rated against 7.62mm depleted uranium rounds, is it?"

"No, Sir."

"A minigun with penetrators could cut that trailer in half, couldn't it?"

"Sir? Yes, Sir."

"You could kill my prisoner, couldn't you?"

"Sir?"

"Widow dash Three, you and your wingman are cleared to fire warning shots only. I want that rig at Coningsby airbase as soon as possible with the prisoner alive. Make sure they stay on the road. Major Quiver, the .50 cal machine guns on the APCs, the M240s on the MRAPs and your trooper's small arms are released for immediate use between here and the RAF airbase. Is that clear?"

"Yes, Sir."

"Then be about it. Clear those Order of Thoth scum off my truck."

"Roger that, Sir," Major Quiver replied enthusiastically.

The line muted. Victoria had her orders. She stared, steely-eyed, at the Order of Thoth operatives riding bold as brass on the MRU's trailer. She tilted her helmeted head to the right, and then to the left. There was a soft cartilage click somewhere near the place her neck connected with her body.

She would just have to wait and play nursemaid for the troops on the ground.

She barked a short, dismissive laugh. A nursemaid! It wasn't what she had signed up with the 'Stateless Warfare Wing,' more commonly known as Squadron F for. 'F' was another one of the squadrons comprising the Special Airborne Service, the famous SAS of the British army. The same, but different; more cutting edge, always outfitted with the very latest technology, and never short of funds. There was a deeper mystery as well, sometimes late at night after she'd shared a bottle of scotch or two with the other pilots, someone would mutter a single word – Shadowstone.

Shadowstone, a nebulous, super-secret outfit that seemed to be operating just out of sight at the highest echelons of government and the corporate world. That was her goal, she wanted into the game, and she wanted in bad.

Being a gunship jockey was just a stepping stone to bigger things.

* * *

The pair of blackwidow gunships paced to either side of the mobile rendition unit. The thunder of their engines muted by the howling ninety-mile-per-hour winds rushing over the heavy vehicle.

Anton crabbed his way along the top of the MRU's trailer, moving from maintenance hand hold to hand hold to avoid the hurricane-like slipstream tearing him off the top of the trailer. He hugged the top of the vehicle, chancing a quick glance over the rear lip of the trailer to see what was chasing them.

A bullet went straight through his hair above his right ear.

He ducked back behind the lip, his earbud communicator broadcasting his voice despite the wind as he swore, "What the hell!"

"Anton?" Li asked.

"There are two armored personnel carriers, and four of those armored Humvee-style vehicles right behind us."

MRAPs, he remembered Peter saying, Mine Resistant Ambush Protected vehicles, he'd talked about them back at the safe house in Maine. Modern, tough, and fast, typically armed with a machine gun or other weapons, and the natural successor to the 'coffin on four wheels,' Peter had called the Humvee.

Yvette said, "The helicopters haven't tried shooting at us."

"Probably don't want to hurt their prize," Jay suggested, tapping the top of the trailer.

Anton stared at his team mates. He was the only one facing forward. Li, Jay, and Yvette, all faced him, more or less in a line across the top of the trailer on the other side of a hatch in the roof. The hatch had no visible means of opening from the outside. Damn it, they needed to get Peter out of the trailer as soon as possible. The top hatch was useless as a means to enter the trailer.

Anton said, "We have no strategy."

"Yeah, no kidding," Jay remarked, staring accusingly at Anton.

Yvette smacked Jay on the shoulder.

"Hey," Jay objected. "Just being honest."

"It doesn't matter how we got here – we're here for Peter," Li declared.

They all looked at each other.

"The rest of the team are in front of us," Li explained. "We need to stay with this vehicle until we can get Peter out of it. Anything else leaves Peter trapped by Shadowstone."

The rest of the team nodded.

Francis called out over the comms link, "We're heading for Coningsby airbase. They're planning to fly Peter out of the country."

Anton shook his head, that was never going to happen, not if he could do anything about it.

Machine gun fire erupted simultaneously from both sides of the MRU, striking sparks off the top edges of the trailer. A moment later, a pair of fragmentation grenades looped into the air from either side, over the edge of the trailer, and began falling toward them.

Anton ramped hard, one of the grenades was heading toward his head. Anchored with his left hand, he drew the Blue Dragon from the scabbard strapped behind his shoulders in a blur. His hand flashed up, the blade arcing around. He twisted his wrist at the very last moment, striking the grenade with the flat of his blade, sending it flying backward.

It dropped out of sight, exploding with a loud crack, a hail of shrapnel rattling against the side of the MRU. The forward rush of the vehicle immediately left the gray smoke of the explosion behind. Jay dealt with the second grenade with the same result on the other side of the trailer.

Machine guns fired again, coordinated bursts from left and right, and from behind the MRU. The only advantage they had, was the height of the MRU's roof forced the Shadowstone troopers to fire up at them, leaving a strip down the middle of the roof that they couldn't hit with their bullets.

The very location they were throwing their grenades into.

Chiara said through the comms link, "Right hand curve coming up in three, two, one—"

Four grenades flew overhead as the MRU shifted to the right.

Jay and Yvette both batted grenades away with their swords. Two of the grenades flew toward Anton, one from the left, and the other from the right. If he allowed himself to rise up too high, he would become an easy target for the gunners. He flipped over, his sword flashing left and right.

The grenades flew away exploding mid-air but out of range to do any damage.

Li scuttled over to take a position next to him.

Chiara directed again, "Left-hand curve coming up in three, two, one, now."

The truck turned back to the left.

Anton glanced at Li.

She caught his gaze and frowned, her large, brown eyes flashing fiercely. "You broke your promise."

"No, I didn't," Anton objected, indignation rising in his voice.

Li shook her head once, her eyes wide. "Don't try and justify what you did … Oh, why do I bother?"

A grenade sailed over the side of the MRU trailer. Anton blurred over Li, striking it away with the flat of his blade. It exploded harmlessly, well behind the trailer. He came back down as fresh machine gun fire flashed overhead. Li had moved to the other side of the trailer, a grenade falling toward her.

Anton yelled, "Watch—"

Li blurred, the Green Dragon flashing above her. The grenade vanished back the way it came. A thin scream of horrified despair wailed on the air as the grenade exploded over the MRAP it had come from.

"—out," Anton said, his voice tailing off.

Li glared at him. "I haven't finished with you yet."

Anton shook his head. Li was disappointed with him. It was happening a lot lately. What did she really want from him? He made himself busy looking for fresh threats. What would happen next? Would the Shadowstone troopers run out of grenades, or would they get lucky?

Bullets whizzed overhead, forcing the team to keep their heads down.

Anton looked past Li, scanning the edges of the trailer.

What attack would Shadowstone try next?

* * *

Peter cocked his head, a hail of metal fragments smashing against the MRU's flank. Their sharp, sudden rattle adding to the muted cacophony of explosions, and almost constant ricochets of bullets hitting the trailer's armored hull.

"L109A2 high explosive grenade," he whispered to himself distractedly, "Standard issue for British special forces."

He returned his attention to the task at hand. Unscrewing one of the handles of the ceiling hatch spinlock. It fell free in his hand. He stepped back from the hatch, comparing the threads of the short handle with another larger one he'd taken from the spinlock on the back door.

The two threads matched, they were the same length and width. They were interchangeable. Peter started working as fast as he could to remove a second of the short handles opposite the first one on the ceiling spinlock and replace them with two of the longer, heavier handles from the lock on the main door.

Soon he would have a second chance with the ceiling hatch, this time with double the leverage.

The second short handle dropped to the floor with a sharp clank, before rolling away beneath a white enameled cabinet. Peter rushed back to the rear door for the replacement handle.

He worked fast – tight and focused.

In a couple of minutes, he would be ready to open the ceiling hatch.

At least, that was the plan.

* * *

The Squadron F trooper tightened his white-knuckle grip on the steering wheel of the MRU.

A bead of perspiration slowly tracked its way from his short, salt and pepper hair down his left temple. He was beginning to wonder if being an MRU driver was such a great career choice, what with the constant shooting, explosions and navigating bends at ninety miles per hour when the speed limit was sixty. He glanced across at his colleague who was riding shotgun, armed to the teeth and grinning like a lunatic.

His thin lips pressed tightly together.

The new blokes were all adrenaline junkies; completely hyped up on 'the juice.' As a driver, participation in the Day Guard program had been optional, and he'd opted out. In another two months, his twenty years of service with the squadron would be up, and he would be taking the package. He'd seen things to give a man nightmares, and enough was enough; it was time to get out.

Director Heathmont's voice came over the comms link, "MRU Driver?"

"Yes, Sir."

"Drive faster," Director Heathmont ordered. "The wind will blow those scoundrels off the top of the truck."

Why on Earth would I want to go any faster?

"How much faster, Sir?"

"Isn't it obvious man? As fast as possible."

"Yes, Sir."

"Do it, man, knock those bastards off my truck."

"Yes, Sir."

The line muted.

The driver blinked. He sucked air in through his nose and let it out in a long sigh, it didn't help. He pushed forward on the accelerator. The turbine behind the cabin roared, and the truck surged forward to one hundred and ten miles per hour.

He wondered what would happen to the poor fools on top of the MRU's trailer. No one could hold on in such winds.

Surely, they're doomed.

* * *

The howling wind threatened to tear the clothes from Anton's body.

Anton tightened his grip on a hand hold, silently thanking the safety conscious engineer who had put maintenance handholds over the top and sides of the truck. He squinted his eyes to look into the wind. Every five or ten seconds, a burst of gunfire would go over their heads, or strike sparks off the side edges of the trailer roof.

Sometimes, grenades would fly up, and they would beat them away. The Shadowstone troopers were mixing things up, holding onto their grenades until the last second so they would explode before Anton and his friends could deflect them away. The team had anticipated the tactic, getting as close to the edge of the roof as possible. The last grenade had exploded a split second after Jay had smacked it back the way it had come. The bulk of the blast had occurred over the head of whoever had thrown it, but Jay sported nasty lacerations along his left arm for his trouble. Blood dripped down his arm in a red streak and pain gripped his face, leaving him scowling and gritting his teeth.

"Yvette?" Anton shouted. "How many rounds have you got left in the MGL?"

"A full load, but we can't use it from here. Their fire is too concentrated."

Anton nodded. "Right." He sheathed the Blue Dragon and scrambled forward along the top of the truck. Yvette gave him the MGL as he passed by, a nonplussed look on her face. He dropped into silence, ramped hard and blurred over the forward lip of the trailer's roof. Dropping down, his boots landed on a triangular articulated frame attaching the trailer to the rig.

He backed up to the rear of the rig's cabin. Sheltering from the wind, he checked the MGL, it was ready to fire. Where he stood, he could see the outside front corner of an MRAP less than six yards away. If he leaned out a bit more, he'd be able to get a clean shot straight into it.

Of course, they would be able to see him too.

Without hesitation, Anton crouched down low on the frame, anchored himself with his left hand and leaned out as far as he could. The dark-gray bitumen of the road whipped past beneath him. The leading wheels of the

MRU trailer thrummed against it. The hurricane force winds tore at his shoulder and arm, threatening to rip the MGL from his grip.

In front of him, a black-clad Shadowstone trooper stood up through the MRAP's hatch. With a grenade in each hand, he drew his arms back to throw them up at the rest of the team.

Anton pulled the trigger, the MGL fired, the grenade lancing forward through the base of the windscreen of the MRAP. Its shaped charge warhead sent a molten copper whip slashing through the cabin, obliterating the crew. The trooper collapsed back into the MRAP as smoke billowed out of the hatch, and the MRAP veered away from the MRU.

The dead trooper's live grenades bounced off the road, promptly exploding next to the rear wheels of the MRU, shredding the rubber on the nearest wheel. The next two wheels behind it took up the load, while a subtle vibration settled into the trailer.

Anton pulled back behind the rig, clambered to the other side, chancing a quick glance to see what was happening. The second MRAP, its roof splashed with blood, was pulling back. A small turret on top of it swiveled slightly, machine gun fire lashed toward him, striking the side of the rig behind him as he pulled his head back.

After the loss of one MRAP, and losing at least one man from the retreating MRAP, sure as hell, Shadowstone were going to change tactics.

Anton ramped again, blurring back up to the roof of the trailer to join his teammates.

* * *

The roadblock consisted of a police car parked at right angles in the middle of the side road, its police lights strobing red and blue, and a set of bright orange witches' hats crossing the intersection with the main road between the Squadron F base and Coningsby.

A loud crack, resounded from the south, a plume of dark-gray smoke erupting into the air. The crunch of a heavy vehicle hitting a tree line followed a second or two later.

A young policeman, fresh out of cadet school and on his first posting placed the last of a row of orange witches' hats. He jogged back to the police car; his face filled with concern. A pair of military helicopters flew about six hundred yards apart, flying parallel with the road and heading straight for them. The roar of their engines grew with every second, becoming a howling thunder, driving the young man to stuff his fingers in his ears.

His partner stood next to the car, lighting a cigarette. Smoking on duty was a reportable offense, but the younger man turned a blind eye to his partner's habit. He may be the youngest officer at his station, but he knew well enough, you didn't rat on your fellow officers for something as minor as smoking a cigarette.

The older man blew a gray cloud of smoke and shouted, "Damn crazy MI5 horse shit. That's what this is."

"MI5?" the young man asked nonplussed, staring down the road. Whatever had crashed was now burning about half a mile away behind a long stand of trees on the side of the road.

The older man nodded knowingly. "Yeah, sure."

A pair of charcoal Range Rovers sped around a shallow bend, racing past the roadblock at more than a hundred miles per hour.

"What tha' hell!" the young man shouted, clutching his police cap tight to his head to stop the wash from the two vehicles blowing it off. "What about them? They're speeding."

The older man shook his head disdainfully, taking another long drag on the cigarette. "MI6, just part of the exercise."

"What about that explosion?" the young man said, pointing down the road at the dispersing plume of gray smoke.

The older man stared at his young partner, with a 'prepare to be schooled,' look and said, "They make it all look realistic for the exercise, they have to. The Stateless Warfare Wing that would be Squadron F for newbies like you, is a force apart. They can go anywhere in the world, fight anyone, and answer to the highest echelons of the government via MI5 and MI6." He waved his hand at the witches' hats. "We're just here to keep the public out of the way."

Something big and fast came around the bend. A snub-nosed semi-trailer rig, its turbine engine roaring, flames shooting from its exhausts, flashed past them. It towed a long trailer, with sloping sides, about the size of a shipping container. The backwash blew over all the witches' hats and sent the young man's cap fluttering away.

Following it were three MRAPs and a pair of armored personnel carriers. The young policeman could've sworn blood splattered the roof of the lead MRAP's roof and numerous dents scored the vehicles armor as if someone had dumped stones all over it.

The helicopters flew overhead, the hard points for missiles on both sides had space for four missiles each, but only carried one.

Where were the rest of the missiles? Had they been firing them already?

The young policeman stood open-mouthed as the convoy of vehicles raced away to the north. His partner took another drag on his cigarette and began casually picking up the witches' hats and putting them back into a neat line.

"C'mon mate, quit gawking and give us a hand."

The young policeman frowned for a brief moment, and then shrugged his shoulders. What did he know, he was a newbie? He joined his partner in making the roadblock whole again.

They had a job to do, and they were doing it.

What more could anyone ask of them?

* * *

The charcoal Range Rovers shot past the police roadblock at close to one hundred and ten miles per hour.

Francis glanced at Juliette, and she said, "They think we're part of the convoy."

Juliette's fingers flashed over her laptop. She used prepositioned Order software to hack into the local police networks. A moment later, her eyes scanned down the list of the day's police reports. "... They think that 'Squadron F,' is conducting an impromptu training exercise between their military base and RAF Coningsby. Shadowstone have ordered them to clear all civilians out of the way."

"That's a small mercy. Any information on how they might be planning to take Peter out of the country?"

"I've checked the available air traffic reports, but there is nothing there."

"Wait," Francis said, ducking his head to look up high in the air. There was a large, gray, four-engine transport aircraft flying a couple of thousand yards above the ground. "That's a transport. It's heading straight for the RAF airbase."

Juliette followed his gaze. "Yes, that is the one. There is no mention of that flight anywhere."

Francis studied the aircraft, relying on his reflexes to keep the SUV tracking along the road. He had to ensure the truck never got onto that plane. With the speed they were traveling at, they were eating up the miles, in minutes they would be at the airbase.

He had to get Peter out of the truck, every other option led to failure and potentially the destruction of the team. The only question was how. Francis didn't have an answer, he would have to trust Jay, Yvette, Li, and Anton to get Peter out before the truck reached the airbase.

With time running out, he didn't like their odds.

* * *

The MRU driver's eyes flicked down to the speedometer. Nothing had changed, it still read one hundred and ten miles per hour. The turbine roared at full power beneath and behind the cabin. Its scream muted by thick armor and noise suppression insulation surrounding the rig.

There was something 'not quite right.' There was a little vibration in the trailer. He dearly wished to be able to slow down. Anything going wrong at this speed could easily create a total catastrophe.

The driver wanted nothing to do with anything remotely approaching such a disaster, not with two months left before retirement.

The comms link, opened up, and Director Heathmont's voice came over the line, "MRU Driver, I have new orders for you."

Oh hell, what now?

"Yes, Sir."

Drop your speed back to sixty miles per hour until further notice."

There really is a God.

"Yes, Sir."

The line muted. The driver pulled his foot off the accelerator and started braking. The big rig began sloughing off speed. He sighed with relief as the speedometer dropped to sixty miles per hour and stabilized there.

Now, maybe the shooting will stop too.

* * *

The MRU slowed down.

The hurricane force winds dropped back to a gale.

"What now?" Yvette asked in exasperation, applying a hurried strip bandage to Jay's upper arm.

Anton stared at Jay, a common realization flashing across their faces as they chorused together, "Boarders!"

Li readied the Green Dragon, crawling toward the back of the trailer. Anton tied the MGLs straps to a hand hold. Gripping the Blue Dragon, he followed Li, taking up a position beside her. Yvette took one of the H&K MP5s in her left hand and her katana in her right, using her feet to hook onto a pair of handholds. Jay flexed his bandaged arm and did the same. Between them all, the team covered the four corners of the trailer.

Fiery tracers from the APC's .50 caliber machine guns flashed overhead. The M240's on the roofs of the MRAPs joined in, their bullets sparking off the lip surrounding the roof of the MRU's trailer.

The firing all stopped at once.

"Now," Anton whispered, ramping hard, along with his teammates.

Black shadows rose up in the air, resolving into the shapes of men. H&K MP5 submachine guns erupted in their hands, short, bright tongues of fire leaping from their barrels.

Anton leaped to his feet, twisting violently, bullets whipping past him. He drove the Blue Dragon up through the torso of the nearest trooper, then pulled the sword out in a wide slash. The man's agonized grunt fled with the wind as he toppled backward off the trailer.

Anton dashed toward the middle of the trailer roof, another two troopers landing to his left and right. Both troopers aimed their MP5s directly at his chest. His left hand blurred, grabbing the first man by his leading wrist, pushing upward against heavy resistance. These troopers were strong. Anton's right foot lashed out, catching the second trooper in the gut. He staggered backward toward the edge of the trailer's roof.

The first trooper's submachine gun started firing, the bullets ripping above his shoulder.

Too close for comfort.

Anton's right hand lashed forward, the Blue Dragon now reversed, the end of the handle breaking the man's jaw. The trooper fell backward, toppling over the edge of the trailer.

The second trooper recovered his balance. Stepping forward he leveled a gun at Anton's ear, snarled and said, "Dodge this, mother—"

Anton blurred aside, the bullets blasting past his head with whip-like cracks. He moved back in close, his hands pushing out on the man's shoulder and hip. A quick thrust with his hip and the man flew screaming through the air off the MRU. The rest of his words lost in the howling wind as he disappeared amongst the trees lining the road.

Anton spun around, all the other Shadowstone troopers were off the MRU, or lying still on the blood-splattered roof.

The team returned to their positions, guarding the corners of the MRU's trailer.

Li grimaced, stretching her right foot out. Anton's heart jumped, and he asked, "You, okay?"

She shook her head, a look of uncomprehending dismay crossing her face. "I don't know how it happened, one of them fell across my ankle, and it got twisted."

"Tell me if it gets worse."

Li paused for a second as if remembering that she didn't like him. "Yes, kemosabe."

A grimly ironic half-grin spread slowly over Anton's face. "Riiight!"

He looked away. The fight had left Jay and Li injured, the team was slowly getting beat up. Sooner or later, they would have to slow down. No one could ramp forever, and then they would be in real trouble.

They had to get Peter out and get away soon.

As soon as possible.

* * *

Peter twisted the last of the large handles into the spinlock on the ceiling of the MRU.

It was good and tight, he grabbed hold of the extended handles of the spinlock, and crunched upward. Planting his big boots to the left and right on the ceiling, he crouched upside down over the spinlock. He focused his mind, descended deeply into silence. The Ramp flowered within, power rippling through him in increasing waves.

He started to push, and push, and push.

Heat washed off him. His face flushed, perspiration running up his forehead and into the dangling shock of thick red hair falling down from the top of his head.

He grunted, and moaned, veins popping on his wrists and hands.

The metal heart of the spinlock resisted his efforts with mute indifference.

He descended deeper into the silence.

The world darkened around him.

He pushed harder than he'd ever pushed anything before.

Nothing happened.

Peter dropped out of the Ramp. Sucking in great lungfuls of air while holding on upside down, he adjusted his position to get his thighs and hips involved in the effort. A second later, he dropped back into the Ramp. His focus on the present moment sharpened to a laser-like point. Silence overwhelmed him. Lightning coruscated from the base of his spine, flashing along his nerves and sinews. His muscles bunched, his knuckles whitened, his fingers almost penetrating the steel of the spinlock handles.

His mouth gaped, a scream from deep within filled the chamber. A noise of suffering, unlike anything heard in that dreadful, antiseptic room before.

Something screeched, as it went beyond all-natural limits of endurance.

Something tore, and something else snapped like a whip.

Peter fell down to the floor.

* * *

A pair of charcoal Range Rovers paced in front of the convoy.

Victoria Hansen double checked her scopes. What she was seeing didn't make any sense. Squadron F, or was it Shadowstone, had optimized blackwidow gunships for ground assault. Nothing the size of a car could move anywhere within five miles of a blackwidow without the helicopter's sensor arrays spotting it. But as far as her ultra-high-tech sensors were concerned, the two SUVs half a mile in front of the MRU didn't exist.

Cyberwarfare. They must be Order of Thoth. I'd better call this in.

"The prisoner's out!" her gunner shouted.

Victoria stared in amazement at the hatch door on top of the MRU trailer. It was standing hard upright, the wind holding it in place like a lonely tombstone. In front of the hatch door, a thick-bodied, red-haired man leaped onto the roof of the trailer.

He blurred left and right, impossibly fast for a human, .50 caliber tracers from one of the trailing APCs flashing past him.

"Madness," she whispered. It was time for a warning shot, she tilted her gunship, swinging it in toward the MRU. All she needed to do was scare him back into the trailer and give him second thoughts about escaping – her 20mm cannon would do the trick.

The red-haired man bent down, grabbing the hatch door, ripping it left and right, an instant later it was in his hands. He twisted and twirled around on the spot like an Olympic level discus thrower before launching the hatch door directly at her.

She shouted, "What the—" Instinctively veering left, the gunship roared, responding like a hawk in flight. The hatch door, spinning perfectly on its axis, flashed four feet to the right of her cockpit.

"Fuck!" she yelled, as something crashed behind her.

Alarms screamed, and red lights flashed, the helicopter twisted around her, diving back to the right, moving with her original momentum back toward the MRU. She pulled on her controls, nothing happened, they were dead in her hands. The Helicopter continued the slow descending turn, starting to twist around its central axis.

She turned around in her chair. The tail rotor hung stationary on a thread of metal; the MRU's top hatch door embedded in its main housing.

Her heart froze. There was no escape, they were stuck in a dead helicopter that was gathering speed as it sailed over the top of the MRU toward the road directly behind it.

The dark bitumen rose up toward her.

Victoria pushed back against the windscreen and screamed, "Fuck! Fuck! Fu—"

In a single crushing instant, her world went black.

* * *

Eighteen tons of blackwidow gunship hit the bitumen of the road at over one hundred miles per hour.

The helicopter disintegrated upon contact with the hard tarmac. The turbines separated from each other, spearing forward with several tons of 'inevitability' each, straight into the paths of the armored personnel carriers.

The APC on the right took one of the turbines just inside the right front wheel and the chassis. The impact flipped the APC over onto its left side. It screeched along the road in a shower of sparks for another twenty yards before it encountered the miraculously intact fuel tank of the blackwidow. The fuel tank promptly exploded in a blinding glare, greasy black smoke fountaining upward in a tall plume. The APC, burning furiously, ground its way into the nearest ditch.

The second APC was not as lucky as the first. The second turbine struck it end on like a giant's fist punching through the front of the APC's hull, obliterating the driver and half the crew as it disappeared somewhere into the belly of the vehicle. The APC careered blindly through the front half of the blackwidow's tumbling cabin, a canister of 70mm Hydra rockets flew through the gaping hole into the APC's interior. The rockets instantly detonated in a colossal explosion, converting the APC into a cloud of burning metal confetti.

While the APCs were taking the brunt of the impact of the crashing blackwidow, the crews of the three remaining MRAPs shadowing the MRU were attempting to evade as best they could. Shadowstone enhanced reflexes dragged on steering wheels, floored accelerators or slammed on brakes.

One of the trailing MRAPs, attempting to avoid flying helicopter debris, ran through the exploding second APC, evaporating itself in a gray-black cloud of burning metal. The second trailing MRAP pulled wide, accelerating snake-like between the two APC wrecks, directly into half the armored hull of the blackwidow. The MRAP flipped vertically into the air, looping over itself before landing on its roof in the middle of the road, its wheels spinning wildly in the air.

The leading MRAP accelerated up to the MRU, a stray section of rotor blade shearing through the M240 mount on its roof. The machine gun fell away, joining the wave of destruction taking out everyone else behind them.

Streaming forward at sixty-five miles per hour, the MRU, trailed by the single surviving MRAP, left the burning wreckage in its wake.

Peter dropped to a prone position, his eyes flashing with excitement. He said brightly, "I told you I'd be on time."

Grinning with a mixture of relief and joy, Anton slapped Peter's shoulder. He shrugged out of the over-sized battle vest and handed it to Peter.

Peter pursed his lips, his eyes shining. "Beautiful."

The team was back together again.

Chapter Six

"The oppression we all face is guarded by what we are unwilling to question." – Juliette Mirovar

* * *

South of Coningsby, Lincolnshire, August 22nd, 12:01

At breakfast, there had been four blackwidow pilots in the mess hall at the Facility, now there was only one left alive.

He put a gauntleted hand over his chin mike, and addressed his gunner, sitting half a dozen feet behind him, "Fuck this. Fucking Director Heathmont can climb up my fucking asshole as far as he wants. I'm not going anywhere near those fuckers on that truck."

"Fucking amen to that, Sir," the gunner swore.

"Well ... unless I've got full weapons clearance."

The comms link activated, the director's voice resounding in his ears, "Widow dash Four, report in."

What the hell am I supposed to say, we just got our asses kicked by one man with a fucking flying frisbee.

"On station, Sir. Three hundred and fifty yards to the right of the MRU."

"Your miniguns are cleared for use," Director Heathmont declared, in tightly clipped tones, like he was reluctant to admit the necessity. "However—"

Of course, what now?

"—we need to recapture the prisoner alive."

The pilot wanted to rub his eyes, but his helmet's visor and gauntlets got in the way. His hands stayed resolutely on the controls of the blackwidow, and his lips pressed into a thin gash.

"Sir, in all honesty, how are we supposed to do that with a blackwidow? We're designed to kill things, not capture them."

There was a short pause over the comms link, while the pilot considered that his career may have just nosedived into the toilet.

"Just to be clear Widow dash Four, I want you to ensure the terrorists on top of our mobile rendition unit do not access the cabin or interfere with the progress of the unit to the Coningsby airbase. I have a ... reception, waiting for them." The director's voice dropped into the freezing range as he inquired, "Are you able to comply Widow dash Four? Or, do I need to find another pilot who can do the job."

The pilot glowered at the targets. His gunner could avoid the body of the truck – if he got closer, but the terrorists were carrying an MGL, and one of those placed in the right spot could kill his bird.

He replied, "Wilco, Sir."

The director's voice warmed from frigid to merely icy, and he ordered, "Carry on, then."

The line muted. The pilot closed the distance between the MRU and his gunship to two hundred yards. He kept a close eye on his targets. They were hugging the roof of the MRU as it accelerated back up to maximum speed.

The pilot covered his chin mike and directed his gunner, "You see any of them point an MGL at us, you shoot those grenades in flight. Right?"

"Roger that, Sir," the gunner replied with quiet conviction.

Within minutes they would be at Coningsby airbase and whatever 'reception,' the director had planned for the terrorists would come into play. In the meantime, the pilot had decided discretion was the better part of valor.

At least it was against these Order of Thoth operatives.

* * *

The hurricane force winds rolling over the top of the MRU stretched the earbud communicators to their limits.

"We have to get into the cabin," Anton yelled.

Li looked doubtful, and shouted, "The last blackwidow has us targeted. You can bet they've orders to stop us doing that."

"Anton," Francis said, his voice was faint but clear over the comms link. "We need to create a distraction to allow us to break contact with Shadowstone."

Juliette said, "Panopticon hazing will start to run out in seven minutes, and not later than twelve minutes."

"We have to break contact in under seven minutes," Francis declared, "and by then, the truck will be at the airbase."

Anton looked around at the rest of the team, they were all facing in, while hugging the roof of the MRU. "This truck is fast, if we have control of it, we can use it as a weapon." He grinned. "We just need to run it into something important."

"And who would be driving it?" Jay asked.

Anton lifted his eyebrows in answer, he wasn't going to ask anyone else to take the risk. He reached over, undoing the straps on the MGL, it still had five high-explosive armor piercing rounds in it. "In the meantime, we've gotta keep pushing at Shadowstone and keep them off balance."

"Anton, wait!" Li yelled.

Anton blurred forward against the wind. He appeared, crouched on the front right corner of the MRU trailer. He anchored himself with his left hand. Raising the MGL with his right hand, he aimed it at the armored door next to the driver. He pulled the trigger, the MGL fired, the noise lost in the howl of the wind. The grenade traveled the three yards to the door in a tiny fraction of a second, exploding in a bright glare. The molten copper of the shaped charge carved a shallow rent all the way along the front right-hand side of the rig.

The door stayed solidly attached.

A burst of 7.62mm rounds speared between the rig and the MRU, barely a yard in front of Anton. He jerked backward, the blackwidow was closing to one hundred and fifty yards. The port side minigun was pointing straight at him.

"Over the side," Peter yelled. The team blurred behind Anton, disappearing over the far lip of the trailer away from the blackwidow. The only thing left trailing the MRU was a beat-up MRAP about fifty yards back, it's M240 machine gun lost miles behind them in the gunship wreck. It was the lesser of two evils.

His friends were in immediate danger from the blackwidow, a red mist descended over Anton's mind. He had to do something. He blurred along the trailer, his finger hard on the trigger of the MGL. The grenade launcher fired three times in the next second, the grenades looping toward the blackwidow.

The port side minigun's barrels whirred, a line of tracers spearing through the air, connecting with each of the grenades in turn. They all exploded in a row halfway between the trailer and the helicopter gunship.

Anton grabbed a hand hold, swinging over the far side of the trailer. He landed next to Peter, who was precariously hanging onto handholds on the trailer's side.

Peter dropped back from the top edge of the trailer and said drily, "That was pure ass on their part—"

The last MRAP pulled into view behind them, a trooper standing up through its top hatch, his assault rifle coming to bear on them. Bullets flew in both directions, Jay firing back with his submachine gun.

"On top!" Peter called out, the team blurring back onto the top of the trailer.

Out of the line of fire from the MRAP, but exposed to the blackwidow pacing the MRU at one hundred and fifty yards on the right-hand side.

Anton stared up at the gunship, the barrels of the minigun were pointing right at him.

They could've taken the shot, but hadn't. They wanted them all alive.

Anton's eyes widened, Shadowstone expected to capture them all.

* * *

The charcoal-colored Range Rover slowed as it entered Coningsby, passing another pair of police roadblocks keeping local traffic off the main approach to the airbase. The SUV peeled to the left, past the entrance to the airbase. The second Range Rover running tight in behind it.

Juliette glanced up from her laptop and stated, "Panopticon cover will begin to run out in two minutes."

Francis glanced back at her, broadcasting to the team, "Thirty plus Shadowstone troopers at the airbase entrance. One commander tank, two APCs and four MRAPs. Sixty plus RAF regiment soldiers with their vehicles."

"C'mon Boss," Peter replied. "That's hardly fair against us. The poor bastards won't stand a chance."

"Can you get off the truck before it hits the airfield?" Juliette asked.

"Sure, we can," Jay confirmed in a clear voice, "but Shadowstone will be all over us. The blackwidow will be able to track us, and we'll never break contact."

"It's too late," Li declared. "We're a minute behind you – we're almost there."

"Get ready to fight," Anton said. "We're hitting this gate hard."

"Don't get caught at the gate," Francis directed. "Breakthrough, we'll reposition to pick you up on the other side of the airbase."

"The MRU is starting to slow," Yvette said.

Anton said with hard enthusiasm, "It's game time."

Juliette and Francis' Range Rover sped along the street parallel to the RAF airbase perimeter fence. The team needed to do something terrible to create a distraction big enough to break contact with Shadowstone.

Innocent people, such as the RAF Regiment soldiers, would die. Juliette shook her head, a sudden sadness lashing through her. The innocent would die and the Mirovar team would pay a price for breaking their own rules.

She was sure of it.

* * *

Francis pulled the Range Rover to a halt on the side of the road. Samuel Luther pulled the second SUV in hard behind the first car.

Francis commanded, "Chiara, MGL, and the spare ammo. You're with me. Luther, follow Juliette. We rendezvous in five minutes on the other side of the base."

"Copy that," Luther said dryly.

Francis frowned, glanced at Juliette who nodded at him. She would be okay. He opened the door, grabbed the White Dragon, and an H&K MP5 with a couple of spare magazines of high-performance rounds. He paused at the edge of getting out, leaned back in and kissed her once on the lips.

"See you soon, mon amour," he promised.

"Yes, mon amour."

He leaped out, shutting the door behind him. Chiara was already crouching near the perimeter fence watching him calmly, her long dark hair snaking down her back in a long plait. Her katana lay strapped across her shoulders, an H&K MP5 dangled from straps at her side, and she carried the Milkor MGL with her hands.

Francis dashed over to her, drawing the White Dragon clear of its scabbard with a smooth flick of his wrist. Barely slowing down, he went through the perimeter fence as if it wasn't there. Leaving a two-and-a-half-yard high triangle gap in the wire mesh, the edges of the metal wire smoking lightly from the impact of the White Dragon.

Chiara followed closely behind him.

There was a fifty-yard stretch to the nearest building, a large gray-metal hangar. They blurred across the open space in under three seconds, coming to a halt, hard up against the wall of the building. They dashed to the right corner and Francis peeked around it.

He pulled back and directed, "Go to the right, I'll go left and watch your back. The name of the game is thunder and smoke. We need as much damage as possible to pull everyone we can away from the main gate."

"Got it, Francis."

"Go."

Chiara blurred around the corner, disappearing into the RAF airbase.

Francis followed after her, his eyes everywhere. Soon, everyone was going to be trying to kill Chiara, and he was the only person there to watch her back.

* * *

The RAF airbase at Coningsby was a model of a modern airbase, large open areas, fresh, clean buildings, and rows of brand-new F-35 Lightning II fighter jets.

Chiara lined the MGL up on an F-35 sitting three hundred yards away and pulled the trigger. The grenade chuffed away, trailing a thin line of smoke that vanished against the leaden sky. A second later, the grenade punched into the body of the fighter aircraft. The plane instantly exploded, sending a plume of black smoke rushing into the sky. Secondary explosions ripped the aircraft apart sending glittering streamers of bright fire in a dozen directions.

"Certainly, burns pretty," Chiara whispered to herself.

With a smile curling the edges of her full lips, she set her eyes on a fuel bowser four hundred yards away.

She blurred deeper into the airbase. No one had seen her yet, there were no alarms, no shouts – nothing. It was her job to make sure that changed. The row of twelve F-35 jets lined up in the open air represented the best opportunity to attract attention.

There were no pilots, no ground crew, or anyone near the aircraft. It was just another Tuesday at lunchtime, they were probably in the mess hall stuffing their faces with 'bangers and mash,' or something else typically English.

The bowser came into range, she pulled the trigger, her second grenade looping away. She didn't wait for it to land. There was too much to do. She blurred along the tarmac for another three seconds, firing another four rounds.

She pulled to a halt.

The bowser was gone, a smoking pit fountaining thick, black, oily smoke had replaced it. Five of the fancy new F-35s lay in tangled fiery wrecks, each attended by a rampant plume of dark smoke. It was as if fire djinns from some ancient fable had come to life, and hovered malevolently over the ruins of each aircraft.

Chiara paused and began reloading the MGL.

Her head flicked left and right, was anyone going to notice what was happening?

* * *

"Oh my God!" the RAF regimental officer uttered under his breath as half a dozen explosions echoed across the base in as many seconds.

"Sound the alarm, we're under attack."

One of his men punched a button, a series of klaxons began wailing across the length and breadth of the base.

A dozen screens occupied a wall in his command center. Four of them remained focused on events at the front gate. A specialized rig was slowing as it approached the gate. Most of his available force was there, along with a contingent of Squadron F troopers. He hadn't been comfortable with shifting most of his resources to one part of the base, but the orders had come from the top. Squadron F command had seconded his RAF regiment soldiers, and that was that – there was nothing he could do about it.

"There," he said, pointing at one of the other screens, a tiny figure crouching in the middle of it. "Who the hell is that?"

One of his men zoomed in the camera. The screen pixelated for half a second and then resolved. It was a girl, with a sword across her back and a grenade launcher. She threw away an empty bandolier. She'd just reloaded her weapon.

Beyond her, other screens showed half a billion pounds worth of ultra-modern jet fighters burning into scrap. Next to the wrecks were another half dozen F-35s; a brief break in the cloud cover opened up, the jets gleamed in the summer sunlight.

The girl lifted her MGL, her long dark plait of hair swinging across her shoulders. Grenades started launching from her weapon.

A horribly sick feeling settled in the regimental officer's guts, this was his worst nightmare come true. Squadron F be damned, the purpose of the RAF regiment was to protect the base, he had to act.

He shouted, "Get our troops away from the gate, secure the base."

"Yes, Sir," chorused a handful of subordinates in the command center.

Rapid commands were issued. The screens displayed the RAF Regiment soldiers leaving the front gate, their armored Land Rovers heading out across the base. Two of the bulky sand-colored vehicles were heading directly for the girl on the runway.

Then she started running, sprinting, blurring toward a hangar. She disappeared off the screen, the camera couldn't pan fast enough to follow her.

Who is she?

What is she?

* * *

The commander tank's main weapons tracked the mobile rendition unit as it approached the gate.

The MRU driver stared at the bore of the 105mm gun. It looked awfully big when it was pointing straight at him. The commander tank sat outside the gate on the left. In front of the driver was an array of Squadron F troopers and their equipment. A pair of armored personnel carriers, their .50 caliber machine guns and 25mm Bushmaster cannons pointing straight at him, sat like iron guardians on each side of the entrance. Another four MRAPs sat in a loose semi-circle in front of them, their M240 machine guns all manned and pointing at him. Most of the Squadron F troopers stood next to their vehicles, armed with net throwers, their intent to capture clear in their choice of equipment.

The RAF regiment soldiers were all leaving the gate, their vehicles streaming into the airbase. In the distance, explosions cracked, and nearly a dozen plumes of dark smoke rose into the gray sky.

An A400 transport descended to land, despite the chaos on the main runway.

"Gods," the driver whispered, what was going on? He hit the release on his seatbelt. He needed to evacuate in a hurry. He reached for the door.

A bright blade appeared through the side door next to him. It jerked downward, slicing through the locking mechanism. Beside him, the Squadron F trooper riding shotgun slammed his H&K 416 rifle against the driver's face, breaking his nose. Collateral damage as the trooper lined up on whoever was about to open the door.

The driver flattened himself back into his seat, blood pouring from his nose.

The door ripped open with a scream of tortured hinges.

The H&K rifle burst into life, flames shooting from its barrel mere inches from the driver's face.

Something shiny flashed past him.

Someone grabbed his arm, jerking him out of his seat. He flew through the air, feeling quite helpless and foolish. He crunched himself up as much as he could, the bitumen of the road rising to meet him. He landed hard, rolled and came to a stop on his back.

Everything hurt, his nose was bleeding, his shoulder felt dislocated, but he was alive.

The troopers at the gate shouted, "Halt! Halt! Halt!"

The rig's engine roared. The vehicle surging forward between the MRAPs and the APCs. Machine gun fire erupted all around, bright tracers lancing toward the rig from half a dozen machine guns at once. A blackwidow helicopter cruised overhead, its guns silent, a lazy bystander given the fury spearing toward the MRU.

The driver lay back.

All the fire was flying above him.

Two months to retirement, it was so close he could taste it.

* * *

Anton floored the accelerator.

Peter squirmed over him, pushing the dead trooper hard up against the far door, then pulled one of his throwing axes out of the man's forehead.

Anton slammed the side door shut, but it hung loose – the locking mechanism cut to ribbons by the Blue Dragon. All around, .50 caliber and 7.62mm machine guns fired at them. The bullets ricocheting off the sides of the rig in a deafening racket.

"What are they trying to do – scare us to death?" Peter asked, more bullets bouncing off the transparent armor of the windshield in front of his face.

"They still want to capture you … us."

Shadowstone troopers lowered their guns, aiming for the tires. The rig continued to accelerate, the turbine roaring as the MRU passed between the APCs and into the base. Fusillades of machine gun fire opened up from behind the MRU. It rocked left and right, its tires shredding on both sides of the rig and the trailer. It kept on rolling, the tires designed to run flat, but for how much longer Anton didn't know. He hoped it would hold together long enough to matter.

"Everyone okay?" Anton yelled.

"We're still holding on up here," Li called back.

Peter pointed forward. "That transport aircraft is heading toward us."

Anton nodded. "Perfect."

"Anton?"

"Distraction – a big fat one."

No doubt, the plane was made of light materials, certainly a lot lighter than the armored mobile rendition unit. The rig reached a quarter mile into the base, accelerating past fifty miles per hour. Behind it the four MRAPs gave chase. The APCs were backing and turning, blocking the commander tank at the base entrance. The shadow of the blackwidow passed over the top of the rig as a brief shaft of sunlight penetrated the cloud cover.

The A400 transport plane rolled to a stop two hundred yards in front of the rig. The pilots stared at the MRU rushing toward them. A pair of RAF Regiment MRAPs, little more than uprated land rovers pulled to a halt near the plane's nose. Soldiers spilled from them, raising their rifles to their shoulders and began shooting at the onrushing rig.

"Get off the trailer. Get up close to the rig," Anton shouted.

Jay, Yvette, and Li blurred over the edge of the trailer and hugged each other directly behind the rig cabin.

Anton stared hard at the transport. The pilot's faces blanched with fear, they pulled on their controls. The aircraft's engines roared, it started to pull forward and turn.

Too late.

It was all too late.

* * *

Francis' hand flashed out, catching the RAF regiment soldier on the side of his chin. The man's head whipped back; he fell stunned to the pavement. Francis scooped up his H&K 416 rifle before it struck the ground.

"You've seen one of these before?" Francis asked Chiara, pointing to a tracked, anti-air gun system next to them.

"Got it," Chiara affirmed, leaping in front of the control console of the weapons system, while Francis scanned the airfield, the captured H&K 416 rifle in his hands. The short range MP5 submachine gun slung for the moment.

Chiara flipped a pair of switches, the massive twenty-foot gun swinging left and right on its base in front of her. "We're hot."

"The gunship first, and then the MRAPs."

Chiara deactivated the identify friend or foe system and selected the lone blackwidow as a target. A fraction of a second later, the gun opened up. It was a short-range anti-air weapon built around a 30mm multi-barreled chain gun. Originally designed for use on A-10 Fairchild ground attack aircraft as an anti-tank weapon, some bright spark had decided it could double as a ground-based air-defense system.

The weapon roared. A tongue of fire leaping another ten feet past the end of the barrels. Empty shells the size of coke bottles flew to the left in a spray as fifty rounds a second of armor penetrating high explosive rounds zeroed in on the blackwidow.

The helicopter gunship evaporated in a mid-air explosion, raining glittering fragments of burning metal onto the runway.

The four MRAPs ran through the descending cloud of debris, and then began diverging away from each other. Still chasing the MRU, but avoiding being easy targets.

Francis frowned. During the whole engagement, the Shadowstone forces had been adapting their tactics at every step of the way. Sooner or later the Ramp wouldn't prove to be enough of an advantage, and his force team's luck would run out.

The MRU was racing toward the gray bulk of the transport aircraft, impact was seconds away.

"Kill the MRAPs," Francis commanded.

Chiara swung the weapon down toward the new targets.

* * *

The speedometer of the MRU ran past seventy miles per hour. Its shredded tires thundering over the runway's dark-gray tarmac. RAF regiment soldiers ran desperately to the left and right. The A400 transport aircraft lurched forward, its four turbines roaring, its propellers ripping at the air.

"Brace!" Anton yelled.

Everyone on the rig ramped hard, holding on with grips of steel. Jay, Yvette, and Li crouched together just behind the rig cabin, the body of the trailer three yards behind them. Peter braced himself against the dashboard.

Anton held the steering wheel with arms hard as iron. Time slowed down, the side of the aircraft looming to fill his vision. He jigged the MRU rig slightly to the left, catching the A400 at the point where the rear of the wing attached to the body of the transport aircraft. The impact rippled through his bones. The skin of the aircraft stretched, and then split, falling inwards as it broke apart. Aluminum struts crumpled and tore. The rig dropped ten miles per hour in a fraction of a second as it carved through the body of the transport, ripping a huge hole through the aircraft. Debris filled the air as the rig punched out the other side.

The trailer kept the aircraft upright as it passed through it, leaving a thin spine running along the top of the plane's body, connecting the front half of the aircraft with the back half.

The MRU completed its passage. The transport aircraft teetering like a wounded dinosaur almost ripped in half by the massive bite of a carnivore. The front and back collapsed inward, the nose and tail rising in the air to make a tragic 'V' shape. Fuel gushed from half-empty wing tanks, pooling beneath the gaping belly wound in the aircraft.

They were through, Anton glanced into the rear-view mirrors, he needed the aircraft to explode. The Shadowstone MRAPs were hot on their tail. He could catch them within an explosion.

He looked forward. A fuel truck sat parked on the tarmac. The rig would pass safely to the right of the truck.

Anton glanced sideways at Peter, pointed at the fuel truck, and said with relief, "Good thing we saw that; we could've hit—"

The left rear axle coupling gave way, the damage done by the grenades on the road approaching the airbase finally reached a tipping point. The rear wheels on the left side of the trailer wobbled for half a second before coming loose and flying off. The trailer lurched to the left, a storm of sparks erupting along the edge of the trailer as it dragged along the tarmac.

The MRU's failsafe systems locked up the steering wheel and switched off the engine.

The MRU was a rolling hulk, pulling to the left and heading straight toward the fuel truck.

"Out! Out! Out!" Anton screamed.

The team blurred away from the rig. Jay, Yvette, Li and Peter all went left; Anton being on the right-hand side of the rig, dived out of the cabin to the right. He rolled, picked himself up and began blurring back toward the space between the transport aircraft and the MRU trailer.

Anton had taken a dozen steps when the nose of the MRU ran into the fuel truck. The bowser detonated with a thunderous roar, a wave of superheated air picking him up and throwing him thirty feet through the air.

His reflexes kept him alive, moving as fast as he was, he was able to land and roll with the blast, diminishing its effect. Burning debris was falling through the air. He was dangerously close to the leaking fuel of the transport aircraft.

He focused hard, launching himself forward, running faster than he'd ever run before. He shot forward, the rest of the team were streaking away, lines of burning fighter aircraft in front of them. Clouds of smoke drifted across the runway, providing cover. They just had to run through it.

The fuel around the transport aircraft ignited, flames leaping and flashing toward the main body of the plane. Explosions ripped the wings off the body. The aircraft exploded in a fireball as reserve fuel tanks detonated with thunderous cracks that echoed across the runway.

Anton blurred forward, the heat of the explosion washing over him, but now too far away to cause real damage.

Thirty to forty yards in front of him, Yvette, Jay, Li, and Peter sprinted in a line through the smoke. Anton blurred, gaining on them. Eighty yards to his left, three Shadowstone MRAPs cleared the smoke, accelerating toward the rest of the team.

Their top-mounted M240 machine guns swung around to target his friends.

All Anton had left on him was the Blue Dragon. He pivoted, drawing his sword, and blurred toward the nearest vehicle.

* * *

The MRAPs were streaming toward the team.

Chiara manipulated the big gun's controls. Its integrated sensor array could pick up a vehicle shrouded in smoke with ease. There were three targets. One of the four MRAPs had been too close when the A400 transport aircraft exploded, and hungry fire had leaped out, claiming the MRAP and its crew as a prize.

She depressed the trigger. The gun shivered, the barrels whirring. Fire leaped as round after round of 30mm armor-piercing high explosive warheads speared down range toward the speeding MRAPs.

It was no contest. The three vehicles evaporated in wild explosions, their crews disappearing in pink mists. A lone Order warrior ducked away from the explosions, blurring toward the rest of the team. Chiara's lips curled into a half smile – only Anton would be crazy enough to attack when everyone else was evading.

The two armored personnel carriers and the commander tank were through the main gate and heading into the base. She selected them all as targets and set the system to auto mode. As soon as there was a clear shot, the gun would take it and keep firing until it destroyed all three targets. While the gun would carve the APCs into pieces, the commander tank was another proposition entirely, and the gun was no place to be when the commander tank inevitably targeted it.

Chiara glanced at the far end of the base. A pair of charcoal Range Rovers sat parked on a side road, just beyond the perimeter fence. The rest of the team were blurring through the wrecks of the F-35s.

It was time to go, she looked at Francis and said, "All set."

"Let's move," Francis commanded.

They ramped hard, blurring away from the big gun. Behind them the big gun ripped into life, roaring like a grounded dragon spewing angry flames. One of the APCs exploding about nine hundred yards away. A second later the other APC lit up with flames shooting out of its top hatch. Then the big gun exploded, torn in half by a tungsten kinetic spike fired from the commander tank.

Chiara kept running, Francis beside her, smoke from the burning aircraft and fuel bowsers, cloaking their escape.

There was only the commander tank left to pursue them.

* * *

Tom Wilkes, 'Tommy,' to his friends picked himself up off the tarmac.

His RAF regiment issued H&K 416 rifle lay in front of him. He'd emptied the magazine firing at the MRU before it ran into the transport aircraft. He fumbled for a moment, pulling a fresh magazine from his combat webbing. The other members of his squad lay around on the tarmac, alive or dead, he didn't know. He dumped the empty magazine and slammed the fresh one home. Cocking the rifle, he took a professional firing stance on one knee.

In the distance, shadows blurred through the smoke – faster than he could believe anyone could move – but it was happening.

He sighted along the barrel; the targets were already near maximum effective range. He pulled the trigger. The gun thrummed in his hands; in full auto mode it sent thirty rounds of high-performance ammunition into the smoke before clicking on empty.

The dark-gray pall thickened and swirled like hostile fog, had he hit anyone?

A bitter hope filled his heart.

* * *

Yvette stumbled, her hands flying out to either side, her hair an auburn halo around her head. She started to fall.

She didn't hit the ground. Jay swooped in from the side, scooping her up in his arms without missing a stride. With no visible loss of speed, he blurred forward to the perimeter fence.

Peter was there first, using his double-bladed battle-axe to carve a hole in the wire. He stepped forward, using his axe to hold the wire back so that Jay could easily carry Yvette through.

Li ran up and put her hand on the exit wound in the upper left corner of Yvette's chest. Blood sluiced between her fingers; Yvette was bleeding badly.

"The cars, we've got to get her away from here," Jay shouted, his eyes alive with fear.

Somewhere in the distance, a commander tank was hunting for them. Smoke shrouded the air between them and the tank. Klaxons wailed all over the stricken base.

Juliette appeared in front of Jay and ordered, "Put her on the back seat of my car, and drive to the rendezvous point."

The team rushed into action. A handful of seconds later, everyone was in the Range Rovers, the SUV's wheels spinning in the loose gravel on the side of the road before finding traction on the bitumen and launching the cars away from the airbase.

They broke contact with Shadowstone. The fading seconds of Panopticon cover as effective at hiding the SUVs from the commander tank's sensor arrays as it had been for the blackwidow's sensor arrays minutes earlier.

In the back of the leading Range Rover Juliette applied pressure to Yvette's wound and said urgently, "Jay, we need to be there as fast as possible."

"I'm on it," Jay snapped, the SUVs supercharged engine snarling in response as he floored the accelerator.

"She needs surgery – now!"

"Damn it," Jay swore.

The Range Rover hurtled along the streets. There was no one to dodge or pass. The streets were clear of traffic. The klaxons continued to wail in the distance. No one was on the streets, with the airbase under attack, the local population had fled to the safety of their homes.

Jay prayed that he would be in time, and Juliette could work her surgical 'magic.'

His heart wrenched. His eye's moistened. He could lose Yvette.

He loved her.

He drove like a man possessed.

His heart felt like it had expanded to fill his throat, robbing him of the ability to speak.

The rendezvous point was clear on the SUV's GPS. The device reported he had two more minutes to get there at the regulation speed limits.

He vowed to arrive in under sixty seconds.

The Range Rovers sped along the streets.

Chapter Seven

Section 2.2.9 False Narratives in Common Media

Summary: Operation of False Narratives

[1] The purpose of this method is to satisfy and exhaust the target populations ability to inquire, with false narratives. Begin by establishing at least two opposed, mutually exclusive, false narratives aligned with the belief systems of separate opposed social cohorts.

[2] Leverage social division between the social cohorts to entrench the narratives as intrinsic to the tribal identity of the targets. Once established as intrinsic to the identity formation of the target population, the narrative will be beyond question and disbelief in the narrative will signify lack of social belonging.

[3] Publish media reports that support the adopted narratives from authoritative members of the social cohorts.

[4] Publish media reports that deny the opposing narrative from authoritative members of the social cohorts.

[5] Provide 'neither confirm nor deny,' statements from senior Government sources.

[6] Provide separate anonymously leaked statements from Government sources that support all false narratives in play.

Detail: Definitions and worked examples

The details of this tactic with worked examples is described below.

[REDACTED]

– Excerpt of Section 2, Methods of Obfuscation, Shadowstone Covert PSYOPS Manual

* * *

Coningsby, Lincolnshire, August 22nd, 12:14

The dark-blue Jaguar sedan pulled to a stop forty yards short of the entrance to the RAF airbase at Coningsby. Two MRAPs filled with Shadowstone troopers in full body armor halted behind it.

Gordon Heathmont looked through his car's front windscreen and surveyed the airbase. Dark-gray smoke sat in a thick pall over the whole site. Sirens wailed, cutting through the base's klaxons as emergency workers strove to contain the fires. The wreckage of a pair of armored personnel carriers burned a hundred yards beyond the gate. They'd been torn open like cans of tuna given to a chainsaw. Someone had used one of the new anti-air guns on them. Nothing was flying, all the blackwidow's were gone. The one major asset left was a fully armed commander tank patrolling the middle of the base.

Gordon consulted his laptop. The commander tank's sensor arrays were clear of threats. The Order of Thoth had vanished like ghosts. The temporary hazing of the Panopticon had passed. Shadowstone cyberwarfare units operating out of Beijing, Saint Petersburg and Seattle, had finally neutralized the Order's attack on the Panopticon.

The Order of Thoth team had successfully broken contact. It was a temporary setback; he consulted his laptop again, the latest flight path for the Order's Embraer jet had been to a private airfield near Goathland in the Yorkshire Moors, about ten miles from Whitby. The location had to be critical to the Order team's mission; they would return to Yorkshire.

There were two angles of attack to reacquire the Mirovar force team. He would lock up the approaches to their target in Yorkshire, and pursue them from Coningsby. The first was a straightforward objective, the second would require detective work. The force team must have used vehicles to escape the airbase. Staying on foot, or nearby would be grossly stupid, and they were clearly not stupid, possibly mad, but not stupid.

They would have vehicles, something that would blend in, but with the streets cleared under standard protocols for an airbase disaster. People would respond to the sirens by retreating into their homes. People who could be curious enough to stare out their windows at what was happening. Perhaps someone had seen something, like a vehicle speeding away from the airbase.

Half of Squadron F had deployed west on a wild goose chase. The Mirovar force team had tricked him with false information provided over the Order earbuds taken from the red-headed Order operative. Those Shadowstone forces were already flying back to the ruins of the Facility. Fortunately, the hangars at the Facility were still operational. His forces would have to refuel before they could head north. It was a terrible delay, but he couldn't avoid it.

A single Order of Thoth team member had captured a commander tank, nearly destroying the Facility. The casualty list at the Facility remained to be tallied, but ten to fifteen percent of the base's working population were in the path of the rogue commander tank. Casualties in the affected buildings would be high. He had also lost four blackwidow gunships and more than sixty Day Guard phase IV troopers. Add in the destruction at the RAF airbase and there were a couple of billion pounds worth of damage that would take more than a year to rebuild and replace. The highest levels of Shadowstone would demand an accounting for these losses. He was on the hook to explain them.

Gordon consigned the original plan to capture and question an Order of Thoth operative to the dustbin. The mission had evolved – he would have to kill every last member of the Mirovar force team before the day was out.

It was the only result that could justify his losses. He would use any and all forces to fulfill this new plan. Any losses or collateral damage was acceptable to reach the new objective.

Gordon briefly considered redirecting the local police force to lock up the northern roads out of Coningsby, but without the rest of Squadron F to back them up, the Order would cut them to pieces. James Haley's words regarding the Mirovar force team, 'don't underestimate them,' came back to haunt him. As much as he didn't want to admit it, recent events forced an obvious conclusion – he'd thoroughly underestimated the Order of Thoth operatives in every possible way.

That would stop now. He would change his tactics. He would position his forces for rapid deployment in Yorkshire and await his enemy to come to him. He would rely on what he had that the Mirovar force team did not – massive firepower.

He reached for his quantum encrypted smartphone. He needed to inform Major Quiver of the change of priorities and the need to tightly monitor the approaches to Yorkshire. He would also send his personal security detail to investigate any breaches in the RAF airbase's perimeter fence and to question the locals living nearby. By the time his remaining Day Guard forces were in place, a mouse couldn't cross into Yorkshire without him knowing about it, and there was a good chance he would know what vehicles he should be looking for.

The net was tightening, and soon the Mirovar force team would have nowhere to run to.

* * *

The rendezvous point was a rundown house on the northern outskirts of Coningsby. Its one redeeming feature was a large four car garage.

A gray and black striped blanket covered part of the garage floor. Yvette lay face up in the center of the blanket, a rag between her teeth. Chiara had cut away her blood-drenched shirt and bra to expose the ragged exit wound above her left breast.

Yvette remained fully awake while Juliette's hands blurred over her chest. Tears squeezed from her eyes as she clenched her teeth on the rag, a soft moan escaping from deep within her body.

Juliette had begun work without the administration of anesthetic. Yvette was doing it 'raw,' relying on her system zero genetics to allow her to cope with the agony of emergency thoracic surgery while awake.

Yvette resisted stilling her mind to escape the pain, ramping would only make the experience seem like it was lasting forever. Her mind kept going to what was happening to her, it was impossible to step away from reality.

Juliette knelt to Yvette's left, her medical satchel resting next to her right leg. Her usual combat surgical equipment and supplies filling it to the brim.

Chiara hovered on the opposite side, a towel spread before her, covered with surgical equipment.

Juliette had already clamped the severed artery running up into Yvette's shoulder. She requested in crisp efficient tones, "Needle."

Chiara passed a stainless-steel needle above Yvette's face.

"Thread."

That also passed over her face.

Juliette's face stilled as she dropped into silence, ramping hard. Metal flashed beneath the overhead fluorescent lights. Her hands blurred, needle and thread moving with machine-like speed and precision. Forty-eight seconds later, she'd stitched the loose ends of the artery back together.

Juliette asked for supplies and Chiara passed them to her. She quickly applied an adhesive, biodegradable gauze netting to reinforce the blood vessel. Then she took up a preloaded syringe and applied anesthetic to the wound sites, front and back. She then stitched up the entry and exit wounds, applied dressings, strappings, a broad-spectrum antibiotic, and then rocked back on her heels and stood up.

"I need some blood donors, any volunteers?" Juliette asked the room in a calm voice.

Everyone volunteered.

"Not you Jay, you've already lost some with your arm. I'll stitch you up next. Okay, Anton and Li," she indicated spots to the left and right of Yvette, "take a seat. Chiara will hook you up. Peter, find the jar of herbal balm. Both Anton and you need it on your faces, and Anton – you're a mess. But given your recent actions, you can't be too badly hurt, I'll tend to you last."

Anton nodded, and moved with Li to kneel on either side of Yvette. Chiara inserted clear lines between Li and Anton's arms, and Yvette's left and right arms. Blood filled the lines flowing into Yvette's depleted veins.

Yvette turned her head to the right, her gaze locking with Jay's. Juliette was stitching up a number of rips in Jay's arm received when a grenade exploded too close to the top of the MRU trailer. The grenade would have shredded a normal man's arm down to the bone or taken it off entirely. Yvette thanked God for the Ramp, and for the genetics that underpinned it. Without it, the Order would not have been possible, and the vampires would rule unopposed.

Jay remained whole because his skin was hard to tear, his bones resisted breaking, his nerves operated multiples faster than normal, and his muscles could exert forces five times more powerful than normal on a pound for pound basis.

She clenched her left fist, power still flowed through her damaged shoulder and arm. Her wounds compromised her, but she remained undefeated. She would heal in the next hour what would take ten hours for a normal human being. By nightfall, she would have experienced the equivalent of nearly four days of healing.

Yvette clenched her left fist again. Anton's and Li's blood was flowing through her veins. Another gift of system zero genetics – every Ramp master was a universal donor/receiver. She was feeling stronger already.

Soon she would be ready to fight again.

* * *

The Range Rovers were leaving the town of Coningsby behind. Anton sat behind Juliette in the lead SUV, with Li next to him, Peter on the far side of Li, while Francis drove. Luther followed in the second Range Rover, with Jay, Yvette, and Chiara.

"Where are the local police?" Anton asked. "A major RAF airbase is in ruins, and there are no roadblocks."

"It's a good question Anton," Juliette said.

"Did they run out of resources?" Li asked. "First, they're blocking side roads on the other side of town, and now perhaps, they're helping out with the airbase disaster."

Peter's lip curled. "C'mon, surely, they'd want to lock the town down and prevent anyone escaping. We just spent an hour in a safe house patching everyone up. They could have brought in resources from neighboring towns."

Francis frowned and remarked, "And yet they didn't."

Juliette sighed. "They're letting us go for now."

Anton gazed into the distance and said, "They don't have the forces to follow us – we gutted their main strength."

"If they fell for our ruse," Francis said, "they would have divided their forces. That other force, it will be returning by now from the west country. Perhaps it is even refueling back at the Squadron F base as we speak."

"We should assume that Shadowstone will send a second force against us," Juliette recommended.

"Yes," Francis agreed, "and they will update their tactics. They've been adapting the whole time we've been fighting them."

"They're stronger and faster than normal," Peter said.

"Yeah, noticed that," Anton agreed.

Li spread her hands apart and said, "It's like they can do a partial Ramp."

Juliette said, "Ramped or not. We can expect them to hit us hard if they get another chance at us."

The cabin of the car became silent for a long moment.

"Stealth to avoid Shadowstone or speed to reach Armitage? We can't have both," Francis observed with a frown, "but we need to make haste. It's already quarter past one. We've lost an hour. I know we had wounded to attend to, but we could ill afford the time."

He looked across at Juliette. "What have you got left to shield us with?"

"It appears Shadowstone do not know we have these Range Rovers. I can run a signal from my laptop with a one-mile radius of effect that will airbrush our cars out of any cameras we pass."

"Cool," Li enthused from the back seat.

"Can't trick eyeballs," Peter remarked, arching an eyebrow.

"You're right Peter," Juliette conceded. "If Shadowstone knows what we are driving, then we're exposed to anyone physically watching for us, or by high flying drones and satellites."

Francis said patiently. "We don't want to assault the dungeon holding Kain after nightfall. We don't know what reinforcements Armitage may have access to. The longer we take, the stronger her position grows and the more information she will take from Kain."

"Are we assuming that Kain will talk?" Li asked.

"He'll squeal like a pig," Anton remarked.

"Anton!" Juliette said. "Manners – he is still the Head of the Order."

"And demonstrably corrupt," Li said.

"Li has a point," Francis conceded with a frown. "The issue is not the man, but the information he holds. We have to assume he has broken and is talking. The longer we delay his rescue, the more damage he does."

Juliette nodded. "Of course, it must be so. If we stay on the main roads, we can reach the manor house by quarter past four. That gives us four hours before sunset."

Francis and Juliette looked at each other. They resolved the arbitrage between speed and stealth with a single glance. The decision made, Francis focused forward, the Range Rover smoothly eating up the miles on the northbound road.

Anton glanced out the window. A sign whipped past. It read, 'Welcome to Horncastle.' In another three hours, they would be on the threshold of confronting Chloe Armitage in her own home. She'd come into Anton's home and taken his parents away from him. She'd ripped his life apart, and now he would be able to extract payment for the debt she owed his family.

Anton took a deep breath and let it out slowly. All the months of training, the blood and the pain, had led to this day. To this opportunity to finally confront Armitage with the consequences of her actions. The need burned deep within him. To see the Blue Dragon flashing in the light. To beat past Armitage's blade. To separate her head from her body and lift it aloft in vengeful triumph.

How his heart would sing.

And then, with the instrument destroyed, he would turn his attention to her master – Cornelius Crane.

The need was so strong he could taste it.

* * *

The humble residents of the town of Coningsby had been fruitful with information.

Gordon Heathmont's men had discovered a pair of coal or dark-gray colored, late-model Range Rovers had sped north out of town. The prize had been an elderly woman who had witnessed them come and go from a house nearly opposite her own. A house without inhabitants and possessed of a large garage. She'd noticed the SUVs because normally no one, apart from a monthly gardener, ever visited the place.

Gordon's sedan rested in the driveway of the abandoned house while his men forced up a pair of roller doors on the garage. He stepped out of his car, he wanted to see for himself what signs the Mirovar force team had left for him.

The faint smell of exhaust fumes laced the air inside the garage. They'd left recently, less than fifteen or twenty minutes before Gordon had arrived. He shivered with delight; he was close behind them. They were fleeing before him, and he would pursue them all the way to hell.

"Sir, you'll want to see this," one of his men remarked, holding up a darkly splattered, gray and black striped blanket.

Gordon peered at the stains. It was blood, mostly dry, but there was a lot of it. At least one of the Mirovar force team had bled badly. They hadn't got off Scott free during the recent engagements, but there was no body.

He scowled, his mood turning dark. The enhancements of the Phase IV Day Guard program hadn't made any difference so far. He silently hoped the new Phase V Day Guard program would deliver a better result. Cornelius Crane had hinted much without offering confirmation of how effective the new program would be.

For the fifth time today, he attempted to contact Crane's personal line. The signal came back null, empty, void – communications with the head of Shadowstone remained down.

Gordon's laptop started pinging, multiple messages arriving at the same time. He returned to his sedan and sat in the back. He opened his laptop; scanning the new messages. His men had not recovered any bodies from the wreckage of the Mirovar force team's Embraer jet. He'd been skeptical that the Order operatives had evacuated the aircraft before it landed. He shook his head once, the evidence was compelling, they'd done precisely that.

How they evaded detection was a mystery that would have to wait for a quiet moment to solve. It was another riddle to add to the growing list of questions he had about the Mirovar force team.

Just how many Order operatives were active in the UK right now? How many were members of the Mirovar force team? Where the bloody hell were they and what was their objective? He had too many questions and too few answers.

One message stood out, the results of the Panopticon searches for cars matching the descriptions provided by the local Coningsby villagers. There were two hundred and forty-eight hits within a sixty-mile radius of the town. all the matching cars remained actively tracked. He filtered the results for pairs of cars traveling together, and the number of hits went to zero.

Had the two SUVs split up outside of Coningsby? Had they swapped vehicles and were now using something else? Were the Order operatives hazing the Panopticon without tripping countermeasures?

If they'd doubled back and were now heading south, east, or west, he had no idea where they might be or what their objective was. It was only to the north that he had any hope of finding them. He put his hands over his face, then dragged them down over his cheeks and jaw. The next decision was critical, he had to make the right move or lose everything.

The one piece of information he could rely on was the flight plan to Goathland – it was the key. There would be no more wild goose chases after phantoms or will-o-wisps. He would not waste time and resources searching anywhere but the north. He needed to adapt. The Order operatives were faster and stronger than he'd anticipated. He needed to apply area of effect weapons to defeat their ability to evade fire. Hellfire III missiles would be the weapon of choice, and that meant nightfalcon and blackwidow helicopter gunships.

Gordon closed his eyes; his thoughts intensifying. He needed to find the Mirovar operatives before he could kill them. With two hundred and forty-eight hits from the Panopticon, it was like looking for a needle in a haystack. His gut instinct was the Order team was somehow still hazing the Panopticon. They would still be in their original cars, running hard to the north and whatever objective they had there.

He broadcast the details of the cars, and photos of Peter Lamb and Anton Smith, to the remaining operational Shadowstone forces in the UK. He issued clear orders; report all contact, track, and do not engage unless fired upon. He then placed a call to his agent on the Privy Council, it was time to get the king to declare a state of emergency and get everyone in the north of England off the roads.

Gordon's phone started dialing. He frowned, glancing at the face of his smartphone, it read 13:32. The wheels of government were slow to move but move they would. In another ninety minutes, perhaps two hours, the traffic would start disappearing from the roads.

Gordon's eyes sparkled, if you can't find the needle, then remove the haystack.

* * *

The road sign flicked past on the left. In another five minutes, they would be entering Scarborough. From there it was twenty miles to Whitby and the manor house holding Kain.

"With a little luck," Francis said, "we'll be there by four o'clock this afternoon."

Peter said, "Is it just me, or is the traffic thinning out."

Juliette looked up from her laptop and frowned. "Camera counts are dropping." She shook her head. "Cars are disappearing from the roads, and hijackable phone cameras are disappearing with them."

Her fingers flew over the keyboard. "Oh no. There is a state of emergency in play. The government have issued orders for everyone to avoid travel and return to their homes until further notice."

"Why didn't we hear about this earlier?" Anton asked.

"The UK government doesn't have your phone number Anton," Li said sarcastically.

Juliette shook her head. "Don't fight. Unfortunately, the technique I'm using to haze cameras as we pass them requires my full attention."

"You're being squeezed," Li said. "Can I help?"

"Not without an implant."

"Lights ahead," Peter noted.

There were a pair of local police cars parked in the distance, their lights strobing blue and red in the universal police pattern. Before them, there was a turn off to the left and a sign above it that read, 'A170.'

Anton asked, "Are the police looking for us too?"

"They could be," Francis answered. "We have to assume they are. We need a new route, is the A170 any good?" Francis slowed the Range Rover, giving Juliette more time to check options. The intersection was approaching rapidly, and beyond it, the police cars were waiting.

Juliette paused for a handful of seconds, her face still, her eyelids closed as if she was dreaming. "Yes, take it. It's the next best route."

"Are they funneling us?" Li asked.

Francis took the off-ramp to the new road. Juliette twisted around in her seat to face Li and replied, "No evidence of that, but cutting traffic is clearly a strategy directed at us."

"With no other traffic," Anton observed, looking at Li. "We'll be easy to find."

"I kinda worked that out, Anton," Li said drily.

Francis directed, "We'll keep the cars as long as we can. Then, we'll leave them, and disappear."

He looked along the road in front of him, there were only a handful of cars and a lone truck visible heading in both directions. He accelerated back up to the speed limit. "No one promised this was going to be easy," he broadcast to the team. "Of course, Shadowstone will do everything they can to find us and kill us. We've got to stay one step ahead of them. Keep your eyes open and your weapons handy. We may need to fight at a moment's notice."

Francis kept his concerns to himself. It would be a miracle if they could get to Whitby without Shadowstone discovering them. They'd been lucky not to lose anyone so far, and he felt in the depths of his soul, that sooner or later their luck would run out.

The team had never been this exposed on a mission.

* * *

The Shadowstone agent put the freshly made cafe latte next to his briefcase.

He'd taken a position in a cafe booth overlooking the main road through Thornton Dale, about four hundred yards before the intersection of the A170 with the Whitby Gate road. The second road was a much-used route north into the Yorkshire Moors, and his superiors had assigned the agent to the task of monitoring it. He'd positioned himself a little to the east of the intersection as he'd liked the look of the cafe he was sitting in.

The agent's case was on the large side for a briefcase, more like a small suitcase. It rested on the table, its lid up, revealing a twenty-four-inch high definition screen and a server sized computer in the body of the case. Four gray spheres rested on the edge of the table. Shadowstone sensor arrays wirelessly connected to the main server in the case. The system was fully operational, covering a hemisphere of territory one mile in radius centered on the case.

The agent sipped his latte; he'd made it himself. The owner of the cafe was sleeping on the floor of the kitchen, struck down by a Shadowstone sleeper dart. He'd be stiff, cold and sore when he woke up tomorrow, but he would still be alive and the previous twenty-four hours would be a black hole, his memory wiped clean.

The agent silently lamented the need to be working. He was on annual leave, holidaying in the north with his girlfriend. Summoned into work by the boss, he had reluctantly left her watching videos in a hotel room while he sat out here in the middle of nowhere watching an empty road. He'd taken a first in psychology from Oxford University and completed a masters in public relations at Bristol University. Acquiring a senior operator role in the PSYOPS directorate of the Shadowstone organization had taken hard work and commitment. But it was days like today, boring days that impinged on his personal time that made him wonder if he'd made the right choices in life.

He stared at the screen, there was not a single hit within a mile of the cafe. The roads remained deserted, everyone had fled to their homes under the state of emergency. A sudden movement caught his eye. He glanced up from the screen, peering out at the main road running past the cafe. A pair of charcoal Range Rovers drove past at speed.

"What the hell!" he said. "Not a bloody sign of them on my scopes."

He grinned triumphantly and dialed Gordon Heathmont's direct line. The director would want to know about this straight away.

* * *

Juliette's laptop pinged.

"Damn," she swore. "Shadowstone just found us again."

"How do you know?" Anton asked.

"There's a big difference between a Samsung, Amazon, or Huawei-Apple camera and what I just hazed. I'm certain it was a Shadowstone sensor array."

"If we hazed it, maybe we're still okay?"

"No chance Anton. A sensor array takes my system about ten seconds to fully resolve. It put the center of the array back up the street. The array's operator was watching the main road through this town, we literally passed them at a range of less than forty yards – they would have noticed we didn't 'show up,' on their scopes."

Francis spotted a side street and cut down it to the left. "Let them think we're heading south. He circled around to the right and a minute later was heading north out of sight of the location where they'd passed the sensor array.

He floored the accelerator, the car barreling along the street. "Now it's speed that matters – we've got to put some distance between us and this town. We'll ditch the cars where they won't be noticed before Shadowstone can re-establish visual contact, and proceed on foot. Where is the nearest main town?"

Juliette consulted her laptop. "Goathland. It's about eleven miles north of here, and ten miles from the manor house at Whitby."

"Goathland – where we were heading to at the start," Peter noted.

"Small world," Anton remarked.

Francis flicked the steering wheel to the right, then left. The car raced through a dogleg corner onto the main road heading north. "Ten miles is close enough. We'll be in Whitby by five thirty, an easy two and a half hours before sunset. Jay, all speed."

The supercharged engines roared as the Range Rovers surged along the road in a tight convoy. There was no other traffic, not even a police presence to slow their progress.

The eleven miles to Goathland would disappear in minutes. Juliette took a deep breath and sighed. Normally serene, the day was beginning to wear on her. How many more things could go wrong?

It was a question she feared to ask.

* * *

The semi-trailer rig spouted steam from its punctured radiator. It lay on its side, its white trailer, emblazoned with the livery of a local supermarket chain, blocking both lanes of the A169 road.

A pair of Squadron F MRAPs were parked tail to tail behind it, carefully hidden from any traffic coming up from Thornton Dale to the south. Eight Squadron F troopers were guarding the main road leading to Goathland or Whitby. Thirty yards in front of the 'crashed,' truck was an intersection with a road leading off the A169 directly to Goathland. The roads had become deserted in the last half an hour, the locals retreating into their homes under the declared state of emergency.

The Shadowstone trooper glanced up at the western sky. The clouds were rapidly darkening, a storm was on its way. There had been an operational weather report fifteen minutes before, warning of strong winds and heavy rain throughout the late afternoon pushing eastward overnight.

Lovely, he thought sarcastically. He hated bad weather and the cold. Work assignments anywhere in the north of England set his mood midway between sour and homicidal.

His mouth was a grim slash, he whispered to himself, "Suck it up, princess." There was work to do, bloody work. They'd lost almost half the strength of Squadron F that morning. The enemy were still at large and had to be found. His orders were clear – report all contacts, track them, and do not engage unless fired upon.

Of course, following orders was a matter of interpretation, and 'fired upon,' – well, sometimes it can be difficult to determine who fired first. He had command of the two squads manning this post, and he'd lost close friends that morning. If the enemy showed up, he would make sure they were not going anywhere else – except, in a body bag.

He checked his squads. Four of his men were inside the MRAPs, the drivers, and the gunners operating the M240 machine guns mounted on top of the armored vehicles. The other three troopers were with him, outside the vehicles and armed with large caliber H&K 417 assault rifles fitted with under-barrel grenade launchers and red dot laser sights. Shadowstone command had provided descriptions of the vehicles the enemy would be driving and photos of two of their operatives. If they came along this road, he and his men were sure to find them.

The trooper took a position just to the left of the tail end of the overturned trailer. He lifted his binoculars and scanned the road to the south. The landscape of the Yorkshire Moors stretched in all directions, the roads gently curving around low hills. Unkempt grass and low mauve bushes covered the land. The sky hung low, a dark-gray sheet tending to black in the west, dimming the sun to a dusk-like shadow.

His binoculars were fully digital, linking seamlessly back to the Panopticon. In the distance a pair of SUVs came over the crest of a low hill, racing along the road toward his position. The Panopticon marked them as matching the description given for the target vehicles. Metadata streamed through the viewfinder; a Shadowstone operative had marked the vehicles as targets nine minutes earlier.

The Range Rovers began to slow, their speed dropping below one hundred miles per hour, down through ninety, eighty, seventy, back to the speed limit of sixty miles per hour. The trailing SUV pulled out to shadow the shoulder of the leading car, and then moved further apart, making full use of both lanes.

They're suspicious. They should be.

The trooper twisted around to face his men. Pulling his sidearm from its holster, he swung the 9mm pistol toward the MRAPs. He pulled the trigger, blowing out the nearest MRAP's headlight with a single round.

"Right men, we've been fired on," the trooper snarled, holstering his pistol. He shouldered his H&K 417 assault rifle and shouted, "Now open up on those bastards!"

The MRAPS surged left and right, racing clear of the semi-trailer, allowing their M240 machine guns to bear on the approaching Range Rovers. A second later both machine guns erupted into life, streams of bright tracers and 7.62mm ball heading down range toward the onrushing SUVs.

All hell broke loose.

* * *

Francis stared through the front windscreen; his heart filled with dread.

Two MRAPs appeared to the left and right of the overturned semi-trailer. The M240 machine guns on their roofs spurted orange tongues of flame, stark against the darkening sky. Black-clad Shadowstone troopers raced on foot behind them, firing large-bore assault rifles straight at the Range Rovers.

A storm of bullets hammered the Range Rovers. The SUVs had been subtly armored, their defenses hidden beneath their ceramic toughened skins. Their windscreens and windows were bulletproof transparent armor designed to mimic glass in appearance. Their tires could run flat with minimal loss of performance. But everything has its limits and enough firepower would overwhelm the vehicles' defenses.

The Range Rover slammed to a halt. Francis shouted, "Weapons, out!"

The second Range Rover ran another twenty yards before the wheels twisted hard left. The SUV bucked like a wild animal, taking off and twisting in a sideways roll through the air. The doors flew wide. Jay, Yvette, Luther and Chiara, all ramped to the max, leaped from the SUV as it spun in a flat arc into the right-side MRAP.

The SUV smashed into the MRAP, coming apart with an earsplitting bang. Metal tearing itself to pieces as two tons of SUV encountered seven tons of MRAP at sixty miles per hour. The Range Rover evaporated to pieces, taking out the crew of the MRAP with it. The front half of the MRAP caved in, the impact shoving the heavy vehicle back a couple of yards, leaving the crew unconscious or dead.

The left-side MRAP continued firing its M240 machine gun at the lead SUV. All the doors of the Range Rover opened at once. The SUV's windscreen starred and cracked, sparks flying from the front panels as 7.62mm rounds ripped into the ceramic armor. Francis, Anton, Peter, and Li blurred from the wreck, rounds from Shadowstone troopers whizzing through the spaces behind them.

Francis ramped hard, blurring away from the deadly trap the SUV had become. He lifted his H&K MP5, firing at the Shadowstone troopers near the MRAP. From his peripheral vision, he could account for everyone else in his team. Jay, Yvette, Luther, and Chiara were looping through the air to land behind the troopers. In moments, they would catch the troopers in a fatal crossfire. Anton and Li had gone left, their guns blazing as they cut the distance to the surviving MRAP. Peter appeared near Francis' shoulder, his submachine gun hammering as he drew a battle-axe from his belt.

His heart leaped into his throat.

Where's Juliette?

He turned in horror toward the SUV, the windscreen shattering as round after round pummeled it.

"No!" he shouted, blurring over the SUV in a mighty leap to the other side.

Francis landed, twisting around behind the armored car door. Bullets streamed a foot over his head or slammed into the open car door.

Juliette lay still in her seat, still strapped in, the left side of her face covered in blood.

"No, no, no," Francis moaned.

* * *

Time slowed to a crawl.

Anton blurred forward, Li at his shoulder, his H&K MP5 vibrating in his left hand as it sent high-performance 9mm rounds at the troopers thirty yards away. He carried the Blue Dragon in his right hand, its naked blade dull beneath the leaden sky. Grenades were looping in toward the surviving MRAP from Jay and Yvette, while Chiara and Luther cut down the two remaining Shadowstone troopers near the smashed MRAP and the ruined Range Rover.

Anton locked gazes with one of the Shadowstone troopers for a fraction of a second, long enough for each man to bring their weapon to bear on the other. The trooper glared at him, moving faster than normal, his H&K 417 assault rifle swung around.

Anton found himself staring down the barrel.

The under-barrel grenade launcher fired, smoke burst from the barrel; 7.62mm rounds and a 40mm grenade flying toward him.

Anton leaned over backward, the bullets flying over him.

Li fired back, her rounds taking the trooper in the face. His head rocked back, blood and bone spraying over the underside of the overturned trailer. He slumped forward, explosions rattling the MRAP before his body hit the ground.

Anton stood upright, the trooper's grenade exploding harmlessly behind him in the scrub. Twisting around he scanned the team, everyone was okay, but there was no sign of Juliette. He sucked air through his teeth, turning back to the Range Rover. Francis was reaching into the front left cabin of the SUV. There was a flash of dark-brown hair, there were flecks of blood on the smashed windscreen.

"What the hell?" Anton whispered.

He dashed back to the Range Rover.

* * *

Francis stepped back from the Range Rover. The look of horror on his face disappearing, replaced by one of utter desperation.

"Chiara, quickly, the—"

Chiara appeared at his shoulder, Juliette's medical bag in her hands.

"—medical kit."

Chiara crouched down next to Juliette, putting her fingers on the right side of Juliette's throat. A handful of seconds later she declared, "She's got a pulse." She started checking her for other wounds. Blood covered Juliette's left thigh in a dark sheen. She reached into the bag and took out a tourniquet, which she placed high on Juliette's thigh. "Two bullets through the left thigh. This'll stop the bleeding – for now."

Francis stepped back, scanning the horizon. "Team, collect what you can from the SUVs and form a perimeter. The only people on the move now are Shadowstone."

He left his command at that, the team members all knew what they needed to do.

The team had to move. Shadowstone would know they'd destroyed this site within minutes. For all Francis knew, Shadowstone routinely wired and monitored the vital signs of all their troopers. Some command center somewhere could be registering a set of flat-lined readouts. At the very least, they would make regular reports, and their command would miss the next report and work out something was wrong.

The perimeter line in place, Francis ducked his head in over Chiara. She was probing Juliette's head wound with her fingers.

Chiara turned her head to look up at Francis, her face filled with concern and said, "The bullet scored her scalp, hence all the blood, but she may have a fractured skull. We need to find a medical clinic with a modern med-sensor."

"Patch her head first," he directed. He stood back, looking at his team. "Li, check the net and see if there is a medical clinic nearby with state-of-the-art sensor equipment."

"Yes, Francis," Li said, pulling her smartphone from a chest pocket.

Francis stepped away from the SUV, hovering over Chiara wasn't helping her focus on her work. He scanned the horizon and his team. Everyone was where they should be, and there was no sign of Shadowstone. He opened up his smartphone and dialed Walker. The phone rang six times before Walker answered it.

"What do you want?" Walker said brusquely.

"Juliette's been shot. I need your help."

"And what do you think I can do?"

"Send two cars, we have no transport."

Walker laughed bitterly. "Surely you could not have missed the state of emergency."

"Yes, I know. We still need cars. We have to get Juliette to a medical surgery."

"Mirovar, it's not possible. Right now, Shadowstone has no idea we're here. I'm not compromising my team or the mission to rescue you from your own incompetence."

Francis seethed, pulling the phone away from his ear and swearing under his breath. He brought the phone back to his ear. Walker was still talking.

"—have to get yourself out of your own mess and get over here with your surviving fighters. We'll need them to assault the manor house."

"I'm taking Juliette to a medical center – you'll have to wait."

"Fuck you Mirovar – the mission comes first."

Francis' eyes became dark hard stones. "We'll be there. Sit tight Walker."

"I'd heard the Mirovar force team was incompetent, now I know it's true."

Francis shook his head, what was the source of Walker's enmity?

"Do us all a favor and put a mercy bullet in her brain," Walker proposed in tight cold tones. "Then move everyone to Whitby now."

Francis snapped, "Vas te faire encule, fils de pute." He hung up. There would be no help from the Walker force team. They were on their own.

"Francis," Li called out. "There is a medical center in Goathland. According to their advertisement, they offer advanced medical facilities. With the state of emergency, the place is probably empty, all I'm getting is voicemail."

He poked his head back into the SUV, Chiara was completing the bandaging of Juliette's head. "Can you operate their medical equipment?"

"Absolutely."

"Excellent," Francis said, a flicker of hope igniting in his chest. "We'll go on foot. Help me with her. Strap her to me, I don't want her head moving around when I carry her."

Chiara stepped back, and Francis scooped up Juliette's limp form, cradling her in his arms. A minute later, Chiara completed strapping Juliette to Francis, ensuring she would be as stable as possible when Francis ran.

Chiara put a hand on Francis' shoulder looking into his eyes. "Watch her breathing, we haven't been able to intubate her, she could stop breathing at any time."

Francis nodded, and then stepped away. "Team, form up on me," he commanded. "Keep your eyes open. We're running hard for Goathland. Li, you're navigating, take us to the medical center."

Li blurred away, Francis a yard behind her, racing down the road. The team paced with them, they had three miles to cover to get to the heart of the town of Goathland.

They would be there in ten minutes.

* * *

The medical center was a two-story white block with a flat roof.

The team left Jay guarding the front door, while Luther ascended to the roof with a set of digital binoculars to guard the approaches. The medical center had been locked up before they arrived, shut down during the state of emergency while the staff evacuated back to their homes. Breaking in had been a trivial task, and the team had followed Francis as he blurred into the empty doctor's surgery.

Chiara released the bindings holding Juliette close to Francis, and he laid Juliette carefully onto the examination table.

Juliette moaned. The first noise she'd made since getting shot. Chiara glanced at the wall clock, it read 16:21, nearly twenty minutes had passed since the last battle with Shadowstone. It was a long time to be unconscious, concussion was a certainty. Now she'd to find out the true extent of her injuries.

Juliette had taken a bullet along the left side of her skull, scoring a long, deep cut along her scalp an inch above her ear. If the bullet had been an inch to the right, it would have taken the top of Juliette's head off. She was lucky to be alive.

Chiara checked the leg wounds. Two bullets had ripped along Juliette's left thigh. There was a lot of blood, but both bullets had gone through muscle on the outside of the thigh, the inner thigh leading to the vulnerable femoral artery was untouched. It was a small blessing.

Li stood on the opposite side of the table and asked, "Can I help?"

"Sure," Chiara said, grateful for any assistance. Having Juliette's life in her hands was a responsibility she didn't want. Normally Juliette would be in charge, and Chiara would take her guidance. Taking responsibility for killing someone was easy. Taking responsibility for saving someone's life, especially when you loved them like a mother was something entirely different.

Juliette moaned again. Was she about to wake up? Her eyelids fluttered and then stilled. Chiara checked her vitals, she was still breathing, and her pulse was a steady thirty-five beats per minute.

Francis stepped closer, frowned and said firmly, "Time is wasting."

"Yes, yes," Chiara said, a touch of exasperation leaking into her voice. She rolled a trolley loaded with high-tech equipment next to the examination table. She fitted a brace around Juliette's head and attached it to the table to keep her still. Taking a long silvery wand, attached to a monitor on the trolley by a slim black cable, she approached Juliette's head. She flicked a switch, a pale light emanated from the tip of the wand. She stroked the tip over Juliette's head, first vertically, and then horizontally. Each stroke about half an inch to the side of the previous stroke. An image of Juliette's skull appeared on the monitor and began to fill in with heat mapped detail.

Chiara concentrated on her work.

Behind her, Francis clicked his fingers and ordered, "Anton, Peter, we need supplies. Find us some food and anything else useful. Be back here in twenty minutes."

"Yes, Boss," Peter agreed, and Anton nodded. The two young men picked up their weapons and backpacks, departing the room moments later.

Chiara sat back and turned to Francis. "Juliette's got a fractured skull."

"C'est un foutu bordel!" Francis swore, pacing the room. "How long before she wakes up?"

"I don't know. We have to wait."

"Deal with her other injuries while we wait."

"Will do," Chiara said, glancing across at Li. "How's your suturing coming along?"

"One of the first things Juliette taught me."

"Excellent, let's get started then."

Chiara and Li set to work to repair the two bullet wounds in Juliette's thigh and save her leg.

Chiara breathed a sigh of relief to be working on comparatively simple bullet wounds. Looking after a brain injury was beyond her skills. She hoped there would be no complications and Juliette would wake up soon with nothing more to complain about then a splitting headache.

Chiara bit back a sob, focusing hard on the tasks at hand. Juliette couldn't die, she'd been a mother to her for half her life.

No, it couldn't happen. She would do everything in her power to save Juliette's life.

"Francis, we'll need blood. You haven't donated yet."

Francis began rolling up his sleeve.

A minute later Chiara returned to her work. Li had neatly cut away Juliette's pants leg revealing the full extent of the injuries. There were four wounds, two entry points a few inches above the knee and two exit holes high up on the thigh. The bullets had carved through the muscles, long but shallow wounds. Much like long stab wounds. Chiara settled in with Li and got to work. Checking to make sure the wounds were clear of foreign material and then suturing them up.

As Juliette's surgical apprentice, it was work she had plenty of practice with.

* * *

Peter looked at the lock on the front door of the home-mart store for a second. His hand blurred forward. The wood and thin metal around the lock tore away, the door swinging free.

"We're in," he whispered to Anton.

"Right," Anton said sardonically, heading along the aisles, filling his backpack with high-protein fitness bars, and anything else that was high calories in a small package.

Peter did the same. Half a minute later he exclaimed, "Bonus!"

Anton jogged over to where Peter was collecting battery powered LEDs. They were general purpose headlamps, small, powerful, and easily hidden.

"Stick these in your pockets," Peter advised. "Just like we said, if Armitage switches off the lights, we'll have a backup plan. Anton smiled; he liked the idea of confounding Armitage if she plunged the team into darkness as part of her 'trap.'

On the wall opposite the LEDs was a rack of climbing equipment. A pair of product signs and a corkboard of photos indicated that someone associated with the store was a climbing enthusiast, perhaps the store's owner. Anton picked up a coil of rope and put it over his shoulder, there was a multi-pronged hook attached to the end.

"Thinking of climbing something?"

"Armitage's house is on a cliff face, isn't it? We might need to come in from that angle."

"Good idea, gives us another option."

"Time to go," Anton observed, patting his full backpack. "Francis wanted us back in twenty minutes."

"Hang on a second," Peter said, rummaging around in the bottom of his backpack. He withdrew a fat wallet stuffed with cash. He pulled out half a dozen fifty-pound notes and placed them on the counter next to the till. "That should just about cover it."

Peter's actions were a relief, Anton was uncomfortable with the idea of 'just stealing stuff,' even if it was a life or death situation, it didn't sit right with him.

Peter grinned at him. "Hey, I came prepared. We're not thieves you know."

Anton smiled; Peter's irrepressible good humor always lifted him. He was lucky to know him; his life could have gone a far different path after the death of his mother and the abduction of his father. It could have easily spiraled into a short-lived hell of wrath and violence.

The friends he had in the Mirovar force team had become more important to him than anything else. A voice nagged him at the back of his mind, it whispered, '*Liar, vengeance is your god now.*'

"No," he whispered to himself, following Peter from the shop but he lacked conviction in his denial.

* * *

Eight turbines roared as the helicopters circled to land.

The four fully-armed nightfalcons descended to a private airfield outside Goathland. It provided a perfect staging point for the remaining elements of Squadron F to cover Yorkshire. A pair of hangars stood mutely in the distance, silent witnesses to the paramilitary force landing in the middle of the airstrip.

An extra Mk-19 grenade launcher sat opposite the 7.62mm minigun on each of the heavily armed gunships. The waist-mounted MK-19 could fire six grenades per second, the perfect anti-personnel weapon to provide an area-of-effect attack on fast moving targets. They also carried their main armament of eight Hellfire III and eight Stinger II missiles for air-to-ground and air-to-air combat respectively. The final element was a pair of tri-barreled .50 caliber machine guns equipped with two thousand rounds of depleted uranium ammunition mounted in the hull beneath the nose of the helicopters.

Each helicopter carried a crew of two pilots, and two gunners, and sixteen fully armed and armored Day Guard phase IV Shadowstone troopers.

The lead craft landed first. Sixteen troopers streamed from both sides of the nightfalcon to create a defensive perimeter fifty yards from it. Major Frank Quiver, tall, slim, and sandy-haired, with a distinctive wing commander mustache was the last to exit.

Major Quiver was the commanding officer of Squadron F and immediate subordinate to Director Heathmont. He strode away from the nightfalcon along the runway tarmac. He glanced at his watch, it read 16:40. It had taken nearly four and a half hours to bring his forces back to the Facility, refuel, rearm and reposition to this airfield.

His wing commander mustache twitched with annoyance. He didn't like a civilian ordering him around like some navvy. Director Heathmont was adamant that the Order of Thoth team had an objective in or around Goathland. Major Quiver had ordered the fitting of the MK-19 multi-grenade launchers to the port side mounts of the nightfalcons. The extra weaponry would be an asset versus the incredible speed of the Order operatives. If Heathmont was right, his men were as prepared and as well-equipped as they could be.

The other helicopters landed, the men moving out from them to take up defensive positions and stretch their legs. The whole force remained on hot standby, the helicopters idling their turbines, ready to take off at a moment's notice. With a two-hundred miles per hour top speed, his force could be anywhere in the north of England in short order.

He stroked his mustache, an unconscious gesture performed out of habit, it soothed his mind and helped him think.

There had been contact with Order of Thoth forces three miles out of Goathland on the A169 forty minutes ago, presumably the Mirovar force team. The enemy had wiped out two squads of his men in the engagement. So far, he'd expended half of Squadron F without claiming a single casualty on the opposing force, it was an unprecedented result.

Major Quiver vowed to concentrate on using his Hellfire missiles, and the Mk-19 grenade launchers to even the odds. His forces would stand off with the nightfalcons and pound the ground wherever the Order of Thoth operatives chose to stand.

They would not catch him out twice. The next time he came into contact with the enemy, he would blow them all to hell.

* * *

Juliette's eyelids fluttered, sharp light edging around them.

She had a splitting headache, and her left leg was on fire from the hip down. The good news was, she was still alive. There was a hard surface beneath her; she had enough medical experience to place it as an examination table without thinking about it.

She whispered, "What damage?" it sounded more like, 'Whaf damf?'

Juliette took a deep breath, her head hurt like hell, but her lungs were working fine.

"Juliette, you're waking up," Chiara said softly. "You've been shot, you took a head wound."

"The others?" Juliette squeezed out; her voice raspy.

"Sip this," Chiara said, offering Juliette a straw in a glass of water.

"Juliette sipped, the water soothing her throat.

Chiara explained, "Everyone is safe, we're holed up here in a small town called Goathland, about ten miles away from Whitby."

A shadow loomed over her; Francis leaned down to kiss her forehead. "Mon amour, you have come back."

Juliette looked up at Francis' face, his concern writ large on his features. His eyes were liquid with unshed tears. She lifted her hand up to stroke his face but never made it.

The last thing she experienced was Chiara shouting, "There's something wrong."

* * *

"She's bleeding on the brain," Chiara shouted. "She needs immediate surgery."

Chiara looked around at everyone in the room – they stared back at her. Her heart sank. There was no one else; she was the best qualified to do the surgery. She just didn't trust that she could do it.

She looked hard at Li. "Okay, let's prep."

The two young women blurred into action.

"Yvette," Chiara half-shouted, pointing to a second trolley on the other side of the surgical theater. "Bring that one over here."

Yvette blurred, the trolley appearing next to the table. Chiara reached over and grabbed the equipment she needed. Yvette started to back away, a shocked look on her face.

"Wait, I need your help," Chiara pleaded, catching Yvette's gaze with her eyes. "Here take this," she requested, handing Yvette an oval balloon the size of a football, with a nozzle at one end. She concentrated on Juliette's mouth, opening it, and inserting a firm tube down her throat. She attached the end of the tube to the nozzle of the balloon.

"Yvette, press on the balloon in a steady rhythm and keep her breathing."

Yvette swallowed, stared at Juliette's chest and kept her breathing with the balloon.

Chiara picked up the silvery wand, activated it, and ran a set of short sweeps over the wound site. The bleed showed up on the monitor as an angry red welt on the screen. It was just beneath the skull. An acute epidural hematoma.

Using the wand, Chiara located the exact center of the bleed, took a black pen and marked a line to the edge of the wound and a second line to make an 'X,' on Juliette's scalp.

There was an electric razor on the trolley. Twenty seconds later, Chiara had cleared a strip of hair away from the 'X.' Disinfectant was next, then she scanned the room, rushed to a cabinet and came back with a drill with a shiny stainless-steel bit.

Chiara paused for a second, staring at Francis. "You may want to look away for this bit."

Francis lifted his gaze away from Juliette for a moment. He looked at Chiara with eyes wide with dread and pleaded, "Do what you have to do, just ... please ... save her life."

"We will," Chiara replied, more confidence in her voice than she felt. She moved the trolley aside to give herself room, there was no time for hesitation.

She ramped, her hands becoming stonelike in their stillness. Time slowed, she activated the drill and placed it precisely on the center of the 'X.' It was essential that she reach into Juliette's skull far enough to allow the collected blood to drain but no further.

Chiara pushed the drill forward. It cut through Juliette's scalp with ease, then struck the bone. She lifted the pressure slightly and the steel bit ground into Juliette's skull.

The whine of the drill cut through the air like a knife. Chiara ripped it back, dark blood spurting from the hole. The flow slowed to a steady trickle. Chiara placed an absorbent pad against the hole and strapped it in place.

"Normally," she noted. "A surgeon would repair the blood vessels and possibly put in a drainage tube. Here, we have to rely on Juliette's system zero genetics to stem the bleeding. We'll need to keep an eye on her now and monitor her progress."

Francis looked at his wife, his face clouded with worry. "When will she wake up?"

"She has to stay still, or she will most likely die. The longer the better, certainly, at least an hour."

Francis looked up at the wall clock, Chiara tracked his gaze. The clock read, '17:12.'

"We're here at least until after six pm," he promised, gently stroking Juliette's hand.

Chiara nodded and prayed silently for Juliette to wake up.

* * *

Thunder cracked overhead, and rain hammered the front windows of the medical center. The street lights had come on, responding automatically to the darkness of the storm.

The clock on the wall read, '18:30,' a little less than two hours to sunset. The team had congregated in the main reception area as they prepared to leave. Everyone had picked up a large black plastic garbage bag from the cleaning cupboard, cutting holes in them for their head and arms, to make impromptu raincoats.

Juliette had woken up twenty minutes earlier. She was sitting in a chair in the waiting area, dressed in a fresh pair of pants. The only visible hints of her recent injuries, the heavy bandaging of her skull, and thick wrapping that tightened the fabric over her left thigh. Her eyes were alert, and she carried her head high.

Anton walked into the room carrying a pair of crutches, went over to Juliette, and said, "I found these, I've already adjusted them for your height."

Juliette smiled. "Thanks."

"Good work Anton," Francis said. His lips tightened, he frowned, catching Anton, Peter and Li's gazes. "I have a very difficult mission for the three of you."

"The best sort," Peter observed, crossing and flexing his fingers, his knuckles cracking loudly.

Anton nodded resolutely and said, "Whatever you need Francis."

Li glanced at Anton and sighed softly. "I will do my best."

"Good," Francis noted. "Juliette's going to conduct another full Panopticon hazing operation. She will center it on her laptop. It will create an information black hole three miles wide for fifteen minutes … However, Shadowstone is on full alert, they will notice the hazing as soon as it starts and they will send all their available forces toward the center of the hazing."

"So, we leave the laptop here and escape?" Anton asked.

"No. We'll send it with you. The hazing begins at 18:45 and will run to 19:00. Between now and then, you will take the laptop as far north as you can go."

Luther looked up from his seat, smiling grimly at Anton. "With all this talk, you've got less than thirteen minutes before the hazing starts. We don't want you starting from here and giving away our position."

Francis threw Luther an irritated glance. "One last thing, the laptop has a thermite charge in its base, it will self-destruct when the hazing ends."

Anton asked, "Why destroy the laptop?"

"A normal hazing is defined on a single geographical location," Juliette explained. "The laptop governing the hazing doesn't even have to be there. This hazing is located on the laptop itself. When the hazing stops, the laptop is going to be in the middle of it. We have to destroy it to ensure it doesn't fall into Shadowstone's hands."

"You don't trust us to be able to escape with it."

Luther stepped forward. "It's standard operating procedure. The Order can't take the risk. When we perform a hazing this way, we always destroy the laptop. It's known as a 'sacrifice play.'" He stared at Anton. "Like when a lizard drops its tail to escape a predator."

Anton fell silent. He became preternaturally still, on the borderline of ramping. Luther's presence always filled him with a sense of veiled threat.

The situation could only last so long before it blew up. He believed the time was coming soon when either Luther or himself would be dead.

"Very encouraging," Juliette said sarcastically, her eyes flashing at Luther.

Luther snapped. "I told you before we left. I would keep this team honest."

Anton shrugged off the incipient Ramp, and stepped forward, crouching before Juliette. "It's okay. Let's get you safe."

Juliette reached out, taking his hands in hers and said softly. "You're just like your grandfather you know, and in the best possible way."

Anton stood up, turning to the rest of the team. "Don't worry about us."

Francis directed, "You must go now, time is short. We will be at the manor house at Whitby in two hours."

Peter nodded, grabbing the laptop in its protective satchel, he made for the door. Anton and Li, shouldering their weapons and gear, following behind him. A moment later, they were out on the street.

"North then," Anton offered, shielding his eyes from the rain with his left hand.

"North it is," Peter replied.

They ran off down the street. In ten minutes' time, the hazing would begin, and Shadowstone would throw everything they could muster at them.

"We're bait," Anton said wryly, his face caught halfway between a grin and a grimace.

"Better get used to it princess," Peter remarked. "It won't be the last time."

"You hope," Li said, running next to them.

Peter didn't have anything else to say.

They ran on in silence, putting a mile every four minutes between themselves and the rest of the team.

Chapter Eight

"Low to medium level wars, proxy wars, and wars by non-state actors all provide excellent cover for the secret war between the Vampire Dominion and the Ramp masters. War within the human community is to be maintained at a level aligned with the goal of providing ready, and believable scapegoats to blame for those occasions when the operations of the Vampire Dominion become visible to humans. Note well, that one of our number is missing from this conference because his reckless ambitions plunged the world into six years of wasteful conflict. Let Dieter Franz's punishment be a lesson to you all – world-wide conflagrations will not be tolerated. I trust I have made myself clear." – Cornelius Crane, King of the Vampire Dominion at the Conference of Generals, New York, 1946.

* * *

Outside Ogton, Yorkshire, August 22nd, 18:58

The storm winds whipped past the open doors of the nightfalcon helicopter.

The gunship was hugging the ground, flying at one hundred and eighty miles per hour at one-hundred yards altitude over the Yorkshire Moors. Four four-man squads of fully armed and armored Shadowstone troopers crowded the main cabin of the craft. Corporal Brian Jenkins strode up and down the aisle, slapping shoulders and checking equipment.

"Well fuck a doodle doo boys, it's showtime," he shouted over the roar of the helicopter, clasping the broad shoulders of one of his men.

The man grinned back, a wild light behind his eyes. They were all participants in the Phase IV Day Guard program. They'd been told it was a UK government program to create a superior fighting force to fight terrorists anywhere in the world. For the last two years, he'd been on a steady program of injected serums, steroids, and stimulants. The effects had been dramatic, Corporal Jenkins could bench press four hundred and eighty pounds and run a marathon with full kit in two hours. He could easily win gold in a host of Olympic events, but of course, he couldn't compete. He was disappointed about that, he was sure there was no 'official,' drug testing regime that could detect the exotic cocktail flowing through his bloodstream.

Jenkin's eyes tightened, he snarled and declared, "Time for some payback."

"Hell, yeah," came back from the men surrounding him.

He thumped an armored shoulder with his gauntleted fist. For a normal man, the blow would have cracked the joint. The trooper grinned back at him, eager, and ready to fight.

"ETA, one minute," came over his tactical helmet comms link.

The major was on this bird, personally commanding Squadron F for this battle. An unknown number of hostiles faced them. They anticipated more than twenty, and perhaps as many as thirty individuals had been warring with the 'F,' all day. The results had been horrific, with nearly half the squadron lost. The four nightfalcons in this flight and the attached eighty troopers were the bulk of the remaining force.

Now they'd found the enemy. They were on the move, heading toward the village of Ogton. Luckily, the squadron had staged at a private airfield east of Goathland, mere minutes away from their targets.

It was a God sent opportunity. The enemy had appeared in their laps, and Jenkins would happily assist in hammering them into dust.

Jenkins looked out through the open cabin doorway; the trooper next to him was manning a Mk-19 grenade launcher. They'd fitted the weapon to the helicopter earlier that day – an equalizer – there had been rumors that the enemy was enhanced with extreme speed; and the capability to fire half a dozen 40mm grenades a second was deemed necessary.

Were the enemy that dangerous? Jenkins stared into the stormy darkness outside the nightfalcon. The street lights of Ogton were just visible in the distance. He was keen to answer that question for himself.

Thunder cracked overhead, lightning flashing nearby, rain fell in sheets. The nightfalcons flew on in the dusk-like darkness without running lights. The whole of the remaining force of Squadron F converging on the hamlet of Ogton.

* * *

The trio ran through the lamp-lit streets of Ogton at Olympic level marathon pace.

Li pulled to a halt, Anton and Peter stopping a couple of yards later, turning back to her.

Thunder cracked overhead, lightning dazzling across the sky, gleaming off the wet black plastic of their impromptu raincoats. Li declared, "They're here, or will be in seconds."

The roar of jet turbines cut through the air, four nightfalcons emerging from the gloom beneath the storm clouds. The wedge formation separated, two helicopters veering to the left and the other two peeling off to the right. In moments, they were flying in concentric circles around the hamlet of Ogton.

Peter twisted around, watching the gunships circle and said sardonically. "Geez, if brute force doesn't work, we might need to use finesse."

The nightfalcons slowed, hovering thirty yards off the ground beyond the edge of the village. Dark lines dropped from the helicopters, Shadowstone troopers followed, rappelling down the lines. They completed the operation in less than ten seconds. The troopers immediately dashing off in the gloom to take up positions in a cordon around the village.

There was a gas station, forty yards away, on the main road leading out of town. Given the state of emergency curfew and the storm, it lay empty. Peter glanced inside the laptop satchel; his face momentarily lit by a faint red glow. "Thirteen seconds to go." He blurred to the station, pulling the laptop from the satchel as he ran.

Anton and Li ran along the other side of the street.

The nightfalcons veered upward, making a single evenly spaced circle around the village. They were flying in a broad circle from right to left, their waist mounted Mk-19 grenade launchers swinging toward the village.

Peter blurred back to their side, guiding them further back from the gas station. A second later the laptop's thermite charge detonated. A bright glare appeared next to one of the fuel bowsers. Half a second later, the bowser erupted in a towering fountain of flame.

"The hazing is over," Peter declared. "That's the distraction, now we break through their lines and escape."

"It's still too light to avoid being seen," Li observed.

Li was right. Shadowstone would have them in their sights and were only positioning to take the final shot. Anton's face became still, his eyes deadly serious in the gloom. "Then we will have to kill them all."

He turned and blurred down the street. He didn't know what he would do yet, but he was sure he didn't want to leave an operational Shadowstone unit hunting them, or the rest of the Mirovar team, alive and on their tail.

The forces circling overhead, and setting up a perimeter around the village, would have to die. It was the only way he could be sure to keep his friends safe.

A dreadful fury boiled within him, his eyes glistening beneath the storm clouds and pelting rain. Ripping away the plastic sheet around his shoulders, he lifted his FN P90 submachine gun from a holster at his side. The Blue Dragon's handle jutted over his right shoulder, ready to swing into action at a moment's notice.

He headed back into town, looking for a high spot to get to, he needed to see all of his enemies so he could see who needed to die.

"Violence will be my friend," Anton uttered, a ferocious light behind his eyes.

He blurred into the shadows, Li and Peter following closely behind him.

* * *

Major Frank Quiver rolled along in his railed chair, scanning the wall of screens in his command nightfalcon. The vital signs of his ground troops were all displayed underneath feeds from their individual helmet cams. Everything was in the green and proceeding according to plan.

The Order of Thoth's hazing operation had just ended, defeated by cyberwarfare counter attacks from Shadowstone units across the world. With the storm and the curfew, the streets were empty; except for three newly identified forms running hot in the infra-red and super-fast toward the center of town.

He ignored the flaring gasoline fire on the edge of town. It was an obvious distraction; he wasn't about to be tricked by something so simple.

With the Panopticon linked into the networked sensors on the four nightfalcons, he had a clear three-dimensional view of the village and everyone in it. This was going to be easier than he'd expected. The enemy had divided their forces. The three operatives discovered in the village at the center of the Panopticon haze lay exposed to every weapon he had at his disposal. But he had to be wary, the Shadowstone mandate was to operate in secret. There was only so much he could do out in the open. He couldn't simply blow away a whole village to get to three operatives. It would be next to impossible to explain, especially on top of the disasters at the Squadron F base, and the RAF airbase at Coningsby.

The Shadowstone PSYOPS directorate was shitting kittens, secrecy was not something he could throw away on a whim. He would have to send in his men and flush the enemy out into the open where his heavy weapons would prove decisive.

He opened his tactical comms link to his squad commanders. They were all on the ground, manning a cordon around the village. He gave the order to flush the enemy to the south. The hostiles were moving toward the center of the hamlet at frightening speed, but it only took him a moment to vector his squads after them. He pulled two of his squads away from the south entrance of town to give the Order operatives a path of 'escape.'

His men would push the Order operatives back to the south, once clear of the village, his nightfalcons would take them out with Hellfire missiles.

They would not be able to escape him this time.

* * *

Thick, dark clouds glowered overhead.

Corporal Brian Jenkins peered through the sheeting rain, looking for the hostiles he was supposed to push south. To his right, a wall of flames consumed a gasoline station. A heads-up-display filled his tactical helmet visor, overlaying everything he saw with metadata provided by the Shadowstone Panopticon. It was too much to take in at the same time, the flames, the storm, and all the high-tech crap clouding his vision.

He lifted his visor.

"There's no one here," he muttered.

Four men emerged from the gloom, running across the street toward the gas station. Each one carried something in their arms. Weapons, bombs, he didn't know, but they weren't Shadowstone. He lifted his H&K 416 assault rifle, letting rip with a long burst. The bullets flashed through the men, cutting them down. The nearest one fell forward, the object he was carrying rolling across the ground.

It was a red fire extinguisher, wet and gleaming in the firelight.

"Stupid bastards."

They were locals.

He signaled his men with a raised fist to advance. He walked past the fallen men, dark pools spreading from their bodies. Shaking his head, his mouth set in a grim slash, he thought, *This is going to get ugly*.

* * *

The command screens reflected the carnage on the ground.

Major Quiver glared at his displays. He didn't need collateral damage. The Phase IV stimulants made his men faster, but they could lead to careless risk-taking. The four bodies cooling in the rain were a testament to that.

A green light flashed in the corner of his set of screens. A call from Director Heathmont was coming in.

He answered, "Sir?"

"What the hell is happening?" Heathmont asked. "Have you killed them yet?"

"No, Sir. We have three hostiles in Ogton."

"They must've split their forces. It will be their undoing."

"Sir, I've sent in my men. I'll flush them into the open and destroy them."

"No," Heathmont snapped. "Don't risk your men. Pull them back now."

"Sir?"

"Take out the town, it's the only way to be sure. It's sitting over a major gas line. We'll explain everything away with a gas explosion. Erase everyone, there can be no survivors."

Major Quiver took a deep breath, and replied, "Yes, Sir."

"Make sure it's done. No survivors."

Without blinking, Major Quiver said, "Roger, Sir."

The line went dead.

Major Quiver didn't hesitate, issuing orders over his tactical comms link to his squad commanders to pull back beyond the edge of town. He followed with orders to his pilots to fire at will at the three hostiles in the center of the village.

The helicopters started to pivot as one, bringing their main weapons to bear on the three operatives highlighted on his screens.

"This will be over soon," Major Quiver whispered to himself.

* * *

The nightfalcons turned.

"Move!" Peter shouted.

Peter, Anton, and Li blurred away from the center of the village. Hellfire missiles streaked through the rain toward where they'd been standing. The blasts ripped away the dusky gloom beneath the storm clouds. Buildings evaporated, windows shattered, dust, smoke, and flame bursting upward in a hellish tower over the hamlet.

The edge of the blast wave hit them like a giant's fist, hurling them along the street. Anton scrambled off the slick cobblestones. Li bounced to her feet a couple of yards in front of him, shaking her left hand. Peter rolled to his feet and shook himself.

"They're destroying the village," Li shouted, glancing down at her bloody hand.

The nightfalcons roared overhead, circling for their next attack.

"We have to stop them," Anton declared. He twisted around and pointed at the tallest structure in the town. "The water tower."

Peter and Li looked at Anton, nonplussed for half a second. Anton threw his FN P90 submachine gun to Peter, and said, "I won't be needing this."

Peter grinned, hefting an FN P90 with each hand and shouted, "Yes! Go! I'll keep 'em occupied down here." He blurred back through the smoke and falling debris, firing short bursts of 9mm rounds from his submachine guns at the circling helicopters.

Anton ramped hard, blurring away to the base of the water tower, loosening the climbing rope he'd picked up in Goathland. He leaped ten feet up to a steel stairway, snaking up and around to the top of the tower. Li followed a step behind him. Blurring up nearly fifty yards of rusting steel stairs, they burst out onto the brick and cement platform at the top of the tower.

One of the nightfalcons was approaching at about forty miles per hour. Its port side gunner firing his Mk-19 grenade launcher down at the village. He was chasing Peter with his weapon, patterns of two and four grenades exploding along the main street. The helicopter was going to pass the water tower in seconds. It was flying about thirty yards higher and another twenty yards away from the top of the tower.

Anton unbound his climbing rope, swinging its hook in a circle. He figured he had one chance, any second now, Shadowstone would notice their presence on top of the tower. He dropped into silence and time slowed down. The steady beat of the nightfalcon's rotors separated out into individual thumps, reverberating through the air. The fires below lit the gunner's helmet, a faint reflection of Anton and Li appearing on his visor. In the distance, the lightning seemed to crackle forever as it reached hungry fingers down to the Yorkshire Moors.

The Mk-19 fell silent. The gunner's stare fixing on Anton.

Anton released the hook, throwing it with all his might. It flew like an arrow into the nightfalcon's main cabin, missing the gunner by a couple of feet.

The gunner swung the Mk-19 up toward the top of the water tower.

Anton whipped the rope, the tri-bladed hook swinging back through the cabin, embedding itself in the gunner's back. He arched backward, his arms swinging wide. The barrel of the Mk-19 dropped as he lurched forward against his restraints.

"Now!" Anton shouted, wrapping the rope tight around his wrist. Li leaped onto his back, her arms wrapping around his neck and her thighs locking around his hips. The rope snapped taut, Anton moved with it, blurring forward, and leaping into the darkness beneath the nightfalcon. The rope snapped tight again, Li and Anton swinging underneath the helicopter. His hands blurred, ascending the rope, shortening their loop as they came up the other side of the helicopter.

They landed in the main cabin. The Mk-19 gunner writhed within his harness, trying to extract the hook from his shoulder. The trooper manning the starboard side minigun reached for his 9mm sidearm.

Li's foot lashed out, taking the nearest trooper beneath his helmet. He slammed backward within his safety harness, then fell forward, dangling in his restraints with his head at an unnatural angle.

Anton drew the Blue Dragon in a horizontal slash, beheading the hooked trooper struggling in his harness. The man's helmeted head fell forward, disappearing into the gloom, his blood painting the ceiling in a dark crimson streak.

Shadows stretching from the cockpit fell across the floor. A hidden submachine gun erupted, 9mm bullets wildly spraying the back of the cabin. Anton and Li sprang forward, taking up positions to the left and right of the entrance to the cockpit.

The co-pilot darted forward, attempting to rush through into the cabin while shooting to his left. He came to a sudden halt, held upright by the

Blue and Green Dragon swords piercing his torso from both sides. The blades swished out; a look of helpless despair flitted momentarily over his face before he slid bonelessly to the floor.

Anton didn't wait for the co-pilot to land, leaping high over his dying body, and blurring forward into the cockpit. The pilot's left arm swung left, a 9mm automatic in his grip. The gun barked, the bullet going beneath Anton as he flew off the opposite wall. The Blue Dragon arced downward, entering the pilot's chest just above the collarbone and diving deep down through his body. He coughed once, blood splattering the console.

Anton drew the Blue Dragon clear of the pilot's body. He leaned forward, snapped the pilot's harness clips, dragging him clear of the cockpit and dropping him next to the co-pilot on the floor of the nightfalcon's main cabin.

He glanced at Li, and then at the 7.62mm minigun. "Can you fire one of those?"

Li ripped the body of the trooper from the harness next to the gun and cast it aside. She arched an eyebrow, glancing at the cockpit. "Can you fly one of these?"

Anton grinned, dashing back into the cockpit, leaping into the pilot's seat. His hands flew over the controls with practiced ease, all the long hours spent in training simulations with Peter back at the safe house in Maine were now paying off.

The nightfalcon had been circling on automatic pilot for the last dozen seconds, and it looked like no one had noticed Anton and Li's capture of the craft. Digital displays showed his weapons inventory. Only four of the Hellfire missiles remained. The tri-barreled .50 caliber machine guns under the nose had full magazines. The prize was the eight Stinger II air-to-air missiles sitting on hard mounts to the left and right of the cockpit.

He flicked off the identify friend or foe system. Reset the combat system for sole pilot control and armed all weapons. A heads-up display painted the windscreen in front of him. It wasn't as advanced as the system deployed in the commander tank, but it was good enough for what he needed tonight. The HUD lay a color-coded ninety-degree wide map centered on the mid-line of the nightfalcon on the front windscreen – the off-boresight field of fire for the Stinger II missiles. He could reliably target any opponent in the front quarter of the gunship with the Stinger missiles.

Anton broke left out of the circle formation, flying hard toward the next two nightfalcon's in front of him. Their port side gunners equipped with Mk-19 grenade launchers, their attention fixed on pummeling the village below.

The sustained use of massive numbers of 40mm high explosive grenades was ripping the village apart. The HUD display showed dozens of warm bodies sprawled in the street. It was a massacre. Anton swallowed hard, pushing the throttle forward. The nightfalcon surged, he targeted the two helicopters flying from right to left before him. They were about three hundred yards away, and he was closing rapidly. He selected the Stingers, firing two at each craft. The missiles launched from the hard points on either side of his cockpit, jagging hard to the left and right, matching up on their designated targets. They speared away, crossing the distance to the nightfalcons in less than a second.

The targeted nightfalcon's defensive systems recognized the threats immediately. Bright flares automatically ejecting to the left and right of each helicopter. Chaff bloomed and glittered above the village fires. The defenses defeated two of the missiles, sending them past their targets to fly harmlessly off into the stormy darkness.

The other two rammed into their marks, detonating with thunderous explosions, the helicopters transforming into furious balls of light and flame. Anton pulled back on the controls, his nightfalcon flying above the falling debris.

He banked his helicopter hard to the left, curving around in a tight circle. It was time to hunt the last surviving nightfalcon.

* * *

Major Quiver's pilot shouted through the tactical comms link, "Falcon dash Seven's gone rogue!"

Quiver leaped from his command chair, rushing forward to the cockpit. The rogue nightfalcon fired two pairs of Stinger missiles. They speared into two of his remaining birds, the gunships exploding in great balls of fire, filling the left half of the nightfalcon's canopy with light, stark against the storm clouds covering the sky. The rogue gunship banked hard left, soaring above the flaming wreckage as it fell toward the ground.

"Take evasive actions. Bring our weapons to bear and take them down!" Quiver shouted.

The rogue gunship wheeled about; in seconds it would be heading straight toward them.

Quiver's pilot slammed the throttles to maximum power, the engines roaring like colossal demons. The nightfalcon veered upward, banking in toward the rogue bird. Whoever reached a firing solution first would have the advantage.

The rogue gunship straightened up, accelerating to pass his gunship on the right. Both pilots fired simultaneously, a pair of Stinger missiles leaping away from each nightfalcon toward the other. Missile warners rang shrill alarms. Dazzling flares shot out to the left and right. Clouds of silvery chaff bloomed, swirling in the backwash from the rotors.

Quiver's Helicopter jigged hard left, running through the chaff of the other bird.

Minigun fire rippled through the chaos, his two gunners screamed in the main cabin. He twisted back, searching for his men. They'd disappeared, carried away by the depleted uranium rounds, their empty harnesses dripping blood. A line of golden fire ripped through the rear section of the helicopter. His nightfalcon shuddered, rising higher under full power. The opposing minigun fell silent, no longer able to bear on his bird.

Engines roaring, Quiver's nightfalcon wheeled hard through the air. The other gunship was also banking hard, the pair of nightfalcons describing a long figure eight over the burning village.

They were going to make another pass at each other. The rogue gunship only had two Stinger missiles left, his bird had six. Quiver shouted to his pilot, "Fire all the missiles."

"Roger, Sir."

This attack would overwhelm his opponent's defenses.

It was an all or nothing play.

One he had to win.

* * *

A hellish version of the fourth of July was erupting over the village.

"Anton," Li shouted. "They'll fire more missiles, open the angle so I can use the minigun."

"On it," Anton shouted back.

Anton pushed the nightfalcon to it limits. The frame of the craft shuddered as it veered left, positioning the opposing bird on the right forward flank.

Li swung the starboard mounted minigun as far forward as she could. She ramped to her maximum extent. Her mind stilled, a supreme calm descending through her, met by surging power from within her depths. Time slowed down. The rotor blades above her entered a lazy rhythm. Individual raindrops resolved as they fell past the open doorway next to the main cabin. The opposing nightfalcon loomed in her vision. The pylons jutting left and right from the cockpit hosted hard points holding four Hellfire and six Stinger missiles.

Anton fired his last two missiles, the Stingers streaking away into clouds of gleaming chaff and spinning flares.

All the opposing Stinger missiles fired at once, spearing toward her like hot silvery talons. Defensive flares sailed lazily to her right, their actinic glare reflecting off the noses of the incoming missiles. She depressed the minigun's trigger. Time dragged as the minigun's electric motor hesitated before spinning the barrels. Flame gouted from the mouth of her weapon, bright tracers lancing in a hotline toward the nearest Stinger. The depleted uranium rounds connected with the missile, smashing it in a bright ball of flame.

Li's eyes narrowed, her face a mask of intensity as she swung her minigun to the right. The missiles were closing fast, accelerating to more than twice the speed of sound. The tracers followed her gaze to the second Stinger, her fire consuming it halfway along its path. There were four missiles left. She reached deeper into the silence, the individual barrels of the minigun snapping past in front of her, long tongues of flame flickering after each shot. Spent shell casings floated to her left like gravity-defying confetti, every fifth round a bright tracer lancing away, the ripping whirr of the gun lost in a wave of rolling thunder.

The third missile evaporated in a bright puff of brilliantly burning debris at sixty yards.

Li's heart paused, waiting for the next beat.

She moved the gun slightly to the right, machine-like in her precision, the fourth missile splitting into a cloud of flaming fragments at forty yards. The fifth missile streaked in, piercing the defensive flares and chaff clouds, before detonating at fifteen yards, a mist of razor-sharp fragments carried forward by momentum reaching out at her with a thousand glittering fingers.

The last missile had been accelerating the longest, hitting its top speed as it reached the cabin doorway eight feet to Li's right.

She blurred left, away from the minigun, pushing herself hard up against the cabin bulkhead. Her arms flew up to shield her face, the lip of the doorway providing extra protection.

The last missile shot through the open cabin without connecting with anything. The debris of the fifth missile close behind it, ripping away equipment and scouring the back half of the main cabin.

Her heart beat again.

She dropped out of the ramp, the opposing nightfalcon disappearing past her behind the shield of its failed missile attack, flares, and chaff. It was already past the field of fire of her minigun.

The captured nightfalcon started banking hard to the left. Anton was going to make another run at the other helicopter.

All the air-to-air missiles were gone. The only weapons left they could use for air-to-air combat were the .50 caliber machine guns in fixed mounts under the nose.

To use them in a face-to-face pass against another nightfalcon would be mutual suicide.

* * *

The two nightfalcons lined up on each other at two hundred yards.

In the HUD display, the topography of the burning village lay drawn in ghostly shapes. One building stood out dead ahead – the water tower.

Anton slammed the nightfalcon's throttle to maximum, the turbines roared, the craft leaping forward. He depressed the trigger for the two tri-barreled .50 caliber machine guns, bright fire leaping from beneath his cockpit toward the opposing helicopter.

The other nightfalcon fired back, tracers streaming toward Anton's craft. Both nightfalcons were traveling at above fifty miles per hour, accelerating and closing. Whoever's weapons hit first would win, killing the other crew, destroying their craft, and then allowing the surviving pilot to bank hard, avoiding a mid-air collision.

The heavily armored noses of the nightfalcon's absorbed the fire, metal-ceramic armor ablating away from the raw metal underneath, the protection would last a second or two.

Anton anticipated a left-hand bank from the opposing pilot, he'd been doing it consistently all battle. Anton made a final adjustment to set the nightfalcon's course to automatically bank hard right in three seconds. He ramped hard, blurring from the cockpit, scooping up the Blue Dragon from the floor as he dashed back to the rear of the craft.

Pulling the tri-bladed hook from the headless body of the trooper who'd manned the Mk-19 grenade launcher, he swung the hook once, hard and fast, snagging the parapet at the top of the water tower as it passed thirty yards underneath.

There were two seconds left before the gunship would bank.

"Time to go," he yelled.

Li ran to him, leaping upon his back. They sailed out through the side of the nightfalcon as .50 caliber rounds cut through at ankle height from the front of the helicopter.

The empty gunship banked hard above them.

They fell together, thirty yards down to the height of the tower, Anton's leap taking them past the tower's top. They fell toward the ground fifty yards below. The rope was just over thirty yards long, Anton looked up along it, silently praying the hook would hold. He ramped hard, silence overwhelming his mind, time slowing to a crawl. His left arm became hard as stone, his grip like iron on the rope. It was a combined sixty-yard fall, with Li's and his weight hanging on his arm, the rope, and the hook.

The rope snapped tight, Anton and Li swinging with their momentum through a long arc coming up above the height of the tower. They paused there momentarily, before reversing back down toward the side of the tower. Hitting the bottom of the swing beside the tower, Anton let go, falling the final twenty yards to the ground below. They landed, rolling smoothly forward on the well-maintained lawn around the base of the tower.

Anton sprang to his feet with Li at his side.

They looked up, the nightfalcons were lurching toward each other.

* * *

The exterior of the rogue nightfalcon started to break up under the sustained fire from his gunship's heavy machine guns.

His pilot banked hard left to avoid a mid-air collision the gunfire spearing past the oncoming machine.

The other helicopter banked hard toward them.

Major Frank Quiver, the leading officer of the ultra-secret Phase IV Day Guard program, stared in growing horror at the nightfalcon rushing toward his bird. His pilot dragged on his controls, the airframe shuddering under the load as it banked harder to the left.

His upper lip stiffened, his wing commander mustache twitched, he raised a hand in helpless defiance.

It was all too late.

The canopy of his aircraft caved in, tearing metal and shattering transparent armor silencing his pilot's despairing scream in an instant.

A tiny fraction of a second later, the nose of the rogue nightfalcon pinned Major Quiver against the bulkhead at the back of the cockpit, and his world vanished forever.

* * *

Peter dashed up to the base of the water tower, flaming helicopter debris crashing to the ground behind him.

He grinned, slapping them both on the shoulders. "Awesome guys."

Li turned, grabbing Anton by both shoulders and giving him a hard shake of annoyance. "See what happens when we work as a team."

"Hey," Anton said, "Where did this come from?"

Li snapped, "You've been off the rails all day."

"I've only done what I needed to," Anton asserted, his eyes narrowing.

Peter leaned in between them. "Hey, we need to be on the move."

Li and Anton stared at each other, emotions boiling beneath the surface.

Anton breathed out, shrugged his shoulders and asked, "When are you going to stop treating me like your student?"

Li frowned, stepped in close and stated, "When you start acting like a master." She tapped him on the chest. "And you broke your promise about handling your emotions and not taking off on your own."

"For God's sake Li, I took the initiative in a combat situation."

"And nearly got everyone killed."

Anton glanced at Peter and said, "I saved Peter."

"No," Li declared. "We saved Peter after you got yourself stupidly stuck in the middle of a Shadowstone base."

"That base needed taking down. It's one less place for them to launch against us."

"Oh, c'mon Anton," Li said, exasperatedly. "They'll just rebuild, and next time they'll be stronger."

Peter put his hands between his friends, pushing them gently apart. He leaned in, a shadow of tension at the edges of his eyes, and declared, "We really need to move now. The window of opportunity is closing."

Anton glanced at him. "Sure, I'm okay. Let's do it."

"Of course, Peter," Li agreed with a pointed glance at Anton. "Very sensible."

"Whitby is pretty much due east of here," Peter noted, leading them away from the water tower.

Li and Anton glanced at each other, she frowned, her lips pressed tightly together.

Anton sighed. *Li is … complicated.*

He fell into step next to Peter. In a couple of minutes, they would be through Shadowstone's perimeter. The troops were in disarray, all their air cover was gone, and their command structure lay broken.

Anton's face hardened in avid anticipation, the next stop was Whitby and Chloe Armitage.

They blurred into the gloom beyond the fires.

* * *

Gordon Heathmont slumped back into his seat in the rear of his Jaguar sedan, his fingers absently stroking the fine leather upholstery as he stared out the window into the storm.

He lifted both hands to his face, rubbed the bridge of his nose, and then dragged them down his cheeks.

There would be repercussions, the day had descended into absolute, unmitigated disaster. He shook his head slowly; it was beyond anything he could have imagined. The capture of Peter Lamb had been a gift, a decisive step forward in Shadowstone's secret war against the Order of Thoth and the Red Empire, but whatever advantage that capture represented was lost the moment an Order of Thoth operative stole a commander tank.

From then on, the day had descended into chaos.

What could he report to Cornelius Crane?

He was numb with shock. He would have to rally the survivors and provide a full accounting of events. His only hope was that he could demonstrate he'd made a reasonable decision at every step.

He sucked air through his nose, had he done everything he could have done?

He shook his head again, he didn't know.

Of one thing he remained certain, Cornelius Crane would decide his fate, and he would decide it soon.

Chapter Nine

"I have no interest in inflicting mindless, empty, meaningless suffering. When I cause suffering, it is always for a greater purpose." – General Chloe Armitage

* * *

Armitage Manor, Yorkshire, August 22nd, 19:11

"Chloe, you need to see this," Marcus declared.

Chloe stepped away from Kain. He hung within his chains, pale and drenched in sweat, strung out from the constant interrogation and blood-hunger over the last thirteen hours. She'd almost wrung him dry of useful information. She walked back to the table in the middle of the room where Marcus had opened up a large, military-style, ruggedized laptop. The screen displayed four separate Panopticon feeds of the aftermath of a devastating Shadowstone defeat seven miles from her manor house.

The Mirovar force team would arrive soon, she'd no doubts they'd survived the best efforts of the UK Shadowstone forces. The delaying tactic had worked perfectly, the Order was now unlikely to be able to mount an attack before sunset. With the onset of night, her freedom to move around outside would return, providing her with a powerful tactical advantage.

This was her home territory, and she knew it better than anyone else. She'd successfully brought her opponents to a battlefield of her own choosing, and tonight would see a telling blow delivered against the Order of Thoth, and the advancement of her own secret agenda.

She pulled out her phone and sent James Haley a text, 'Communications status?'

His reply came back in seconds, 'Still down. Order of Thoth operations continue to disrupt direct communications to the head of Shadowstone.'

Chloe smiled; her eye's alight with the game. James was using neutral language, he was most likely with someone, and taking action to keep her secrets. The communications links to Crane's direct lines were all down. Crane was in the dark and would stay that way for a while longer.

She sent another text, 'Where is he?'

'His personal drone, departing Israel for New York.'

Crane was in transit from Jerusalem after supervising the evacuation of his assets in the Middle East. His personal drone was not a quad-pod vehicle like the shadowstar drones, it was single crew craft with vertical take-off and landing capability. He would land in his citadel's main hangar in about ninety minutes time. As soon as he stepped from the drone, his executive secretary Ursula Zielinkski would meet him, and she would tell him precisely what was happening with his Shadowstone forces in the United Kingdom.

His fury would be epic.

Then nothing would happen – for a while. Crane was not one to engage in precipitous action. He would assess what had happened, sit back and strategize a fresh approach to achieve his goals. Chloe frowned slightly, there was no way for her to attack Crane directly, but a succession of rapidly changing events would undermine the foundations of his world until he made a mistake and put himself in a position where she could bring him face to face with her weapon – Anton Slayne.

There was one last critical piece of information she needed from Kain, she moved back to stand in front of him. She leaned in close, her face a handful of inches from his. His blood-hunger was a physical stench, like rotting meat, it had been steadily getting worse for more than half a day. She hid her disgust; she needed the information in his mind.

She inquired, quietly and with perfect diction, like she was asking a polite question in pleasant company, "Where and when will the next Order conclave be held?"

"I don't know," Kain spat, his eyes rolling on the edge of delirium. "Of course, I don't know."

"Come on Ramin, don't be difficult," she encouraged, lifting his chin with her finger, forcing him to meet her gaze. He stared back at her for a second before averting his eyes. She said, "You know I'll find out sooner or later. Here," she moved the bucket of congealing blood closer, "I promise you, this is the last question, and then you can have the rest of this blood."

Kain's pale face twisted into a grimace of thwarted desire, he panted, and stated, "I really don't know, I'm told by my staff."

"Hmmm," Chloe stepped back. "Then tell me how the process works?"

Kain started, and shouted desperately, "That's another question. You promised!"

Chloe sighed. "It's still the same question, describe the process of how a modern conclave is called, and I will have the answer to my last question."

Kain stared at the bucket of blood in silence, a thin line of drool running from the side of his mouth.

"Answer me in full, and not only will you have this bucket, but you will also have fresh, hot blood, as much as you desire, and your freedom before the next dawn."

Kain's eyes stilled and widened, fixing tightly on Chloe's face. He licked his lips and said urgently, the words tumbling from his mouth, "A force leader calls the conclave. Justin Blake will call the next one. The loremasters use their implants and secured cloud access to spread the word. The notice is always short, a matter of days."

"With your 'disappearance,'" Chloe observed, arching an eyebrow. "They will call another one soon. The Order must have a head." She frowned for a second, an idea on the edge of her mind. Something important, resting just beyond her awareness. She just needed to tease it into the light. "What happens if you can't use the loremasters to spread the word?"

Kain looked at her for a long moment. "There is a default protocol. A message defined at the last conclave that provides a once only predefined conclave location, the date and time are variables encoded into the message. The Order broadcasts the message in the general media – it will look like an advertisement. Only the force leaders will know the truth."

"Why not use your quantum encrypted smartphones to simply spread the details?"

Kain glared at her, a semblance of sanity re-establishing itself. "As we both know, after you hacked my phone during breakfast a couple of months ago, if the quantum signature is known, anyone with the skills can compromise the phone. We designed the default protocol to be foolproof."

Chloe stepped in close and whispered, "And the encoded message is?"

Kain whispered the answer, and she remembered every word perfectly. She stepped away from him, turning to stare into space. A handful of seconds passed before a slow smile crept across her face. "We need to adapt our plans. Give him all the blood – we need to move quickly."

Marcus passed the bucket to Kain, and he plunged his face into it. He leaned back, the bucket upturned over his gaping mouth, blood slopping down his throat, the excess spilling in great splashes around his feet.

If she could force the Order to use the default protocol, she would find out the date, time and location of the next conclave. Her smile broadened, filling her face with light. "What an opportunity."

She knew exactly what she needed to do.

* * *

The Raven's smartphone vibrated silently in their hip pocket.

They dropped back to the rear of the group, and brought the phone out, shielding it with their body from the rain pelting down. It was a message from the other Red Empire agent – Chloe Armitage.

Perhaps now was the critical moment where the Raven could deceive Armitage to her doom. They glanced once at the phone, the message filled the screen and read, 'The Red Empire is running a mission with Chloe Armitage and Marcus Drake against the Vampire Dominion. The Red Ghost has tricked the two vampire traitors into capturing Ramin Kain. All the secrets of the Order now belong to the Red Empire – this is our victory, not theirs. Detail the disposition of the Order forces and the exfiltration paths. Armitage and Drake will die. Victory is ours!'

Armitage still believed they were ignorant of the truth – it would be her undoing; the advantage still lay with the Raven.

The Raven lifted their smartphone, their fingers flashing over the phone's surface, they replied with, 'Understood. The Walker team is in place, and the Mirovar team is approaching with an ETA of 20:30. There are injuries, but the fighting capability of the Mirovar force team is nearly at full strength. I will send exfil data once I have it.'

It was not yet the time to deceive. Telling the truth now would maintain the illusion the Raven was still a loyal servant of the Red Empire, and an ally of the 'Red Empire agent.'

Soon, the time would be ripe, where they could cause maximum damage to Armitage's plans, perhaps even kill her. The Raven hoped for such an opportunity but was willing to see how the night evolved before making a decision. Perhaps the exfil data would prove conclusive, if they sent Armitage in the wrong direction at a critical moment, it could make all the difference.

They would wait and see.

* * *

Storm clouds thundered overhead, rain sheeting down upon the town of Whitby.

Richard Walker stared at the manor house on the cliff overlooking the town, his eyes narrow, his body tense. The manor stood alone, wreathed in dismal shadows. The sun had just set, and with the storm raging overhead it might as well have been midnight.

The Mirovar force team had failed miserably. If they'd arrived during daylight, he could have used their fighters to mount a combined daylight assault with a high probability of success. Instead, night had fallen, and they were mostly still absent.

He barked at his loremaster, "Joan, contact Mirovar and find out their latest ETA?"

"Yes, Sir," she responded. Joan Lewis sat in one of the black Range Rovers ten feet away, her laptop out of the rain. She closed her eyes for twenty seconds, attempting to commune with Juliette Mirovar via the quantum encrypted cloud used by the Order of Thoth.

"She's offline."

"What now?" Richard asked, his disdain for all things Mirovar nakedly visible in his voice.

"She's offline," Joan repeated, her mouth opening in a small 'O,' of concern.

"Damn it," Richard swore, pulling his smartphone from a chest pocket beneath his raincoat and voice dialing Francis Mirovar's phone address.

The phone rang three times before Mirovar picked it up and answered his obvious question coldly, "We're coming. We'll be there in fifteen minutes."

Three of the Mirovar team had arrived ten minutes before, wet and weary, with little to offer except their personal needs for food and water. Peter Lamb, Li Wu, and Anton Slayne, with a tale to tell of defeating a Shadowstone force seven miles away. It had been a miracle Shadowstone hadn't followed them. It seemed that Shadowstone in the UK were currently out of action, a small mercy given all the other problems his team faced.

"Nightfall was a minute ago. You have given our enemies the advantage by arriving late."

"We'll be there, and we will be ready to fight."

Richard snorted. "I certainly hope so."

He stared at the manor house and put his phone away. Lights had come on within the ground floor of the main building. The vampires would be active now and not afraid to hide. He cursed loudly, "Damn it all to hell."

Lamb, Wu, and Slayne looked up at him as one from beside one of the Range Rovers. Lamb arched a quizzical eyebrow, Wu wore an impassive expression that masked her feelings, and Slayne frowned, his eyes flashing with sharp emotions.

Well, let them judge him, they would be going in first. They could serve a useful purpose by springing any traps that might be waiting for his team.

* * *

The other three members of the Red Empire fist team followed Tamsah al Ramil into the library.

The ground floor room was one of the larger chambers in the manor house, it held several classic pieces of furniture including a grand piano, several antique reading desks and divans. A host of leather-bound books filled shelves lining all the interior walls from floor to ceiling. Heavy curtains shrouded the windows. His initial site inspection had revealed transparent armor had replaced the original window panes. Electric lamps dialed down slightly from their normal levels lit the library with a soft indirect illumination. A door leading into an armory stood on the right-side wall.

A long table beneath the windows lay draped with a sheet of heavy black fabric, four, vaguely human-like forms, appeared to rest beneath the sheet.

What was she hiding here? The question tore at Tamsah. Perhaps, Ms. Armitage would answer it; she stood in the middle of the library, with her tall, blond henchman behind her left shoulder. She'd changed her clothes since the morning. She wore fresh combat fatigues in a tiger print of dark grays, tans, and blacks. Her combat webbing carried a holster with a 9mm automatic, four hand grenades, and her katana, the Red Dragon, lay strapped to her waist. She stood relaxed and ready in her combat boots, with a black cap crowning her head. Drake wore his praetorian armor, a broadsword and a double-bladed battle-axe belted on the left and right side of his hips.

"Yes, Ma'am?" Tamsah asked.

"To be clear," Armitage stated, her eyes fixed on Tamsah's face, "your orders are to obey me unless I order you to kill each other or attack the Red Empire. I have done none of those things. You must continue to obey your oaths to the Red Ghost, is that correct?"

A sliver of fear threatened to worm its way into Tamsah's guts, but he pushed it aside, he was too experienced to be intimidated by the vampire standing opposite him. But still, why would she ask this particular question? What were her intentions?

"Yes," Tamsah nodded, "it is so."

"Excellent, then you should accept what follows."

Tamsah's mind raced. Her words were laden with threat. To his left, one of his men staggered, but nothing had happened to cause it. He sniffed, a faint, delicate sweetness filled his nostrils.

Gas.

His throat froze, his voice fleeing as his vocal cords constricted painfully.

"It doesn't affect vampires," Armitage remarked, lifting one eyebrow, "but humans – it's almost instantaneous—"

Tamsah crashed face down on the carpet with his men, darkness to rival the storm clouds over the manor house claiming him.

* * *

Chloe stepped forward and prodded the short Red Empire assassin's shoulder with the toe of her boot. He remained senseless to the world, breathing quietly.

"That was the last of our knock-out gas?" she asked.

Marcus replied, "Yes."

Her eyes widened in avid anticipation and she commanded, "Fetch the staff, it is time to bring them all here."

Marcus smiled. "Yes, Chloe."

She caught his gaze and asked, "How is your appetite?"

He grinned broadly, his fangs descending into attack position. "Famished."

Chloe inclined her head slightly. "Excellent."

Marcus left the library.

Chloe turned, walking to the long table at the back of the room. She pulled the black sheet away, and let it drop to the floor. The bundles beneath the sheet stood revealed, their matte-black surfaces dull beneath the dimmed lights. She reached out a finger, tapping the hard surface of one of them. The material absorbed the impact of her tap, muting the sound. The combat armor was up to specification; especially ordered, built and delivered from a manufacturing unit on the east coast of the United States. Brought into the room the day before by her retainer, David.

David had always been a loyal and efficient aide to her cause and had provided decades of service, it was a pity that he would not survive the night. However, she must make such sacrifices when needed, the end goals were too important to allow hesitation, remorse or regret.

She allowed herself a moment to reflect upon her immediate plans. Soon, she would make Anton Slayne's most dreadful fear manifest, and then he would be at his most vulnerable. He would be unable to resist as she drew him deeper into her web of control.

"Time to start," she whispered, kneeling next to Tamsah al Ramil. She tilted his head, exposing his throat. Her fangs descended over her bottom lip. She lunged forward, her fangs tearing into his neck, a trickle of blood rolling past her lips, falling onto the library's carpet.

The sounds of her feeding were the only noises in the library for the next five minutes.

* * *

The rain fell steadily, peacefully, the lightning and thunder had recently moved further east, promising a respite not yet fully delivered.

Juliette ignored the aches in her left thigh and skull, pushing on through the rain and dark on her crutches. Francis, Jay, Yvette, Chiara, and Luther surrounded her, holding phosphorescent glow sticks to light her way. A short distance in front of her were more lights reflecting faintly off a pair of Range Rovers parked on the edge of a stand of trees. Half a mile away on the left, a manor house stood on top of a cliff overlooking the ocean. Pale light emanated from some of the ground floor rooms, but heavy curtains shrouded the interiors blocking any casual inquiry.

Three figures broke away from the group near the SUVs and came rushing toward her. Anton, Peter, and Li resolved out of the gloom, Li was the first to arrive, hugging her tightly. Peter and Anton surrounded her, their hands on her shoulders and back.

"I'm not surprised to see you here," Juliette said, "I always believed in you."

Li stepped back. "Shadowstone is broken, they will not trouble us tonight."

Juliette nodded once at the manor house and said with a note of apprehension creeping into her voice, "We'll have enough to deal with over there."

Peter leaned in and whispered, "Walker is not happy with us, thinks we're more or less useless."

"It's expected – but, we'll still work with him," Juliette said, limping the rest of the way up to the Range Rovers.

Walker pushed himself off from the trunk of a tree and stepped forward, the rest of his team moving into a semicircle behind him. "It's about time – now we need to get down to business. How are your ammo stocks?"

"Anton, Li and I are out," Peter stated, looking at the assembled team members.

"You were supposed to bring your own," Walker snapped. "You weaken us all showing up without adequate supplies."

Juliette's head throbbed, the incessant politics in the Order was making her headache worse, she leaned against Francis and whispered, "We need to end this tonight if we can. Something terrible is building."

Francis squeezed her arm and whispered back, "I'll see it done."

"There will be enough to go around," Francis declared loudly, flipping his spare FN P90 magazines to Peter, Li, and Anton. "Just be careful with your fire, stay on three round bursts and avoid full auto." He looked back at Walker as his team adroitly caught the magazines and locked them into place on their weapons. "We have wounded. Juliette and Yvette are not able to fight, I will designate two of my team to guard them here."

"No, I need all your fighters in the mix," Walker directed, his eyes intense in the soft light, he indicated three members of his team. "I'll assign Joan, Mary, and David to protect your wounded."

Francis frowned momentarily, nodded and stated, "So be it."

Walker stood tall, glancing around the assembled Ramp masters. "Complete your preps, we move in three minutes. Loremaster operations will be with Joan Lewis, as Juliette Mirovar is out of action. The exfil location is a clearing on top of the cliffs, four hundred yards on the Whitby side of the manor house – is that clear?"

The combined team gave their assent and moved into action: cocking weapons with sharp clicks, lifting and checking swords one last time, and putting the finishing touches on the configuration of the tactical comms link. Everyone adjusted their Order nightglasses and aligned them with the encrypted tactical network. In short order, the teams were ready to assault the manor house together.

It was rare for two Order teams to join forces. It was only the presence of a high-value target that aligned the Mirovar and Walker teams to a common cause. Normally Order teams worked the jurisdiction of their own territories, hence why Walker was in charge of the assault, the United Kingdom was his territory.

If there were any enemies in the manor house, the combined strength of the two teams would slaughter them, and if Ramin Kain were still alive, they would rescue him and bring him back to the United States.

Juliette put her hand gingerly to her aching head.

At least, that's the plan.

* * *

Francis strode over to Anton and tapped him hard on the chest.

"You, come with me now," he ordered, his voice filled with tightly controlled anger.

The two men walked thirty yards away from the rest of the combined team. Francis stopped first, turning to stand a couple of feet in front of Anton. "What the hell do you think you were doing pulling a crazy stunt like that? You nearly got us all killed? The whole of the UK is looking for us now. You can bet they've got photographs of everyone who was on that truck."

Francis paused for a second, his eyes narrowing. "Worse, you put yourself ahead of the team, you acted selfishly, recklessly and without thought for the consequences." He shook his head, and declared in disappointed tones, "I expected better of you Anton."

Anton stood silently for a long moment, frowning slightly.

"Do you have anything to say for yourself?" Francis asked.

"Yes, I do," Anton began, "Firstly, Peter's capture was a time critical scenario. Without quick action, we would have lost any opportunity to save him, and right now, we would be down one man."

Francis' lip curled.

"Secondly, the UK Shadowstone force has been more or less destroyed. Yes, they wounded some of us in the process, but everyone will heal."

Francis' eyes became flint-like black stones, "Juliette nearly died, Yvette could easily have been killed."

Anton said quietly, "Aren't we all at risk?"

Francis' mouth dropped open for a second, then he declared harshly, "This isn't a debate. You are a member of the Order of Thoth, you have to obey your force leader, especially when on operations – that must be crystal clear."

"I'm not a member of the Order of Thoth."

Francis blinked, and then snapped, "And perhaps you never will be." He tapped Anton on the chest again. "We have a mission to do, this isn't over, we'll have 'words,' when this is done."

Anton nodded.

Francis stepped past him and returned to the team.

Anton turned around; the rest of the combined team were busy getting ready for the mission. He walked back toward them and whispered to himself, "Saving Kain or killing Armitage, I know which mission I'm on, does everyone else?"

* * *

As the rest of the Order teams worked, the Raven stepped behind the nearest Range Rover.

They opened their smartphone, composing a short message to Armitage. The vampire had asked for the exfiltration coordinates, now was the perfect opportunity to send her on a wild goose chase. They could send Armitage in the opposite direction, and when the teams left the manor house, Armitage would never find them in time to stop them escaping with Kain. But she would also know that the Raven had betrayed her.

It was a one-shot tactic.

The mission had barely started, there may be a far more useful time to deceive Armitage in the near future, and the Raven didn't want to waste the one opportunity they had. They completed the message and told Armitage the truth.

Armitage would know the exfil point.

The Raven put their phone away, lifted their weapons and rejoined the teams.

* * *

Francis leaned gently against Juliette, pressing something into her right hand. It was a short-handled dagger, sheathed in a forearm holster.

"Take this blade," he whispered.

"Silver?" Juliette asked, raising an eyebrow.

"Yes. If need be, it'll be your last defense."

"Thank you, can you help me put it on?" Juliette balanced on her crutch, extending her right arm.

"Of course," Francis agreed, strapping the dagger in place. A moment later, her sleeve covered it, hiding its presence from all but the most thorough examination.

They hugged each other for a long minute as the teams bustled around them.

"I love you," Francis whispered in her ear, his lips soft against her cheek.

"I love you too," her heart caught in her throat, her eyes welling with sudden tears. She hugged him tightly and implored, "Come back to me mon amour."

His head nodded next to her own. "I will see you at the end of this."

"I will hold you to your word," she promised with every fiber of her being.

Francis leaned back, a smile gracing his lips, his eyes shining in the soft lights carried by the team. "I would expect nothing less."

The combined team began to move. They broke apart and joined the rest.

* * *

Walker lifted his hand, bringing the teams to a halt on a fork in the path halfway to the manor house.

"We split now," he commanded over the tactical link. "The wounded will go along the left path to the exfil point. With the state of emergency still in effect, we can't use the Range Rovers, we will have to abandon them for now. We have an Order helper with a boat down at the Whitby docks. We will go from the exfil point to the docks and then travel up the coast. Any questions?"

The Raven choked on their words, grunting briefly and almost silently.

Juliette reached out, placing her fingers on their arm and inquired softly, "Are you okay?"

The Raven shook their head once. "It's nothing." They jogged over to where Walker was turning toward the right-hand path. "Sir?" they asked. "I should join the group defending the wounded."

Walker stopped, whirling back toward them. "Are you joking? ... No, you're serious aren't you." He turned back to the path and declared loudly over his shoulder, "Request denied."

The Raven followed him, catching up and pulling on his left arm. "Sir?"

Walker blurred around, his arm slipping free of the Raven's grasp. "Are you a coward? We're in the midst of a combat mission, you will follow orders, or else. Is that clear?"

The Raven, stood for a second, blinking in the rain. "Yes, Sir."

"Fall back, and take up your assigned position."

The Raven stepped aside, letting the other team members walk past until they could re-enter the line. They slipped back into position, their heart in their throat. They'd assumed the wounded and their guards would stay with the Range Rovers, and were nonplussed when they had joined in on the march toward the manor house. Now they were heading away toward the exfil point, a location Armitage knew they would all go to. She could be waiting for them there right now. The Raven shivered, they may have just handed Juliette, Yvette, and the three UK Order team members to Armitage. Walker had sent his own loremaster, Joan Lewis, with the wounded, obviously not wishing to expose her to the risks of assaulting the manor house. There were two loremasters together, defended by three warriors, one of whom was at half strength due to her own wounds.

The Order didn't have loremasters to spare.

They couldn't reveal the risk to Juliette and the rest without exposing who they were.

The Raven's stomach cramped with nausea.

What had they done?

* * *

Manicured gardens and a low stone fence surrounded the manor house.

The gates were wide open, a long driveway lit by low lamps along its sides led up to the main building. External lights lit the manor house, and many of the rooms on the ground floor shone from within. The upper two floors lay shrouded in darkness, the roof of the manor barely discernible against the storm clouds.

The teams halted in the shadows outside the stone wall, about forty yards back from the entrance to the manor grounds.

Anton frowned, the way into the manor was apparently unguarded. Armitage was expecting them. If it were up to him, he would simply blow the site to kingdom come from a distance and be done with it. Kain couldn't reveal any secrets if he were dead, but the Walker team and the Mirovar's were adamant that they must save him.

It was a trap, an obvious trap, and God only knew who would come out alive.

Peter nudged his left shoulder and whispered, "You know ... if one of us doesn't make it out of here."

"What?" Anton snapped, glancing across at him.

"I just wanted you to know that it was all worth it," Peter said quietly, grinning in the darkness.

Anton almost laughed out loud, stifling it with a hand over his mouth, but Peter's words broke the tension.

"How do you do that?" Anton whispered. "This looks like madness."

"Were fighting vampires – what do you expect? A walk in the park? We're gonna go in there and mess them up. What did you think – you're gonna survive all this?" Peter rubbed his hands together, then interlaced his fingers, cracking his big knuckles with a sound like stones colliding. "You've gotta love the challenge of it all. You could have a long and boring life, or you could fight vampires, really tough vampires, and on their home territory no less ... could you walk away from that?"

Anton studied the manor house, his gaze intense, his heart thudding in his ears. "No way."

"Then don't worry about it. We'll be together," Peter said, he glanced across at Li, who was listening intently on Anton's right. "That's right Li, we've got each other's back."

Li whispered without taking her gaze off the manor house, "Always."

Walker signaled 'advance,' with a waved fist. The team broke up into smaller combat teams to avoid presenting a single target and to allow each small team to cover the other teams. Anton, Peter, and Li advanced together.

Anton put his game face on – shit was about to get real.

* * *

Anton walked on point, Peter, and Li behind him.

He preferred being in front; point was dangerous, the person occupying the role was most likely the first person to contact the enemy. He preferred it because he didn't want to see his friends hurt, not if he could help it. Too many people he loved had died, he wanted it all to stop – and if he could, he would stop it. There would never be any questions left to ask after a battle. Could he have done more? Had he given his all? Did he do everything he could to save his friends and defeat those who would kill them?

There would be nothing left undone.

He broke into a garden clearing dominated by a stone pool lit by lamps under the water. The lights lay artfully placed to illuminate an elegantly carved statue of a crane. The stonework was impeccable, dragging the eye to the curving neck and majestic head of the bird. An apparently simple subject lifted into a sublime expression of repose and alert watchfulness.

Anton stared at the stone, faintly sparkling in the soft, buttery light.

Crane.

* * *

The front doors of the manor house stood before Anton.

Walker's command whispered over the tactical link, "Lamb, Slayne, Wu, take us inside."

Anton half crouched with Peter and Li on either side of the main door, under cover of the eave. Rain continued to patter softly down onto the graveled driveway. The rest of the team members waited in pairs within the gardens, scanning the approaches and searching for threats. At Richard

Walker's direction the combined team was composed of smaller combat teams; Anton, Peter and Li, Jay and Chiara, Francis and Luther, Walker and his youngest team member James Cox, and another pair of experienced warriors, Karen Chapman and David Khan.

Walker had put Anton on point, and the majority of the Mirovar force team at the front of any action. It seemed like people within the Order were still trying to kill him, or was that just paranoia?

Anton didn't give a damn – they could get in line with the Vampires and the Red Empire – he glanced over his shoulder at Peter and Li.

They both nodded, they were ready.

Anton tried the door handle. The unlocked door glided open on well-oiled hinges. The interior light spilled out in a warm glow on the doorstep.

There was no response from anyone inside, the only greeting was silence. Anton lifted his FN P90 submachine gun in both hands. Its magazine loaded with high performance armor piercing rounds; every fifth bullet made of silver. The Blue Dragon lay strapped to his back, its handle reaching up over his right shoulder. He paused for a moment, lifting his nightglasses aside and running a gauntleted hand down his face, wiping away the moisture. The last thing he needed was a stray drop of water dripping into his eye at the wrong moment. Fixing his nightglasses back into position, he dropped into silence. He ramped hard, time slowed, and he blurred over the threshold with Peter and Li behind his left and right shoulders.

The manor's foyer opened up into a large hall, Anton, Peter, and Li blurred to the far corners of the foyer, scanning the hall beyond. The interior of the hall reached up from the ground floor through the first and second floors. Balconies running the lengths of the left and right walls connected with staircases down the walls to the floor.

At the base of the far wall was a large stone fireplace, lit with a roaring fire. Three brilliant chandeliers hung from the ceiling, banishing all shadows from the hall.

A single large painting stood over the fireplace. A portrait of a tall, slim French nobleman dressed for war and carrying an ornate broadsword. His eyes were brown, his hair long and dark. His face rested impassively, as if unconcerned by anything that others may do.

Anton dropped the barrel of his gun slightly, his gaze drawn to the portrait.

"Is that Crane?" he whispered. "Is that what he looks like?"

Peter shrugged his shoulders, and Li whispered, "Could be."

Footsteps padded quietly in the foyer. Jay and Chiara taking up position behind Peter, and Francis, and Luther falling in behind Anton and Li.

Walker commanded over the tactical link, "Clear the upper floors, we don't want any surprises before we go into the dungeons."

Anton glanced behind him; everyone was ready.

He led them into the Manor house.

* * *

Anton, Peter, and Li worked to clear the ground floor, the other teams had moved up the stairs to the left and right to search the first and second floors.

There was one wing left to clear on their current floor. Anton blurred into a room; it was an armory composed of a pair of aisles to either side of a line of cabinets. Unlike the other ground floor rooms, this chamber had no windows. A centuries-old tapestry depicting a French castle covered the outer wall. A baronial shield rested on each corner of the tapestry: a blue crane over a silver field.

In the bottom left-hand corner was a short sentence woven in dark-blue thread, 'Le Baron Cornelius de Grue.'

de Grue, Anton thought, *the Crane.*

A cold fire burned in his heart, he turned to face the opposite wall. A portrait of a young dark-haired woman was the sole display. She stood dressed in silver, red and black, in the classic style of a 19th century Order of Thoth warrior. A training arena surrounded her, the sun above and behind her. She sported a silver rapier in her right hand and a pistol lay holstered at her belt. She wore a relaxed expression, a slight smile playing at the corners of her mouth.

Anton seethed; it was Chloe Armitage – unchanged to the day he'd last seen her. He approached the painting, a metallic gleam catching his eye. He turned in horror, the cabinet beneath her picture held the assassin's rapier she'd used to torture and behead his mother.

Memory flooded back – as clear as if it had happened a second ago.

His stomach clenched with nausea; this nightmare had to be over soon. He pushed the last door open, taking a step into the last room on the ground floor.

It was a library, in the center was an open space where half a dozen human forms lay covered by a black sheet of fabric. Anton, Peter, and Li entered the room ramped, scanning the walls, ready to respond instantly to any threat.

They circled the sheet, Anton dropping out of his ramp. He knelt next to the sheet and lifted it aside from the first form. He was a tall, lean man, perhaps in his late fifties, with sandy-gray hair and dressed in a well-made black suit.

He was dead, his throat bitten through, his flesh pale with blood loss.

Anton tore the sheet away, revealing six dead, still dressed in their household uniforms and all with the marks of vampire attack.

Peter looked on grimly. "They've killed the manor house staff."

"She's not planning on coming back here," Li observed.

Anton nodded. "Let's make sure she doesn't leave – ever."

"Copy that," Peter remarked, his eyes hard and bright.

Li caught Anton's gaze and said, "Time to bring this to a close."

Anton nodded. "Once and for all."

He stood up, glanced around one last time, and led the combat team back out into the hall, he tapped his earbud and reported, "The ground floor is clear."

"Roger," Walker responded.

The rest of the Order team moved into the great hall, joined by the other combat teams descending from the floors above.

It was now time to go below.

Into the dungeons.

* * *

The ill-fated mission of Francine Parker and Michael Wilson had charted the secret stairwell.

Their fatal path captured by their Order nightglasses and recorded by Joan Lewis onto her laptop. Data now reused to chart a path through the dungeons to Kain's last known location. Each team member could see the path as a ghostly green line overlaid on what they could see with their Order nightglasses.

Anton was the first to reach the bottom of the spiral staircase and take a step onto the second level of the dungeon complex. They'd cleared the first level minutes before, and found nothing of interest. The combined team proceeded forward, observing mission silence by using hand gestures for communication. Anton was still on point and tactically leading the advance into the dungeon.

Fluorescent lamps bolted onto the stone ceiling a dozen feet overhead lit the corridor in front of him. Twenty feet in front of him the corridor branched to the left and right. Another thirty feet past the intersection, the corridor opened up into a well-lit room. The green light ran the length of the corridor and ended in the open room – where Francine Parker and Michael Wilson had died.

Somehow Armitage and Drake had surprised them despite their training, and their failure had cost them their lives.

Anton pushed out into the corridor in front of him, hugging the right-hand wall with his shoulder, his FN P90 submachine gun held up high, pointing exactly where he was looking. Peter and Li were on the other side of the corridor and pacing him as he advanced forward.

Anton glanced back, Jay, Chiara, Francis, and Luther were all in the corridor, the rest of the team had reached the bottom of the stairwell. He lifted his left fist to signal a halt, he caught Peter and Li's attention with a flick of his hand, indicating the intersection left and right. They would check it thoroughly before proceeding, he didn't want Armitage and Drake to catch them the same way Parker and Wilson had been.

Anton, Peter, and Li moved into the intersection and then advanced down the left and right corridors. Both were dead ends, running about seventy feet before reaching bare stone. Jay, Chiara, Francis, and Luther took up positions at the intersection, keeping watch while Peter and Li cleared their end, and Anton cleared his.

A secret door would work here, he thought. Was anything disturbed? He found it moments later, a little mortar fragment on the floor. Five feet above the fragment, sat a stone brick in the wall without any trace of mortar around it. He prized the brick free, and put it quietly on the floor, revealing a six-inch deep cavity hiding a black-metal lever.

Anton left the lever alone, backing back to the intersection where Francis watched him with proud eyes, and Luther scowled.

Anton pointed to his eyes and back at the lever – they would need to watch this intersection.

Francis nodded and signaled Anton to advance.

Peter and Li came back, their corridor was empty. Together they moved up to the room where Francine Parker had died, and Ramin Kain was last seen alive.

It was empty, except for a set of chains and manacles attached to the left-hand side wall. The flagstones on the floor in front of the chains were still damp, and water had pooled in the grooves between the stones.

Had someone tried to wash something away?

Anton walked over to the chains, stooping down to examine the water. He dipped his finger in it and lifted it up to the light, there was a faint pinkish tinge – traces of blood. Was it Kain's? It seemed likely it was.

Anton shook his head, traces of blood meant nothing, Kain could still be alive. He stared down the last corridor, it opened up into a much larger space. He flicked his left hand toward it, it was time to go down it. It was the last unexplored space under the manor, it had to be where Kain would be if he were still here.

Anton reached the threshold first. He sidled up to the edge of the opening and looked inside, the well-lit chamber was sixty yards across and twice that deep. The ceiling must have been at least twenty feet high. Two corridors branched off into darkness on both sides, and the chamber narrowed to a final corridor that led to the external cliff face, a cold draught coming from that direction.

It was empty.

"What the hell!" he whispered harshly. How could it come to this? All that effort for nothing, Kain was gone. Armitage and Drake had already left – unless they were hiding in the corridors branching off the chamber – but, why do that? What could possibly be the advantage of doing that?

"Silence Slayne," Walker barked. "Joan just went dark, comms are down."

A figure emerged from the far-left corridor and proceeded to walk into the chamber – it was Ramin Kain.

"RK!" Luther called out, pushing past Anton.

"Sam," Kain declared, smiling, and opening his arms wide. "I knew you would rescue me from this hell hole."

Luther jogged forward, his katana still sheathed, his FN P90 carried before him.

Walker shouted, "Sam, stop."

Luther ignored him.

Francis snapped, "Defensive positions everyone."

Walker whirled on Francis and thundered, "Don't give orders, this is my jurisdiction."

Francis stared incredulously at Walker, pointed at Luther running toward Kain, and shouted, "Mon Dieu?"

Luther's voice rang out, "Ramin! You're safe?"

"Quite so," Ramin said, his smile broadening.

"I knew you would survive."

"And right you are Sam. Loyal Sam, good Sam, I knew I could trust you above all others to find me."

Anton watched in horror as Luther got within touching distance of Kain.

Kain's eyes gleamed with hunger.

Chapter Ten

"You shall not allow a vampire to live." – Quote from The Way of the Faithful, a book of Red Empire lore.

* * *

Armitage Manor, The Dungeons, Yorkshire, August 22nd, 20:46

Li ramped hard, power coruscated through her body, time slowing down to a crawl.

Even ramped, Kain's movement was quick, striking like a snake, his hands snapping forward to grasp Luther's shoulders, his face lunged forward, his mouth agape, his new fangs gleaming in the overhead lights.

He hit Luther's throat hard, blood jetting to the left and right.

Li lifted her FN P90, the barrel lining up on the center of Kain and Luther's bodies. Luther was falling to his knees, Kain following him down – still horrifically attached to his neck. Luther was doomed, there was no way he was going to survive the violence of Kain's hunger. She pulled the trigger, her submachine bursting into life, the bullets flashing down toward the two men.

She never saw them land.

* * *

Li's world turned to mirrors.

A mirrored corridor appeared around her.

The three-round burst she'd just fired disappeared through a mirror a handful of feet short of where Kain and Luther had been standing. The mirror absorbed the rounds, three wave-like ripples emanated out from an inch-wide point four feet off the ground, flexing across the mirror before disappearing along its edge.

"What?" she whispered.

She whirled around; the mirrored walls ran from floor to ceiling. A long-mirrored corridor on all sides stopped at the rear wall of the chamber. The mirrored corridor boxed her in.

She tried to remember in exact detail how the mirrors had come into existence, they'd grown in an instant, congealing, seemingly out of thin air.

Voices started swearing across the chamber. Whatever was happening, it had trapped everyone else too.

Li touched the nearest mirror with the barrel tip of her gun, it was solid with a slightly plastic 'tap,' sound on contact. While perfectly reflective, its behavior when shot indicated it was nothing like a regular mirror.

She put her FN P90 down, allowing it to hang from its straps at her side. The Green Dragon hissed clear of its scabbard, its majestic blade reflecting into infinity within the mirrored hall.

Whatever was about to happen, she would settle it with the blade and nothing else. She advanced forward, approaching her image in the far mirror.

The image of herself distorted. The walls moved, running like fluid as they reshaped to a new configuration. Her teammates shouted warnings to each other. The hall around her shortened, the far wall evaporating to reveal a doorway into a larger chamber.

The maze fell into silence; everyone watched and waited.

A chill clawed at her heart, she blinked, pushing it away – fear would only slow her down.

"Your move Armitage," she whispered. "I'm ready."

* * *

Gossamer!

The quantum field activated smart material had been on the drawing board when the Red Ghost inserted the Raven into the Mirovar force team. As the Red Ghost's child, they'd studied the strategies for technical advancement pursued by the Red Empire. Clearly, their former instructors had perfected the Gossamer technology.

There had to be a control system nearby. A system that would be compatible with the Red Empire software hidden on their smartphone. They held back a couple of steps from the other Order team member trapped with them. They needed to be careful, what they were about to attempt could not be discovered and would have to be done fast. Gossamer was perfect for maze traps, and its deployment here meant that Armitage must need all of its special capabilities. Now was the opportunity to thwart her plans by bringing the maze down.

Armitage may not even realize how her plan had come undone as it would appear as if the system had simply failed.

The Raven smiled slightly, putting their hand into the pocket at their hip. They'd taught themselves long ago how to use their phone by touch and timing alone, able to operate all of its sophisticated functions in silence with minimal risk of detection. But in such close confines, all they needed was for their teammate to turn around at the wrong moment, and they would be exposed.

They activated the phone, quickly delving into the hidden functions that operated the array of Red Empire software at the heart of the machine. Invisible fields washed through the room, probing for the control system. In moments, they would find it, then they would hack it, and once through its defenses, they would command the Gossamer, and the trap would be undone.

The phone vibrated silently; they'd found the master controls.

Now all the Raven had to do was penetrate its defenses, silently, by touch and timing alone, while hiding their actions from their Ramp master teammate standing three feet in front of them.

The Raven had come home.

* * *

They would fall amongst the trapped Order of Thoth operatives as wolves amongst sheep.

Tamsah al Ramil, aka 'Sand Crocodile,' ramped hard. The iris beneath his feet would be open for less than a tenth of a second to maximize the element of surprise. If he weren't careful, the device would cut him in half. He couldn't rely on gravity to complete the passage – he would launch himself downward, a matte-black armored missile, armed with a razor-sharp longsword.

Abomination! Screamed a voice in the back of his mind. Vampire blood ran through his veins, lending strength and speed to his already extraordinary capabilities.

He'd fed upon another human being. He'd become everything he abhorred, and yet he still lived, he was still bound by his oaths of allegiance to the Red Ghost and the Red Empire. Armitage's words haunted him, 'Your orders are to obey me unless I order you to kill each other or attack the Red Empire.'

She'd done none of those things – instead, she'd converted them into monsters, vampires who had all tasted the exquisite elixir of human blood.

Anathema! He and his men deserved nothing but death, but were not free to take their own lives, trapped in the service of Chloe Armitage, General of the Vampire Dominion.

A sworn enemy of the Red Empire.

How had this come to pass, he must have made a severe error of judgment, or committed a grave moral failure – this 'thing,' he'd become exceeded the moral framework of 'The Way of the Faithful,' the revered text at the foundation of the Red Empire.

'Death before dishonor,' was at the core of Red Empire belief. He paused for a second, the future weighing upon him. He could exist in this state for years ... decades ... centuries, before he could end his shame.

The iris opened. Tamsah pushed off from the ceiling of the secret chamber above the Gossamer maze. He shot through the opening and twisted in the air, landing in a crouch, his blade gleaming in the weird Gossamer light. Behind him, one of his fist team landed with the soft scuff of armor composite against stone. He forgave the man his lack of complete silence, neither of them had experience wearing the matte-black armor of one of Crane's praetorians.

A dozen feet away, a tall man with close-cropped gray hair and a callow youth were ramping, their katanas poised in perfect stillness over their shoulders.

Tamsah blurred forward, the youth leaped toward him.

It was time to fight, but not for honor, and if not for honor, then what did he fight for? A vampire can't have honor – not in any way understood by the Red Empire.

His mind clouded with questions, and that would never do – he pushed them aside and allowed his skills to flourish. Now it was time for blood, steel, and death, and that was an arena in which he'd long been a master.

* * *

James Cox leaped forward, engaging the shorter of the two praetorians, their blades clashing in a shower of sparks. Weapons struck each other in the next corridor, Khan and Chapman made contact with the enemy.

The short praetorian's counterstrike ripped through Cox's torso, his heart's blood spraying across Richard Walker's face.

With his eyes shrouded in red gore, Richard spun forward, his sword lashing out at the second vampire. Their blades struck each other, sparks flying, the vampire's sword pushed in toward him. He spun in the reverse direction, allowing the blade to go past him, his spinning kick sending the praetorian flying backward along the corridor.

Richard strode forward, his katana snapping back into a high guard position, his best hope lay in keeping both opponents in front of him, if they surrounded him, survival would be that much harder.

A woman's voice fell to silence mid-scream, Chapman was down. His heart tore, his team was dying. He cursed the day – could it get any worse?

The short praetorian rushed forward, Richard blurred to meet him, his blade slashing down in an overhead strike. The shorter man caught the katana with his longsword, angled his wrist, allowing the blade to slide past him on the right, his blade flicked over, trapping the katana against the gray flagstones.

The vampire appeared inside his guard, looking up at Richard with flat, brown, merciless eyes. His left fist punched through his gut, a gauntleted hand grasped his spine, ripping down and out in a single motion.

There was a sickening crack, the world tilted, all sensation below his chest vanished. He landed on his back, staring upward, gasping for breath.

A longsword flashed above him, descending in a blur.

A sharp fire ignited across his throat, and Richard Walker, Order of Thoth force leader for the United Kingdom, descended into infinite darkness.

* * *

Why do I feel like bait?

Li frowned, her lips pressing together. She edged forward, close to the mirrored wall. Her senses were fully awake, alert to every sound and movement around her. She held the Green Dragon above her, its blade reaching back over her right shoulder, poised to strike.

The noise of combat ebbed away. The tactical links remained jammed, but sound carried well through the mirror maze, and it was clear the Order had just taken losses.

"Walker, Chapman, Cox, Khan?" Francis called out.

No one answered.

Francis called to the team again, "Sound off."

Anton, Peter, Jay, and Chiara all called back. They were somewhere behind her, caught in the maze – she was alone.

"Li," she called out. It was enough to let everyone know where she was.

She passed through the doorway into the large chamber beyond. It was square, about ten yards on a side, she moved carefully toward the middle of the room. There was a faint susurration, her head whipped back, the doorway vanished, the wall congealing behind her.

An opening appeared in the wall to her right, four praetorians blurred into the chamber, forming a line half a dozen feet inside the room. The vampires held their weapons perfectly still, their blades dripping blood onto the flagstones of the dungeon floor.

The wall reformed behind them, the lights brightened overhead, the walls of the chamber became transparent. The walls of the maze beyond the chamber vanished as quickly as they'd appeared. The surviving members of the Order rushed to the wall around her and started pounding on it with their weapons.

Li moved backward to the center of the chamber, shifting the Green Dragon to a horizontal position in front of her face, her eyes tracking the vampires circling around her. The katana's blade gleamed mirror-like in the lights, reflecting the vampires maneuvering behind her.

Four praetorians? The vampire's features beneath their armored helms spoke of Kazakhstan, Mongolia and Tibet, not regions noted as recruitment grounds for Cornelius Crane, but well known to provide recruits for the Red Empire.

"What the hell is this?" Li whispered.

"Your death," the shortest of the four remarked with dreadful certainty. His voice was at odds with his eyes, conflict lay reflected in their dark brown depths, a harsh intensity overlaying a deep well of emotions barely held in check.

She'd be damned if she waited for them to attack.

Li feinted left, the vampire on that side moved to block the attack, her father's voice whispered in her mind, *The four-foe defense.*

Silence overwhelmed her, the vampires blurred toward her, blades arcing in, she leaped over the bright ring of steel. She landed, the Green Dragon sweeping through a broad arc behind her, forcing two of the vampires to leap high over her blade to avoid instant bloody death. She reversed instantly, tumbling forward through the empty space they left behind.

In the silent depths of her mind, she knew one certain fact, no matter how skilled her defenses, the vampires would outlast her.

No one could ramp continuously for more than a handful of minutes.

* * *

The lights in the dungeon dimmed around the walls, leaving a bright spotlight focused on the transparent cage in the middle of the chamber.

Luther's body lay slumped on the floor beyond the cage. Kain stood a dozen feet behind him in the shadows, grinning smugly, a light akin to madness gleaming in his eyes.

Anton had to break Li free of the trap. He brought the Blue Dragon down hard, slashing the katana against the transparent wall.

The meteoric-iron blade scored the wall, leaving a thin white mark floating in mid-air for half a second before it vanished. The material regenerated before his eyes, capable of endless reformation, it could absorb any punishment that didn't instantly destroy it.

"NO!" he screamed in frustration, smacking the wall with his open hand and pressing his face up against it.

Li blurred within the cage, ramping at maximum speed, her face still with concentration, her eyes filled with ferocious intent. She whirled, dodged, leaped and rolled, her blade a gleaming blur amongst the praetorians.

Sparks flew as blades clashed, her defenses were amazing, but unless one of the vampires made a mistake, she had no opportunity to reduce the odds against her.

Anton's heart sank.

Four against one was a death sentence.

* * *

A longsword arced in toward her.

Li snapped the Green Dragon up against it. The angle was perfect, the genius-forged meteoric-iron of the Green Dragon's blade shearing through the lesser sword in a shower of sparks.

The vampire's eyes widened with shock as his sword shattered before his eyes.

Li whirled, her booted foot catching him in the solar plexus. He folded around her strike, flew through the air, crashing against the side of the cage. He slid down the wall into a stunned heap on the flagstones.

Her follow-up attack had left her exposed, all three of her remaining opponent's swords striking down at once.

She swept the Green Dragon over her head, catching all the blades, redirecting them over her while she tumbled forward between their knees.

Li came to her feet, the vampires whirling in pursuit, she ran vertically up the nearest wall. Lifting her FN P90 with her free hand, she launched herself into the air, using the submachine gun to split her opponents, its hammering fire cutting a line and putting one of the vampires to one side of the room.

She landed near the lone vampire. His blade slashed down toward her. The Green Dragon snapped up to meet it, deflecting it aside. She moved in close, firing a three-round burst directly into the vampire's chest.

He staggered back in a cloud of gray smoke, blood streaking the transparent wall behind him.

Li whirled away, and tripped, the vampire she'd stunned with a kick had grasped her ankle. The one she'd shot was slumping to the floor. The other two were leaping in, weapons angled to kill.

She pushed back toward the vampire holding her ankle, the Green Dragon arced down, the blade slamming into his upper back, pinning him to the floor like a bug. She swung the FN P90 underneath her outstretched right arm toward the vampires coming in behind her and pulled the trigger.

The gun fired once before a blade slashed through its barrel silencing it forever. A second blade fell flat on her wrist, knocking her hand away from the Green Dragon.

She spun, her foot lashing out at the nearest vampire, he was short, not much taller than herself, he caught her foot mid-air, twisted backward, spinning her over and onto the floor.

The blow knocked the air from her lungs.

Hands like steel grabbed her arms and pulled them tight.

They'd caught her.

* * *

I am a vampire's puppet.

Revulsion grappled with admiration in the pit of Tamsah's soul. The young woman had fought with exemplary skill, and a rare authority of technique that had left him awed. An awe that had turned his blade at the last minute to knock her hand from her sword rather than cut it off. The only reason she hadn't claimed the lives of at least two of his team was the dark alliance of Red Empire fist team skills with vampire blood.

Two of his men held her arms with vice-like grips, the third stood to the side, his fist jammed into the rent in his chest armor where the young woman had almost killed him. Tamsah marveled again at her swordsmanship, what a pity the Red Empire had never inducted her, and what a loss in the war against the vampires her death would be.

But he'd taken oaths, more than one, and he would not go against his word. It was time to follow Armitage's instructions and begin the theater this strange killing would be.

Tamsah stepped in behind the young woman, forced down to her knees in front of him by his two teammates. He pulled back his long blade and declared sternly, "By order of Cornelius Crane, Li Wu is hereby sentenced to death. Her sentence to be carried out forthwith."

She twisted her head up and back, her gaze caught his with a proud, defiant look, filling him with a dreadful shame.

He hesitated for a brief moment, his teeth clenched, then leaned forward and whispered harshly, "You're a foolish girl, this place was always a trap for you."

She stared back at him, indomitable and without fear, and demanded, "Who are you? You're not a praetorian."

Tamsah's eyes widened with shock. The truth of her words tore at his heart and he whispered without thinking, "I'm someone who has given an oath to obey, and obey I will, but your death serves the vampires, which I abhor with every fiber of my being."

He stood up, lifted his blade, the moment stretching, the sword poised above the young warrior, ready to plunge down and tear out her life.

Something snapped within, breaching a forbidden barrier, Tamsah took a long shuddering breath.

Let Armitage believe what she will, after all, where is the honor in serving a vampire?

He must perform his next action perfectly. The slightest error would foil the plan burgeoning like a wildfire in his soul.

He adjusted the angle of the blade slightly and thrust down, the longsword disappeared into the young woman's body.

She gasped.

He tapped her once on a pressure point just to the left of the C5 vertebrae and her eyes mercifully closed.

He held the blade still for a long second, silence filled the hall, then a young man screamed in anguish less than twenty feet away.

Tamsah pulled the sword clear, the young woman slumping bonelessly forward into a heap at his feet.

It was done.

Armitage had never explained what would happen next.

* * *

Li fell to the flagstones.

I'm too late to save her!

The Raven breached the final defenses of the control system and prepared to issue the command to shut down the Gossamer system. Their fingers raced against the surface of their smartphone.

The transparent walls composing the cage around Li and the four praetorians vanished. The Raven halted what they were doing, someone else had shut down the system.

Anton was the first to move, blurring forward, directly at the short praetorian who had stabbed Li.

The praetorian stepped back, his gore-streaked blade snapping into a high guard position.

The rest of the Mirovar force team raced forward to engage the other vampires.

What just happened? The Raven blurred forward with the rest of their teammates, a chill racing up their spine.

Whatever was happening was nothing like what they'd thought it would be.

* * *

It was real, Li was dead.

Anton's soul exploded with rage, a red fire consuming him from the inside. His vision narrowed upon the short praetorian stepping away from Li's body, his wet longsword slick with her blood.

Power blew through him like a hurricane, he blurred forward, appearing in front of Li's killer. The Blue Dragon arced down toward the vampire's head, a gleaming thunderbolt of retribution.

The praetorian moved, faster than any vampire Anton had ever confronted. His blade angled up, his body flew backward, the swords connected briefly, sparking once – it was enough to deflect Anton's strike.

Anton launched himself after the retreating vampire who was reversing at speed toward the single corridor leading to the cliffs.

The wild Ramp was ebbing, a crazed burst he couldn't sustain. Anton reached into the silence, drawing forth an edge of speed, and closed on the praetorian.

Anton lashed forward with the Blue Dragon, and struck a second and a third time – the short vampire deflecting each blow at the last moment. He slashed across the vampire's chest with a reverse cut, the blow didn't land.

The short praetorian leaped high into the air, flipping upside down, running steps along the ceiling before dropping back amongst his comrades.

Anton whirled around, his focus on Li's killer, his back to the shadows leading to the cliff edge. His rage was subsiding, becoming cold fury, his senses reached out through the chamber.

Kain laughed madly, swinging a sword wildly. Jay cut off his laugh as well as his head, which bounced and rolled along the flagstones.

Francis, Peter, and Chiara fought the other three vampires, the one disarmed by Li, was now wielding Luther's katana.

With the short praetorian joining his comrades, it would be five against four. Anton strode forward, a dreadful certainty filled his soul – he would have vengeance tonight or die trying.

* * *

Chloe embraced Marcus, whispering into his ear, "For love and duty."

She stepped back, they looked down along the corridor into the Gossamer chamber. She'd shutdown the Gossamer system, it had fulfilled her purpose perfectly. Li Wu was dead, and the situation was descending into chaos, the Mirovar force team falling upon the Red Empire vampires like vengeful angels. Kain had allowed himself to be drawn into the fight, suffering the intoxication of blood drunkenness, he'd believed himself to be invincible.

The Mirovar force team had closed off the loose end of Ramin Kain for her.

"Buy me five more minutes, it's all I need to advance our cause."

Marcus nodded grimly.

Chloe leaned up, kissed him for the last time and promised softly, "Your courage will not be forgotten."

He nodded again, and said with quiet sincerity, "I've always loved you."

She stared into his face for a long moment and said, "I know."

He turned away, walking down the corridor toward the chamber, rolling his shoulders, and limbering up his battle-axe and a nine-foot-long whip-like black chain.

She expected him to do his best, if it was enough to survive, then Anton Slayne was not the weapon to defeat Cornelius Crane, and she would begin again. If Marcus didn't survive and Anton Slayne did, especially if Marcus died by Anton's hand, then the game was very much alive.

It was time for Anton to walk the true path of vengeance, a pathway soaked in blood, suffering, and wrath.

She stepped out to the edge of the cliff face. Dark clouds obscured the sky, the rainfall had reduced to a fine drizzle. Sheer rock walls rose a hundred feet above her and fell another hundred feet below her to the ocean. She leaped twenty feet upward, fingers like steel stabbing into the rock face. She moved upward, scaling the rock wall with ease, in moments she reached the upper cliff and stood tall on the precipice.

Her manor house rose before her, the ground lights illuminating the purpose written in the hard intensity of her face. The lights of Whitby glimmered in the distance, she turned toward the town, making her way to the rendezvous point.

Chloe had barely four hundred yards to travel, the way lay shrouded with stands of ancient trees growing back from the cliffs. In the distance a clearing waited for her. One known from her childhood so many years in the past. She advanced toward it, it matched the coordinates provided by the Raven. She needed to meet Juliette Mirovar and Joan Lewis. She had business to complete with the loremasters of the Order of Thoth.

It was the next essential step in her plan.

* * *

"Behind you!" Peter shouted.

Anton whirled around, ducking instinctively, a thick black chain slashing through the air above his head, sparking and scoring an inch-deep groove on the stone wall.

The chain clattered to the flagstones, before skittering away behind Marcus Drake. He stood a dozen feet in front of Anton, the length of chain dangling from his right hand and a massive double-bladed battle-axe in his left. A corridor stretched behind him, wreathed in ever-deepening shadows until it merged with the pitch-black night beyond the cliff.

They stared at each other for a brief moment, Anton's mind immediately shifting gears to meet the new threat.

"Where's my father?" Anton demanded, circling to the left, fury flowing like a river of ice through his soul. He hoped to pull Drake deeper into the light.

Drake's eyes tightened, as he counter-moved to the right. "As if I would tell you?"

Anton stepped backward, perhaps he could draw Drake forward. "You will tell me before this is done."

Drake grinned, but his eyes were glacial. "You are a child, full of idle boasts. Kill me and the secret of your father's location will die with me."

He's trying to make me hesitate.

"You've killed him anyway," Anton spat, watching Drake carefully. He'd never fought anyone using a chain before. It would be like a whip, the tip moving lightning fast would rip through anything in its way. It was too late to attempt to use a gun against Drake, by the time he drew his weapon and it fired, Drake would be upon him with the battle-axe or the broadsword sheathed at his hip.

"No," Drake offered slowly, shaking his head. "He is very much alive."

Drake's words rang true, and Anton's heart sank. "A vampire?"

"And imprisoned in silver," Drake declared, taking a step forward, putting Anton within range of the chain. "Unlike the Order, we keep our promises."

Drake's right hand blurred, the chain speared forward toward Anton's chest.

Anton blurred to his right, the tip of the chain brushing past his left shoulder, before slithering back behind Drake.

"Your parents lied to you for your whole life. You join the Order, and they lie to you again and again. You know nothing."

Anton bit back a reflex denial, he had to admit Drake was speaking the truth, but it didn't matter – not this time – Drake was trying to bait him, to fill him with doubts and weaken his ability to fight.

Anton stared hard at Drake and promised, "I will free my father."

Drake arched an eyebrow, moving back toward the shadows. "You will let a vampire loose on the world?"

Anton followed him, grim-faced, and promised darkly, "I will free him."

Drake laughed, a grim, barking sound. The black chain lashed forward out of the gloom.

Anton blurred left, away from the nearest wall, straight into the path of a thrown battle-axe. The leading edge of the axe was a thick crescent shape of dark iron between the two blades, it slammed into his chest, catching the flat of the Blue Dragon's blade in a diagonal across his body.

The meteoric-iron of the katana saved Anton's life, distributing the force of the blow across a much larger area as the axe lifted him off the floor and threw him backward twenty feet.

A white sheet of agony flashed through him. He rolled as he landed, coming back to his feet, his katana on guard, his chest heaving as he attempted to get air back into his lungs. A pair of shallow cuts beneath his nipples from the tips of the axe's blades began bleeding into his shirt.

Drake, his broadsword drawn, the black chain whistling through the air like a demonic serpent was upon him a moment later.

The fight hadn't started well.

* * *

For love and duty.

The words echoed in Marcus' mind. He knew that Chloe didn't love him, it was enough that he loved her. He would kill the boy. It would prove he wasn't what she believed he could be – a genuine threat to Crane.

With Anton Slayne out of the way, there would be time to find another way to breach Allemande's curse, and he would be where he belonged – at her side again.

By sheer luck, the boy had survived his thrown battle-axe and was still on his feet. He'd evaded Marcus' follow-on attack with an astonishing burst of speed.

They stood a dozen feet apart, the boy's face paled, his blue eyes stared with a wild intensity at Marcus, a thin line of foam appearing on his lips.

What the hell is happening to him?

Whatever it was, best to kill the boy quickly, he flourished his sword and prepared his next strike with the chain, striding forward to bring the boy within range.

* * *

Anton's Ramp went wild, dark lightning coruscating through his body.

Anton's right hand reversed on the Blue Dragon's handle, grasping it like an oversized dagger for an overhead strike. He blurred forward, suddenly appearing in front of Drake. He hammered the Blue Dragon down in a stabbing motion, piercing Drake's armored breastplate between his heart and his left shoulder. The meteoric iron of the blade tore through the ceramic nano-fibers of the armor, skewering flesh and bone before disappearing up to the hilt, half the blade appearing outside Drake's back, sending a red ribbon of his blood splashing into the shadows behind him.

Drake staggered back under the impact of the blow. His eyes widened, he snarled, his right fist wrapped with chain links pummeled Anton's chest, sending him spinning backward a dozen feet without the Blue Dragon.

The chain followed; a lethal black whip whistling through the air.

Anton landed, twisting blindly back toward Drake. The tip of the chain slammed into the side of his face, entering next to his left eye. It continued forward, obliterating his nightglasses and gouging a furrow an inch deep through his left eye and the top of his nose.

A red mist composed of his own blood and fragments of bone bloomed in front of him. His heart burst with a torrent of rage, pain, and grief. The wild ramp overtook him again, he instinctively drew upon his training in hooded darkness and blurred forward, reaching across his body for the Blue Dragon with his left hand.

Drake's broadsword had been in his left hand, his counterstrike would come from Anton's right. Anton's right hand flashed up in a block, his forearm connecting with Drake's wrist, he was within Drake's guard, his broadsword had over-reached past Anton's right shoulder.

The Blue Dragon's handle smacked into his left hand; his grip tightened around it. There was heavy resistance to moving the blade, it remained embedded in Drake's chest, and surrounded by armor front and back.

Drake cried out, "No!"

Anton screamed in inarticulate agony, his muscles rippling; he drew the Blue Dragon out in a massive draw cut, the blade shearing through Drake's heart, spine, right lung and chest wall.

Anton stepped backward.

Drake slumped to the floor in front of him, blood splashing across the flagstones in a torrent.

The Blue Dragon crashed to the floor. Anton's left hand rose to his ruined eye. His heart thudded in his chest, he sobbed once, a vision of his mother's head falling to the floor assaulting him like a lash from beyond the grave.

He sucked in a great breath, whirled around, searching for Li with his good right eye. She still lay where she'd fallen, the battle between the Mirovar force team and the praetorians raging near her body.

"Li!" he cried, scooping up the Blue Dragon, he rushed toward her body and the fighters swirling around her.

* * *

Li woke up, her eyes were already open, but she couldn't move them.

She couldn't move anything.

Oh my God, I'm paralyzed.

The battle stormed around her, she'd crumpled forward unconscious and lay with her face to one side. She'd been stabbed. The entry wound between her left shoulder and neck had stung, then everything had gone black.

Why am I still alive? I should have bled out by now.

Her father's voice whispered in her mind, *There are secret strikes that don't cause any real damage but appear deadly.*

But what had knocked her unconscious? The vampire had tapped her next to the spine, it must have been a pressure point technique. That was good, the paralysis would most likely wear off in a while.

Most likely ... but what on Earth was his motive?

A praetorian blurred into view. Anton and Jay overwhelmed his defenses in a flurry of strikes, and he slumped to the floor, his heart's blood spreading in a pool beneath him.

The battle was turning, the two forces had been evenly balanced, but as one team gained ascendancy, numbers would become telling, and suddenly it would be over.

There was a gurgle behind her, and a low grunt, weapons clattered to the stone floor.

Francis called out, "Non, Anton! Let him go, come back and bring Li's body, we don't leave anyone behind."

Footfalls rapidly retreated into the distance; two final pairs approached on the flagstones.

Anton knelt down next to her and rolled her over onto her back. His face was a mess, covered with blood, his left eye socket ripped open – a red ruin. Tears had carved furrows amongst the blood and grime covering the rest of his face.

He pushed his hands underneath her shoulders and hips, holding her close with tender gentleness. He rocked backward, smoothly lifting her as he stood up.

Peter's voice, his tone grim, came from somewhere behind him, "C'mon Anton, follow me, we have to catch up with the others."

Anton whirled around, running after Peter.

Li was able to scan the chamber as Anton turned, she counted six bodies, Kain, Luther, Drake, and three praetorians. The short vampire who had stabbed her and seemed to be the strange praetorian's leader had vanished.

She appeared to owe him her life.

Anton held her close, jogging steadily up the spiral staircase to the manor house. His chest was tight as a drum, his heart thudding near her ear. His breathing would catch on every breath. He couldn't breathe properly, he'd been badly hurt, more broken ribs and perhaps a cracked sternum to add to the smashed eye socket.

But it wasn't the physical damage that tore at her heart, it was his words whispered over and over, "Not Li too, not Li, not now, not her too..."

Li's heart rate had dropped to the single digits per minute, and she was breathing too slowly to be noticeable.

What on earth did that vampire do to me?

I hope they work out I'm not dead?

A vision of her grave overtook her. Clods of dirt falling onto her limp body, lumps of clay catching in her open mouth, darkness obliterating everything. She screamed once in utter silence before regaining control of her emotions.

Surely it wouldn't come to that?

C'mon Anton, see me, I'm alive.

I'm alive!

Chapter Eleven

"Never give up on your friends. Never give up your faith in them. It's when everything is worse than you could ever imagine it could be, that you'll need your friends the most." – Juliette Mirovar

* * *

Armitage Manor, The Cliffs, Yorkshire, August 22nd, 20:52

Black clouds bloomed over a night sky, backlit by a brilliant sea of stars. The edge of each cloud illuminated with a ghostly, silvery light that was millions of years old.

Chloe moved stealthily beneath the trees, her steps silent on the soft grasses and wet leaves. She caressed rough bark on the trunk of the nearest tree, the air was rich with the scent of the ocean and the recently passed storm.

The clearing was in sight, there were two Order warriors on guard, facing out into the darkness and wearing what appeared to be sunglasses. The same technology the pair of Order operatives who had infiltrated the dungeon that morning had been wearing. They stood in wary watchful postures, well equipped with light intensifier technology overlaid with data supplied by their loremasters.

Kain had indeed been a treasure trove of information.

Chloe positioned herself next to a tree, she was about forty yards back from the clearing. The two guards stood clear of the rest, a young, blond woman, and a tall man with a touch of gray in his hair. They looked like a pair, not lovers, but trained to fight with each other, together they would not be a simple kill.

Beyond them were three others, Juliette and Yvette Mirovar, and Joan Lewis, the loremaster for the United Kingdom force team. The loremasters were not much of a threat, it was Yvette that presented a risk, but she was favoring her left arm. Chloe arched an eyebrow for a moment. The young Mirovar must have taken a wound earlier in the day and was not at full strength.

That would make all the difference.

It pained her that Yvette was here. It was possible she was the Raven; it would be a setback to lose the Raven at this point in the game. It was a risk that was now unavoidable, everyone in the clearing would have to die.

Chloe stepped away from the tree, there was no time to waste, she drew the Red Dragon and blurred toward the rendezvous site.

* * *

Juliette leaned back against the trunk of a large tree.

With the help of her Order nightglasses, the world was a twilight-lit realm instead of pitch-black night. From where she sat, she could see the lights of the manor house in the distance. She'd picked her seat in the hope of seeing Francis, and the rest of the team come toward the rendezvous site.

Joan Lewis, the local loremaster sat next to her. She'd been working feverishly on her laptop for the last eight minutes in a vain attempt to break the jamming of the tactical comms link.

To Juliette's left was the cliff edge, where Yvette stood looking out into the night. Mary Turner and David Wilkinson guarded the approaches to the clearing. They stood watch, armed with H&K MP5 submachine guns and their katanas.

She was worried, this was the first time the team had been in combat without her tactical oversight, and the long running battles had exhausted their strength. With the loss of communications there was no way of knowing what was happening, and to make matters worse, the identity of the Red Empire spy was still unknown.

But … all the pieces of the puzzle suddenly snapped into place. The spy had confronted Walker about guarding the wounded once he announced the split to the rendezvous point. Juliette had asked them if they were okay. They were frightened of something, and they'd wanted to be here – to protect the wounded.

But that would mean—

A figure clad in black, gray, and tan combat fatigues, and wielding a dragon-blade katana flew through the air toward the middle of the clearing.

Juliette gasped out. "Armitage!"

The threat was overwhelming and instinctive, Juliette ramped on reflex.

Turner and Wilkinson opened up with their H&Ks: flames stabbing from the throats of their submachine guns, bullets slashing through the clearing, rounds striking bark from the trees, and zipping off into the night,

Yvette's sword hissed free of its scabbard.

Juliette reached for her crutches, she had to get to her feet.

Joan leaped to her feet, stretching out her hand to grasp Juliette's arm. She shrieked a single word, "Run!"

* * *

The deadly streams of 9mm rounds reeked of silver.

Chloe landed in a fighting crouch between the two Order warriors. They both stopped firing to avoid hitting each other. It was the wrong move, they should have kept firing to guarantee a hit regardless of the risk to each other, but a fighting pair became instinctive about not hitting each other in a melee.

It was an exploitable weakness, allowing Chloe to draw them into a fight on her terms. However, whoever she attacked first, the other would advance on her undefended back. A skilled and experienced pair of Order warriors was not to be trifled with.

There was no time for uncertainty, she drew upon her capability for a supreme Ramp. Time slowed precipitously, her heart paused between beats, energy exploded from the base of her spine, flooding through bone, sinew, and nerve.

Her mind raced.

The male warrior was coming toward her, his blade arcing through a diagonal slash that would cut her from shoulder to hip – if it landed.

Chloe moved to her right, the Red Dragon snapping up to her left to meet his descending sword. The two blades connected, his katana deflecting away to her left in a shower of sparks as her sword consumed its edge. She kept moving, rotating her wrists flat, running the Red Dragon horizontally across his abdomen as she passed him on the right.

She whirled to face the clearing.

The man was faltering, falling forward, bright blood splashing to the left and right.

The girl rushed upon Chloe, her gaze intense, ferocious, her mouth a grim slash, her sword angled for Chloe's heart.

Chloe's supreme Ramp was peaking, she waited until the final moment to bring her katana into play. The tip of the Red Dragon's blade met the tip of the girl's sword, pushing the opposing blade aside by a matter of inches. Chloe leaned away to her left, her sword traveling along the length of the girl's blade.

The girl realized the danger and began moving aside – too late.

Chloe's katana ripped through her chest, as the girl ran upon the Red Dragon, its bloody tip appearing a foot outside her back.

Chloe ripped the sword out through the girl's side, opening her up like a gutted fish. She blurred to the left, the Red Dragon flicking up into guard, the supreme ramp fading.

Yvette's first strike slammed against her sword, and then Yvette was past her.

Chloe circled back into the middle of the clearing, Yvette pacing her at a dozen feet.

The two women faced each other, Chloe with the Red Dragon, dripping with fresh gore, Yvette with her katana poised in guard position over her left shoulder, her red hair storm-swept and wet on her forehead.

Their gazes met with deadly intent.

* * *

Yvette stared at Chloe Armitage.

To her left, Joan helped Juliette to her feet.

Her left shoulder hadn't healed from the gunshot wound, even with system zero epigenetics she'd only experienced the equivalent of four days of healing in the last nine hours, and it wasn't enough to restore her to full strength.

Still, she was no novice, and she would rather die than leave her adoptive mother and Joan Lewis to Armitage's tender mercies.

Her heart thudded in her chest, her body instinctively recognizing the predator standing opposite her. Armitage had cut through Wilkinson and Turner like they'd been standing still. Her speed was amazing – if she could continue at that pace, Yvette knew she wouldn't last much longer than the others had.

Lasting long enough was the key to her strategy. She had to believe the rest of the Mirovar force team were on their way. If she could survive long enough, Francis, Jay, Peter, Chiara, Li and Anton would arrive, and together they would end Armitage forever.

She had to buy time, she had to play a defensive game – the sort of game she excelled at.

A breeze blew in off the ocean, riffing Armitage's hair beneath her cap, she sighed with disappointment. "With your wounds, there is no honor in killing you, but take your life I must."

"Why?" Yvette asked dryly, wondering how much time Armitage would burn talking.

Armitage glanced at the loremasters, then looked at Yvette and shrugged her shoulders. "You're in my way – I'm sure you won't tolerate what I need to do."

"Which is what?"

Armitage smiled. "I admire your bravery, and of course, you hope to slow me down long enough for help to arrive – but you will not succeed."

Yvette scowled. "Just bring it!"

"With pleasure."

Yvette drew upon every ounce of training she'd received at the hands of Francis Mirovar, and Jay Creeley, her primary training partner. She'd mastered an array of defensive techniques that had proved impervious to everyone except a berserk Anton Slayne. She reached deep into silence, her mind dropping into a fathomless quiet, golden light bloomed from within her deepest being and stormed along her limbs.

Armitage flew toward her, the famous Red Dragon arcing down for a head strike – a sudden death move designed to end the fight before it began.

Her katana, a faithful blade gifted to her by Jay Creeley, arced forward. She blurred hard to the left, her sword catching the Red Dragon in a deflection to her right.

The shock of the blow reverberated along her arms; her left shoulder threatened to tear apart. She barely avoided the near irresistible force of Armitage's strike; blurring further to the left, she swapped positions with the vampire general.

Armitage had done her best to kill her and failed, all she had to do was keep defending at the same level, and she would hold Armitage here until help arrived.

Armitage inclined her head respectfully and promised, "I will not forget you."

"You won't get the chance," Yvette promised in turn, happy to steal every second she could.

Armitage blurred toward her, the Red Dragon arcing down in a perfect diagonal slash.

Yvette's blade rose to meet it.

It was a feint, Armitage pulled the blade back, her left foot lashing out to catch Yvette in the solar plexus.

Yvette twisted aside, turning Armitage's kick into a glancing blow. She whirled away, her sword lashing instinctively toward Armitage, whose own blade swept back against her own with a clang.

Armitage, it seemed – was impossible to touch with an edged weapon.

They stood opposite each other again.

The storm clouds were breaking up, bright stars appearing overhead. A cool sea breeze caressed Yvette's face.

Joan Lewis pulled on Juliette's arm, it was time to flee, but her mother resisted. It was no more possible for Juliette to abandon her daughter to Armitage than it was for Yvette to abandon her mother.

Their destinies were bound together. The skills of Yvette's masterful defenses versus Chloe Armitage's terrifying capabilities would determine their fate tonight.

Armitage frowned, the first show of concern. Yvette took it as a small victory of sorts, perhaps Armitage would make a mistake Yvette could capitalize on. Time was on Yvette's side, if she could drag this out long enough, she would survive, and her friends would destroy the vampire facing her.

Armitage's eyes narrowed, her face stilling with intense concentration. She launched herself forward, the Red Dragon arcing down toward Yvette.

Thousands of hours of training and combat experience kicked into high gear. Yvette's movements flowed like a perfectly formed symphony, her silence complete, her mind a still point of certainty. Her blade rose to meet

Armitage's descending sword, her body moving toward the left to avoid the inevitable deflection.

The Red Dragon smashed through her katana, cutting straight into her right shoulder a couple of inches away from her neck. Tiny droplets of superheated steel struck the side of her face. The glow of the blooming cloud of metal illuminating Armitage's face before her, her eyes gleaming with a silvery light.

Armitage's strike continued deep into her chest, her right arm disappearing from her awareness. Cold steel ripped through flesh, blood, and bone with relentless force, a wave of shock and horror slammed through her.

Her sword fell from nerveless fingers.

The inevitable draw cut came an instant later, followed by merciful oblivion.

* * *

Juliette cried out in grief.

Yvette crashed to the ground, Armitage stepping away from her, the Red Dragon flicking through the air to rid itself of Yvette's blood.

Juliette stood in front of the same tree she'd been sitting at, Joan at her side.

Joan pulled a 9mm automatic from her hip and fired at Armitage. She blurred left and right, the bullets flying harmlessly past her. The pistol clicked on empty, Joan threw it away and blurred to her right.

Armitage blurred toward Juliette.

Juliette attempted to move aside, but her left leg wouldn't carry the forces of a ramp, and she barely moved half a foot.

The Red Dragon's impact pushed her up against the tree. The cold meteoric-iron blade running through her chest, thudding into the trunk behind her with a wooden crack that echoed away from the cliff.

Juliette's world faded, it was a heart strike – she was dying, her blood running freely past the blade to soak her shirt.

Joan appeared to her right, Wilkinson's katana in her hands, swinging in hard toward Armitage.

Armitage dragged back on the Red Dragon, but it was stuck fast in the tree. Her left foot kicked out, connecting with Joan's blade which swung wide.

Armitage dragged on the blade again with more force, this time it came free, just in time to impale Joan Lewis as she attempted to strike a second time.

Juliette staggered forward a step, dragged in a ragged breath, stilled her mind and ramped. Her right hand blurred forward, the silver dagger given to her by Francis, appearing in the middle of Armitage's right forearm.

The pointed tip, red with Armitage's blood jutted three inches out the other side. Her face chalk white with horror, she staggered back a step and launched herself with a mighty leap backward over the cliff edge.

Juliette, her strength spent, slumped to her knees and toppled forward. Joan rocked backward and forward and then fell next to her.

Twin pools of blood began spreading slowly from their bodies, soaking into the grass.

* * *

The silver dagger pierced Chloe's right forearm.

A dreadful numbing cold raced up her arm. Her fist had frozen on the handle of the Red Dragon, if the knife had been in her opposite arm, she wouldn't have hesitated to cut it off with her sword.

She flew backward through the air. She had a single chance to rid herself of the thrall of silver or be lost forever to a catatonic paralysis until the dagger was removed.

Her left hand brushed clumsily at her right arm, her left arm felt like a wet noodle, barely under her control.

Had she struck the dagger clear, she couldn't feel enough to tell. Her body became rigid, she descended past the cliff edge, falling toward the rocks and ocean below.

Rocks and ocean … rocks and ocean … rocks and ocean.

* * *

The Raven followed Francis and Jay into the clearing, the rest of the Mirovar force team were behind them.

Francis and Jay rushed toward Juliette and Yvette; their voices filled with desperate hope. Hope, the Raven knew would evaporate like snowflakes on hot stones as reality sank in.

Everyone was dead, Juliette was slumped with Joan Lewis next to a tree, a few feet away Yvette lay in disarray, while the other Order team fighters lay in pools of their own blood and entrails.

The Raven watched, dissociated from events, numb, their mind in perfect denial of what their eyes could plainly see.

Then their world shifted violently, their breathing became ragged, their chest heaving helplessly, their heart thudding in their chest. A wave of nausea overwhelmed them, and they fell to their knees, vomiting the thin contents of their stomach onto the wet grass.

It wasn't the brutality of death; they'd seen worse. It wasn't the loss of a beloved mother and sister, although the thin, cruel talons of grief were already clawing at their soul.

It was the dark, inescapable guilt rising like a tidal wave over everything else.

The Raven staggered to their feet; their eyes wide, unable to look away from the horror before them.

Jay cried out, holding Yvette's body in his arms while rocking back and forth, his voice lost to strangled sobs.

"Mon Dieu, her silver dagger, it's gone," Francis wailed, flailing around for the lost dagger as if its recovery would restore Juliette to life.

Their other teammate stood still, their face stricken with helpless horror, their hands on their head in disbelief.

Francis fell forward over Juliette, his arms cradling her blood-soaked torso. He prayed for release with thin, desperate words.

The Raven looked back down the path, Anton was running toward the clearing, Li's body in his arms.

It was too much, the loss, the catastrophe; the guilt was beyond what they could bear. They turned toward the cliff edge, blurring forward to the enveloping darkness beyond it.

They hit the edge stepping off into space. A strong arm snaked around their waist, and a hard body tackled them sideways to the ground.

Anton rolled them over onto their back, away from the cliff edge, his face was pale, angry but controlled. He shouted at them, "Do you think we can afford to lose you too?" he slammed his own chest and grimaced through the pain. "Do you think your hurting worse than everyone else here!" he leaned in close, his one good eye holding a mixture of intense wildness and adamantine purpose. "We don't stop here. We move forward. We fight for each other, and we damn well fight back."

Anton rocked back on his heels, stood up and snapped his hand out. "Get up. You're coming with me. I can't do this without you."

The Raven stared at Anton for a second, then took his hand and stood up. Inwardly, they lay lost, drowning in a dark sea, but Anton's hand was strong, his bearing filled with purpose, his command a lifeline to a safe harbor.

The Raven, tears streaming down their face, accepted Anton's leadership.

They were no longer an agent of the Red Empire, that time was past. They would follow Anton to whatever end, and perhaps, one day they would find honor again.

If it was still possible to find honor.

* * *

"What's this?" Anton asked, staring at something on the ground a foot back from the edge of the cliff.

He picked it up, it was a silver dagger, still slick with blood. He studied it for a long moment, piecing together a likely sequence of events. A grim smile touching the corners of his mouth; apparently, someone had stuck Armitage with a silvered blade.

Peter said behind him, "That's Juliette's, I think Francis gave it to her earlier." He strode to the cliff edge and peered over into the darkness.

Anton joined him. The ocean was rolling in, wave after wave crashing against great black rocks. If Armitage had taken a hit of silver before falling over the edge, she might have died upon the rocks below.

The violence of the waves scoured the rocks clear every ten or twenty seconds. The sea would have taken her body almost immediately.

"Without her body," Anton declared. "We must assume she is alive until proven otherwise."

Peter raised an eyebrow. "It's the only safe assumption."

The two men stepped away from the cliff edge, Anton tucking the dagger into his belt, he would give it back to Francis later.

Once they'd reached some measure of safety.

"We all take a body – no one gets left behind," Anton commanded. "Francis with Juliette, Jay with Yvette, Chiara, and Peter can manage the other three, and I will carry Li. Quickly now, down to the docks before anything else happens."

Francis was too distraught to argue Anton's assumption of command. Jay nodded his assent, his face streaked with tears.

Less than a minute later, the remnants of the Mirovar force team left the blood-drenched clearing and strode single file down the hill toward the Whitby docks.

* * *

The fishing trawler was driving north, half a mile off the Scottish coastline.

Anton stood with Peter on the deck, leaning on the rails, facing out toward the ocean. He shook his head, a rueful smile kept appearing on his face despite the circumstances.

Li was alive, she'd woken up, and started moving. It had freaked everyone out when it had happened. Anton's first thought had been that she was coming back as a vampire.

Then she'd hugged him and then slapped him for not realizing that she was alive. He was happy, things were back to normal between them.

Francis had asked Chiara to retrieve the implants from Juliette's and Joan's forearms. The implants were at the forefront of Order technology and could not be lost.

Most of the team were asleep, Peter and Anton had taken the first watch. The Order helpers, a pair of old salts in their sixties who knew this coastline and waters better than they knew their own wives manned the trawler.

Li was sleeping, her wound was surprisingly light, somehow the blade had missed every vital organ in her body. Clearly, the short vampire had his own agenda. Whatever it was, Anton was thankful there appeared to be at least one vampire who was working against Armitage and Crane.

He blinked and looked up at the stars overhead. It would be easy to be overwhelmed by the challenges ahead. The UK team had been utterly destroyed, the Mirovar force team had just been smashed, and the loss of two loremasters was a third of the Order's total complement.

There would be no way to mask their operations or travel from the Panopticon.

Now there was a target, Anton thought, if only they could find it, they could blind the Vampire Dominion.

Peter clasped his shoulder and said, "We'll have to get you an eye patch."

Anton stared out at the sea with his one good eye, his left hand lifting reflexively to the bandages covering the left side of his face. "It will have to be black."

Peter nodded. "Fitting…"

The two young men stared out at the rolling waves. The storm had exhausted its fury, a wreath of stars graced the heavens, providing a faint ghostly light beneath a shroud of infinite darkness.

Marcus Drake was dead, proof that Anton could take down his enemies. Now there was only Armitage and Crane to destroy, and he would have justice for his mother and father.

Juliette had been lost and Yvette with her. The Mirovar force team was badly wounded, its leaders dead or maimed with grief. There was work to be done, they would have to rebuild, and refocus on a new mission.

It was time to step up and make a real difference to what was happening in the world.

Armitage was gone, but he felt she was still alive, still out there, still an agent of her master's will. Without her cold body as definitive proof, it would be foolish to assume she was dead, but it was Crane who was the architect behind her actions. It was Crane who had ordered the murder of his parents. It was Crane who had to be destroyed. With Kain's secret collusion with the vampires exposed, it was time to take the battle to the Vampire Dominion.

Anton said quietly, "We must cut off the head of the snake."

"Amen to that," Peter responded.

The ocean's endless darkness drank in their quiet words, a mute answer to the crystal purity of their shared purpose.

Anton stared out into the night and considered his visions. He had thought to discuss them with Juliette, she'd asked him to do exactly that after the vision of Peter's death, but now she was dead that conversation was never going to happen.

It probably didn't matter, there were too many real world things to do. They didn't seem to be causing any harm and might even be helpful, hadn't the vision today indicated the importance of saving Peter?

Anton decided to remain silent on the topic of visions. There was no need to tell Li or anyone else, after all, there were friends to keep safe and vampires to kill.

And that was enough for any man to deal with.

* * *

Chloe was the sole occupant of the cabin of her Spike 512 supersonic business jet. It was half-past ten at night, the flight was more than fifty thousand feet above sea level over the mid-Atlantic.

The pilot and co-pilot, her surviving retainers, had stayed at the airport during the day. As humans, and mistakenly deemed innocents, they'd been left alone by the UK force team when they'd investigated the hangars that morning.

Her mind turned to recent events.

Juliette Mirovar had nearly claimed her life with her silver dagger.

Chloe had leaped far enough out from the cliff to miss the rocks – just barely. She'd been underwater for nearly thirty minutes and swept out into the North Sea. The silver-induced catalepsy had reduced her metabolism to a level that had ironically saved her from drowning.

With the dagger removed, she'd revived in time and swam back to shore. Coming out on a beach a couple of miles north of Whitby. She'd run back through the night at speed, making for her private airport outside Goathland.

Now onboard her flight, showered, and wearing an elegant silk dressing gown, she relaxed in her favorite chair with a glass of chilled Krug champagne. She studied the high-def screen in front of her, it displayed recorded feeds from the Gossamer chamber at her manor house.

Li had died as planned, and Anton had killed Marcus in a frenzy of violence.

He had a talent, just like his grandfather. A capacity for an enhanced burst of speed, much like her supreme ramp. He was becoming the weapon she needed to defeat Crane, although he did seem to be quite berserk when he went off on a rampage.

She'd watched the footage of the death of Marcus three times, from different angles. Anton had moved so fast; he'd penetrated inside Marcus' defense before he could move. It was quite stunning, and then using the Blue Dragon like it was a dagger – she pursed her lips, *What was in control when that was happening?*

Chloe tilted her head slightly, *Talents – there's always one or two quirks in there.*

She took another sip of champagne; it really was excellent and the perfect ending to a difficult two days. She could visualize Crane and Anton in combat, it would be a bloody mess, but there was no certainty that Crane would win. She looked absently at the bubbles rising in her glass and decided that Anton was indeed the 'one,' to kill Crane for her. He'd proven it tonight when he'd killed Marcus.

Marcus – she would miss him, but omelets, broken eggs and all that.

Anton would one day free her, an act that would usher in an entirely new world.

She took a deep breath and sighed, *Mechanics.*

The Raven was still in place, an essential link into the Mirovar force team. Their information on the rendezvous point proved they were still working to her advantage.

But still, there was a question over them, would they remain loyal? She determined to test the Raven soon, to ensure they were still committed to their mission. Upon reflection, it had become clear the Raven had not gone to the rendezvous site and must be either Peter Lamb or Chiara Romano.

Her thoughts turned to her destination, and Cornelius Crane.

Crane was a terror in combat, faster and stronger than any other vampire, except herself – if she used her supreme Ramp, she was faster, stronger, harder, but Crane knew nothing of her power, and she couldn't use it due to Allemande's curse.

The source of Crane's powers was a mystery, he'd hinted it was due to his great age, being nearly a thousand years old, but Chloe suspected it was something else. Crane was a man who kept his own secrets.

She finished watching the recordings and wiped the data, the images preserved forever in her eidetic memory. There was one last thing to do to complete the evidence for the story she would tell Crane. She set her screen to a sole camera feed at the entrance gate to her manor house. The camera swiveled around to face the manor.

She ran a command on her smartphone. Less than a second later, the manor house silently disappeared in a fountain of fire, dust, flying masonry and billowing clouds of smoke.

Chloe sipped her champagne. She would tell Crane a tale about many splendid things: Red Empire assassins targeting her, battling with the UK Order force team, brave Marcus fighting them all to the death, and finally, the bombing of her ancestral home.

She lifted her champagne flute and watched bubbles stream to the surface. She would detail how the encounters of the UK Shadowstone squadron with the Mirovar force team had produced Order losses, including Ramin Kain, his head of staff, Samuel Luther, the warrior Yvette Mirovar and the loremasters Juliette Mirovar and Joan Lewis.

While Crane's forces had paid a high price, the events of today had eliminated the Order in the United Kingdom, diminished their force of loremasters and seriously weakened the Mirovar force team, a result Crane could easily deem a victory for the Vampire Dominion.

The smoke cleared from the screen, the light intensifiers on the camera feed revealed a great gouge in the ground, like a giant's hand had reached down and scooped the manor house, the dungeons underneath, and half the cliff away and deposited it into the North Sea.

Chloe drank the last of her glass of Krug, savoring the exquisite and refined flavors. She put down the glass and declared softly to the empty cabin, "The past must die so the future may live."

It seemed apropos.

Chloe spent the rest of her flight reviewing her plans. The Order would hold a conclave that she must disrupt to cement her position with Crane. There were new allies to recruit to her cause, members of an ancient predator species whose powers would be extremely useful in the coming war.

For war would come, and chaos would be its avid handmaiden.

She would have her liberty, and she would bring a new order to the world, one that reflected the truth of how the world really worked.

She would make deception obsolete.

It was her destiny.

* * *

Standard operating procedure for the Red Empire when building a camera sensor network was to build in a secret pathway through it.

After breaking contact with the Order force team, Tamsah al Ramil had left the manor house using the pathway he'd built himself. He expected Armitage would scan the camera feeds, and his exit from the manor house would remain hidden. His deception would leave her with the belief he'd remained in the doomed manor house.

He'd seen the explosion on the horizon far to the south, she would think he was now dead, his body consumed in the destruction of her original home.

He felt betrayed, he and his fist team had been sold to the vampires for no discernible gain. It was against the precepts of the Way of the Faithful. It was wrong in so many ways, and there must be an accounting for the Red Ghost's actions.

If necessary, Tamsah vowed that he would be the agent of a terrifying and remorseless retribution, the Way could not be denied – there would be justice, or there would be death – there were no other options.

He passed through a stand of trees; dark shadows illumined in silvery starlight. He was tracking a fishing trawler north along the coast, the ship visible a mile offshore. He moved through the darkness like a shadow, easily keeping pace with his quarry. He would have to find shelter soon, for the sun would rise in a couple of hours, but he would pick up the trail again come nightfall.

There was a girl onboard the trawler, a young woman of extraordinary skills. She interested him, there was something about her that resonated within himself. She was a key of sorts, a key to his own strange fate. There were powers swirling around her and her friends, and he planned to find out who those powers were, and if appropriate, he would thwart them.

She'd spoken truth to him, and he'd felt deeply ashamed, and it seemed a lifetime had passed since that last happened.

He'd done nothing wrong. He'd acted with honor at all times, and yet, he was now a vampire. The only answer was that a power beyond his understanding was moving through his life. There must be a greater purpose behind what was happening. The only thing he had left was his faith in the Way, and it would be his sole guiding light.

It would have to be enough.

Tamsah al Ramil, the Sand Crocodile, initiate of the second level of the test of the Olgoi Khorkhoi and Red Empire fist team leader vowed to bring justice to the world.

He smiled slightly, he now had two guides: faith and justice. Since honor remained denied to him, they would fill him up.

Tamsah would be their willing and terrible servant, for none could stand before the might of faith and justice together.

He stared out at the trawler. He must protect the truth speaker; her fate was his fate. There was something there, something beyond definition or knowledge, a calling beyond oaths or allegiance.

As the Way proposed, in the end, there was only 'the truth,' and those who were shameless before the truth would be honored above all others. Her words had cut him more deeply than any sword could have done. She'd awakened a fire within him that once lit, could not be extinguished. There were those like the Red Ghost who had lost the 'Way,' and would need to be corrected, but the truth speaker was someone else, she was something else.

If need be, Tamsah would protect her with his life.

The End

The story will continue with the next instalment of The Metaframe War.

The Day Guard

IT'S A HOT WAR.

Cornelius Crane, King of the Vampire Dominion has his eyes fixed on the final destruction of the Mirovar force team and Anton Slayne.

The Day Guard is ready. Crane's new super-soldiers can fight the Ramp masters of the Order of Thoth and the Red Empire during daylight.

The Order of Thoth has called a secret conclave to decide who will lead. The faceless men who run the Order will stop at nothing to ensure Francis Mirovar does not become the next Head of the Order

Rogue vampire general, Chloe Armitage, seeks a new alliance with an ancient foe. A terrible power Anton Slayne has never seen before.

Will the Day Guard tip the balance of power in favor of Cornelius Crane? Will the faceless men of the Order secure their grip on power? Will Chloe Armitage advance her enigmatic cause?

Will Anton Slayne and his friends prevail, or will the last true hope of humanity versus the vampires be extinguished forever?